Grant tightened the focus and stared

Lowering the binoculars, he gently disengaged the detonation cap from the plastique compound, unpocketed his trans-comm and pressed the button to open Kane's channel.

His partner's voice filtered out of the palm-size radiophone. "You set?"

"You might say that," Grant replied, softening his deep rumbling voice. "We've got company. Roamers."

He easily pictured the look of incredulity crossing Kane's face. "Roamers? You sure?"

"It's a safe bet they aren't Mormons."

"How many?"

"Looks to be about twenty," answered Grant, "though there are a few stragglers on foot."

"Arms?"

"Home-forged muzzle-loaders. Blades and axes. The usual."

The small comm unit transmitted Kane's deep sigh of irritation. "Come on down, then. You've planted the C-4, right?"

"Right, but I'd rather not patch in the proximity detonators with the Roamers around."

"That," Kane said grimly, "depends on the Roamers."

Other titles in this series:

JAMES AXLER

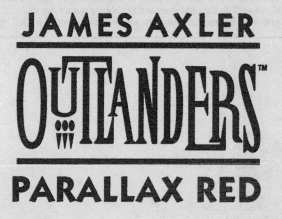

OUTLANDERS™

PARALLAX RED

First edition October 1998

ISBN 0-373-63818-4

PARALLAX RED

Special thanks to Mark Ellis for his contributions to the Outlanders concept, developed and created by him.

Copyright © 1998 by Worldwide Library.

A GOLD EAGLE BOOK FROM
WORLDWIDE®

TORONTO • NEW YORK • LONDON
AMSTERDAM • PARIS • SYDNEY • HAMBURG
STOCKHOLM • ATHENS • TOKYO • MILAN
MADRID • WARSAW • BUDAPEST • AUCKLAND

First edition June 1998
ISBN 0-373-63818-3

PARALLAX RED

Special thanks to Mark Ellis for his contribution to the Outlanders concept, developed for Gold Eagle Books.

Printed in U.S.A.

We dance on the angle,
From the edges we dangle
    and circle the parallax square—
When the fires of night consume us,
we've gone only so far as we dare.
    —"Millennium Fever," by Gavin Nebraska
        published by Explorer Press, Mt. Airy, NC,
        Dec. 2000

The Road to Outlands—
From Secret Government Files to the Future

Almost two hundred years after the global holocaust, Kane, a former Magistrate of Cobaltville, often thought the world had been lucky to survive at all after a nuclear device detonated in the Russian embassy in Washington, D.C. The aftermath—forever known as skydark—reshaped continents and turned civilization into ashes.

Nearly depopulated, America became the Deathlands—poisoned by radiation, home to chaos and mutated life forms. Feudal rule reappeared in the form of baronies, while remote outposts clung to a brutish existence.

What eventually helped shape this wasteland were the redoubts, the secret preholocaust military installations with stores of weapons, and the home of gateways, the locational matter-transfer facilities. Some of the redoubts hid clues that had once fed wild theories of government cover-ups and alien visitations.

Rearmed from redoubt stockpiles, the barons consolidated their power and reclaimed technology for the villes. Their power, supported by some invisible authority, extended beyond their fortified walls to what was now called the Outlands. It was here that the rootstock of humanity survived, living with hellzones and chemical storms, hounded by Magistrates.

In the villes, rigid laws were enforced—to atone for the sins of the past and prepare the way for a better future. That was the barons' public credo and their right-to-rule.

Kane, along with friend and fellow Magistrate Grant, had upheld that claim until a fateful Outlands expedition. A displaced piece of technology...a question to a keeper of the archives...a vague clue about alien masters—and their world shifted radically. Suddenly, Brigid

Baptiste, the archivist, faced summary execution, and Grant a quick termination. For Kane there was forgiveness if he pledged his unquestioning allegiance to Baron Cobalt and his unknown masters and abandoned his friends.

But that allegiance would make him support a mysterious and alien power and deny loyalty and friends. Then what else was there?

Kane had been brought up solely to serve the ville. Brigid's only link with her family was her mother's red-gold hair, green eyes and supple form. Grant's clues to his lineage were his ebony skin and powerful physique. But Domi, she of the white hair, was an Outlander pressed into sexual servitude in Cobaltville. She at least knew her roots and was a reminder to the exiles that the outcasts belonged in the human family.

Parents, friends, community—the very rootedness of humanity was denied. With no continuity, there was no forward momentum to the future. And that was the crux—when Kane began to wonder if there *was* a future.

For Kane, it wouldn't do. So the only way was out— way, way out.

After their escape, they found shelter at the forgotten Cerberus redoubt headed by Lakesh, a scientist, Cobaltville's head archivist, and secret opponent of the barons.

With their past turned into a lie, their future threatened, only one thing was left to give meaning to the outcasts. The hunger for freedom, the will to resist the hostile influences. And perhaps, by opposing, end them.

Chapter 1

Washington, D.C., had been dead for a very long time. How long and what had killed it was still a matter of conjecture.

In predark days, some opinionated and learned people put forth persuasive arguments that Washington, the capital city of the most powerful nation on earth, had expired spiritually and morally sometime after World War II. The means of death was attributed to a confusing variety of blunt political instruments, wielded either by liberals or conservatives, foreign interests or government bureaucrats themselves.

The arguments and accusations ceased abruptly on January 20, 2001, at 12:00 p.m. EST. The one-megaton blast in Washington, D.C., on a presidential-inauguration Saturday, pretty much decided the question of the city's living or dead status. The detonation of two other nuclear warheads in and around the District of Columbia left no leeway for further debate. The citizens of Washington, D.C., liberal, conservative, independent or apathetic, perished so thoroughly it was a question for statisticians whether they had ever lived at all. Of course, the question was never addressed because no statisticians remained to conduct the necessary surveys.

The complete and utter destruction of the city began a chain reaction, and by 12:03 p.m. World War III was in motion. Within the next six hours, the face of the world disappeared beneath soaring fireballs and vast mushroom clouds. By the end of that Saturday afternoon, the nuclear winter began. Massive quantities of pulverized rubble had been propelled into the atmosphere, clogging the sky for a generation, blanketing all of earth in a thick cloud of radioactive dust, ash, debris, smoke and fallout.

The exchange of atomic missiles did more than slaughter most of Earth's inhabitants. It distorted the ecosystems that were not completely obliterated and sculpted the face of the planet into a perverted parody of what it had been.

After eight generations, the lingering effects of the holocaust and the nuclear winter were more subtle, an underlying texture to a world struggling to heal itself—except in Washington, D.C., where the injuries had never healed, but simply scabbed over.

Only a vast sea of fused black glass occupied the tract of land that once held the seat of American government. Seen from a distance, the crater lent the region the name by which it had been known for nearly two centuries. Washington Hole was a hellzone, still jolted by ground tremors and soaked by the intermittent flooding of Potomac Lake. A volcano, barely an infant in geological terms, had burst up from the rad-blasted ground. The peak dribbled a constant stream of foul-smelling smoke, mixing with the chem-tainted rain clouds to form a wispy umbrella stinking of sulfur and chlorine.

The smell was so cloying and so fetid that new arrivals found it necessary to wear respiration masks until they grew accustomed to it. Of course, there weren't many new arrivals. The shantytowns that once ringed

the outskirts of Washington Hole had been razed long
ago, during the first year of the Program of Unification.
Most of their inhabitants had succumbed to rad sickness years before. The former District of Columbia fell
under the jurisdiction of Sharpeville, and the baron was
not inclined to abandon any piece of his territory to
squatters, even those that he would have had difficulty
giving away.

Although the center of Washington and all of its sub-
urbs had dissolved in the first three minutes of the
nukecaust, the outer rim still contained a few crumbling
ruins. Beyond the shells of buildings lay an expanse of
rolling tableland, broken by ranges of hills. To the
north rose a rampart of tumbled stones.

The landscape lay dead, lifeless, except for an ad-
vancing mechanical movement.

STENZ SLID BACK the Sandcat's canopy and poked his
helmeted head out, inhaling a whiff of the astringent
air. Coughing, he fought back his gag reflex and resisted the impulse to rub his irritated mucus membranes. Sweat flowed like water down his cheeks. He
endured the discomfort silently. A Magistrate who had
twice been cited for meritorious service had to endure—at least that was the constant claim of Ericson,
his division commander.

The Sandcat churned its way across the flatlands,
twin plumes of grit curving up from the clattering metal
tracks. The controlled roar of the 750-horsepower engine sounded uncomfortably loud, even through the
polystyrene lining of his helmet.

Built to serve as a FAV, or Fast Attack Vehicle,
rather than a means of long-distance ground transpor-
tation, the Sandcat had a low-slung, blunt-lined chassis

supported by a pair of flat, retractable tracks. An armored topside gun turret concealed a pair of USMG-73 heavy machine guns. The wag's armor was composed of a ceramic-armaglass bond which offered a shield against both intense and ambient radiation.

The interior comfortably held four people. At the front of the compartment, right beneath the canopy, were the pilot's and co-pilot's chairs. In the rear, a double row of three jump seats faced each other. Four Magistrates in full armor stared at each other, anxious for the nine-hour journey to end and their mission to commence.

Stenz was anxious for it, too, but only because the air-recycling system in the Cat wasn't working at maximum efficiency. When he opened the canopy, he hoped for a fresh breeze, but he wasn't particularly surprised when he was disappointed.

Below, from the pilot's chair, Presky called up, "Sir, we've got a midrange-orange rad count. You shouldn't be exposing yourself any longer than necessary."

Stenz did not respond, either to the young man's words or to his tone of agitation. Presky had only been awarded his duty badge last year and had never been outside the walls of Sharpeville. As a Magistrate, he was still a cherry, not used to the rigors of duty or wearing the black polycarbonate battle armor for a longer period than weapons drills. He obviously wasn't accustomed to traveling through a hellzone, sharing cramped, poorly ventilated quarters with five other men.

Stenz forced a bitter smile. It was a new experience for him, too. He had served in Sharpeville's Magistrate Division for the past eighteen years, and though his hair had gone gray and his face become scarred in its service, he had never been assigned to penetrate the dark territories of Washington Hole. The D.C.–New Jersey–New York Corridor comprised the largest and most dangerous hellzone. All of the Eastern Seaboard had been hard-nuked, but Washington Hole was still the most active hot spot in the country.

Ericson had briefed him on the whats and wherefores of the op, but the whys were still incomplete. Stenz wasn't sure if he didn't prefer it that way.

According to Ericson, all of the nine baronies in the ville network were engaged in a cooperative mission— to recce the redoubts in their individual territories for any recent signs of use or entrance.

Stenz had been stunned into dumbfounded silence when Ericson blandly mentioned the redoubts. Anyone who served in one of the ville divisions had heard whispers about the redoubts, the Continuity of Government stockpiles, perhaps even caught a murmured word here and there about the scientific marvels they contained.

Over the course of postnukecaust generations, strange stories, rumors, campfire tales circulated about these bizarre places buried deep in what were known as the Deathlands. The legends claimed these subterranean enclaves were stuffed with breathtaking technological treasure troves. It was even hinted that these redoubts provided escape routes to some happy land, lying beyond the scoured hellscape of the continental United States.

When Ericson, his pale gray eyes as cold as his voice, confirmed matter-of-factly that the folk tales had a basis in reality, Stenz's stomach slipped sideways. He went on to state that a major component of the Program of Unification had been the seeking out and securing of all redoubts within the territories of the villes. Anyone who spoke of having knowledge of them, even based on hearsay, was ruthlessly hunted down and exterminated. Inside of a generation, tales of the redoubts were suppressed to such an extent that they became baseless legends, much as stories about Atlantis and Avalon had been dismissed in earlier centuries.

Stenz felt no pride that he was being allowed to share a dark secret of humanity's past. Fear filled him as Ericson told him more things he would have rather not known. He mentioned the Totality Concept, an umbrella designation for supersecret American military researches into many different arcane and eldritch sciences, working to ensure the safety of the United States against all aggressors. Stenz didn't voice his opinion if that was the stated aim, then the program had failed miserably.

One of these esoteric researches involved matter transmission, relying on a device known as a gateway. Ericson provided him with a thumbnail description of its function, though Stenz didn't comprehend it to any meaningful degree.

Project Cerberus, a subdivision of the Totality Concept, dealt with the mat-trans gateways. Ericson claimed the project's purpose was to explore the possibilities of mass teleportation of surplus population.

Stenz couldn't help but ask, "Teleport them to where?"

Ericson shrugged and spoke of colonizing planets in the solar system without requiring the time and money of the predark space program.

When Stenz asked him if such an undertaking had

been accomplished before the nukecaust, Ericson replied bleakly, "I don't know."

Despite his growing fear, Stenz had felt a bit sorry for him—sorry for a man who seemed to know so much, yet still didn't know enough.

Regardless of whether the goals of Project Cerberus had been achieved, a gateway unit had been installed in every Totality Concept redoubt. The installation near Washington Hole had been code-named Redoubt Papa.

Stenz's assignment was to go there. Ericson had provided him with the information of how to gain entrance to the redoubt and check the mat-trans gateway control systems. He left it up to Stenz to handpick the Mags to accompany him on the journey to ground zero.

Because of the unpredictable geothermals in the region, Ericson deemed the trip too risky to make by air. After all, men were easier to replace than Deathbirds. To blunt any objection that Stenz might lodge, Ericson had employed his own personal cliché: "A Magistrate must endure."

Although Ericson didn't mention the reasons behind the op beyond the fact it sprang from a recent council of the nine barons, Stenz had heard rumors. In fact, the Magistrate Divisions were wellsprings of rumor. Intel officers would pass on scraps of information to a friend, and that friend would pass it on to someone else, like a covert relay race.

When the scraps reached Stenz, he found them too fantastic to believe but too disturbing to ignore. Some months back, a couple of Mags in Cobaltville had fused out, gone renegade and disappeared. Less than two weeks ago, they had returned and kidnapped a high-ranking archivist, allegedly right under the nose of Baron Cobalt. Combining that rumor with his assignment, Stenz came to the conclusion that the turncoat Mags knew about the gateways and used them to elude apprehension.

Magistrates had deserted and bolted for the fragile freedom offered by the Outlands before. It rarely happened, but it wasn't unprecedented. In this instance, Stenz had heard murmurs of the involvement of the Preservationists, a shadowy conspiracy whose alleged objective was to overthrow the baronies.

That could be the only reason for the mission to Redoubt Papa, but Stenz made no mention of this to Ericson. His commander hadn't said that the information he had imparted was classified, under threat of termination if he ever spoke of it. He didn't have to say it—Stenz picked up the implication from the man's eyes, voice and bearing. As it was, he couldn't help but wonder how long he would live after completing the op and returning to Sharpeville.

Now Stenz tried to ignore his fear, just like he tried to ignore the stink of the hellzone. He focused his gaze on the great heap of tumbled stone lying at the foot of a slope several hundred yards away. Impatiently he brushed sand particles away from his helmet's visor.

Presky slowed the Sandcat, steadily applying the brakes. Stenz's eyes traveled up the huge chunks of rock and concrete, seeking the vanadium sec door Ericson had briefed him about. It was situated inside a rock-ribbed hollow about halfway up the slope. Clumps of scraggly brush grew around it, masking the depression so effectively it was only by chance he glimpsed the dull reflection of light against the smooth alloy.

Stenz dropped back down into his seat as Presky brought the wag to a complete halt. He glanced at the rad counter on the instrument panel. The glowing scarlet arrow wavered erratically across the scale, ticking uncomfortably close to the red band.

Presky keyed off the engine, and Stenz announced sharply, "Disembark." His command was transmitted through the helmet transceivers.

The four Magistrates in the jump seats obeyed his order without comment, climbing out through the rear storage hatch. Presky flung open the gull-wing door on the driver's side and stepped out. All five of them formed a line in front of the Sandcat, standing stiffly at attention.

Stenz surveyed them swiftly, silently. All of them—Miller, Hughes, Lewis, DeCampo and Presky—wore the black polycarbonate body armor. The lightweight exoskeletons fit snugly over undersheathings made of Kevlar weave. Small disk-shaped badges of office were emblazoned on the arching left pectoral, depicting the stylized, balanced scales of justice superimposed over nine-spoked wheels. The badges symbolized the Magistrate's oath to keep the wheels of justice turning in the nine villes.

Like the armor, their helmets were made of black polycarbonate, and fitted over the upper half and back of the head, leaving only a portion of the mouth and chin exposed. The red-tinted visors were composed of electrochemical polymers and connected to a passive night sight that intensified ambient light to permit one-color night vision.

Stenz snapped, "Lock and lock."

In unison, the Magistrates raised their right arms, bending them at the elbow. They extended their index fingers. Five tiny electric motors whined as they tensed their wrist tendons. Sensitive actuators activated flexible cables in the forearm holsters and snapped the Sin

Eaters smoothly into gloved hands. Since the big-bored automatic handblasters had no trigger guards or safeties, the pistols fired immediately upon the touch of crooked index fingers.

They stood quietly, barrels pointed toward the lead-colored sky. Though they were too disciplined to show it, Stenz knew they were all worried about the high rad count. He nodded, not in approval of their silent acceptance of the risks, but in acknowledgment. "I'll take the point. Let's move out."

He clambered up the pile of lichen-patched stone. Though Ericson hadn't said so, he figured the massive slabs and chunks of rock had once been the upper floors of a multilevel complex. Sheared-away reinforcing rods jutted out of the edges of some pieces like rusty, skeletal fingers.

A tiny six-legged lizard, its skin bleached a dingy brown, flopped sluggishly out of his path. Its eyes were covered by a gelatinous film. Stenz inhaled sharply at the sight of the mutated reptile. The acrid air seared his throat, and it took a great effort not to succumb to a coughing fit.

The climb was not particularly rugged because the heaps of fallen rock and concrete formed a crude stairway. Beneath a shelf of granite stood the wide sec door. As Ericson had described, a square keypad was positioned within the recessed double frame. Taking and holding a deep breath, he punched in the three-digit entrance code, 3-5-2.

Stenz released his breath when a grinding, squeaking sound of buried hydraulics and gears began to build. He stepped back, eyeing the shuddering portal nervously. The vibration triggered miniavalanches in the surrounding stone, small pebbles pattering down amid sifting showers of grit.

Though he couldn't be positive, the laborious groaning of the mechanisms indicated that the door hadn't opened in a long time, perhaps not since before the nukecaust.

Like a curtain of steel, the massive door slowly inched upward. With a squealing grate of rust breaking free and a prolonged pneumatic hiss, it slid into slots between the double frame channels. Solenoids snapped loudly as they caught and held. The rumbling, grinding noise ceased abruptly. The Magistrates behind him drew back uncertainly.

A wide, square corridor yawned on the other side of the threshold. Inadequately lit by a single light strip stretching along the center of the ceiling, the glow was a dim, misty white. Stenz saw an undisturbed layer of dust covering the floor.

He activated the tiny image enhancer on the forepart of his helmet. The corridor leaped into clear, sharp, one-color focus. A musty odor tickled his nostrils. Feeling the pressure of the eyes of the squad on his back, Stenz squared his shoulders and took the first step beneath the sec door and into Redoubt Papa. The Magistrates followed him, fanning out across the passageway in the standard wedge deployment of personnel and firepower.

Stenz wasn't surprised that the overhead light still functioned. He'd been told that the redoubts were powered by nuclear generators, which were buried in the deepest part of the installations, just like the mat-trans gateways. As he walked along, heel to toe, he kept alert for any sign of a stairwell or an elevator shaft.

The corridor turned sharply to the left. Splits and

bulges showed in the walls and ceiling where the vanadium alloy had buckled. Redoubt Papa may not have received a direct strike, but even a thermonuclear near miss had come very close to collapsing it.

Stenz suddenly froze, gesturing behind him for the squad to halt. The patina of dust filming the floor showed markings, but they were so unlike footprints he couldn't quickly identify them.

Easing down to one knee, he silently cursed the feeble light. As he gazed at the marks, he felt his heart suddenly trip-hammer inside his polycarbonate-encased chest. A cold hand seemed to stroke the buttons of his spine.

The prints were small, like a child's, but they didn't look like feet. They resembled the impressions made by distorted, malformed hands, with all the fingers the same length and a stubby thumb crooked at a forty-five-degree angle. He experienced a momentary irrational suspicion that a gang of mutie children had broken into the complex and walked around on their hands simply to bewilder any Mags that might stop by one day.

Stenz knew that the prints were recent and, judging by the other markings, whoever made them had alternately pulled and pushed a heavy object. Double rows of straight lines cutting through the dust suggested wheels.

He rose to his feet, whispering, "Triple red."

Moving forward again, he cautiously peered down unlit side passages before passing them. After a dozen yards, the corridor dead-ended at a closed sec door, the green control lever on the frame in the down position.

Turning to Presky, he said quietly, "I'll throw the switch. You stand ready."

Stenz stepped into the corner between the frame and the wall and gripped the lever in his left hand. He waited until the rest of the squad shifted around the corridor so they could fire without hitting Presky.

The lever was stiff, but Stenz wrenched it up. Presky tensed as the squeaking hiss of hydraulics filled the passageway, holding his Sin Eater in a two-fisted grip.

The slab of vanadium alloy slid upward far more smoothly than the main entrance door. Stenz was dismayed by that, knowing it meant the sec door had been operated in the recent past.

The door's upward progress stopped, clicking into place. The squeal of the lifting mechanism faded and seemed to blend with a new sound—a faint, high-pitched whine so distant that Stenz couldn't really be certain he heard it.

Presky thrust his head forward. "Nothing. No lights. All dark. Can't see a thing."

Stenz began to step away from the lever when he felt a tingling, pins-and-needles sensation all over his body, as if he were skirting a low-level electrical field. The tingling became a prickle. The fine hairs all over his body seemed to vibrate, to bristle. The air pulsed like the beating of a gigantic, invisible heart.

Presky opened his mouth and half shouted, "I see a light—"

With a ripping whiplash sound, the door seemed to gush a torrent of blood. A wavering funnel of intolerably bright crimson light washed from the darkness and splashed over Presky. For an instant, his body swayed as if he stood in the path of a stiff wind. He rocked back on his heels. In the space of a heartbeat, his armor bubbled like boiling tar, then flapped away in black streamers, splattering the walls and floor with thick, semiliquid tendrils.

The twenty 9 mm rounds in the magazine of his Sin Eater exploded simultaneously in a flare of flame and an eardrum-jarring concussion. Presky didn't fall. His body flowed, smearing itself across the floor like a viscous ebony pudding bearing only the vaguest suggestion of a human outline.

Stenz stood wedged between the door frame and the wall, paralyzed by terror and shock. His eyes watched Presky ooze over the corridor, and his ears heard moist, slithery sounds as the man's jellied remains stretched slowly along the passageway.

Then all the Magistrates began to scream, to curse, to retreat in panic. Stenz slammed down the lever in a spasmodic movement, but the sec door didn't drop. Hughes and DeCampo, on the run, swiveled around to hurl indiscriminate blasterfire in the direction of the open doorway, forcing Stenz to jam himself sideways against the wall to avoid the wild slugs.

Under other circumstances, he would have shouted orders to bring his men under control. Instead, he began to sob, hot tears springing from his eyes and scorching their way down his cheeks.

A red, shimmering spear engulfed DeCampo's head. Polycarbonate, hair, bone and flesh slapped against the wall as if someone had tossed a basinful of sludge there. As the man's headless body toppled to the floor, the liquid mixture of flesh, bone, brains and polymer trickled down the wall like silt.

Stenz kicked himself away from the corner and caught a fragmented glimpse of a light dancing in the darkness beyond the doorway. A periphery of radiance shone around it like a ghostly halo.

His boots gouged gashes in Presky with the sound of a man running through a bog. As he leaped over DeCampo's decapitated corpse, he thought he heard another sound—voices raised in malicious, drunken laughter.

Stenz risked a quick over-the-shoulder glance and he cried out in horror. He had a fleeting vision of a broad, inhumanly flattened head peering over the threshold. Pendulous lips writhed, twisting in a wet smile of glee. Beneath the head, he saw a monstrously misshapen, stunted body.

Stenz ran, bleating in terror with every step. He ignored the hot stream of urine running down his leg just as he ignored the flow of tears burning his skin. He raced down the corridor, the drumming footfalls of Hughes, Miller and Lewis rebounding from the floors and walls ahead of him.

Even when he turned the corner and was presumably out of sight of the thing behind the door, he didn't slow his pace. The square of light in the open entrance gaped like the gates of salvation. The three Magistrates were already plunging through it, scrambling recklessly down the rock face.

Stenz followed them, jumping from ledge to ledge. He had stopped bleating, stopped sobbing. The only sounds were his harsh breathing and the crunching of boot soles on stone. His racing thoughts settled into a slightly more rational rhythm. The other marks he had seen in the dust indicated that whatever weapon had been unleashed in the redoubt was mounted on wheels. He had no conception what kind of weapon it could be or its operating principles. The Sandcat, with its shielded, armored hull, might offer some protection—

Stenz stumbled, his grasping hands catching only

thin air as he plummeted downward to strike his head at the bottom of the slope. Only his helmet saved him from a fractured skull. As it was, he lay stunned for a long moment. When he heard the roar of the Sandcat's engine, he sat up groggily, gritting his teeth against the surge of nausea.

The Sandcat lurched backward, gears clashing. Stenz struggled to his feet, shrieking, "Don't leave me, you fucking slaggers!"

A column of light burst from the recessed doorway of the redoubt. It touched the Sandcat, washing it down in a stream of crimson luminescence. For an instant, it acquired the red hue of the light. Then a billowing orange-yellow fireball swallowed it.

The shock wave slammed Stenz off his feet, the wave of superheated air instantly drying the tears on his face, blistering the exposed flesh. The concussion rolled over him like an extended thunderclap. Pieces of the vehicle banged and clattered all around him, bouncing from the rock tumble.

Lifting his head, peering through his soot-blackened visor, he watched the brilliant beam of scarlet carve a churning crescent in the ground around the smoldering, split-open husk of the Sandcat, then lance toward him. With stones against his back, he had nowhere to go. He flung up an arm.

As the polycarbonate sheath on his forearm splattered away like droplets of black wax, he thought bitterly of Ericson's tiresome refrain: "A Magistrate must endure."

Chapter 2

Grant pressed his back into the cliff face and tried very hard to look like a rock. His dark brown coloring and equally dark clothing helped him blend in with the shadows cast by a granite cleft.

He turned his head, scanning the gorge floor some fifty feet below. He saw nothing but outcroppings and thickets. Still the sound of shod horse hooves reached him, beating distantly like flint against steel.

He had climbed to this point to plant the three-pound block of plastic explosive. Now he felt like a target, advertising not only his presence but that of Kane and Brigid Baptiste, who worked somewhere deeper in the gorge.

Turning slightly, he tilted his head, looking at the black bulk of the Bitterroot Range silhouetted against the late-morning Montana sky. The narrow canyon was the only path through the foothills into the high peaks. Once it had been a two-lane highway, and even now patches of the blacktop showed through the tangles of overgrowth. There was even a hint of a white line painted down the center of the road.

The cracked and twisted asphalt ribbon skirted yawning chasms and precipices. Although acres of the mountainside had collapsed during the nuke-triggered earthquakes nearly two centuries ago, much of the road remained intact. The highway pitched and turned treacherously, but it could still be negotiated by determined travelers in all-terrain vehicles. It led to only one place—a mountain plateau and the Cerberus redoubt.

They had come down from the plateau to find a way to either disguise the road or make it completely impassable. The latter option was a blade that cut two ways—though the mat-trans unit in Cerberus was the primary means of transporting people and matériel into and out of the sanctuary, maintaining an open overland route made sound tactical sense.

After the events of the past ten days, the road was, more than ever, a channel for a full Magistrate assault. Although the Cerberus gateway was listed on all ville records as utterly inoperable, Lakesh extrapolated that Baron Cobalt would leave no redoubt unopened in his search for him. A hybrid spawn of human and other he might be, but the baron was no fool.

The baron had witnessed a group of interloping seditionists using his own personal gateway to transport elsewhere, so logically his quarry had to have a destination—and that meant another functioning mat-trans unit. The matter-stream modulations of the Cerberus unit were slightly out of phase with other gateways, so they couldn't be traced. The baron's only alternative was a hands-on, physical verification. Kane usually argued with Lakesh on issues of strategy, frequently just to be contentious, but not this time. If he were in the baron's place, he would have done the same thing.

Besides the desire to rescue his trusted adviser from the grasp of people he believed to be murderous insurgents, there was something else at stake: Baron Cobalt's monumental vanity and ego. Kane had twice humiliated the baron, and that was three times too many for a creature who perceived himself as semidivine.

Grant prodded the explosive charge jammed into the cleft of the gorge wall, making sure the radio-activated detonation cap was securely affixed to it. The combination of RDX and polyisobutylene plasticizer was very stable. Even if it fell, the C-4 compound wouldn't go off, since its impact sensitivity was 0.75 kilometers per minute.

After careful examination of the canyon walls, Grant had decided the cleft was the best place to plant the block of C-4. At this height, the cliff rose in a series of ledges of dry, crumbling stone, separated by vertical slabs of granite that decades of wind, acid rain and snow had eaten away. Tons of delicately balanced and overhanging rock could easily be dislodged by the right kind of demolition charge, planted in the proper place.

He glanced down into the gorge again, taking a certain pride in looking for and not being able to spot the Hussar Hotspur Land Rover. He had done an exemplary job with uprooted shrubbery and camouflage netting.

At the faint squeak of saddle leather, Grant turned his head, looking out past the mouth of the gorge, feeling for and finding the compact binoculars attached to his web belt. Bringing them to his eyes, peering through the ruby-coated lenses, he swept his gaze over the gently rolling, pebble-littered hills beyond the defile. He wasn't looking for Magistrates, who would have made too much noise, with Sandcat engines roaring or Deathbirds dropping out of the sky.

Intruders on horseback most likely meant Indians, from the small settlement of Sioux and Cheyenne. Many tribes of American Indians believed the nukecaust was the purification promised by ancient prophecy, and over the past two centuries they had reclaimed what was left of their ancestral lands, protecting them ruthlessly from invasion.

Still, the settlement was over a hundred miles away, according to Lakesh, and in the years since the nuke-caust, the Indians had ascribed a sinister mythology to the Bitterroot Range. Because of their mysteriously shadowed forests and deep, dangerous ravines, they were known as the Darks. Most people, white or red and otherwise, gave the mountains a wide berth.

Squinting through the eyepieces, Grant caught a flicker of movement. Swiftly he tightened the focus and the microbinoculars' 8×21 magnifying power brought the distant details to crystal clarity. He stared, dumbfounded. A troop of people mounted on horseback rode up out of a declivity in the grasslands. They advanced purposefully toward the entrance of the gorge.

He estimated at least twenty of them, most riding in a single file, but with a few spread out in flank. Armed with blasters, long, clumsy flintlock affairs, the riders also carried swords, pikes and battle-axes strapped to the saddles of their mounts.

As they drew closer, Grant made out their harsh, strong features, hair ranging in color from dark to fair to brindled red, the men with drooping, leonine mustaches. They wore a complicated arrangement of garments—vests covered with metal wafers, sky blue shirts, baggy breeches that were either checked or striped or polka-dotted. Long, beribboned cloaks trimmed with fur hung from their shoulders.

Their headgear was no less eclectic—red scarves, turbans, broad-brimmed leather hats decorated with feathery plumes and dangling foxtails. The women wore skirts slit at the sides above the thigh, and their unruly mops of hair were bound up with rawhide thongs. Necklaces of painted bone and wolves' teeth banded their throats. In fact, all of them, men and women alike, had the bearing and feral expressions of wolves.

A lean man riding point caught Grant's attention. His dark, shoulder-length hair showed a stippling of silver, and his face was deeply creased with lines of suffering and the scars of combat. A strip of wolf pelt encircled his broad, deeply furrowed forehead. Beneath a drooping mustache, the grim slash of his mouth had a lupine quality to it. His black eyes, under bushy dark brows, were like chunks of obsidian.

Grant let a slow, disgusted breath hiss out between his teeth. Lowering the binoculars, he gently disengaged the detonation cap from the plastique, unpocketed his trans-comm and pressed the button to open Kane's channel.

His partner's voice filtered out of the palm-sized radiophone. "You set?"

"You might say that," Grant replied, softening his deep, rumbling voice. "We've got company. Roamers."

He easily pictured the expression of incredulity crossing Kane's face. "Roamers? You sure?"

"It's a safe bet they aren't Mormons."

"How many?"

"Looks to be about twenty," answered Grant, "though there are a few stragglers on foot."

"Arms?"

"Home-forged muzzle loaders. Blades and axes. The usual."

The small comm unit transmitted Kane's deep sigh of irritation. "Come on down, then. You've planted the C-4, right?"

"Right, but I'd rather not patch it in to the proximity detonators with the Roamers around."

"That," said Kane grimly, "depends on the Roamers."

Grant pocketed the trans-comm and squinted through the eyepieces of the binoculars again. As a general rule, Roamers were dangerous only to isolated outland settlements. Outlaw nomads, they used resistance to ville authority as a justification for their raids, murders and rapes. Inasmuch as they stayed as far away as possible from the villes, Grant often wondered who they thought they were fooling by paying lip service to a political cause.

As he focused on the man riding point, a memory from a Magistrate briefing a couple of years before ghosted through his mind. He attached a name to the face of the man—Le Loup Garou, the Wolfman, chieftain of the most vicious Roamer band in the western Outlands.

Hanging by a looped thong from his saddle horn was a curiously shaped handblaster. Though Grant was familiar with all types of guns—predark and postdark—it took him a moment to identify the pistol as a tap-action flintlock, or an imitation. A double-barreled weapon, it featured a design that allowed one lock to fire each barrel in turn.

Seeing such an archaic blaster didn't surprise him overmuch. One of the first priorities the drafters of the Program of Unification had set for themselves was the disarmament of the people. Still, books and diagrams survived the sweeps, and self-styled gunsmiths continued to forge weapons, though blasters more complicated than black-powder muzzle loaders were beyond their capacities.

Even such a rudimentary firearm in the hands of Le Loup Garou would have earned him an immediate termination warrant, had Grant still been a Magistrate.

He lifted his gaze beyond the mounted people. On foot behind them staggered six women and four children. Stark naked and tethered to each other by thick leather collars and lengths of rawhide, they made a chain of human misery. All of them were copperskinned with the flowing, jet-black hair of Indians.

A pair of Roamers marched beside the stumbling captives, urging them along with curses and strokes of long whips that raised blood-edged welts with every flail.

Grant ground his teeth, no longer wondering at the presence of the raiders. They had attacked the Indian settlement, and the captives were either the sole survivors or those they were able to steal. Despite the loathing he felt for the Roamers, he almost hoped the first possibility was the case. If not, then Sioux and Cheyenne warriors would be on the coldhearts' trail. If they were, the Roamers' route through the Darks was not arbitrary or whimsical. They hoped the superstitious regard in which the Indians held the mountain range would discourage pursuit.

Grant knew very little about the culture of the few scattered Indian bands living in the hinterlands, but he didn't think that a tribal taboo would prevent the warriors from rescuing their women and children.

Stowing the binoculars, he screwed the detonation cap back into the explosive block, then began picking his way carefully down the cliff face. His fingers gripped cracks in the stone, and rivulets of gravel started beneath his boots, rattling and clicking. The descent was more difficult than the ascent, and not for the first time he wished Domi were with them. Nimble and strong, she could climb like a scalded monkey.

He huffed and puffed and swore as he clambered to the gorge floor. He dropped the last ten feet. Brigid and Kane were there to meet him.

"What the hell are Roamers doing out here?" Kane demanded harshly.

An inch over six feet, every line of Kane's supple, compact body was hard and stripped of excess flesh. His high-planed face held a watchful expression, as did his narrowed gray-blue eyes. His thick dark hair was tousled, and his left hand pushed through it impatiently. He kept his right hand, his gun hand, free. His holstered Sin Eater was strapped to the forearm.

Brigid said, "They're wanderers, like gypsies were supposed to be. They can be anywhere."

She was tall, full breasted with a willowy, athletic figure. A curly mane of red-gold hair spilled over her shoulders and upper back, framing a smoothly sculpted face dusted lightly with freckles across her nose and cheeks. The color of polished emeralds glittered in her big eyes.

Grant massaged his sore shoulder muscles and worked his stiff fingers. "There's a reason why they're in this particular spot. They've got Indian prisoners taken from the settlement. They're probably hoping to throw warriors off their track in the mountains."

A few years older than Kane, a few inches taller and more than a few pounds heavier, Grant was a very broad-shouldered man. A down-sweeping mustache showed jet-black against the coffee brown of his skin. Beneath it, his heavy-jawed face was set in a perpetual scowl. Like his companions, he wore dark trousers and a shirt of tough whipcord.

"I think it's Le Loup Garou's little social club," he added.

Kane's eyes flickered in recognition of the name, and he sighed in angry exasperation. "Why can't anything be simple?"

Grant ignored the query, assuming it was rhetorical. He nodded toward the mouth of the gorge. "We can't let them through the pass. The road leads only to Cerberus."

Tersely Kane replied, "There are too many to fight. So that leaves the time-honored tactic of the bluff."

Brigid raised a skeptical eyebrow. "How do you propose we run a bluff on twenty barbarians?"

"Not we," answered Kane. "Me."

Grant groaned. "Here we go. Don't you ever get tired of making up shit as you go along?"

Smiling crookedly, Kane opened a pouch on his belt and removed a small oval of black plastic. He extended a thread-thin antenna and pointed it toward the cleft above them.

"Wait—" Grant began.

Kane depressed a tiny stud on its surface. "The charge is armed."

Eyes flashing green sparks of anger, Brigid snapped, "We've just spent two hours setting up the microwave sensor perimeter. Blowing the plastique ourselves isn't part of the plan."

"I'm making shit up as I go along," Kane reminded her dryly. "If I can't bluff the Roamers into turning tail, we'll have no choice but to drop the hammer. Besides, what difference does it make if Mags touch off the proximity sensors or if we're the ones to light the charge? The results will be the same. Boom."

Pausing, he scanned their faces before clarifying his

take on the situation. "I don't want Roamers knocking at our door any more than I want Mags."

Neither person said anything.

"Look," Kane continued, trying for a reasonable tone, "if they can be scared off, we'll disarm the charge and go back to the original setup."

"What about their captives?" asked Brigid.

Kane shrugged. "Not our business. If warriors are following them, it's their lookout to rescue the prisoners, not ours."

"The Cerberus policy of isolation," Brigid muttered darkly.

His voice and eyes went cold. "Now you're getting it."

He tossed the transmitter to Grant, who caught it gingerly with both hands. Affixing the trans-comm to an epaulet on the left shoulder of his shirt, Kane said, "Keep your comm channel open. Depending on what I say, you may have to ignite the charge, but don't do it unless I say so specifically. Get over to the wag and stay out of sight."

Brigid and Grant gave him lingering, bleak stares, then did as he said, turning and walking toward the thicket some thirty yards away. Kane strode down the blacktop to the very mouth of the canyon. Finding a granite boulder, he leisurely leaned against it and crossed his arms over his chest, hiding the Sin Eater from view. He hoped he wouldn't have to use it.

Chapter 3

Within one minute, he heard the steady clopping of hooves, the jingle of harness and the murmur of voices. The gorge mouth was narrow, only a dozen yards from wall to wall, and it wouldn't permit more than three riders abreast along the furrowed blacktop.

Inside of two minutes, the Roamers turned a bend in the rock wall. Le Loup Garou caught sight of Kane immediately and he reined his horse up so sharply it whinnied in protest. He froze motionless with astonishment and lifted his left hand to halt the people behind him. A half shout went up, reins were jerked and weapons drawn. Instantly several rifles were leveled at Kane, but the sudden shock of finding one man lolling casually against a boulder stayed their fingers on the triggers.

Le Loup Garou and Kane inspected each other silently. Slowly a smile stretched the chieftain's lips. "What is your thought, encroaching on the territory of the Roamers?" His soft voice was touched by what might have been a French accent a long time ago. Now, decided Kane, it was just an affectation.

"Since when do Roamers have territories?" he retorted.

The man's smile widened into a disdainful grin. He was missing two teeth, and the others were darkly stained and cavity speckled. "Any piece of ground we cross becomes ours simply by dint of our passage."

"Not this particular piece."

Le Loup Garou furtively eyed the undergrowth, the canyon walls above and behind Kane, suspecting the stranger had blastermen hidden on all sides.

Calmly he said, "We wish only to go to the mountains. That is all."

"Sorry," Kane replied, "the mountains and this pass are private property."

Le Loup Garou's eyes narrowed, puzzled and uncertain. "The property of who?"

"Me."

"Claimed by one man?" demanded Le Loup Garou incredulously. "Just what kind of man are you? You're too smooth for an outrunner, too pale for a *peau-rouge*."

"A *peau* what?"

"Redskin."

Kane imitated Le Loup Garou's scornful grin. "I am an expatriate."

The Roamer chieftain rubbed his chin contemplatively. "I have never heard of that tribe."

"It's not a tribe. It's more of an occupation."

Le Loup Garou nodded. "Ah. We pursue our own occupations."

"So I've heard. Chilling, robbing, enslaving."

The man shrugged. "I wish only to pass. If you so desire, I will pay you a toll."

"No," Kane said flatly.

Le Loup Garou's shoulders stiffened. "I offer you a gift, then. A red girl, still young and juicy. She claims to be a virgin, but with savages, who can say. I chose her for myself, but a man like you will appreciate her as much as I."

"I don't take gifts from scum."

The man raised his voice slightly in anger. "I do not care for your manner."

"Not many do. I've had complaints about it before."

"For a single man facing many, you are being extraordinarily argumentative."

Kane ignored the observation. In a soft, icy whisper, he said, "I've no more to say to you. Turn about and go. I won't tell you again."

Le Loup Garou snarled like his namesake. Quick rage flickered like a flame in his black eyes. Behind him, the Roamers peered at Kane, their inclination to chill him conquered by curiosity and apprehension about hidden guns.

Thrusting his head forward, Le Loup Garou growled, "I won't tell *you* this again—be practical. Let us pass or you will die."

Kane eyed the hollow bores of the rifles pointing at him, then tensed his wrist tendons. The Sin Eater unfolded, and the butt slapped into his palm. Casually he brought it into view, but he didn't aim it. Le Loup Garou stared, gaping open-mouthed. He leaned back in his saddle, away from the handblaster.

"Chilling you may serve no practical purpose," said Kane coldly, "but by God, you tempt me."

The chieftain struggled to regain the composure he had lost at the sight of the Sin Eater. "I've seen blasters like that before, in the hands of sec men."

"Sec men" was an obsolete term still applied to Magistrates in hinterlands beyond the villes. A low murmuring, in thick, hate-filled tones, passed among the Roamers. Magistrates were feared and despised all

over the Outlands. To chill a Mag was the fondest hope
of marauders like the Roamers.

Though he didn't otherwise move, Le Loup Garou's
hand crept toward the tap-pistol hanging from his saddle horn. Kane swore silently. Regardless of what else
was said, the chief intended to draw his pistol. He had
no choice. If Le Loup Garou backed down in front of
a sec man, his people wouldn't forget and his position
as their leader was doomed.

"I'm not a sec man," Kane declared. "I told you
what I was."

Le Loup Garou's hand continued to creep toward the
blaster.

"This isn't necessary." A steel edge slipped into
Kane's voice. "Nobody has to die. Do as I say and
ride out."

Le Loup Garou's hand stopped moving, his slitted
black eyes locking on Kane's. The tension suddenly
went out of the man's posture. His shoulders heaved
in a dismissive shrug, and he half turned in his saddle
toward the people behind him as if to say something
to them.

Kane hissed softly in disgust. "Ah, shit."

The chieftain's attitude of resignation didn't deceive
him. As far as the human wolf pack was concerned,
their leader had been challenged by a hated enemy, and
failure to accept the challenge was tantamount to a
death sentence.

Le Loup Garou swiftly twisted in the saddle, his
hand darting for his blaster. At the same instant, Kane
lunged around the base of the boulder. Only his steel-
trap coordination saved him as three rifles exploded
more or less simultaneously.

The balls gouged white scars in the rock, ricocheting

away with high-pitched whines. Le Loup Garou bellowed orders, and the nearest Roamers dismounted, others heeling their steeds forward, jostling and bowling over their people on foot. Horses neighed, reared, throwing riders from their backs. The attack was so disorganized, so impulsive, that Kane almost laughed.

Leaning around the boulder, he saw savagely screaming Roamers swarming at him from both sides. He aimed and fired a triburst. The bullets impacted against flesh at 335 pounds of pressure per square inch. Shooting to wound with a Sin Eater was rarely an option. Even a bullet striking a limb resulted in hydrostatic shock.

The rounds he fired didn't strike limbs. Three Roamers rushing forward in a shoulder-to-shoulder wedge absorbed the trio of 248-grain rounds with their upper bodies. They went down together, legs flailing madly in reflex motion.

Kane caught a glimpse of Le Loup Garou thumbing back the locks of his pistol, trying to frame his head in the sights. Kane drew back as the twin barrels belched flame and smoke, spattering the boulder with lead. He crouched lower, knowing that making a break for the gorge would be dangerous. He could be riddled before he made a dozen yards. A crude single-shot muzzle loader could chill him just as effectively as an autoblaster.

Le Loup Garou shouted a fierce command. Kane hazarded a quick look around the base of the boulder and saw a Roamer, ragged garments flapping around him, racing toward his position, flintlock rifle at his shoulder.

Kane pressed the Sin Eater's trigger, and the round caught the Roamer in midstride. With a wild screech, he staggered, jackknifing at the waist. He crashed head-long against the opposite side of the bullet-pocked boulder.

The Roamers sprinted for cover outside the mouth of the gorge, unnerved by Kane's uncanny marksmanship and the deep-throated reports of his pistol. Still, they were too infuriated to engage in a complete retreat. They pulled their neighing, stamping horses out of the zone of fire, for which he was relieved. He had no stomach for shooting animals, especially horses.

Brigid's voice, tight with worry, filtered from the trans-comm at his shoulder. "What's going on?"

"They don't want to leave," he replied. "Stand by. I'm going to make a run for it."

Kane sprang up and dashed into the gorge. As soon as he showed himself, he heard an angry howling burst from the throats of the Roamers. He was a swift runner, but the loose and treacherous rocks underfoot prevented him achieving his full speed.

Mushy pops echoed up and down the canyon, and gravel gouted all around him. Glancing back, he saw Le Loup Garou running around the boulder, discolored teeth bared in a grimace. Smoke dribbled from one of the bores of his tap pistol. Well over a dozen of his band, men and women alike, followed him, pounding close-packed between the gorge walls. They triggered their flintlocks as they came, their pace spoiling their aim. The high canyon walls magnified the gunfire, making it sound as if an entire battalion fired volley after volley.

Still, Kane heard a little whump of displaced air as one ball passed close to the right side of his head, fanning his cheek with a swirl of cold air. He returned the fire with his Sin Eater, knew he missed and didn't try again.

His eyes sought out and located the cleft high in the wall where Grant had planted the charge. Into the transcomm, he shouted, "Light it!"

Brigid's voice, crackling with tension, responded, "You're too close!"

A bullet plucked at the sleeve of his shirt. He shouted again, louder, "Light it!"

With an earsplitting, teeth-jarring crack the block of C-4 erupted in a flash of orange flame and white smoke. The concussion shoved him stumbling forward, but he managed to maintain his footing. Kane risked an upward glance. The air went on shivering with the echoes of the explosion as ugly black fissures spread out in a spiderweb pattern around the cleft. Then the entire cliff face appeared to be in motion. It tottered, seemed to suspend itself in midair for a long moment, then toppled.

As it fell, it sheared away the softer ledges beneath, breaking them apart. A seething avalanche of roaring rock slabs and dirt cascaded along the steep face of the cliff, augmenting its bellowing fury with tons of stone torn loose by its rush. Great crags and shards came raining down.

A thousand tons of granite and shale thundered down into the gorge floor, boulders skipping and bouncing. Dimly, above the grinding rumble and crash, Kane heard the screams of Roamers as they were crushed and buried beneath the falling cliff.

A boulder almost the size of the Hotspur rumbled end over end past him. Kane sprinted madly toward a jutting shelf of stone projecting five feet above the ground. He ducked as a small rock no larger than a pumpkin hurtled over his head and smashed itself into five pieces against the blacktop road.

He bounded at the ledge, clawed at the rim and heaved himself atop it to huddle in a shallow depression beneath an overhang. Before a whirling dust cloud obscured his vision, he saw a wave of shattered stone sweeping across the floor of the gorge to crash like tidal surf against the base of the opposite cliff. The impact sent black cracks zigzagging through the wall of rock, triggering new falls.

Kane sheltered his face from flying fragments, squeezing his eyes half-shut against the stinging particles of pulverized rock. A couple of stone splinters nicked his hands, and an egg-sized chunk of granite fetched him a painful smack on his left hip. He crouched there as the earth heaved and trembled around him.

The shuddering crash of tumbling, rolling rock slowly faded as the avalanche bled itself out. Settling stone continued to click and grate. Lowering his arms, peering through the thick pall of dust, he saw a vast, high heap of broken earth, shale and titanic boulders completely filling the gorge. He stood ankle deep in loose dirt and pebbles. Yet only a trickle of the rockslide had reached his ledge.

Unless the Magistrates—or the Cerberus personnel, for that matter—wanted to undertake a major excavation project, there was absolutely no chance of getting through the pass even with the most advanced ATVs.

Of the Roamers, he saw no sign, except for a few blood-and-grit-encrusted arms and legs protruding from the litter of the avalanche. Perspiration trickled into his eyes, burning them until he blinked it out.

"Kane!"

Brigid's voice had an odd, stereophonic quality to it, emanating from both his trans-comm and faintly, somewhere on the other side of the dust cloud.

"I'm all right," he said into the trans-comm clipped to his shirt, squinting through the shifting planes of gray powder.

"What happened?"

He coughed, fanning the air in front of his face. His tongue was coated with dust. "Looks like we chilled two birds with about a million stones. Settled the Roamer problem and blocked the pass at the same time."

"Do you need us?"

"Negative. Stay where you are. All this shit is still settling. I'll make my way to you. Stand by."

He moved cautiously out into the rubble. His visibility was limited, and the sun was veiled by the clouds of swirling dust. The welter of chipped stone clattered loudly under his boots—so loudly he didn't hear the crunch of feet on gravel until it was too late to evade the attack.

Le Loup Garou landed a blow on Kane's left shoulder with the butt of his tap-pistol. Pain exploded up and down his arm, into the base of his neck. He heard the splintering of the trans-comm's plastic casing as he fell onto sharp-edged rocks. Training and experience turned his fall into a roll so that a clubbing hammerblow missed his skull by mere inches.

Kane came to his feet, skidding on the pebbles and soft dirt beneath him. Not truly aiming at the shadowy figure in the dusty gloom, he pressed the trigger of the Sin Eater. It refused to move, frozen in place by tiny particles of grit.

Le Loup Garou hurled his pistol at Kane, but it

passed well above his head, spinning end over end. He crossed his arms at his waist, then spread them out in a flourish, a knife gripped in either fist. One was a slender stiletto barely five inches long, the other a wickedly curved, foot-long *kukri* with a spiked knuckle-duster hand guard.

Kane pushed the pistol back into its holster and took a long backward step as Le Loup Garou took a long forward one. The Roamer chief's clothes hung in tatters, revealing shallow lacerations on his hairy torso. His hair was plastered with sweat, and he breathed deep through expanded nostrils. Purple veins stood out on his temples like bas-relief carvings. Froth flecked his lips, the ends of his drooping mustache. Coated from head to foot in a shroud of dust, like some gray phantom of vengeance, he said nothing.

Le Loup Garou slashed the *kukri* in a whistling stroke that threatened Kane's groin. As he leaned away from the mirror-bright blade, the stiletto flashed in and opened a rent in his shirt and the flesh beneath. Only his reflexes kept the knife from plunging between his ribs.

Kane backpedaled carefully, the Roamer chief following, swinging and stabbing. Both men's movements were slowed by the uncertain footing. A stone turned beneath Le Loup Garou's boot, and he stumbled. As he regained his balance, Kane's right hand shot down and closed around the nylex handle of the combat knife in its boot scabbard. His fingers touched the positive-release push button.

He whipped up the fourteen-inch, tungsten-steel, titanium-jacketed blade. The double-edged, razor-keen metal was blued so it would have reflected nothing had any light penetrated the dense canopy of floating dust.

Le Loup Garou's expression of homicidal fury didn't alter at the sight of the knife. Instead, he feinted with the *kukri*, thrust with the stiletto. Kane parried both blades, steel clashing loudly against steel. He kicked at the Roamer's left knee, but dirt slid beneath him and he almost fell.

He staggered, going to one knee and avoided a scything, decapitating back swing from the *kukri*. Kane slashed at his calves, hoping to hamstring him, but Le Loup Garou skipped backward with the agility of a wolf. His heels struck a stone, and he sat down heavily.

Kane lunged, knife held out before him. The Roamer chief launched a kick that connected solidly with his chest. Kane went with the force of the kick, threw himself to one side as a vicious follow-up swing of the *kukri* missed his face by a finger's width.

Both men scrambled to their feet and stood for a moment, panting and glaring, chests heaving. Le Loup Garou stank with a strong, vile smell as human as it was animal. Neither one dared to take deep breaths, fearing the dust-saturated air would trigger coughing fits. Kane knew Grant and Brigid lurked somewhere near, concealed by the curtain of grit-laden mist. With his trans-comm broken, he could only hope they would hear and follow the sound of the struggle but wouldn't distract him by calling his name.

He also hoped that when visibility improved, Grant would be near enough to shoot Le Loup Garou and so end the duel. The fight wasn't a matter of honor. The bastard had brought it upon himself by ignoring Kane's warning and refusing to withdraw when he had the chance.

Kane understood the thirst for revenge that drove the Roamer chief, but he had no sympathy for it. The man was beyond all appeals to reason or concern for his own life.

Le Loup Garou bounded to the attack again, flailing with his glittering blades. Kane parried desperately, metal clanging and rasping. One of the stiletto cuts got through his guard and sliced into his right shoulder. Fiery pain streaked down his arm.

Wrenching his body backward, he awkwardly blocked an overhead strike of the *kukri*. The force of the blow staggered him. As he fought to recover his balance, a large section of the rockfall collapsed beneath his weight, sliding away like a wave of earth and gravel.

Kane tried to surf it, but the dirt shifted, crumbled, and he was carried down in a head-over-heels tumble. He fell heavily on his back, and a blanket of stone-littered earth half buried him.

Coughing, blinded and nearly smothered, he struggled against the pressure of the dirt covering him from boot tips to his chest. He craned his head, desperately blinking away the kernels of grit stinging his eyes. He dug frantically with his left hand, but for every bit of dirt he scooped aside, another collapsed in its place.

Le Loup Garou leaped into view above him, standing on the crest of the pile of rubble. His weight caused more soil and stones to spill down. Kane spit and sputtered, forced to squeeze his eyes shut to keep them from filling with dirt. He swished his combat knife in menacing arcs.

He heard the man husk out a low chuckle, a savage, gloating sound. Kane thrashed wildly, trying to free himself from the suffocating, pinioning weight. Le Loup Garou snarled out his laughter and stomped on the lip of the earth slip. Dirt rivered down, heavy clods thudded onto Kane's chest, nearly driving all the air from his lungs.

The Roamer chief no longer cared about cutting out his heart; he was intent on burying him alive. Kane tried to find the oxygen to call out for Brigid or Grant, but only a gasping rattle passed his lips.

For an instant, images of all the enemies he had either chilled or escaped flitted through his mind. The notion that a rag-assed Roamer bastard would be the one to put him under—literally—was at once grimly amusing and humiliating.

Then he heard a smacking sound like a heavy rock dropped into mud, and the pelting of rock and soil stopped abruptly. Clearing his vision with a fast, desperate swipe of his left hand, Kane opened his eyes just in time to see Le Loup Garou plummet straight down toward him.

Instinctively Kane swept his right arm up and out. The Roamer chief fell directly onto the upthrust blade of his combat knife. Le Loup Garou hung there for a moment, folding in the middle, transfixed by the fourteen inches of steel piercing his solar plexus. Kane felt and heard the point grate against the spinal column.

Black eyes wide, they showed no expression but confusion. The man's mouth gaped open, and a sharp spur of metal glinted at the back of his throat. Bloody bubbles formed on his writhing lips. They popped, and liquid strings of scarlet drooled down onto Kane's face.

Making a wordless utterance of disgust, Kane heaved the body aside, letting it drop heavily facedown onto the ground beside him. For the first time, he saw the long wooden shaft projecting at an angle from the back of the man's neck, at the base of his skull. The arrow was tipped with bright red feathers.

Looking around, trying to work his knife free from Le Loup Garou's guts, Kane kicked at the heap of dirt trapping his legs. He calculated the arrow's trajectory and turned his head in that direction. Through a momentary part in the dust cloud, he saw a rangy form standing atop the tall, primary pile of rubble that had fallen from the gorge wall.

The man's long black hair fell in two braids halfway to his waist, and he appeared to be wearing fringed buckskin. What Kane could see of his face was painted in bright yellow jagged designs, like lightning bolts. He held a wooden bow in his right hand. He stood about thirty yards away, well within arrow range, and he held the high ground.

The man didn't nock another shaft. He gazed at Kane in silent surmise, then called out, *"Wopila, hota wanagi! Wopila!"*

A breeze wafted a streamer of dust in front of him. When it dissipated, the man was gone.

Kane exhaled a deep breath, then determinedly began to dig himself out. He was free to his thighs when he heard the crunch and scutter of feet above him. Dirt and pebbles pattered down, covering the part of his body he had just cleared. He swore loudly.

"Kane?" demanded Grant, his voice hoarse from inhaling dust. "Where the hell are you?"

"About six feet under if you're not careful," he called out.

Grant cautiously leaned over the edge of the earth fall, then shouted over his shoulder, "I found him."

Carefully climbing down, eyeing Le Loup Garou's arrow-impaled corpse dispassionately, Grant kneeled beside Kane. Brigid joined him a moment later. Both of them were so coated with gray dust they looked like wraiths.

As they helped to dig him out, Kane tersely told them what had occurred. Grant nodded. "I figured the Indians were on their trail. Guess they got their people back and their revenge at the same time."

Kane kicked his legs loose, crawled back a few feet, then unsteadily rose. "The bowman yelled something at me. Probably a threat to do me like the Wolfman the next time he saw me."

"What did he say?" Brigid asked.

Kane repeated the words, stumbling over the pronunciation. To his surprise, she laughed. He asked, "What's so funny, Baptiste?"

She slapped at the layer of dirt covering his clothes. Dust puffed up in little clouds. "He wasn't threatening you. He was thanking you."

Kane raised a skeptical eyebrow. "Don't tell me you speak Indian among your other languages."

"I don't, but when Lakesh told us our nearest neighbors were Sioux and Cheyenne, I read the Lakota-to-English dictionary in the database."

She didn't add that she'd memorized it. She didn't have to. Brigid Baptiste's eidetic memory had proved useful more than once over the past few months.

"What did he say?" Grant asked.

"I can't be sure, never having heard the language spoken, but I think he said, 'Thanks, gray ghost. Thanks.'"

"Gray ghost?" echoed Kane. "Why'd he call me—?"

He broke off, glancing first at Brigid, then Grant, then down at himself. Judging by their appearance, he was at least as ghostly gray as they were.

Gingerly he probed at his rib cage. Though his fingertips came away shining with blood, the wound was superficial, as was the one on his shoulder.

Brigid took him by the arm. "Let's get back to the wag and treat you."

He allowed himself to be pulled along. Surveying the carnage, the vista ruin all around them, he remarked, "A job well-done is a job done well."

"Imagine that," Grant said dourly. "Especially since you were making up shit as you went along."

"We accomplished what we set out to do, didn't we?" retorted Kane.

"Of course we did," Grant drawled sarcastically. "We blocked the pass, buried some human garbage in our own little landfill and scored a public-relations coup with our nearest neighbors. You got shot at and stabbed and damn near buried alive. Yeah, I'd say we accomplished a lot."

Brigid smiled wryly, shaking dirt particles out of her mane of hair. "Regardless, you can't deny this day has been better than most."

Grant opened his mouth to voice heated rebuke, thought over her words, then closed it. She was right.

Chapter 4

Lakesh found Domi standing on the edge of the precipice. He eased out of the partially open sec door, wincing at the twinge of pain shooting across his lower back. The place where Pollard had kicked him was still sore, and though his body was tender elsewhere, his bruised kidneys flared up if he moved too quickly. He'd been lucky to have been rescued from the covert interrogation session carried out by Salvo in Cobaltville.

DeFore had released him from the wheelchair a few days earlier, and despite the polyethylene joints in his knees, his legs felt weak and wobbly. He walked carefully across the plateau, not wanting to startle Domi. The abyss beneath her plunged straight down a thousand feet or more to an old streambed. The rusted-out carcasses of several vehicles rested there, more than likely old personnel carriers.

His step was soft, and adjusting his eyeglasses, he paused for a moment to admire the highlights the setting sun struck on Domi's slight white form. Suddenly she turned toward him, crimson eyes blazing. Her hearing, honed from her upbringing in the Outlands to razor sharpness, detected the faint rustle of his bodysuit despite his stealthy approach.

The blaze in her eyes faded, and her lips twitched in a slightly abashed smile. Domi looked heartachingly small and fragile standing there against the awesome backdrop of the glowing western sky and towering, grim, gray rocks. Small as she was, a little over five feet tall and weighing a shade over a hundred pounds, she wasn't frail, even by the loosest definition of the word.

Her skin was perfectly white and beautiful, like a fine pearl, and her little, hollow-cheeked face was framed by ragged, close-cropped hair the color of bone. Her eyes, as bright as rubies on either side of her delicate, thin-bridged nose, looked at him with melancholy.

Like him, she wore a white, tight-fitting bodysuit. Unlike him, her right arm was crooked at the elbow and pressed tightly over her torso by a canvas body brace. Her shoulder bulged unnaturally, swathed by heavy bandages.

"Darlingest Domi," Lakesh said by way of a greeting. "You may be pushing the envelope of your recovery time."

Domi tried to shrug, caught herself and replied, "Been bit worse by bedbugs back home."

Lakesh didn't doubt that, since home for Domi had been a squalid settlement on the Snake River in Idaho. Guana Teague, pit boss of Cobaltville, spotted her on one of his periodic forays into the Outlands and was smitten by her exotic looks and spitfire personality. In return for smuggling her into Cobaltville, she gave him six months' sexual servitude. When Teague tried to change the terms, she cut his throat and escaped with Kane, Grant and Brigid into the Outlands. Her people back in Idaho were all dead now, murdered by the forces of the villes.

The Cerberus redoubt was now her home, though

Lakesh preferred to think of the trilevel, thirty-acre facility as a sanctuary for exiles.

Constructed in the late 1990s primarily of vanadium alloy, the redoubt boasted design and construction specs that had been aimed at making the complex an impenetrable community of at least a hundred people.

It held considerably fewer than that now, an even dozen human beings, counting Kane, Brigid and Grant. Balam couldn't be counted, inasmuch as he was a prisoner and not truly human.

The redoubt contained a frightfully well-equipped armory and two dozen self-contained apartments, a cafeteria, a decontamination center, a medical dispensary, a swimming pool and even holding cells on the bottom level. Its mat-trans gateway unit was the first one built after the prototype proved successful.

The ragged remains of a chain-link fence enclosed the plateau. Though they couldn't be seen, it was also surrounded by an elaborate system of heat-sensing warning devices, night-vision vid cameras and motion-trigger alarms. A telemetric communications array, uplinked to the very few reconnaissance satellites still in orbit, was nestled at the top of the mountain peak.

The main multiton security door opened like an accordion, folding to one side, operated by a punched-in code and a hidden lever control. Nothing short of an antitank shell could even dent the vanadium alloy.

Lakesh shivered as a chill breeze gusted up from the chasm. He'd been born in the tropical climate of Kashmir, India, more than two hundred years earlier, and his internal thermostat was still stuck there. Although he had spent a century in cryogenic stasis, and though it made no real scientific sense, he had been very vulnerable to cold ever since.

Patting Domi's right shoulder, he said, "The sun is going down, darlingest one. Let's go inside. They'll not try the road at night."

"Wait a while longer," she replied. "Nothing else to do."

Lakesh's thin lips quirked in a sad smile. Among the Cerberus polymath personnel, only Domi possessed no specific area of expertise. Half-feral, very nearly illiterate, she had arrived at the redoubt more or less by accident.

He had arranged for the escapes of the staff from various baronies when they ran afoul of one ville law or another. Domi's speciality lay in simple survival, and the injury she had recently suffered severely curtailed her skills in that.

DeFore, the redoubt's medic, had rebuilt her shattered shoulder with an artificial ball-and-socket joint only a few days before. Any kind of major reconstructive surgery exacted an emotional toll, as well as a physical one—as Lakesh had reason to know.

Upon his revival from cryogenic sleep, he had undergone several operations in order to prolong his life and his usefulness to the Program of Unification. His brown, glaucoma-afflicted eyes were replaced with new blue ones, his leaky old heart exchanged for a sound new one and his lungs changed out. The joints in his knees weren't the same as those he had been born with, either. Though his wrinkled, liver-spotted skin made him look exceptionally old, his physiology was that of a fifty-year-old man's.

He swept his gaze again over the mountain peak looming above them. Lakesh's single purpose in life had been devoted to science, to dispelling the unknown, reasoning that was the only way to save the idiot, half-insane world from itself.

For that purpose, he had studied most of his life, learned twelve languages and then left the country of his birth to work for what he truly believed was a way to restore sanity on earth. His devotion and belief had been as utterly and thoroughly betrayed as it was possible for a human being's to be and not commit suicide out of despair.

Lakesh shivered again and winced as his half-healed abrasions pulled. Domi noticed the wince.

"You go back," she said. "No reason for you to be out freezing ass off because of me."

Domi's eyes suddenly widened, and she tilted her head in the direction of the road stretching away from the perimeter of the plateau. "Hear something."

Lakesh strained his ears but heard nothing except the sighing of the wind. He didn't question her. If Domi claimed she heard a sound, then she heard it.

A moment later, he detected a distant moaning drone, rising, falling, then rising again. As it grew louder, he recognized it as the noise made by a laboring engine as the vehicle upshifted, then downshifted.

"It him!" Domi cried with relief, turning away from the precipice and striding swiftly to the point where the narrow road broadened onto the plateau.

Lakesh followed her, noting wryly she had said "him" rather than "them." He called, "Be careful. We don't know who it is."

"Who else it be?" she retorted.

Who else indeed, thought Lakesh. As unlikely as it seemed, he didn't rule out the possibility of an assault force of Magistrates. There had been no Deathbird recon flyovers, but he attributed that to the unpredictable down and updrafts swirling among the peaks of the Bitterroot Range. The reengineered Apache 64 gunships were rare, difficult to repair and almost impossible to replace. Cobaltville had already lost two of its fleet in the past six months, and Lakesh doubted that Abrams, the Magistrate Division administrator, would care to risk another one. An attack by land made the most strategic sense, and it was certainly the most cost-effective, in terms of ordnance.

"Recognize engine sound," Domi piped up. "It him—I mean them—all right."

Lakesh felt comforted by her assurances, but he didn't fully relax until the Hussar Hotspur's dull gray shape hove into view. The six-wheeled Land Rover was one of two all-terrain vehicles stowed in Cerberus. Its blocky, armored chassis was very unprepossessing, but it was a bit more maneuverable than the Sandcat on the mountain road.

Kane braked the vehicle at the edge of the tarmac and opened the metal shutters of the driver's-side ob slit. Lakesh and Domi peered in. Though Brigid and Grant were dirt streaked, Kane looked as if he had just that moment climbed out of a barrel of flour.

"Didn't have time to wash up," Kane said, speaking loudly in order to be heard over the controlled throb of the powerful engine.

"I didn't expect you back so soon," replied Lakesh. "It's a five-hour trip down to the pass."

Grant spoke up. "We finished early."

Lakesh caught the cryptic note in Grant's voice. "What do you mean? Did you set the proximity sensors?"

Kane gestured impatiently to the sec door. "Let us in and we'll explain."

Lakesh regarded him doubtfully and he and Domi crossed the plateau to the door. He raised the control to the midway point, and the heavy vanadium panels creaked aside, folding one atop the other until the opening was wide enough to admit the Land Rover.

Kane stopped just inside the door, and Brigid and Grant climbed out. He steered the vehicle down the twenty-foot-wide main corridor to the storage depot.

Lakesh used the lever on the interior wall to close the sec door all the way. Painted beside it was a large, luridly colored illustration of a three-headed black hound. Fire and blood gushed between yellow fangs, the crimson eyes glared bright and baleful. Underneath it, in ornate Gothic script was written Cerberus.

The painting had been done sometime prior to the nukecaust but after Lakesh's reassignment to the Anthill complex in South Dakota. Though he couldn't be positive, he figured Corporal Mooney was the artist, since its exaggerated exuberance seemed right out of the comic books he was so fond of reading. He had never considered having it removed. For one thing, the paints were indelible, and for another, it was Corporal Mooney's form of immortality. Besides, the image of Cerberus, the guardian of the gates of hell, representated a visual symbol of the work to which Lakesh had devoted his life.

He turned back to Grant and Brigid. Domi stood very close to Grant, beaming up into his face. He smiled nervously down at her, obviously discomfited by the adoration shining from her ruby eyes. Everyone in the redoubt knew she was in love with Grant and very jealous if she perceived he paid attention to another woman. Lakesh was also aware that the girl had tried in the past to seduce him, though as far as he knew, Grant had managed to evade her attempts.

"You're all safe?" Lakesh asked.

Brigid nodded. "Kane needs minor medical attention."

"Why?"

"A knife fight," Grant replied matter-of-factly.

Lakesh's eyebrows rose toward his hairline. "A knife fight? With whom? The country beyond the foothills is unpopulated for at least a hundred miles. There's no one around except for—"

He broke off, frowned, then groaned. "Not the Indians. Please don't tell me Kane made enemies of the Indians."

"No," replied Brigid with a smile. "But Indians were involved."

As they walked along the corridor made of softly gleaming alloy, beneath curved support ribs of metal, Brigid related all that had happened to them since they arrived in the pass at midmorning.

Lakesh listened without interruption, tugging at his long nose in bemusement. As Brigid concluded her report, he said, "I didn't envision blocking ingress to the redoubt in such a manner, but that's not a new experience. Nothing I conceive ever seems to match its eventual reality."

"Kane is accustomed to improvising," Grant said a bit defensively.

"You called it something else a few hours ago," Brigid remarked. "Anyway, it's the end result that is important."

Lakesh nodded. "Except in this instance, the end result may hem us up here without a viable escape route."

"We'll just have to improvise another," announced Kane, walking out of the vehicle depot. Everyone caught his sarcastic emphasis on "improvise."

Lakesh gazed at him sourly. "Other than parachuting off the peak, what do you propose, friend Kane?"

Kane's eyes went thoughtful. "That's really not a bad concept."

Domi shifted uncomfortably, working her right shoulder as best she could within the confines of the brace.

Grant asked, "You all right?"

"Hurts a little," she admitted. "Tight."

"DeFore should take a look at it," said Brigid sympathetically.

Suddenly Bry's voice cut down the corridor from behind them. "Sir! There's something I think you should see."

The slight, round-shouldered man sounded agitated, which was not particularly unusual. He always sounded as if he were on the verge of nervous collapse. He poked his head out of the doorway of the control complex, running a thin-fingered hand through his copper-colored curls.

"What is it?" asked Lakesh, deliberately affecting a calm, almost bored cadence in counterpoint to Bry's stressed tone.

"We've got activity on the mat-trans network," Bry called. "Redoubt Papa, of all places."

The designation meant nothing to Kane, Domi or Grant, but Brigid's and Lakesh's eyes widened in surprise. Lakesh pushed his way past Kane, moving swiftly. "Let's see it."

The central control complex was the nerve center of the installation. A long room with high, vaulted ceilings, the walls were lined by consoles of dials, switches and readout screens. A double row of computer stations formed an aisle. Circuits clicked, drive units hummed, indicator lights flashed. A Mercator-projection map of the world spanned the width of the far wall. Pinpoints of light flickered in almost every continent, and thin, glowing lines networked across the countries, like a web spun by a rad-mad spider. The map not only delineated the geophysical alterations caused by the nuke-caust, but it also displayed the locations of all functioning gateway units the world over.

One light glowed with an intense, unremitting yellow glare. Bry pointed at it, his words tumbling out in a staccato rhythm. "See? We've got an autosequence-initiator read showing a destination target lock, but not one indicating a departure point. It just flashed on a few minutes ago."

Lakesh squinted at the map. "That can't be possible."

"Perhaps," ventured Brigid, "an intruder broke into the redoubt and activated the unit accidentally, without actually transporting themselves anywhere."

"No," declared Bry firmly. "It's a definite transit line, a positive materialization. Someone transported themselves there, but the modulation frequencies can't be traced." He added blandly, "Just like our own unit."

Kane turned toward Lakesh. "Looks like some genius has rigged a gateway the same way you did."

Lakesh stiffened as if offended. "There's only one person alive who knows enough about the quantum interphase mat-trans inducers to do that. Me."

"You're sure it's not a sensor glitch, transmitting an incorrect signal?" Brigid asked.

A bit crossly, Bry gestured to a computer console. "That was my first suspicion, so I ran a level-two diagnostic on the sensor feed. No, it's a true read, a real signature. The unit in Redoubt Papa was activated."

Kane shook his head in exasperation. A little cloud of dust floated out and up from his hair. "What's so damn important about Redoubt Papa?"

Sinking into a chair before a station, Lakesh replied, "It was the only Totality Concept–linked installation in the vicinity of Washington, D.C."

"D.C.?" echoed Grant. He gazed at the map. "Washington Hole?"

"Exactly." Lakesh's lips tightened in a grim line. "As such, it was of extreme importance as an escape route to politicians and members of the military and intelligence community. It's probably been sealed for two hundred years."

"Washington Hole is a hellzone," said Kane. "The hottest in the country. Who'd be stupid enough to crawl around there?"

"More important," Brigid interjected, "who would know the redoubt even existed?"

"The barons," declared Grant. "Baron Cobalt called a council of the nine. They're turning over every stone, checking out every mat-trans unit trying to learn where we jumped to. Just what we were afraid would happen."

Turning to Lakesh, he asked, "You listed the Cerberus redoubt as unsalvageable on ville records, right?"

Lakesh nodded. "That I did. But under the circumstances, Baron Cobalt, in the interest of thoroughness, may still decide to verify my information. Inasmuch as he sounded the clarion call to the other barons, he'll have little choice.''

Bry cleared his throat. "With all due respect, whether the barons are searching the redoubts is beside the point. Whoever entered Papa did so via the gateway not by the front door. We don't know where they came from. If they altered the matter-stream modulations—''

"I think it's more likely that a gateway unit not registered on the index was the origin point," Lakesh interrupted acidly.

"Is that possible?" asked Brigid.

Lakesh spread his hands in a helpless gesture. "Who can say? I tried to keep track of all the modular units and to where they were shipped, but some may have escaped my notice."

No one responded to his comment. Lakesh had told them that after the initial success of the prototype gateway unit, Project Cerberus staff had been ordered to mass-produce them in modular form so they could be shipped and assembled elsewhere.

He sighed heavily. "Friend Kane, blocking the pass was not prematurely done, after all."

"Is that a compliment, or a statement of fact?"

"A bit of both. You've bought us time so we can properly investigate this anomaly."

"How can we?" demanded Kane. "If the modulation frequencies have been altered, then we can't trace them. If it's an unindexed unit like you suppose, we're still in the dark."

"The molecular imaging scanners," Brigid said crisply. "All mat-trans control units contain them, right?"

Lakesh gave her a fond smile. "As rain, dearest Brigid. Every record of every gateway transit is stored in the scanner's memory banks. They can be downloaded and reviewed.''

Grant's brows knit together. "But that means we'll have to physically pull 'em from—" He broke off, then growled, "Wait just a goddamn minute."

Lakesh nodded sagely. "Yes, friend Grant, the memory banks will have to be removed from the control unit in Redoubt Papa."

"You're proposing to send us to Washington Hole?" Kane wasn't asking a question; it sounded more like he was making an accusation. "The hellzone of hellzones? Why don't you just inject us with isotopes of plutonium and have done with it?"

"Oh, come on," Brigid said with sharp impatience. "You know all redoubts are rad shielded. Even if we pick up a dose, that's why we have a decam facility here."

Kane passed a weary hand over his dusty face. "I suppose I'm really a stupe—" He paused, providing the opportunity for anyone to refute his statement. When no one did, he continued, "But I fail to see the importance of this, much less the urgency."

Patronizingly Lakesh replied, "The escape route we discussed a few minutes ago, remember? If another untraceable mat-trans gateway exists somewhere, it would be a simple solution to the problem of where to go if and when the barons come calling."

Realization glinted in Kane's eyes, but he said nothing.

Lakesh turned toward Bry. "Continue monitoring that signal and cross-reference it with any recent satellite pix we may have of the region. Apprise me immediately if you see further activity."

Chapter 5

Kane ground his teeth together tightly as DeFore ruthlessly ripped off the field dressing and sloshed antiseptic into the knife cut along his rib cage.

"Does it hurt?" she asked.

"Think I'd tell you?" he retorted.

Naked to the waist, he sat on the edge of an examination table in the small dispensary as DeFore efficiently treated his injuries.

"Pretty clumsy to get stabbed by a Roamer," she said. "I thought Mags were invincible...or is that only when you're in armor?"

She probed the edges of the slash, and he winced as sharp pain cut into his side. "Superficial," she declared. "Very lucky."

"Lucky I didn't get chilled or hurt worse?"

DeFore sniffed disdainfully. She used an aerosol can to spray on liquid bandage. A skinlike thin layer of film formed over the cut along his ribs and the puncture in his shoulder. The substance contained nutrients and antibiotics and would be absorbed by the body as the injuries healed.

As she worked, DeFore said, "Before you, Grant, Domi and Brigid came here, I'd go months without removing so much as a splinter from a finger."

"Yeah, well," replied Kane gruffly, "before I came

here, I'd go years without so much as stubbing my toe. What's your point—that we're accident prone?"

DeFore's full lips pursed. A stocky, buxom woman with deep bronze skin, braided ash-blond hair and liquidy brown eyes, she was one of the first Cerberus exiles and accustomed to speaking her mind. "One of you, anyway. It might be appropriate to say you're risk prone."

Kane climbed off the examination table. "Is that a diagnosis?"

"In your case, it's more of a prognosis. It's past time we discussed this."

"Discussed what?" He bit out the words. "Every day you're alive is just another spin of the wheel. Winning is just breaking even. When your number is up, it's up and you're dead. End of discussion."

"Very colorful metaphor, Kane," DeFore said coldly. "But you're not playing a lone hand, even if you think you are."

"Get to the goddamn point, if there is one."

She fixed an unblinking stare on his face. "Point one—you're displaying early symptoms of combat fatigue. It used to be called post-traumatic stress disorder. I already told Baptiste—"

"You did what?" Kane broke in, his gray-blue eyes taking on an icy gleam.

Unruffled, DeFore went on. "I'd hoped she would talk to you, but obviously she didn't consider it very important. I do. You're emotionally exhausted and you're overcompensating. Your powers of judgment are unreliable. Taking Salvo on your last mission proves that."

Glaring at her from beneath a lowered brow, Kane snapped, "What happened on that mission had nothing to do with my decision to take Salvo. Events would have unfolded in the same way, whether he had come along or not."

She shook her head. "That's debatable. What isn't is your decision to rely on a man who lived only to hate you. I understand that during your years as a Magistrate, you set great store by your instincts."

"They saved my life—and others'—more than once."

"Now they're failing you. You're not prescient, not invulnerable. You're burning yourself out and putting the redoubt at risk." She inhaled a deep breath. "That's my diagnosis."

"And your prognosis?"

"Stand down for a while. If you don't, the odds are high you'll get yourself or someone else chilled."

"What if I don't agree?" His voice took on a low, menacing note.

"I'll enforce it if I have to, Kane. Believe it."

Kane tried to lock gazes with the woman, to prove his implacable will, to show her he wasn't intimidated. He couldn't. Too easily he recalled his self-anger when Salvo turned the opportunity Kane had offered to redeem himself into a continuation of their blood feud.

He couldn't deny he had brought Salvo on the op in hopes of salvaging a soul. Instead, the confidence in his instincts had been severely damaged. DeFore had put into words Kane's desperate fear that the next time his instincts faltered, someone close to him would die.

He picked up his shirt, draped it around his neck and strode out of the dispensary, his pace suggesting both anger and preoccupied thought. He passed Grant and Domi without speaking to them. Grant glanced after him, then turned toward DeFore, an eyebrow raised questioningly.

She nodded. "I told him. I don't know if I made a dent. Maybe you should talk to him."

Grant snorted. "Since when did I have any say over Kane?"

He steered Domi over to the examination table. "She mentioned her shoulder was bothering her. Maybe the brace needs adjustment."

"I'm not surprised," replied DeFore irritably. "Ever since I released her, she's done nothing but pace around."

"Get bored," Domi declared, allowing Grant to help her up on the table. She wasn't overly fond of DeFore, suspecting that the medic had her sights set on Grant. As far as Grant knew, it was a completely unfounded suspicion.

As DeFore busied herself unbuckling the canvas body brace, she said broodily, "I told Kane that he's on the verge of burnout. I told you and Baptiste the same thing so one or the other of you could talk to him about it."

Grant shrugged. "He wouldn't have reacted any differently to us than to you. Forcing him to stay behind while there's a mission to perform wouldn't help him."

DeFore peeled the brace off, noting how Domi momentarily sank her teeth into her lower lip. "Does that hurt?"

"Think I tell you?" Domi snapped.

DeFore made a wordless utterance of annoyance. "Did everybody get together and decide that would be the standard Cerberus response to my questions?"

Neither Domi nor Grant responded. As DeFore carefully unzipped the girl's bodysuit, she said, "From what I heard, Kane royally screwed the New York op."

"That's not what I heard," Grant replied defensively. "He did what he always does—turning disadvantage to advantage."

"All he did was solve the Salvo problem." DeFore frowned, examining the heavy padded bandage swathing Domi's right shoulder. She lifted up an edge to peer beneath. "Big deal. That wasn't the objective."

Harshly Grant said, "Stick to medical matters, DeFore. Leave the armchair generaling to Lakesh."

DeFore turned angry eyes toward him. Domi repressed a grin, enjoying the heated exchange between them. "I intend to lodge a formal protest to Lakesh," DeFore stated. "I'll recommend Kane be confined to quarters until I can do a full psych workup. If necessary, I'll arrange for him to be placed in a holding cell, under armed guard if it comes to that."

Grant folded his arms over his broad chest. He didn't speak for a long, tense moment. When he did, his tone of voice far exceeded hers in frosty resolve. "Recommend away, DeFore. But ask yourself one question before you do."

"What?"

"Which asshole will volunteer to die trying to lock him up?"

THE SMALL POOL on the second level had only recently been made functional again, and Brigid was eager to try it out. She hadn't been swimming in a very long time, and she didn't count her near drowning in the Irish Sea a few weeks ago as an enjoyable pastime.

She passed through an open area filled with weights, stationary exercise cycles and workout mats. The pool and exercise rooms had been built to provide the original inhabitants of Cerberus with a means of sweating off the stress of being confined for twenty-four hours a day in the installation. After the nukecaust, just staying alive was probably just as much exercise as they needed.

She pushed through the double doors into the pool room. Round and curve walled like an upside-down bowl, it was dimly illuminated by overhead track lighting. Brigid's pace faltered when she heard the splashing of water. A little dismayed, she saw someone swimming toward her, pale legs kicking languidly beneath the clear surface. She stopped at the edge as Rouch heaved herself out of the water and onto the tiled lip of the pool.

A fairly new arrival in Cerberus, from Sharpeville, Rouch had exchanged only a few words with her. Brigid didn't know what position the woman had held in her barony or what crime she may have committed against it, but Rouch had to be a specialist in some area or Lakesh wouldn't have offered her sanctuary.

Rouch looked to be a few years younger than Brigid's twenty-seven years. Her eyes were oval, almond, true Asian and appeared in the dim lighting to be jet-black. Her mouth was wide and sensuous, her ears and nose tiny and delicate. Glistening black hair fell nearly to her waist.

"Baptiste," she said in a low voice.

"Rouch. How's the water?"

"A little cold."

Brigid noted wryly that Rouch didn't need to tell her that. The woman was completely naked, and the nipples of her pear-shaped breasts jutted out like wooden pegs.

Brigid unzipped her bodysuit and slid out of it. Though she wasn't particularly modest, she didn't take off her underclothes. Nor did she test the water's temperature with a toe before plunging into the pool in a flat dive.

Just like Rouch said, the water was cold, but not frigid. Still, she surfaced gooseflesh and gasping, raking her heavy hair out of her eyes.

"Told you," said Rouch, crossing a pair of exquisitely molded legs.

"I'm an empiricist," Brigid replied, backstroking to the far end.

Rouch cocked her head at a quizzical angle. "What's that?"

For a moment, Brigid wondered if she were joking, but the young woman's puzzlement seemed genuine. She swam back to her, propping an arm on the edge of the pool.

"You're from Sharpeville?"

Rouch nodded, leaning backward to pull a towel from a shelf.

"What level did you work on?"

Bending forward, Rouch wrapped the towel around her wet hair like a turban. "D."

Brigid knew her eyebrows drew down to the bridge of her nose in a frown, but she couldn't help herself. All the villes were built along the same specs, conforming to the Program of Unification's standards—fifty-foot-high walls with Vulcan-Phalanx gun towers mounted at each corner.

Inside the walls, the elite lived in the Enclaves, four multileveled towers joined together by pedestrian walkways. Each tower was connected by a major promenade to the Administrative Monolith, a massive cylinder of white stone projecting three hundred feet into the air, the tallest building in the villes.

Every level of the Administrative Monolith fulfilled a specific ville function. Alpha Level held the administrative offices, Beta Level housed the Historical Division and the Magistrate Division was on Level C, which deviated from the Greek Alphabet upon which the names were based, but maybe it was a tribute to the Magistrates in some way—that they were different from the rest. D, or Delta, Level was devoted to the growth, preservation and distribution of food stuffs. Epsilon Level was a manufacturing and construction facility.

"Were you a nutritionist?" asked Brigid.

Rouch blinked at her in mild surprise. "No, I was in the packaging department."

It was Brigid's turn to blink in surprise. An expert in food packaging seemed about as essential to the work of Cerberus as an expert in flower arranging.

Hoping she didn't sound rude, Brigid said gently, "Certainly that's not your only field of expertise, or you wouldn't be here."

Rouch's lips stretched in a confident smile, slightly touched with superiority. "Oh, now I see what you're asking. I'm here because of my—how did Lakesh put it?—exceptionally strong female drives. I'm also very fertile."

Brigid narrowed her eyes. "I don't get you."

"I guess I'm what you'd call a breeder. And that's something I want to talk to you about. Are you and Kane together?"

Mind reeling with surprise and extrapolations, Brigid murmured again, "I don't get you."

Rouch inched closer to her, her confident smile becoming conspiratorial. "I mean are you fucking him? Not that it makes any difference to me, but the sooner I get started with him, the sooner we can find out how strong his seed is. Lakesh said it was potent, but—"

Brigid raised a preemptory hand, sloshing water on the woman's ankles. "Hold on," she said firmly, doing her best to keep anger out of her voice. "I'm not sure I understand. You're saying Lakesh brought you here solely to be impregnated—by Kane?"

Rouch laughed, a musical tinkling sound. "Not just by him, but he's the one I want to strap on first. Lakesh told me the other women here have fertility problems or genetic abnormalities, like that little albino."

Rouch continued speaking, but her words were muted by the pounding of furious blood in Brigid's ears.

She knew the Overproject Excalibur division of the Totality Concept dealt primarily with bioengineering. One of its subdivisions, Scenario Joshua, had its roots in the twentieth century's Genome Project, and shared the goal of the mapping of human genomes to specific chromosomal functions and locations. The end result had been in vitro genetic samples of the best of the best. In the vernacular of the time, it was referred to as purity control.

Everyone who enjoyed full ville citizenship was a descendant of the Genome Project. Sometimes a particular gene carrying a desirable trait was grafted to an unrelated egg, or an undesirable gene removed. Despite many failures, when there was a success, it was replicated repeatedly, occasionally with variations. Lakesh had admitted that Kane was one such success, one that he himself had covertly been involved with.

Some forty years ago, when Lakesh determined to

build a resistance movement against the baronies, he rifled Scenario Joshua's genetic records to find the qualifications he deemed the most desirable. He used the Archon Directorate's own fixation with purity control against them. By his own confession, he was a physicist cast in the role of an archivist, pretending to be a geneticist, manipulating a political system that was still in a state of flux.

Brigid had assumed from his confession and his genuine expression of regret that Lakesh had learned his lesson. Rouch's blithe words proved he had not. Moreover, the implications that he found her—and presumably Domi and DeFore—lacking in the ability to produce the desired type of children did more than anger her. It stunned her, grieved her beyond the power to put it into words.

From a strictly clinical point of view, what Rouch claimed made sense. To ensure that Kane's superior qualities were passed on, mating with him was the most logical course of action. Without access to the techniques of fetal development outside the womb, the conventional means of procreation was the only option.

But acknowledging its logic did not make her feel better. Intellect and emotions rioted within her. She had always feared to closely examine her feelings for Kane, frightened they were far too intense for her to deal with.

Their relationship was guarded, sometimes tense. Brigid assumed it was due to the fact she took pride in cool analytical thinking while Kane exhibited emotionalism, citing his instincts more than rational analysis. But she knew there were far deeper factors at work, as well.

Twice over the past few months Brigid had faced,

then turned away from, the possibility that her soul and Kane's had been intertwined for a very long time, reincarnated over and over, destined to always find each other. Neither one of them had cared to seriously entertain such a concept. They were not and never had been romantically involved.

He had risked his life on a number of occasions for her, but only once had he ever called her by her first name. Only a few days before, he had kissed her, but it had been an impulsive act, something to celebrate the fact that they had survived their trip back into time. Afterward he seemed a little embarrassed.

Rouch leaned forward, commanding her attention again. Her eyes shone, and Brigid knew she was thinking of Kane, too, but only of his virility and of the novelty of bedding a former Magistrate.

"Tell me," she urged. "What's he like? What does he like? Is he rough? I'll bet he is—"

Brigid clenched her fists, struggling with the almost overwhelming desire to punch the young woman in the face.

The double doors slammed open. Kane stood there, bare-chested, shirt around his neck, his mobile features set and drawn into a grim mask.

Chapter 6

Rouch gazed at Kane boldly. Her eyes rested for a long time on his groin, and Brigid saw her lips move in what could only have been anticipation.

The sight of the naked woman didn't appear to move him at all. Kane gave Rouch an incurious, dispassionate glance, then said, "Baptiste, we need to talk. Alone."

For a long, tense moment, no one moved or spoke. Then, languorously, Rouch rose to her feet, made a deliberately slow show of unwrapping the towel from her hair and dropping it to the tiles. Hips swinging, she sauntered over to the shelves and pulled down a robe. She took a provocatively long time putting it on and closing it up. The words *gaudy slut* leaped unbidden into Brigid's mind, but she managed to keep them from her tongue—just barely.

As Rouch padded barefoot past Kane, one of her long fingernails traced a line on his arm. "Let's do dinner," she said, her voice a husky, seductive croon. "Or breakfast."

For the first time, Kane took notice of the woman, with a swift, slightly irritated flash of the eyes. They were eyes that appraised Rouch, yet were already focused on something else.

As the doors swung shut behind her, Kane declared,

"I understand DeFore expected you to talk to me about being fused out."

Brigid stared up at him, feeling his anger, but too busy wrestling with her own to address it. "Do you know why Rouch is here?"

His eyes narrowed in sudden surprise. "No, and I don't really care. Why didn't you—?"

"She's here to mate with you," Brigid interrupted. "To improve the breed of Cerberus exiles."

Kane's surprise became astonishment. He turned to look at the doors Rouch had just walked through. "Really? Nobody told me."

"Oh, she would've gotten around to it eventually," snapped Brigid bitterly.

"She told you that?"

"And a lot more. First, she wanted to know if you and I were—" she paused, groping for a delicate term "—involved. Not that it would make any difference to her, mind you. It's all business, though she isn't above mixing a little pleasure in with it."

Kane shook his head fiercely. "I don't want to talk about that."

"Will you?" she demanded hotly.

"Will I what?"

"I hate it when you're obtuse. Answer my question."

"Answer mine," he countered.

"You didn't ask me one."

"That's because you didn't give me the chance. DeFore told you that I was fused out."

"That's not a question."

Kane snarled, knotting his fists, turning a complete circle in angry frustration. "Goddammit, let's stay on the subject!"

Brigid heaved herself out of the pool in a splashing rush of water. She snatched up the towel Rouch had dropped and furiously began drying her hair. "Fine. I suppose it makes perfect sense, Lakesh continuing to practice his own version of purity control. It would have been polite to have briefed us on what he had in mind, but then we're just an ex-archivist and an ex-Mag. Exiles all."

Kane gazed at her, finally reacting to the unmistakable edge of barely repressed fury and hurt in her voice. He said the first thing that occurred to him. "You're jealous. For God's sake, Baptiste, you're jealous. You're acting like a—"

He caught himself before he uttered the final word, but Brigid guessed it and spoke it herself. "A woman. That's what you were going to say—I'm acting like a woman."

He shifted his feet uncomfortably. Lamely he replied, "Well, you are."

She stood up quickly. The speed and grace of the motion gave a slight hint of the athlete's coordination within her slender frame. Kane couldn't help but gaze at her admiringly. He had seen her nude before, but the brief brassiere and panties she wore struck him as strangely arousing.

His thoughts whipped back to that night months before in Cobaltville when he had first met her. He had recognized her as a truly beautiful woman then, and with a slight sensation of shock, he recognized a truly beautiful woman now.

Brigid's mane of thick, unruly hair, darker now because it was wet, tumbled artlessly over her shoulders. Her slim body was rounded and curved, long in the leg. Her full, taut breasts strained at the fabric of her brassiere, and through the wet cloth of her panties was plastered to the soft, honey-blond triangle at the juncture of her thighs.

She radiated a beauty far deeper than the physical, a force intangible yet one he had felt since the first time he laid eyes on her, an energy that triggered a melancholy longing in his soul. That strange, sad longing only deepened after a bout of jump sickness both of them suffered during the mat-trans jump to Russia. The main symptoms of jump sickness were vivid, almost-real hallucinations.

He and Brigid had shared the same hallucination, but both knew on a visceral, primal level it hadn't been gateway triggered delirium, but a revelation that they were joined by chains of fate, their destinies linked.

They never spoke of it, though Kane often wondered if that spiritual bond was the primary reason he had sacrificed everything he had attained as a Magistrate to save her from execution. The possibility confused him, made him feel even more sad.

Kane didn't like that melancholia, so over the past six months he worked very hard at burying it, at rerouting all of the repressed passions he felt toward Brigid to a dead circuit board inside of his mind.

The circuit board sparked to life every so often, as it had in New York, on New Year's Eve, 2000, when it impelled him to kiss her. But the melancholy filled him like a cup, and he pushed her away before the sadness overflowed to such a degree he would never be able to contain it again.

A few weeks before, when Kane had protested to Morrigan that there was nothing between him and Brigid, the Irish telepath had laughed at him. She said, "Oh, yes, there is. Between you two, there is much to forgive, much to understand. Much to live through. Always together…she is your *anam-chara*."

In ancient Gaelic, Kane learned, *anam-chara* meant "soul friend."

He wasn't sure what that meant, but he knew he felt curiously comfortable with Brigid Baptiste, at ease with her in a way that was similar, yet markedly different than his relationship with Grant. He found her intelligence, her iron resolve, her wellspring of compassion and the way she had always refused to be intimidated by him not just stimulating but inspiring. She was a complete person, her heart, mind and spirit balanced and demanding of respect.

Only a few days ago, when cornered by Salvo's questions about his reasons for sacrificing everything for a woman, he could think of only one, clumsily phrased response: "Because I know her. Because I need her."

Kane privately acknowledged the perversity of making such a confession to a man who was his sworn enemy, rather than to the woman in question, but he was unable—or unwilling—to speak the same words to her.

Brigid reached down to pick up her bodysuit, shouldering Kane aside. He recoiled, making a swiftly stifled exclamation of pain, his hand moving to the wound on his ribs.

When Brigid straightened up, she saw the ruby bead of blood shining at the edge of the film of liquid bandage covering the cut. "I'm sorry," she said.

"Me, too," he replied ruefully, probing at the injury with careful fingers.

She pulled in a deep, calming breath, pushed it out

and said softly, "I have no right to give you hell about Rouch."

"That's for sure," he agreed. "Direct it toward Lakesh."

"I don't have the right to give it to him, either," she replied. "Objectively his reasoning is sound. I have no hold over you."

Kane frowned, not liking what she said but unable to dredge up anything to refute it. He reached a hand out toward her, but Brigid turned her back and stepped into the bodysuit.

Thrusting her arms into the sleeves, she said brusquely, "DeFore mentioned to me that she was worried about your emotional stability. The coma you suffered after the Irish op threw a scare into her."

Kane said nothing.

"She's afraid you'll develop a full-blown psychosis. She interpreted your insistence on taking Salvo with us to New York as evidence of it."

Zipping up the suit, she turned around to face him, her eyes and voice level. "She thinks that was the reason the mission failed."

Kane opened his mouth, closed it, shook his head and said falteringly, "She might be right. Maybe my instincts can't be trusted anymore."

Brigid's lips curved in a wry smile. "If the mission to change history failed, it had nothing to do with your instincts or Salvo. We gained important data from it. We now know the true purpose behind Operation Chronos."

"Why didn't you tell me about DeFore's worries when I first suggested bringing along Salvo?"

Brigid's green eyes gleamed strangely in the dim light. "What good would it have done except make you doubt yourself? She doesn't know you, doesn't know that you're at your best when faced with seemingly impossible challenges."

He crooked an eyebrow at her. "And you know that?"

She nodded. "I do. DeFore thinks you have a deluded self-image of yourself, that you believe yourself to be an arrogant superman, glorying in your power over life or death."

Kane smiled thinly. "I seem to recall you saying much the same thing on occasion."

Brigid waved aside his comment. "I was referring to your Magistrate's persona. I can see beneath it."

"And what's there, Baptiste?"

Very quietly she answered, "A lonely and frightened man who is doing a job that needs doing. That doesn't make you fused out, Kane. It makes you human. I saw no reason to mention that DeFore diagnosed you as human."

Kane swallowed the hot lump swelling in his throat, felt his heart thud within his chest. He averted his face from the intense pressure of her emerald eyes, knowing they peeled away the carapace to see the pain beneath. He felt the familiar, longing ache and tried to bottle it. Brigid sighed and stepped around him toward the doors.

He turned toward her. "Baptiste?" His low-pitched voice was barely above a whisper.

She paused. "Yes?"

"You were wrong about one thing."

"What's that?"

"About you having no hold over me."

Brigid said nothing, but inclined her head in a short nod before pushing open the doors.

you done yourself? She doesn't know you, doesn't know that you're anything but what blood will create ... ugly impossible creatures ...

He croaked softly... "I ... AH ... No you know that."

She said ... "I do. Do you think you have a little self-image of yourself that you believe yourself

Chapter 7

Like most of the territory surrounding the ville that took his name, Baron Sharpe had been dead for a long time, but spiritually really dead only for the past eight years.

One day he had succumbed to an infection, some airborne filth that had wafted up from either the Pits or floated in from the rad-rich Outlands. Baron Sharpe coughed up blood-tinted phlegm for two days before falling into a coma. Members of his personal staff had whisked him, via mat-trans gateway, to the bioengineering facility in Dulce, New Mexico. There, geneticists who were intimately familiar with all the limitations of the hybrid immune systems, worked on him for a week.

At the end of those seven days, Baron Sharpe opened his big blue eyes and sat up. They told him he was cured, that his metabolism had been adjusted, his tainted blood replaced and detoxified, his damaged organs replaced. They told him he was cured, but the baron knew better. He was dead, regardless of the fact that he walked, talked, ate and breathed.

At first his condition disturbed him since no one else seemed to notice it. After a few months, he grew accustomed to being dead and found it oddly liberating, even exhilarating. Very infrequently, the notion that he might not be dead but simply deluded intruded on

Baron Sharpe's peace of mind. He was unique among the members of the baronial hierarchy, of the hybrid oligarchy, and therefore he had responsibilities to the Directorate that he couldn't shirk, alive or dead, deluded or sane.

Unlike Barons Ragnar, Cobalt, Palladium and all the others who were polyglot mixtures of human and Archon DNA, Sharpe was a direct descendant of the first baron who had claimed the environs in and around Washington Hole as his sovereign territory.

Of course, that baron's genes had been mixed, matched and spliced with Archon material, but nevertheless, there was no question of his illustrious human antecedent, four generations removed. He'd seen old pix of his great-grandfather, and the resemblance was certainly striking.

He had inherited the same close-cropped blond hair, broad shoulders and chilling milky blue eyes the color of mountain melt water. What he didn't have was the man's six-foot height and one hundred percent human physiology.

Unlike his ancestor, his blue eyes were very large, shadowed by sweeping supra-orbital ridges, and his hair possessed a feathery, duck-down texture. His cranium was very high and smooth, the ears small and set very low on the head. He also had inherited a few of his namesake's eccentricities, though he knew some few referred to them as insanities.

One of his eccentricities was a fondness for picking through predark articles of clothing stored in the archives of the Historical Division and wearing whatever struck his whim at the moment. Depending on his fancy, Baron Sharpe would outfit himself in white tie and tails, complete with a silk top hat and silver-knobbed walking stick. On another day, it might be a backless evening gown of gold lamé, with a teased-out bouffant wig as a shock-value fashion statement. It didn't matter much if the clothing was on the verge of falling apart with age. He was dead, and entitled to indulge his impulses.

Still, the fact that nobody else—his personal staff, the Baronial Guard or members of the Trust—wanted to acknowledge his condition irritated him, made him question himself. To settle the internal conflict once and for all, Baron Sharpe sought the counsel of a doom-seer, a mutant gifted—or cursed—with the psychic ability to sniff out forthcoming death.

Under other circumstances, locating a doomie would have been exceedingly difficult, if not impossible. Most of the mutie strains spawned after the nukecaust were extinct, either dying because of their twisted biologies or hunted and exterminated during the early years of the unification program. Stickies, slowies, scabbies, swampies and almost every other breed exhibiting warped genetics had all but vanished.

Fortunately part of his legacy from his great-grandfather was a small private zoo of creatures that had once crept and slithered and scuttled over the Deathlands. The monsters had been fruitful and multiplied over the decades, and one of them was a doomie called Crawler.

It was more of a title than a name, bestowed upon him after his leg tendons had been severed. The psi-mutie had displayed a great cunning and propensity for escape from his compound, no doubt employing his mental talents to find the most opportune time and means to do so. After he had been crippled, his psi-powers availed him nothing, inasmuch as he was restricted to dragging himself around his cell by fingers and elbows.

Baron Sharpe visited Crawler one still, sultry summer midnight. He gazed in revulsion at the human face staring back at him from a wild, matted tangle of gray beard and long, filthy hair. The baron had no idea of Crawler's age, but he understood that he was one of his ancestor's last acquisitions before his mysterious disappearance, some ninety-odd years before. He knew the doomie was very old, but some muties possessed remarkable longevity.

Ignoring the thick waft of mingled stenches the cell exuded, Baron Sharpe commanded Crawler to approach him. The creature scrabbled forward, to the iron bars, heavily muscled arms dragging him along. Dark calluses crusted his elbows, and his atrophied legs trailed behind him, like a pair of boneless, filthy tentacles.

Crawler's dark eyes blazed from behind a screen of stringy hair. Baron Sharpe very nearly turned and ran from the fierce heat of the doomie's eyes, especially when he sensed the wispy, cobwebby caress of a psi-touch.

"I have a question," Baron Sharpe announced. "About my death."

Wheezing whistles issued from Crawler's hair-rimmed lips. For a moment, the baron thought the mutie was undergoing an asthma attack and would expire, but then he recognized the sound as laughter.

In a high, whispery voice, Crawler said, "That question has no meaning, my Lord Baron. You have died and crossed back. You no longer need fear death, for it is behind you, not ahead of you."

Baron Sharpe was so delighted he came close to

bursting into tears of gratitude. His hopes had been realized, his fear that he was mad proved groundless. That very night, he ordered the release of Crawler from his cage, saw that he was bathed, fed, shaved, cropped and pampered. He installed him as a high counselor, ignoring the outraged reactions of his personal staff.

A few weeks later while pawing through the archived clothing, he made a discovery that became his personal uniform and statement of belief. It was a violet jumpsuit, with huge belled legs, flame-colored satin facings and a bat-winged collar. Long fringes streamed from both sleeves. Worked in glittering rhinestones on the back were three letters: TCB.

He remembered Crawler's phrase and knew the letters meant To Cross Back, and thusly the baron decided that by wearing the outfit, he said to the world that he had died and crossed back to the land of the living.

Baron Sharpe was so attired when he greeted the members of the Sharpeville Trust. He met the eight men in his drawing room on Alpha Level of the Administrative Monolith. He had insisted on recreating a Victorian parlor, a cozy sitting room where gentlemen of good breeding received visitors. As a hybrid, his breeding was more than good; it was the pinnacle of genetic achievement.

Every ville had its own version of the Trust. The organization, if it could be called that, was the only face-to-face contact allowed with the barons, and the barons were the only contacts permitted by the Archon Directorate.

Baron Sharpe had never met an Archon, only other hybrids, though he was certain they existed, simply because the gene pool of the baronial hierarchy was a collection of superior traits derived from both human and Archon DNA.

He understood that the entirety of human history was intertwined with the activities of the entities called Archons, though they didn't refer to themselves as such. The term was very ancient, referring to a mystical force that acted as a spiritual jailer, imprisoning the spark of the divine within human souls.

The Archons' standard operating procedure was one they had employed since time immemorial—they established a privileged ruling class dependent upon them, which in turn controlled the masses for them. In ages past, the Archons' manipulation of governments and religions was all-pervasive. However, as time progressed, the world and humankind changed too much for their plenipotentiaries to rule with any degree of effectiveness.

Hence came January 20, 2001, and the greatest megacull in the long, confusing history of the world.

Now, nearly two hundred years after the nukecaust, the population was only a fraction of what it had been and far easier to manipulate, with most nonessential and nonproductive humans eliminated.

Still, the existence of the Archon Directorate remained a ruthlessly guarded secret. The Trust acted more or less as the protectors of the Directorate, and its oath revolved around a single theme—the presence of the Directorate must not be revealed to humanity. If its presence became known, if the truth behind the nukecaust filtered down to the people, then humankind would no doubt retaliate with a concerted effort to wipe them out, and the Directorate would be forced to visit another holocaust upon the face of the earth. No one, not even the barons, wanted that. The planet was now orderly, and another catastrophe would cause a great deal of distressing chaos.

The Trust stood in a formal semicircle around the high-backed leather armchair in which Baron Sharpe sat. Crawler didn't stir from his rug near the hearth, not even lifting his close-cropped head from a satin pillow as the men trooped in. All of them studiously avoided looking in the mutie's direction.

There was a sound reason for not questioning or even acknowledging Crawler's presence in the room. Only a few days after the administrator of the Manufacturing Division lodged an objection to Crawler's input, he had vanished. His replacement, a man named Tobak, knew Crawler had claimed the man harbored disloyal, seditious thoughts. Every member of the Trust did his utmost not to draw the doomie's attention. That was all it took nowadays to disappear—simply come to Crawler's attention.

Baron Sharpe listened graciously to the reports from the Trust, despite his disinterest. He always found it a great effort to pretend he cared about anything his subordinates considered of import.

Ericson, the Magistrate Division administrator, spoke last, in his characteristic colorless monotone. "At the request of Baron Cobalt, I dispatched a recon party to Redoubt Papa."

Baron Sharpe stirred in his armchair, his high forehead furrowing a bit as he ransacked his memory. "Redoubt Papa?" he murmured. "Where is that again?"

Ericson answered blandly, "Washington Hole, my Lord Baron."

Sharpe nodded distractedly. "And why did you send a recon party there?"

"To honor a request made by your brother baron in

Cobaltville." Ericson softened his clipped speech pattern, hoping he sounded unctuous. "To search for the renegades who used a gateway to kidnap a member of Baron Cobalt's Trust. Quite the outrage."

Baron Sharpe flipped a diffident hand through the air. Impatiently he said, "Yes, yes, now I recall. Something about a renegade Mag who humiliated Baron Cobalt beyond his ability to endure. Pompous fool. So?"

"The party I dispatched should have returned by now. They are nearly a half day overdue."

"And that's bad?"

Ericson lifted a shoulder in a shrug. "Merely disquieting at this juncture, my Lord."

Baron Sharpe narrowed his eyes. "Why do you think they have yet to return?"

Ericson cleared his throat. "I can only speculate on the possibilities."

"You have the floor—speculate to your heart's content."

"They encountered mechanical difficulty with their conveyance."

"Which was?"

"A Sandcat. Or they encountered a difficulty that they could not cope with."

The baron sighed. "And which do you feel is the most likely?"

"I cannot say, my Lord. Due to the extremely high rad count in the vicinity of Redoubt Papa, it is impossible to establish radio contact with them."

Baron Sharpe steepled his fingers beneath his chin. "And you are hesitant to send out another party of Mags to ascertain their fates."

"Just so, my Lord."

Baron Sharpe turned his head toward the hearth. "Crawler!"

The doomie slowly raised his head from the cushion. "My Lord Baron?"

"Can you sniff the dooms of the team of Magistrates dispatched to Washington Hole? Will they return?"

Crawler's eyes widened, his lips peeling back from discolored teeth. He shivered, moaned softly, clutched at his brow. Ericson had witnessed the mutie's performance before, as if invisible antennae sprouted from his psyche and quested for answers to the baron's questions. He thought it was a sham, but a very good piece of improvised theater on the part of the doom-sniffer.

Blinking his eyes rapidly, Crawler stared around as if he expected to see some place other than the parlor. In a strained, aspirated voice, he whispered, "Colors. Red and black, black and red. Red for joy, black for death. Those you seek have crossed over. They are happy, they are at peace. Black. Red. Black."

Crawler lowered his hand from his brow, closed his eyes drowsily, then placed his head back down on the pillow.

The mutie's pronouncement stunted conversation in the room for a long tick of time. Baron Sharpe broke it with a laugh and an expansive gesture. "There you have it, Ericson. I hope your curiosity has been satisfied. Now, if there is no more pressing business—"

"With all due respect," Ericson interjected, "if my Magistrates are dead, there are far more questions than answers. Washington Hole is not inhabited. My men were well armed and outfitted. Who—or what—could have killed them?"

Baron Sharpe's lips pursed in petulant disapproval. "You doubt the words of my high counselor?"

Ericson shook his head vehemently. "By no means, my Lord Baron. But you must consider the full implications of his own words—six of your Magistrates, your servitors, your soldiers, have met their deaths in your own territory. Such an incident cannot be allowed to lie without a thorough investigation."

The baron's eyes glinted hard with suspicion. Ericson continued hastily, "If they were murdered, then it is an affront to your authority. Think of the terrible precedent if we do not apprehend the malefactors. We must undertake swift action. Simply command me, and I shall dispatch another team forthwith."

Baron Sharpe sat silently, then a wintry smile drifted over his face. He bounded to his feet, long fringes swishing. "That you shall, Ericson. I command you to dispatch another team, this time by air. And I shall go with you."

"You, my Lord?" Ericson's voice was a faint, shocked whisper.

"Me and my Crawler. Neither one of us gets out very much, you know."

The members of the Trust knew that, and they stared disconcertedly at their lord. Barons, by tradition, almost never left their aeries atop the Administrative Monoliths. Once a year, they visited a subterranean installation in New Mexico for infusions of fresh genetic material, harvested from healthy humans. They traveled by mat-trans, not by Deathbird or Sandcat. They couldn't have reacted with more incredulity to his pronouncement had the baron declared his intent of naming an outlander child as his heir.

Kowper, the senior archivist, said uncertainly, "My Lord, you must take into account the dangers."

"That's why Crawler will be with us." A boyish

grin of enthusiasm and anticipation stretched the baron's lips. "An adventure. I've heard about them, but never dreamed I'd go on one."

"My Lord," intoned Tobak, "Washington Hole is a hellzone."

Baron Sharpe flung his arms wide, the fringes dangling from the sleeves dancing. "I cannot die anymore. I've crossed back." He turned to Crawler. "Isn't that right, Crawler old boy?"

The mutie raised his head from the pillow. "As right as anything in this world, my Lord Baron."

Gazing at Ericson, he asked, "What other baron can make that claim? Prepare three of your Deathbirds. Pick your men, arm them heavily. We leave immediately."

Ericson began to voice a heated protest, then shifted his eyes toward the hearth rug. Crawler stared over the ruffled edge of the pillow, an insolent, triumphant smile creasing his face. Realizing the lethal set of events that could be set in motion if he spoke his mind, Ericson swallowed his objection.

Baron Sharpe swung his right arm out from the shoulder in a fringe-whirling circle, then stabbed a finger directly at Ericson's face. "Let's take care of business."

Chapter 8

Lakesh faced Brigid across the top of his small desk in his spartan office and tried desperately to think of a way to deflect her anger. He knew very little about women in general, and worse, Brigid knew it, too.

"Believe me, dearest Brigid," he said, trying his best to sound warm notes of reasoned sympathy, "Rouch overstated her reasons for being here."

"And what about *your* reasons for bringing her here?" she snapped, a steel edge in her voice.

Lakesh sighed and massaged the deep grooves in his forehead with gnarled knuckles. "Would you not agree that above all else, we must consider the future? What we would term as true humanity is an endangered species. The population of hybrids expands as we diminish. The ville-bred are raised to be servants, vassals, dray animals, and we cannot factor them into an equation dealing with the future of humankind."

"Whether I disagree or agree is beside the point," replied Brigid. "You should have consulted us about your plan to improve the breed, to turn Cerberus into a colony rather than a sanctuary."

"Why should I have?" he demanded.

"Because you're not god, this isn't the Garden of Eden and none of us came here to be Adams and Eves." She inhaled a deep, steadying breath. "What you say about humanity's dwindling population is valid. But I question the means of reversing it. We're not set up here to raise children.''

Lakesh nodded. "As of yet. But circumstances change." He dropped his voice. "Tell me—have you ever thought about motherhood?"

Brigid blinked and shook her head. "I admit I haven't. These last few months, I've been too busy trying to keep my own life intact to think about creating another one. But as you said, circumstances change."

Lakesh leaned back in his chair, absently drumming his fingers on the desktop. "At present and for the foreseeable future, you are too valuable to Cerberus to have your time, energy and resources expended on maternity."

Brigid's lips twitched in a cold, humorless smile. "And since Rouch isn't as valuable as me, she can afford to waste her time with pregnancy?"

Impatiently Lakesh retorted, "I'm not saying that at all. But it is a fact that some people—men and women alike—are better suited for parenthood than others."

"And Kane is a good candidate for fatherhood?"

"Genetically speaking, yes," Lakesh answered bluntly.

"And what about me—genetically speaking?"

Lakesh's finger drumming stopped. "I don't want to have this conversation. These are medical matters, best discussed with DeFore."

"And because DeFore is a woman, you think I should hear the bad news from her?"

"Yes—I mean, no. I mean—" Lakesh broke off, lifted his hands and dry-scrubbed his hair in frustration. He noted how her rosy complexion had suddenly become a shade paler. "You're twisting my words."

"Untwist them, then. Tell me the truth."

Lakesh stared levelly at the woman who had a memory like a computer, reflexes as quick as a scorpion and equally dangerous, but who was still a woman. He was surprised by the sensation of fear her jade bright, jade hard eyes awakened in him.

Softly, sadly he said, "Dearest Brigid, remember the radiation you were exposed to a couple of months ago in the Black Gobi?"

She didn't answer. She wasn't likely to forget the shimmering golden haze that permeated the disabled space vessel and burned like a tiny fire in the blood. Nor would her memory ever relinquish its hold on the tortures inflicted on her by the Tushe Gun, trapped in the genetic mingler—

Brigid straightened up in her chair. For a second, the floor and walls of the tiny office seemed to tilt crazily around her. She was only dimly aware of whispering, "Oh, my God."

Lakesh nodded miserably, his seamed face collapsing in pain. He saw the horrified realization reflected in her eyes, on her suddenly stark and stricken face. Gently he said, "Chromosomal damage, due to the effects of the radiation and the Tushe Gun's devilish device. To what extent and to what degree of permanency is still undetermined."

Her tongue felt like a dry twig, but she managed to ask, "How long have you known?"

"Only a short time. DeFore discovered the condition after examining you upon your return from the Irish mission. As you recall, she was too busy treating Domi and myself to perform a thorough test immediately. When she did, she was still hesitant to make an extended prognosis."

Brigid's shoulders slumped. She squeezed her eyelids shut against the hot sting of tears. Despising the quavery catch in her voice, she said, "You brought in Rouch a week after we returned from the Black Gobi. You and DeFore knew then."

"No. DeFore suspected you might have suffered some sort of damage, but her early tests were inconclusive. The plan to spirit Rouch away had begun a full month before you went to Mongolia. You know how far in advance I like to work. Remember, you were contacted a year before you arrived here."

Brigid ran her hands through her hair, sitting up straighter. "You'll bring in more women like Rouch, won't you?"

"If necessary." Lakesh leaned forward, elbows on his desk, voice pitched low. "Everything I do, everything I plan, is geared toward our survival. As much as I may wish otherwise, I cannot allow an individual's personal situation—no matter how much I empathize with it—to take precedence over the good of the many."

Dully Brigid asked, "And Domi? Is she also unsuited for procreation?"

"Perhaps not emotionally or biologically. But genetically is an open question. Her years spent in the Outlands, living near hot spots, may have negatively altered her ability to bear normal offspring. I don't want to take the chance that she might give birth to a mutant or a child with injurious mental or physical abnormalities."

"What about the potency of the other men here?"

Lakesh shifted in his chair uncomfortably. "What about it?"

"For example, Kane and Grant traipsed all over hell-zones in the performance of their Mag duties."

"I can't be sure of Grant," Lakesh replied wearily. "But as you know, I took a personal hand in breeding into Kane a number of superior adaptive traits. Resistance to disease, to rad poisoning are some of them."

"And," Brigid said in a quiet, uninflected tone, "his seed is strong. Did you take a personal hand in that?"

"I did," declared Lakesh flatly. "And it should be passed on."

"But only to a partner who has—to quote Rouch—'exceptionally strong female drives'?"

"If you view the situation objectively, you must agree." He waited a beat and inquired, "Don't you?"

Flatly Brigid said, "I view the situation as yet another one of your arrogant assumptions."

Lakesh's eyebrows rose, then curved down. The intercom on the desk suddenly blared with Bry's tight, agitated voice. "Sir?"

Lakesh poked a button, knowing he couldn't conceal the relief he felt at the interruption. "What is it?"

The speaker accurately conveyed Bry's tension. "We've got activity on the anomalous mat-trans-inducer signature."

Lakesh threw Brigid a forced apologetic smile before levering himself out of his chair. She followed him out of the office, down the corridor and into the control center. Bry's eyes were fixed on the wall map. As they watched, the bright light indicating the Redoubt Papa gateway unit winked out.

Gesturing to a computer terminal, Bry said, "The autosequencer read is a definite dematerialization."

Lakesh crossed his arms over his chest and fingered his chin musingly. "Then we should, by all rights, receive a rematerialization signal from the destination unit.''

They stood and waited and stared at the map. And waited. Brigid knew the transit process was not necessarily instantaneous, despite the perceptions of those in quantum interphase transition. She really didn't understand more than the basics of mat-trans operations and sometimes she wondered if Lakesh, despite his former position as Project Cerberus overseer, knew as much as he claimed.

As one of the major components of the Totality Concept's Overproject Whisper, the quantum interphase mat-trans inducers opened a rift in the hyperdimensional quantum stream, between a relativistic here and there. She knew the mat-trans units required a mind-boggling number of insanely intricate electronic procedures, all occurring within milliseconds of one another, to minimize the margins for error. The actual matter-to-energy conversion process was automated for this reason, sequenced by an array of computers and microprocessors. According to Lakesh, Cerberus technology did more than beam matter from one spot in linear space to another. It reduced organic and inorganic material to digital information and transmitted it along hyperdimensional pathways on a carrier wave.

In 1989, Lakesh himself had been the first successful long-distance matter transfer of a human subject, traveling only a hundred yards from a prototype gateway chamber to a receiving booth. That initial success was replicated many times, and with the replication came the modifications and improvements of the quantum interphase mat-trans inducers, reaching the point where they were manufactured in modular form. As Brigid understood it, the Cerberus redoubt had been primarily devoted to mass-producing the gateway systems.

Although the jumps through the quantum field were not at the speed of light, rarely did they comprise more than three or four minutes. One of the lights on the map should have flashed yellow, whether the destination lock had been set for Texas or Japan.

No light flashed in any state, country or continent. Lakesh turned away, frowning deeply. "This shouldn't happen. The odds are so astronomically high of anyone having the knowledge or technical expertise to alter the modulation frequencies, they aren't even worth entertaining."

Addressing Bry, he asked, "Did you locate a satellite pix of the region?"

"Yes, sir." He thumbed a pair of buttons on a console's keyboard. "On the main monitor."

Lakesh and Brigid moved to a four-foot square of ground glass. The screen displayed a high-altitude view of a dark, barren terrain. The image was dominated by a black crater, like an ugly puncture wound punched through the crust of the earth to its center. Brigid had been very surprised to learn that Cerberus was uplinked with a Vela-class reconnaissance satellite, as well as with Comsat communications. Like everyone bred in the villes, she had been taught that the few satellites still in orbit were free-floating pieces of scrap metal.

The Vela carried narrow-band multispectral scanners that detected the electromagnetic radiation reflected by every object on Earth, including subsurface geomagnetism. The scanners were tied into a high-resolution photographic-relay system.

The Comsat kept track of Cerberus personnel when they were away from the redoubt through telemetric signals relayed by subcutaneous transponders. The transponder was a nonharmful radioactive chemical that bound itself to the glucose in the blood and a middle layer of epidermis. Based on organic nanotechnology, it transmitted heart rate, brain-wave patterns, respiration and blood count.

Scowling at the image on the screen, Lakesh demanded, "Did you run it through the multispectral scanners?"

"I did," replied Bry a bit defensively. "I detected nothing out of the ordinary—that is, out of the ordinary for Washington Hole. That pix is only about a week old and shows no activity in the vicinity whatsoever."

Lakesh made an impatient spitting sound. "This is really irritating."

"Are you reacting to this problem as a cerebral one, or a visceral one?" Brigid asked.

Lakesh swung his head around toward her. "Explain."

"Are you sure your ego isn't the tiniest bit threatened by the possibility that someone other than you can tweak the gateways?"

He snorted disdainfully. "Don't be ridiculous. I was the project overseer. I knew more about the transducers two hundred years ago than anyone alive. I certainly know more about them than anyone who might be alive now."

Shaking his head, he eyed the image of Washington Hole, then the Mercator map. "It's a matter that needs investigating, that's all."

"The latest in what seems like an endless line," Brigid said sharply. "Who gets to play detective for you this time? Who do you volunteer to take the risks?"

Lakesh's rheumy blue eyes widened behind the

lenses of his spectacles. Reproachfully he replied, "You sound more like Kane than yourself."

"In which case, it's probably for the best he and I can't produce offspring." The instant the words left her tongue she regretted them. Bry swiveled his head toward her in surprise, then he quickly found something else to occupy his attention. Lakesh blinked in owlish embarrassment.

Lowering her voice, Brigid said, "I apologize."

Lakesh cleared his throat. "No need. Besides, you raised a stingingly pertinent point. I shouldn't always be so arbitrary in my selection of—" he paused and smiled "—volunteers. Particularly since this mission is of a technical nature. Mr. Bry—"

"Oh, no!" Bry's normally high voice hit a shrill note of angry, dogged determination. "I do *not* volunteer to jump into a hellzone. No way, no how. You can boot me off the cliff, but I categorically and unequivocally *refuse* to go."

Patronizingly Lakesh said, "Young man, I was not going to ask you to go anywhere but to the workroom and put together a precision toolkit for me."

Bry reacted with surprise. "For you?"

"I can't pull the imaging-scanner memory banks with my bare hands, can I?"

Brigid stared, then gaped at him. "You?" she demanded. "*You're* going?"

He lifted his shoulders in a negligent shrug. "And, of course, anyone else who might care to accompany me."

Lakesh angled an ironic eyebrow at her. "Can you think of any volunteers?"

tokens of his stealth. Regretfully, he replied,

"You sound more like Close than yourself."

"In which case it's probably for the best he and I
can't produce offspring together," she bit off her
tongue, she realized he might follow it by gazing at the
same Act in surprise, then he quickly found something
else to occupy his attention. Lakesh blinked at outside.

Chapter 9

Kane opened his eyes and stared at the hexagonal island upon which he lay. He blinked, and his sense of perspective returned in piecemeal fashion.

He sprawled not across an island, but on a glittering metal floor plate in the shape of a hexagon, interlocking with others that comprised the jump platform of the gateway. Beneath it, he heard the emitter array's characteristic hurricane howl fading away to a high-pitched whine.

He lay on his side, his stomach spasming, and his head swam dizzily. The vertigo was routine by now, a customary side effect of rematerialization. The nausea ebbed, but he knew better than to sit up until the light-headedness went away completely.

All things considered, temporary queasiness and dizziness were small prices to pay in exchange for traveling hundreds, sometimes thousands of miles, in a handful of minutes.

Occasionally the toll exacted was terrible, as when he, Brigid and Grant jumped to a malfunctioning unit in Russia. The matter-stream modulations couldn't be synchronized with the destination lock, and all of them suffered a severe case of debilitating jump sickness, including hallucinations, weakness and vomiting.

Hearing a rustle of cloth behind him, Kane gingerly eased himself up on one polycarbonate-shod elbow,

looking around slowly. Brigid and Lakesh stirred from
their supine positions on the platform. The floor plates
had already lost their silvery shimmer, and the last
wisps of spark-shot mist disappeared even as he looked
at it. Lakesh claimed that the vapor wasn't really a mist
at all, but a plasma wave form brought into existence
by the inducer's "quincunx effect."

Brigid was the first to sit up, blinking at the armaglass walls enclosing the jump chamber. The beautiful
shade of clear, cerulean blue told her they had completed the transit to Redoubt Papa. The six-sided chambers in the Cerberus mat-trans network were color
coded so authorized jumpers could tell at a glance
which redoubt they had materialized into.

It seemed an inefficient method of differentiating one
installation from another, but Lakesh had once explained that before the nukecaust, only personnel holding color-coded security clearances were allowed to
make use of the system. Inasmuch as their use was
restricted to a select few of the units, it was fairly easy
for them to memorize which color designated what redoubt.

Lakesh hiked himself up on his elbows, turned a
wince into a squint and declared, "Transition achieved,
I take it."

Climbing carefully to his feet, Kane made a swift
visual inspection of his armor, making sure all the sections and joints were sealed. He bent down and picked
up his helmet, slipping it over his head and activating
the image enhancer. It worked perfectly, for which he
was grateful. A few weeks before, the light-amplifica-
tion microchannel feed to the visor had been damaged.
It had taken the Cerberus techs days to repair it, and

he had been warned that rough treatment might yet cause it to malfunction.

Extending a black-gauntleted hand to Lakesh, he said, "How are you feeling, old man?"

Rather than taking his hand, Lakesh passed him up the compact tool kit, replying, "Invigorated."

He and Brigid stood up. She consulted the small rad counter clipped to the belt girding her bodysuit. The needle wavered in the low-end-yellow range.

"Tepid readings," she said. "I guess the radiation shielding has held out to some extent. It's tolerable as long as we don't overstay."

Lifting his left wrist, Kane turned toward the door. Strapped around it was a small device made of molded black plastic and stamped metal. A liquid crystal display window exuded a faint glow. The motion detector showed no movement within the radius of its invisible sensor beams.

"It appears we're alone," he said. "Let's get to it."

Gripping the handle, he heaved up on it. With a click, the door of dense, semitranslucent material swung outward on counterbalanced hinges. Manufactured in the last decade of the twentieth century, armaglass was a special compound combining the properties of steel and glass. It was used as walls in the jump chambers to confine quantum-energy overspills.

Kane cautiously shouldered the door aside, fairly certain in advance of what he would see. All of the Totality Concept–connected installations followed standardized specs—the jump chambers led to small anterooms, which in turn led to the control rooms.

When the door swung wide, he wasn't surprised by what he saw, but he was more than a little dismayed by its condition. The anteroom was a shambles of broken plaster and heaps of masonry dust that had fallen from the ruptured ceiling. The surface of a long table bore a thick film of gray white powder. Feeble light spilled from the control center, where a third of the overhead light strips offered no illumination whatsoever.

Brigid and Lakesh moved to either side of him. She murmured, "This place was hit very hard."

"Washington was ground zero," Lakesh reminded her, his reedy voice strangely hushed. "Frankly I'm amazed the gateway still functions."

They stepped carefully and quietly toward the control room, Kane taking the point as always, toeing aside ceiling tiles and slabs of drywall. He studied the floor as he walked, noting signs of recent disturbance in the patina of dirt and dust.

"Somebody has been here," he commented. "Not too long ago, either."

The control room showed extensive damage, but it appeared to be primarily cosmetic. Long black cracks spread out in jagged patterns from the corners, and a considerable amount of the ceiling had fallen in. Looking up through the ruptures, he saw vanadium-alloy sheathing gleam dully.

Still the consoles flickered with power, lights on panels and boards blinking and shining. Kane saw places where dust had been brushed away from readout screens. Wadded up on the floor glinted several small aluminum bags.

"Self-heat rations," he said. "Whoever visited here had a picnic."

Lakesh grunted in disinterest, picking his way swiftly through the rubble to the main console. Puffing out his cheeks, he blew a cloud of dust away from the keyboard.

"Here is the memory matrix for the imaging scanner," he announced. "Tools, please."

Kane handed him the kit. Undoing the latches, Lakesh raised the lid and removed first a flashlight, then an array of small, shiny metal instruments. Kane watched him for a moment, then asked, "You need any help?"

Lakesh shook his head impatiently, fitting the blade of a tiny screwdriver into the slot of an equally tiny screw on the underpart of the panel. "A one-tech task. This has to be done just so, in a certain order, or the microprocessors could be damaged."

"I think I'll do a little exploring." He glanced toward Brigid. "Care to join me in a little recce, Baptiste?"

She looked uncertainly at Lakesh. "You sure you don't need any help?"

"I'm sure. Just stay aware of the time. Ideally the removal shouldn't take more than fifteen minutes."

She reached out, removed his trans-comm from his belt and placed it near the toolkit. "Keep your channel open."

He grunted in acknowledgment. Kane walked deeper into the control room. Before following him, Brigid unleathered the stub-barreled Mauser from her slide-draw holster at the small of her back and cycled a .32-caliber round into the chamber from its extended magazine.

The double sec doors that separated the mat-trans section from the rest of the redoubt were open. Kane pointed out tracks cutting through the detritus on the floor. Several sets of parallel grooves stretched this way and that.

"Something on wheels," he said. "Something fairly heavy, like a dolly. It was rolled out of here, then rolled back."

Brigid turned on the Nighthawk microlight strapped around her left wrist. She shone the brilliant amber beam ahead of them, then along the ceiling.

"The sec cameras are dead," she observed, playing the light on the small vid boxes clamped in the high corners of the room. "There won't be a record of who was here before us."

In the passageway just outside the arched doorway, Kane kneeled to study a scattering of prints. At first glance, he wasn't sure if they showed hands or feet. Brigid focused her light on them and murmured wordlessly in surprise.

"What do you make of this, Baptiste?"

She bent down, squinting, taking out and putting on her former badge of office, a pair of wire-framed, rectangular-lensed eyeglasses she wore when an archivist. "Like the hands of children...or the feet of monkeys."

Kane swung his head toward her. "Monkeys?" he echoed incredulously.

She gazed at the prints with critical eyes. "Too big for monkeys," she said at length. "Apes, maybe."

"Oh, come on," Kane said skeptically.

"See that shape like an opposable big toe?" Brigid replied briskly. "Still, it's too narrow to have been made by an ape."

Kane stood up. "That's good to know. I can't quite picture apes or monkeys teleporting themselves from wherever and digging into a self-heat-rations feast."

"Me, either," she replied. "Could be some unrecorded species of human or animal mutant that some-how got in here. Or—'' She broke off, brow furrowing.

Kane completed her sentence. ''Or a hybrid.''

She didn't respond, but she nodded grimly. More than one type of hybrid had been spawned since the unification program, although the genetic mixture of human and Archon, as typified by the barons, was by far the most numerous. England's self-proclaimed Lord Strongbow and his Imperial Dragoons were mutagenic alterations of human biology, and Colonel C. W. Thrush was a blend of human, machine and Archon.

For that matter, Lakesh had told them that even the mutie species that had once roamed the length and breadth of the Deathlands were less the accidental by-products of radiation and environmental changes than the deliberate practice of pantropic science—a form of genetic engineering devoted to creating life-forms able to survive and thrive in the postnuke world.

Brigid and Kane moved farther down the corridor. The rad counter's needle slowly crept toward the end of the yellow field, closing in on the orange. ''The farther we go, the warmer the count. Not dangerous yet.''

The damage became more pronounced along the passage. The cracks and splits riven deep in the con-crete walls and ceilings spilled piles of masonry and heaps of dirt. In some sections, buckled vanadium showed through the holes. Many of the light strips were completely dark.

Kane alternated making motion-detector sweeps and eyeing the disturbed dust on the floor. The echoes of their steady footfalls chased each other back and forth. Whoever the interlopers had been, he didn't blame them for vacating the installation. Redoubt Papa was as grimly depressing a place as he had ever been, haunted by the ghosts of a hopeless, despairing past age. The walls seemed to exude the terror, the utter despondency of souls trapped here when the first mushroom cloud erupted from Washington on that chill January noon.

They climbed four sets of wide stairs, Kane noting the tracks that came and went on the risers and landings. The fourth stairway led to an open area with several corridors branching off, all but one of them blocked by sec doors. The overhead lights shone dimly, and they saw tracks extending straight ahead into the gloom, toward the single unobstructed doorway.

As they approached it, Kane saw a small form slumped in the shadows near the square frame. He slowed his pace, stiffening his wrist tendons. With a faint whir of a tiny electric motor and a click of the actuator, the Sin Eater snapped from his forearm into his waiting palm.

Brigid saw the shape, too, and at first she took it to be nothing more than a heap of discarded clothing. Still, she approached it cautiously, right hand tightening on the butt of her Mauser.

Outlined by Brigid's microlight, and enhanced by Kane's night-vision visor, the shape formed into that of a man, but in no way resembling any human either one of them had seen before, mutated, hybridized or otherwise.

The corpse floated in a pool of half-congealed blood that had flowed from a bullet-holed torso. He was no more than four feet in height, but he reminded Kane of a stunted giant, not a dwarf. The gnarly arms were disproportionately long in comparison to the legs. The splayed, square-tipped fingers had curved, bevel-edged nails.

The body was thick and powerful, the low, sloping brow topped by a tangle of lank white blond hair. His complexion was very dark, though the features were not negroid. The blunt features held an expression of dull ferocity, fleshy lips peeled back over stumpy, discolored teeth, black glassy eyes wide and staring. He wore a one-piece coverall garment, a drab olive green in color where it was not black with blood.

Brigid shifted her light down to his feet. They were bare, small, callused an inch thick on the soles with nine long, under-curving toes on each one. The tenth toe was exceptionally long, nearly the length of the foot itself, projecting out at a forty-five-degree angle near the heel. It looked like a double-jointed thumb, topped by a yellow horny nail, caked with dirt to the cuticle.

Kane moved first, tentatively dropping to one knee beside the body, avoiding the blood. He gave the body a swift visual inspection. "Shot to death," he said, unconsciously lowering his voice. "Nine millimeter, two rounds. One in the upper right thorax, the other straight through the pump."

He dipped the tip of one gloved finger into the pool of dark scarlet. "Still wet. He didn't die all that long ago."

Picking up the corpse's right arm by the sleeve, he waggled it, testing the elbow joint. It moved, though stiffly. "Rigor is just now setting in."

Brigid inhaled a breath through her nostrils, then wished she hadn't. The coppery tang of blood and the sulfur-ammonia stink of evacuated bowels and bladder made her stomach lurch.

"What do you estimate his time of death?" she

asked, imitating Kane's low tone. "Twelve, fourteen hours ago?"

He dropped the arm, and it landed in the blood with a splat. "A little more, maybe sixteen."

Standing up, he performed a motion-detector circuit of the area beyond the doorway. No readings registered, so he stepped out in the corridor. Brigid followed him, fanning her microlight around. Small brass objects on the floor reflected the amber beam. Kane plucked one up, revolving it between thumb and forefinger.

"Shell casings," he said with a note of grim surprise in his voice. "They're 248 grain. Standard Magistrate Division issue."

Brigid frowned. "Are you saying Magistrates chilled that…troll?"

Kane smiled crookedly. "Troll?"

She returned his smile, though wanly. "That's what he reminds me of."

Tilting his head back, Kane examined the upper walls and ceilings. He pointed to several small, flattened dark blobs, adhering to the vanadium alloy. "See the slugs? If Mags were the blastermen, their firing pattern was pretty damn wild."

He silently counted the bullets impressed into the walls and ceiling. "At least two blasters, maybe three."

Brigid stepped back, directing the beam of her light along and around the door frame, seeing the scars of ricochets. "Mags aren't known for firing wild, are they?"

"Generally speaking," admitted Kane, "no."

"Perhaps it wasn't Mags."

"Think of how those Roamers were armed, with one-shot muzzle loaders. That kind of primitive firepower is about the best anybody without a pipeline into a ville armory can manage. No, whoever hosed these bullets around used top-of-the line autoblasters."

Brigid took another backward step. "Still—"

Something squashed under her left foot, as if she had stepped in mud. Blurting wordlessly, she skipped forward, pulling her boot free with a slight sucking sound. Pointing her microlight down, she saw a viscous, two-inch layer of what appeared to be semiliquid obsidian. "What the hell is this?"

At the startled timbre of her voice, Kane took two long steps and gazed with mystified eyes at the gelatinous mass extending eight feet across the floor toward a bend in the wall. Lumps of the substance clung to the walls.

With a repellently moist, slithery sound, the black matter slowly re-formed around the impression Brigid's boot had made.

"What is this shit?" Kane demanded, thrusting his head forward and sniffing the air. "Looks almost like tar, but it doesn't smell."

Brigid studied the protoplasm and felt the hair at the nape of her neck stir. With a detached sense of horror, she recognized rough human contours, elongated and very nearly liquefied.

Stretching out her arm full-length, she splashed the amber beam down the corridor and her breath caught in her throat. A body lay slumped on the floor, directly beneath a thick smear of the black substance. She whispered, "Look."

Kane looked, stiffened, muttered something beneath his breath and strode quickly to the body. She joined him as he turned it onto its back. The red badge affixed to the molded polycarbonate pectoral caught the light.

"A Magistrate," he said, his voice sounding hollow. "But where's his head?"

Brigid didn't try to repress the shudder that shook her frame when she saw the red-rimmed cavity between the corpse's shoulders. What little flesh was visible had a translucent, rubbery look to it, as of meat boiled far too long.

Mouth filling with sour saliva, she cast her eyes away. They rested on the tarlike lump splattered against the wall. In a dispassionate tone, she declared, "There."

"There what?" asked Kane, continuing to examine the decapitated body.

"His head. There it is."

He looked up, stared and recoiled, sensing the unknown and the unnatural and cringing from it. He stood up, glaring from the headless body encased in armor to the black ooze smeared over the wall. Brigid's mind functioned in a matrix of mounting fear and keen analysis.

"Some force, some kind of weapon, broke down their molecular integrity," she heard herself saying. "Whatever it was, everything holding their bodies together became unstable."

"I never heard of a weapon like that. It can't exist," Kane said, but he didn't sound as if he believed it. "What would be its operating principles?"

"Electromagnetic, particle-beam acceleration, who knows? There were a lot of experimental energy-based weapons in development before the nuke."

Kane's lips compressed in a straight line of tension. "We may not know what did this to the Mags or what that troll really is, but we know somebody who probably has a pretty good idea. Let's get his ass up here."

He activated his helmet's comm-link. "Lakesh, status report."

After a moment, Lakesh's voice filtered into his ear. He sounded distracted. "I'm just about done here. Another minute, and I'll have the memory pulled and we'll be on our way to reasoning out this conundrum."

"Good," replied Kane. "Add a couple more to the laundry list while you're at it."

Lakesh's response was a laconic "I don't know what you mean."

"You will when you see them. Or maybe not. I'm sending Baptiste back down to fetch you. Try to be done by the time she gets there."

Chapter 10

While waiting for Brigid to return with Lakesh, Kane checked the passageway around the bend. It stretched out for about twenty yards, ending against a massive sec door. The film of dust on the floor showed scrape and scuff marks, as of fast-running feet.

He tried to keep from conjecturing about what had happened in the redoubt, to the Mags or upon the identity of the troll. At the door, he reached for the green control lever, took a deep breath, held it and lifted it to the midpoint position.

The huge portal shuddered, then slowly rose upward, raised by the buried systems of gears and hydraulics. Dropping to one knee, Kane peered out into late-afternoon sunlight, slanting down from a partially overcast sky. He saw outcroppings of dark, flintlike rock sloping downward to a sere and sterile plain. The black bulk of a mountain rose on the near horizon, its summit lost to view amidst a cloud of vapor. A faint, rotten-eggs odor irritated his nostrils. The air tasted foul and acidic, making him want to spit.

The door reached the halfway point, and locking solenoids clicked into place. Kane made a motion-detector sweep and cautiously edged out onto a broad shelf extending from the rock-ribbed recess.

At the lip of the tumble, he stopped, scanning in all directions. He saw only barren flatlands. West and east, the view was identical. Southward, he saw a vague black line, a hint of the vast crater that had replaced Washington nearly two centuries ago.

Looking down at the base of the slope, he stiffened, eyes slitted. A double set of treaded tracks was visible in the dry earth. He followed them with his gaze to a heap of slag, metal that had turned molten, then hardened again. It had no identifiable configurations, but Kane guessed by the tracks the slag had once been a Sandcat. Sooty steel fragments lay scattered around it. A looping, crescent-shaped scorch mark had fused the ground to black glass, and it intersected with the heap of metal.

Creeping out farther on the ledge, Kane looked straight down. Spread out over the boulders at the foot of the slope, he saw a splattering of obsidian gel. By staring hard, he was just able to discern what might have been a forearm and hand, now glued to the bulwark of stone.

"Kane?"

Brigid's voice transmitted into his ear caused him to jump and bite back a startled curse. "Here," he said.

"We're nearly there."

"Acknowledged."

He returned to the redoubt, leaving the sec door halfway up. The diffuse sunlight was an improvement over the pallid illumination provided by the ceiling light strips, though it didn't penetrate very far down the corridor.

By the time he came around the corner, Lakesh and Brigid were already standing over the stunted corpse. In a flat, quiet tone, Lakesh declared, "Advanced achondroplasia, with indications of acromegaly."

"I know achondroplasia is a form of dwarfism," said Brigid, "but I'm not so sure about acromegaly."

"It's a disturbance of the growth process affecting bone and muscle development. Usually it's the result of oversecretions from the pituitary gland." Lakesh adjusted his eyeglasses, frowning over the rims. "I'm no expert, but generally acromegaly is associated with giantism, not dwarfism."

"Whatever, he's an ugly little spud," commented Kane. "What about his feet? Ever see anything like them?"

Lakesh shook his head. "Not on *Homo sapiens*. Obviously a mutation, but whether it was deliberately induced or simply a freak of nature, I hesitate to say. It is apparent, though, that the foot bones have been remodified to become hand bones, suitable for gripping."

"Gripping what?" Kane demanded. "Self-heatration packs?"

Lakesh regarded him with an irritated glance. "I don't know. We'll take him back to Cerberus with us for a full examination and postmortem."

"We know what chilled him," retorted Kane. "Too much lead in his diet."

Brigid indicated the open doorway with a nod. "Let's give you a look at our other mystery."

If Lakesh had been fairly phlegmatic upon viewing the bullet-riddled troll, his reaction upon glimpsing the sludge spread out over the corridor floor was the exact opposite. His expression registered incredulity, then horror. He stared unblinkingly at the black protoplasm, reaching out to touch a smear of the substance on the wall, then jerking his fingers back before they made contact.

"An MD gun," he said in a heavy, halting voice.

"Almighty God. I can scarcely believe it. An MD gun!"

"What's an MD gun?" Brigid asked.

Lakesh wet his lips nervously. "Molecular destabilizer. A weapon that was in development by Overproject Whisper's Operation Eurydice in the late 1990s. As far as I knew, it never evolved beyond a few rudimentary prototypes. Bulky things, requiring superconducting battery packs. I saw a couple of tests."

Kane eyed the ooze, then Lakesh. "How do they work?"

"By the application and release of subatomic particles. Organic tissues and structural matter experience molecular de-cohesion, almost as if every binding atom—gluons, they're called—unravels."

"Is the MD gun Archon technology?" demanded Brigid.

"The basic principles, probably," Lakesh answered dolefully. "All attempts at miniaturizing them failed...or so I was told."

Kane gestured to the floor. "We've got wheel tracks. Maybe the MD thing was mounted on some kind of small wag." He hooked a thumb over his shoulder. "Outside I found what's left of a Sandcat and another Mag. Both of them had been unraveled."

Lakesh nodded thoughtfully. "Dispatched from Sharpeville, no doubt. They found more than they were looking for."

He sighed wearily. "Let's get out of here. I left the memory matrix downstairs."

Kane started down the passageway. "Give me a minute to lock up."

He stepped over the decapitated Mag, turned the corner and walked quickly to the sec door. He paused before pulling down the lever, his ears catching a faint, rhythmic swish of sound from outside.

Easing his body beneath the half-raised vanadium slab, Kane duck-walked out onto the shelf and peered over the rock-littered edge. His heartbeat sped up, and he shivered as a jolt of adrenaline shot through his system.

Three Deathbirds alighted on the ground near the slagged remains of the Sandcat. Dust devils corkscrewed in the rotor washes. All three of the compact craft were streamlined and sleek, painted a nonreflective matte black.

The reengineered Apache gunships carried two full pods of missiles beneath stub wings, and multibarreled .50-caliber Chain guns protruded from turrets beneath the tinted foreports. Kane knew the choppers were equipped with infrared-signal-processing circuitry, and like a stupe, he had exposed himself and his body-heat signature to their sensors.

Even while the vanes still spun, black-armored men tumbled out of the craft, all of them wielding Copperheads, deadly Mag-issue subguns. Chopped-down autoblasters, only two feet in length, the gas-operated Copperheads had a 700-round-per-minute rate of fire. They were equipped with optical image-intensifier scopes and laser autotargeters.

From the center Bird bounded a blond man wearing a ridiculous-looking coverall garment. The breeze churned by the rotors set the fringes hanging from his belled sleeves to dancing and looping. Even from a distance, Kane recognized the gracile body structure, prominent facial bones and big slanting eyes of a hybrid.

From another chopper slid a grotesque man-shape,

powerfully built around the arms and upper body, but sickeningly diminished below the waist. His bare legs looked like afterthoughts. They flopped flaccidly behind him as he crawled headfirst out of the aircraft.

The Magistrates fanned out in a wedge formation, facing the base of the slope. Kane didn't wait to see what they did next. Backing swiftly away from the edge, he ducked back beneath the sec door and pulled down on the lever. Then he turned and ran down the corridor, hearing the portal drop down to floor level with a faint crunching thud. He knew the Mags had the code to open it from the outside, but even slowing down their progress a half minute or so could buy precious time.

Lakesh and Brigid must have heard his drumming footfalls, since when he rounded the corner they were waiting for him, faces taut with questioning anxiety.

"Mags on their way up," he grated. "A hybrid with blond hair is with them."

Turning toward the doorway, Lakesh said grimly, "Baron Sharpe."

"Do you know him?" asked Brigid.

"I saw him at the Dulce facility a couple of years ago, during the barons' annual genetic treatments. He's mad, like Emperor Caligula was mad. He never goes anywhere without a crippled doom-seer called Crawler."

"I think he's with him, too," Kane said.

Lakesh gestured to the body of the dwarf. "Friend Kane, if you would be so kind as to carry the corpse of our departed troll, we will exit, stage down."

Kane hesitated, then bent and hauled up the little body. It came free of the tacky pool of semidried blood with a sticky smack. The dwarf weighed very little, probably no more than sixty pounds. Still, it was sixty pounds of dead, unresponsive weight Kane settled over his shoulder in a fireman's carry.

The three people retraced their steps, moving as stealthily and swiftly as they could manage to the stairwell.

ERICSON HADN'T WORN the battle armor in a number of years, and far from feeling nostalgic about being encased in the polycarbonate exoskeleton again, he was distinctly uncomfortable. In fact, he hated it. Sweat seeped beneath the Kevlar-weave undergarment and his skin, making him feel like he was wearing a swamp. His own admonishments to his men about enduring hardships came back not to haunt him, but to laugh in his face.

If that weren't irritating enough, Baron Sharpe countermanded his every order with exuberant whoops and the maddeningly repetitive chant of "C'mon, boys! Today is a good day to cross over!"

The baron bounded up the rock face like a bipedal mountain goat, and at his heels Crawler dragged himself up and over the chunks of stone. Ericson's warning that the on-board sensor circuitry had detected a human infratrace made no difference to Baron Sharpe.

He behaved as if he were on a field trip and determined to have a grand time. He saw no significance in the slag puddled where the Sandcat's tracks terminated, nor in the black goo spread out over the base of the rock slope. Ericson and his three Magistrates had no choice but to follow their lord and his high counselor, no matter where they led.

Crawler stopped his scrabbling ascent long enough to plunge an arm into a crevice between two stones.

When he withdrew it, a bloated, six-legged lizard squirmed fitfully in his fist. Without hesitation, Crawler closed his jaws over its head, bit if off, spit it out and began climbing again, sucking at the blood-spurting neck stump.

Ericson's belly turned over with cold disgust. He tried to avert his gaze from the mutie and his snack. Crawler peered at him, a mocking up-from-under look, red-filmed teeth grinning around the feebly kicking body in his mouth.

Doing his utmost to maintain a stoic expression, Ericson continued to climb. Crawler slithered and lunged beside him, the lizard's tail flopping back and forth, slapping his cheeks lightly. The doomie kept pace with him, as if it were a race to see who could reach the summit first. Ericson fleetingly considered stomping on Crawler's head, attributing it to a misstep.

By the time they reached the wide ledge, Baron Sharpe stood before the recessed sec door. He cast a smirk over his shoulder, snickered and rapped on the portal with a feyly bent wrist. "Let me in or I'll huff and puff and blow your house in."

He tilted his head, pretending to hear a response from within, then piped in a falsetto, "Not by the hairs of our chinny-chin-chins."

The three Mags gained the shelf and spread out in a semicircular formation in front of the door. Quietly Ericson said, "Please, my Lord Baron. I must insist you stand away from the door."

Baron Sharpe regarded him with ingenuous blue eyes. "Danger?"

"Quite possibly."

The baron hugged himself, fringes quivering in excitement. "Oh, I truly hope so. Crawler, what colors do you see?"

Crawler's lips went slack, and the lizard dropped from his mouth. The Magistrates watched sourly as the doomie went through his performance, clutching at his brow, shivering and moaning. Ericson wished the crippled bastard would expand his repertoire.

In his whispering, aspirated voice, Crawler said, "White clouds, golden sunshine and serenity. All is happy. All is golden. Friends from afar await."

Ericson couldn't help himself. His voice was a loud, harsh blare as he demanded, *"What?"*

The baron's smooth features displayed his disappointment. "No danger?"

Crawler husked out, "No danger. Only friends who wish to invite you to join their games."

Ericson glared at the mutie in furious suspicion, then wheeled on the baron. "My Lord, your high counselor is mistaken. He must be."

Irritation flickered in the big blue eyes. "Why must he be?"

The Magistrate administrator groped for a response. Knowing he trod on exceedingly treacherous ground, he said matter-of-factly, "The first squad did not return from this place. There are indications that they are dead. For your own safety, I demand we operate on the assumption that we are in dark territory, regardless of your high counselor's assessment."

Baron Sharpe's lips pursed. He flicked his eyes down to Crawler's upturned face. Ericson watched the brief eye exchange between them. Crawler inclined his head in a curt nod.

The baron's shoulders slumped. In a weary, resigned

tone, he said, "Oh, very well, then. Ericson, be so kind as to lend me a blaster."

Ericson handed him his Copperhead, first making sure the firing-rate selector was switched to single shot. He wasn't foolish enough to give a subgun set on full or even semiauto to a novice.

Baron Sharpe hefted the weapon in his hands, as if trying to guess its weight. Then, with smooth, deft motions, he planted the bore of the Copperhead under Ericson's exposed chin and squeezed the trigger.

The report, muffled as it was by flesh and bone, had a flat, lackluster quality to it. There was nothing lackluster about the effect of the 4.85 mm steel-jacketed round. It punched a path through tissue and jaw, driving up through the roof of the mouth and deep into the brain. Only Ericson's helmet kept his cranium casing from coming apart in fragments.

He toppled backward without a sound. All of the Magistrates saw the crimson-edged, ragged stellate wound where his chin had been. A sooty halo ringed the lower portion of his face. The sweetish odor of cordite mixed with the stink of seared human flesh.

Baron Sharpe cast a swift glance toward Crawler, his eyes shining like a pair of newly minted coins. Crawler smiled in approval. "Well played, my Lord."

The three Magistrates stood rooted in place, overwhelmed by the brutal shock of their superior officer's murder. In a clear, cold voice, Baron Sharpe announced, "All of you will follow me. New friends and games await. If you disobey me, you will not be allowed to play."

Not bothering to gauge their reactions, the baron heeled around to face the door, stepping to the keypad. With exaggerated stabs of his index finger, he entered 3-5-2.

Chapter 11

Kane's vision went dark, and the steps vanished from beneath his feet. Legs flailing, top-heavy with the dead, unresponsive weight of the troll, he pitched headlong down the stairwell. He clawed out for a handrail, missed it by inches, then tried to hurl the corpse off ahead of him.

A shattering impact numbed his body, and he tumbled head over heels into darkness, bouncing and caroming off and down the steps. Dimly, from behind and above him, he heard Brigid's alarmed, questioning outcry.

Kane slammed down onto the landing with a clatter of polycarbonate and an explosive exhalation of profanity-salted air. A flare of pain blossomed in his right knee, so fierce and excruciating that nausea surged.

He managed to push himself into a half-sitting posture, the troll's corpse still draped limply around his shoulders. He dragged it off, its skull striking the concrete with a hollow chock.

Brigid loped down to the landing, shining her light into his face. "Are you all right? What happened?"

Gingerly rubbing his knee, Kane said between clenched teeth, "My night-vision gear went out. Missed my step."

Lakesh joined them, saying breathlessly, "Taking

two and three steps at a time jostled loose the in-feed circuit. Could have been worse.''

Voice hoarse with barely repressed pain, Kane demanded, ''How?''

''You could have been behind us. Brigid and I might have gone down with you and broken our necks.''

''That puts it all in perspective,'' Kane retorted with icy sarcasm. Unlocking the under-jaw guard, he yanked the helmet up and off his head, glaring at the tiny image enhancer mounted above the visor. ''Piece of shit.''

''That piece of shit probably saved you from a fractured skull,'' Brigid observed. ''Can you walk?''

A faint, distant murmur of voices reached them, wafting down the stairwell. He said, ''Guess I have no choice.''

Hoisting himself erect with the handrail and using the wall as a brace, he got to his feet. Experimentally he rested his weight on his right leg. The pain was sharp, but not quite as knife-edged as it had been.

''I don't think it's broken,'' he said quietly, ''but I'll slow you up. You two get going. I'll cover your backsides.''

Brigid and Lakesh regarded him with troubled eyes. The muted overhead lights and the amber glow of the Nighthawk cast wavering, stark shadows over their features. Voices echoed above them, this time a bit louder, but the words were indistinguishable.

''Get going.'' Kane gestured to the corpse. ''Leave that thing to me.''

Brigid shook her head, reaching down to secure a grip on an ankle. ''You don't need to be any further encumbered. Lakesh—''

Reluctantly Lakesh grasped the troll's other ankle. "We'll wait for you in the gateway."

Kane nodded. "If you see a Mag that isn't me, make the jump. I may have to go to ground somewhere."

"Then what?" asked Brigid.

"You know what. If my transponder is still transmitting my vitals, then tell Grant to come a-jumping. And if they're not—" He shrugged, and his teeth flashed in a hard, humorless grin. "If they're not, then tell Rouch she'll get over it."

Brigid's lips worked as if she were about to spit at him. Then she matched his expression with a to-hell-with-you grin of her own. "I will. I'll also tell her she won't be missing much."

Kane almost demanded, "How would you know?" but a scuttling noise from above turned his question into a barked command. "Go!"

They went, dragging the body with them, its head bumping against the steps with a castanetlike knocking rhythm.

Consulting the motion detector, he saw five green dots marching across the LCD. He frowned slightly. He had counted six people disembarking from the Deathbirds. At the bottom edge of the display, digits changed and flickered as the distance between him and the intruders narrowed.

The Sin Eater filled his hand, and holding it in a double-fisted grip, he looked up the yawning stairwell, waiting and listening. Shrouded as it was in murk, Kane couldn't see its mouth. Faint footfalls reached him, and then a brief burst of gay laughter.

The Mags wouldn't be employing flashlights, relying instead on their night-sight visors. As a hybrid, Baron Sharpe's eyes possessed a natural sensitivity to high light levels, and so his vision functioned more efficiently in shadows.

Kane knew very little about Sharpeville or its baron, simply because there was little to know. All villes in the network were essentially the same, laid out identically, each with its own Magistrate Division. The contact between different Mag divisions in different villes was a routine exchange of Intel, and most of that was forgettable.

Still, Kane knew he faced four hard-contact Magistrates, presumably just as highly trained and as zealous in the performance of their duties as he and Grant had been. He knew what to expect from them. Baron Sharpe and his vertically impaired doom-sniffer were the random elements, the wild cards. A baron's presence on a dark-territory probe was utterly without precedent, sane or otherwise.

Under his breath, Kane repeated Lakesh's thumbnail description of Baron Sharpe: "He's mad, like Emperor Caligula was mad."

Whatever that meant, it didn't sound encouraging.

A melodic voice, brimming over with cheery high spirits, echoed down the throat of the stairwell. "I know you're down there, my friend. Is the game to be hide-and-seek, then? If so, let me warn you—I'm very good at it."

Kane's jaw sagged open slightly in astonishment. His finger rested on the blaster's trigger.

"Here I come, ready or not!" cried the voice in a lilting singsong.

A shadow shifted far above. Kane pressed the trigger.

THE BULLET SMASHED a shard out of a step ten feet below the stairwell opening. The round ricocheted away with a buzzing whine, like an angered insect. It bounced four times from wall to wall before finally crashing to a stop.

The deep boom of the shot reverberated for some seconds. All three of the Magistrates instantly recognized the report, and the type of blaster that produced it. Cameron was the first to exclaim, "A Sin Eater! Some bastard is shooting at us with a Sin Eater!"

Baron Sharpe cast mildly interested eyes in his direction. "Your point being?"

Cameron swallowed hard, glancing from Deylen to Miles for support. They didn't step away from him, but they studiously avoided making eye contact.

Clearing his throat, Cameron said, "It's the official Mag Division side arm, Lord Baron."

Baron Sharpe lifted a brow ridge haughtily. "Indeed? Am I supposed to find that significant?"

Cameron had no easy response. Ericson had briefed them on the op, glossing over the reasons why the first squad had been sent out. He had touched only briefly on the subject of renegade Mags from Cobaltville. If the baron didn't know about them, it certainly wasn't Cameron's place to repair his lord's ignorance.

"No, my Lord Baron," he muttered at length.

Baron Sharpe shook his head in exasperation and looked down at Crawler. "I confess I am a bit bemused," he said. "If my new friends want to play a game, why are they shooting at me?"

Crawler's face creased in a relaxed grin. "Isn't it apparent? They know you cannot die—therefore the use of firearms is only to add spice to the game. Something like tag."

Comprehension dawned in the baron's eyes. "Oh, I

get it. Instead of tapping each other with our hands, we use bullets instead, right?''

''Just so.''

A line of concern appeared on Baron Sharpe's normally smooth forehead. ''But if I tag my new friends with bullets, won't they die?''

Crawler chuckled patronizingly. ''By no means. They, too, have crossed over and back. That's why they want you to join them in their play. Afterward all of you will have a celebration in honor of your immortality.''

Baron Sharpe laughed, clapped his hands in delight and nearly dropped his Copperhead. He caught it, aimed it down the dark stairwell and squeezed off a round. The shot echoed hollowly, followed by the whine of a ricochet.

Uttering a grunt of irritation, the baron fiddled with the selector switch, put the Copperhead at his waist and depressed the trigger. The blaster stuttered, shell cases raining from the ejector port, tinkling down at his feet. Whooping loudly, he directed a full-auto stream of bullets down the stairs.

Cameron groaned, ''Oh, fuck us.''

KANE CURSED and skipped clumsily to the far edge of the landing as a hailstorm of slugs chopped out chunks of concrete and ripped long gouges in the walls, striking sparks from the handrails.

Far above, a smear of orange flame danced in the shadows. Over the steady hammering of the Copperhead, he heard a high-pitched yell of exuberance.

Holding his helmet in his left hand, he backed down the stairs, wincing at every step, keeping very low. Ricochets zipped through the air over his head. Pieces of stonework pattered down around him. At the bottom, he began limping down the corridor.

The fusillade stopped, and so did Kane. Taking advantage of the respite, he put his helmet back on, hoping he might be able to eavesdrop on comm-link chat between the Mag squad. He heard nothing, which didn't surprise or disappoint him overmuch. Sharpeville Magistrate frequencies were different than Cobaltville's. If nothing else, the visor would protect his eyes from flying pieces of concrete if the autoblaster opened up again.

The baron's musical voice, raised in a shout, carried down to him easily. "Did I tag you? If I did, you have to tell me! That's the rule!"

Kane grunted in disgust. Baron Sharpe sounded as fused out as a Pit jolt-walker, and the notion disturbed him. Although he had reason to know the baronial oligarchy was not semidivine, it had never occured to him members of it could fall prey to insanity.

The possibility should have comforted him, since it was another indication of the barons' vulnerability, that they weren't the anointed god-kings they claimed to be.

Instead, the madness of Baron Sharpe shook him at a primal level, and he wasn't sure why. Perhaps his reaction stemmed from thirty years' worth of conditioning, over half of that spent in the service of a baron.

Intellectually he knew the barons were born of science, of bioengineering, not mysticism, but his ville breeding caused him to hold them in superstitious regard.

Or maybe the concept of a madman wielding the power at Baron Sharpe's command frightened him the most. Where there was one mad baron, there was bound to be another, sooner than later.

"Here we come!" trilled the baron's voice. "Ready or not!"

Crackling autofire erupted from above, the muzzle-flash an orange twinkling of flame. Kane looked around for cover, saw very little and decided he was as ready as he would ever be.

BOUNDING DOWN THE STEPS two at a time, flanked by Crawler, Baron Sharpe fired the Copperhead in short bursts, voicing ebullient shouts each time. Cameron, Miles and Deylen followed at a more conservative pace, spread out across the width of the stairwell.

Into his helmet's transceiver, Deylen whispered, "Are we just going to go along with this bullshit?"

The question was transmitted to the comm-links of his companions. Bitterly, bleakly Cameron responded to the query with one of his own. "What else can we do? He's the baron."

Miles said, "That fuckin' mutie whoreson is planning something."

"Like what?" Deylen demanded.

"Like how in the triple-fireblasted hell would I know?" Miles raised his voice a bit in baffled anger. "Like, what the fuck really went on here with the first squad? What's that black shit all over the place? How'd that guy lose his head?"

Cameron shushed him, but there was no need. Neither the baron nor Crawler could hear anything over the uproar they were making.

"You think we got a Mag down there?" Deylen asked, bringing his Copperhead up to his shoulder.

Miles murmured, "I think we'd be better off if we never found out."

KANE TOOK UP POSITION a dozen yards down the corridor from the foot of the staircase. He flattened himself against a closed sec door within its recessed double frame. He chose the spot because of its location within a patch of shadow. The light strips overhead were completely dark for about ten feet, yet closer to the stairwell, they still functioned, albeit weakly. He would be able to establish visual target acquisition before he was spotted or before he came within the twenty-five-foot range of the Magistrate's light enhancers.

A whisper emanated from his helmet's trans-comm. Brigid's voice asked, "Are you there?"

Very, very quietly he replied, "Here."

"When we heard the shots—"

He interrupted, "Are you in the gateway?"

Peevishly she responded, "Yes, and we're waiting for you."

Laughter floating down the passageway commanded his attention. "You'll have to wait a little while longer."

Scrambling sounds echoed, and the blond-haired figure of Baron Sharpe appeared on the third-from-last step of the stairway. Crawler dragged himself along at his heels. The mutie swiveled his head to and fro, like a hound casting for a scent. A trio of black-armored wraiths followed at a distance of fifteen feet, pausing on the landing.

Baron Sharpe hummed to himself, swinging the barrel of the Copperhead in short arcs. Crawler reached out and tugged him to a halt by a wide pant leg.

"Your friends don't want to play with them," he

said petulantly, gesturing behind him to the Magistrates. "Tell them to wait here for you."

Baron Sharpe obligingly turned around, waving the Mags back. "Stay there. Don't follow me. You'll spoil the game."

"But, Lord Baron—" began Miles.

Crawler twisted half around, screeching, "Obey your baron!"

The Magistrates stared, dumbfounded, at the crippled creature. Despite his status as a favorite of the baron, he was still a mutie, and muties did not speak disrespectfully to norms, especially if the norms were Magistrates.

"You piece of shit," snarled Deylen, "who do you think you're talking to?"

Crawler made a derisive, spitting sound. "Show him, Lord Baron."

"Okeydoke," replied Baron Sharpe amiably, and squeezed off a 6-round burst from his subgun at the Magistrates.

The baron's aim was pathetic. Out of the six rounds he fired, only two found living targets, and then on the inoffensive Cameron and Miles. The bullets didn't penetrate the armor, but the kinetic shock hurt them, numbed them, sent all three men, crying out in pained surprise, retreating hastily up the stairs.

Kane watched the events with wide, confused eyes. He didn't feel relieved or grateful to Crawler for taking three opponents out of the play. Rather, his mind raced with suspicions and extrapolations. The doomie had an ace on the line, but Kane had not the slightest shred of an idea what it might be.

Crawler tugged peremptorily on the baron's belled pant cuff. "Let's go."

If Baron Sharpe noticed the distinct lack of deference in the mutie's tone, he didn't show it. He obeyed as Crawler slipped off the steps onto the floor and took the lead.

Within moments, they were abreast of Kane's hiding place. He tracked the baron's overlarge head with his blaster, intending to allow him to pass by, then step out behind him once he was certain he had the drop.

Instead, Crawler came to a halt. Thrusting his head forward, he peered into the darkness. Kane sensed a wispy touch, reminiscent of the time the blind psi-mutie Morrigan had telepathically probed him.

The sensation vanished almost immediately. Crawler, with a harsh laugh in the back of his throat, pointed directly to Kane. "There is your playmate, my Lord."

Baron Sharpe turned swiftly on his toes. Eagerly he exclaimed, "Good! This game was starting to tire me. Come out! Olly-olly-oxen-free!"

Treading stealthily, Kane stepped out of the doorway, leading with his Sin Eater. Quietly he said, "Both of you make like statues. Lose the blaster, Baron."

Baron Sharpe gazed at him for a moment, then his high-planed face registered deep disappointment. "He's only another Magistrate. You've truly let me down, Crawler."

The mutie ignored the accusation. Addressing Kane, he rasped, "What are you waiting for? Chill him."

Both Kane and the baron's eyes fixed on Crawler. Kane instinctively knew the astonishment glimmering in Baron Sharpe's eyes was a mirror image of that in his own. His face worked through a number of emotions, finally settling on an expression of incredulous anger.

He kicked Crawler full in the mouth with the toe of his boot. He barked, "What kind of cheap trick is this?"

Crawler spit out blood and trembled with laughter. "A trick to rid the world of a disease!"

Baron Sharpe cried out in fearful fury. He stepped back, swinging up the Copperhead, leveling it at Kane. "Treachery! My own servants plot against me!"

Crawler wiped at the scarlet streaming from his lacerated lower lip. "He knew nothing about it. It was the plot of only one—a broken man, a man your poxed great-grandfather ruined, a man you turned into a beast."

Baron Sharpe snarled, "You're not a man!"

Crawler laughed again. "Once I had a wife, and sons and daughters and property. That made me a man. Then my sons were murdered by Sharpe's sec men, my wife and daughters raped and slaughtered. I was tossed into a stinking cell in a zoo. I was crippled. I was no longer a man, so I was left there to rot and die. But I glimpsed the future and knew that if I struggled to stay alive, I would one day regain my manhood and have my revenge!"

Kane felt like a spectator to the final curtain of a generations-long drama. At the moment, all he could do was watch the last act wind down to its conclusion.

The baron's eyelids flickered madly, as if he were trying to stem a flow of tears. He stammered, "I took care of you, Crawler. Nurtured you. Loved you."

Crawler shrieked with hate-filled laughter, blood spraying from his mouth. "If you loved me, it was as a pet! I heard an old saying once...'every dog has its day.' *This* is my day, hellspawn!"

The baron trained the subgun on Crawler's head. "Your last day. Your life is over."

"If I had a hundred lives, I'd sacrifice them all to buy your doom." Crawler's gaze slid back to Kane. "Chill him now. I saw the hatred you harbor for the barons in your heart. This is your opportunity to release it. Chill him."

The temptation to do so was so intense, Kane's finger fluttered over the Sin Eater's trigger. He had not followed through on killing Baron Cobalt, even when he had throttled the half-human monster unconscious.

Baron Sharpe stared at him, wide blue eyes wondering, not frightened. Kane realized the insane, hybrid wretch didn't truly comprehend what was happening.

Kane relaxed his finger on the trigger. He wasn't about to be manipulated, used like a pawn to commit someone else's murders. He had done enough of that as a Magistrate.

"No," he said in a whisper. "You do it."

Crawler croaked desperately, "I have no weapon."

"I thought you could sniff death in the offing. Didn't your doom sight clue you in that if you want this sick son of a bitch dead, you'd have to do it yourself?"

Baron Sharpe tilted his head up at an arrogant angle. "I cannot die." He turned his back, the rhinestone letters TCB glittering dully. "Do you know what that stands for?"

Kane ventured, "The Creepy Bastard?"

"No!" The baron whirled back around, fringes whipping to and fro. "It means I have already crossed over and back."

Crawler's shoulders shook, his body heaved as if in a spasm. Throwing his head back, he laughed until the walls of the passageway rang. Tears flowed down his cheeks in a floodtide.

Baron Sharpe stared down at him impassively, then his lips twitched, parted and he began to laugh, too, a high, quavery titter with notes of hysteria in it. Kane watched and listened and felt slightly ill. He recognized the emotional bond between these two, a symbiosis of hatred and dependence so complex and strong it was the only passion either one of them felt.

Like the interdependent relationship he had shared with Salvo, they needed that hatred as a confirmation they were alive. But Kane had ended his relationship with a bullet.

Crawler plucked urgently at the baron's leg. "Chill me, my Lord," he said, his voice choked by sobbing laughter. "Do me this one favor."

Baron Sharpe cackled. "You got it."

He leaned down and placed the bore of the Copperhead against Crawler's forehead. "Crossing over isn't that bad, you know."

"I'll wait for you in Hell," Crawler promised.

"Don't do it, Baron," Kane said warningly.

Baron Sharpe glanced at him, stuck out his tongue impudently and returned his gaze to Crawler.

Kane's finger reflexively pressed the Sin Eater's trigger. The blaster thundered once, a short spurt of flame licking from the muzzle. The bullet caught Baron Sharpe high in the chest, smashing through the clavicle, the sledgehammer impact shattering ribs and bowling him off his feet. The Copperhead clattered to the floor.

The baron fetched up in a half-prone posture against the far wall. He continued to voice ghastly laughter through a gurgle of blood gushing from his mouth. "Oh, bay-*bee,* that *hurts!*"

The mutie crept over to the baron, picking up the subgun as he did so. In a liquidy burble, Baron Sharpe announced, "I'll cross back and we'll play another game, right, Crawler?"

Cradling the baron's head in one arm, Crawler crooned, to no one in particular, "My vision was a true one. One last prophecy to fulfill."

Reversing his grip on the blaster, he put the bore under his chin and without even a microsecond of hesitation, pulled the trigger. The bolt of the Copperhead snapped loudly on an empty chamber.

A keening wail worked its way up Crawler's throat. His finger closed around the trigger twice more, producing nothing but dry clickings. He cast a look Kane's way, tear-clouded eyes shining with a mixture of guilt and horror. He flung the gun away from him as if it had suddenly scalded him.

"Do you think he knew?" Crawler's question was a parchment-dry rustle.

Kane lowered his arm. The Sin Eater dangled at the end of it, seeming to weigh half a ton. "You're the doom-sniffer. Why ask me?"

A great stain of wet crimson spread out over the white front of the baron's jumpsuit. His chest rose and fell spasmodically. Crawler moaned.

"He's dying," Kane said gently. "Leave him. Come with me."

"To where?"

"Sanctuary."

Crawler smiled sadly, flicking a strand of fine blond hair away from Baron Sharpe's forehead. "No, I'll stay. Just in case he crosses back. I expect he'd want me to."

Kane stood for only a moment longer, then wheeled

around and stalked down the corridor. He took no notice of the twinges of pain in his right knee.

He knew what Crawler's fate would be once the Mags tired of waiting and decided to investigate the commotion. He refused to look back. The image of a crippled mutie hovering over and giving comfort to a dying hybrid, fatally wounded by a human, was impressed forevermore in his memory.

Human, hybrid and mutie, engaged in a dance of the damned, loathing but relying on one another. He had often wondered where lay the future of the Earth. Kane hoped with every fiber of his heart that the trinity of hatred wasn't it.

Chapter 12

Lakesh swore. Then, in desperation, he hit a button on the keyboard and rotated the image on the screen, turning it upside down.

"Might as well not have the imaging scanner's memory," he said angrily. "For all the bloody use it is."

"You could reverse the read pattern," Bry suggested. "It might have a hidden encryption."

"Like what?" snorted Lakesh. "'The walrus is Paul'?"

Bry regarded him blankly. "I don't understand."

Lakesh didn't respond, propping his chin on a fist. Bry sensed his bad humor and scooted his chair away. Bry attributed Lakesh's foul mood to more than trying to make sense of the spidery webwork of intersecting lines and crisscrossed hatch marks glowing on the screen, and he was right.

From Lakesh's viewpoint, Kane's actions during and after the confrontation with Baron Sharpe seemed sloppy and dangerously open-ended. Not making certain of the mad baron's demise was one error, but compounding it by leaving the psi-mutie alive to tell his story had the potential to be the most serious.

Reluctantly he admitted that had he been in Kane's place, he more than likely would have reacted in a similar fashion. But he was not Kane. One of the reasons he had recruited the man was his willingness to take violent action, the ruthless streak that had earned him several Magistrate Division decorations.

Perhaps it was inevitable that a different man would emerge from the black armor after learning what he had about humanity's secret past. The open question was whether the new Kane could function effectively without incurring lethal consequences for everyone.

He returned his attention to the screen. Dizzying, swirling spirals superimposed themselves over the straight lines. Attempting to isolate the different carrier-wave signatures into separate components was a far more difficult undertaking than he had imagined.

Activated mat-trans units opened a hyperspatial shortcut, avoiding a clash with relativity and causality by moving in a direction at right angles to every possible direction in normal space. Therefore, hyperdimensional space was fiendishly complicated in configuration.

Bry's suggestion about reversing the play order of the patterns refused to leave his mind. Certainly the standard method of tracing a quantum transit line wasn't proving fruitful. If he could not discover where Redoubt Papa's visitors had come from, then perhaps he could learn where they went.

Lakesh hazarded a surreptitious glance over his shoulder, making certain Bry was otherwise occupied. He tapped the keyboard in the reverse sequence. The program came on-line, machine language blurring over the screen, the drive units humming purposefully. He leaned back in his chair to wait as the memory of the imaging scanners booted in through the framework-correlation logarithms.

The control complex had five dedicated and eight

shared subprocessors, all linked to the mainframe behind the far wall. Two hundred years ago, it had been an advanced model, carrying experimental, error-correcting microchips of such a tiny size that they even reacted to quantum fluctuations. Biochip technology had been employed when it was built, protein molecules sandwiched between microscopic glass-and-metal circuits.

The bright outlines of computer-generated images flashed on the screen. Three-dimensional geometric shapes, circles, spirals and squares, appeared and disappeared. The graphics were, of course, simplified representations of a hyperdimensional pathway. Actual reproductions were impossible, beyond the capabilities of either human or electronic eyes to see.

A broken, glowing line raced across the screen, brilliant orange against depthless black, piercing the floating shapes. It scrolled back and forth until it literally filled the monitor.

"What is this?" Lakesh asked in a stunned whisper.

Bry heard him, turned in his chair and stared. "Never saw anything like that before."

"The transit trace has gone beyond the indexed Cerberus network," Lakesh declared.

Bry wheeled his chair closer, eyes narrowed. "Shit," he husked out in awe. "It's like it's following a trail that leads off the damn planet."

As soon as he said it, the lines faded from the screen, replaced by bright green words: "Destination lock achieved." In the lower left-hand corner, a rectangular window flipped through a dozen sets of numeric sequences.

Bry stared, shook his head and stared again. "What kind of coordinates are those? Even if the gateway was perched on the top of Mount Everest, we wouldn't get readings like that.''

Lakesh pursued his lips contemplatively. "Wait until the correlation program has run its course.''

Within seconds, an image formed on the screen, a side view of a wheel, turning slowly on a cylindrically shaped axis. In the window, a block of copy appeared. Bry read the heading aloud: "'USSPC.' What's that?''

Distractedly Lakesh translated, "United States Space Command."

Bry frowned as the graphic display on the screen altered, showing a cutaway view. In the window, the words "Parallax Red" appeared. He demanded, "What's a Parallax Red?''

In a hushed murmur, Lakesh replied, "I'm almost afraid to find out.''

IN THE TWO HOURS since returning from Redoubt Papa, Kane's knee swelled and turned an unhealthy shade of blue. It throbbed with a dull ache so persistent he decided to swallow his pride and visit the dispensary, if not for treatment, then for a pain reliever.

As he limped stiffly down the corridor from his quarters, a door opened ahead of him. Rouch stepped out of her apartment, zipping up her bodysuit. She caught sight of him, did a double take and smiled broadly. She let the zipper stay where it was, just below her breasts, not exposing them but allowing Kane to see she wore no underclothes.

In mock admonishment, she said, "You didn't take me up on dinner.''

As he made a move to hobble around her, he said gruffly, "I was busy.''

Her expression and manner changed. "You're hurt,''

she said sympathetically, reaching out for him. She latched on to one of his arms.

Kane's first impulse was to wave her away, but when she slipped an arm around his waist and leaned into him, he felt the surprising tensile strength in her slim frame. He decided to accept her help.

He couldn't help but be a little intrigued by her, and she was certainly attractive. Maintaining a steady grip on him, Rouch walked down the corridor, keeping up a steady stream of chatter about inane topics.

No, he corrected himself, not inane. Merely ordinary, about everyday things, with no connection to schemes, ops, hybrids, Archons or sudden death.

To his surprise, he found himself able to keep up his end of the conversation on matters mundane. He realized a bit sourly that he and Baptiste almost never talked. They discussed, they frequently argued, but sitting down and conversing about the simple elements of life with each other never seemed to occur to them.

As they approached the dispensary, Rouch said, "I sort of wanted to study medicine, but my early placement tests showed I didn't qualify. Just as well. The sight of blood makes me sick."

The treatment room of the dispensary was deserted, all the beds empty. From the adjoining surgery came voices and the clink of metal. Kane caught a stinging whiff of chemicals, the tart smell of sterilizing fluids. When they reached the open doorway, Rouch stiffened and made a dry-heave gagging noise.

DeFore, her aide, Auerbach, and Brigid stood around a dissecting table. The bright overhead lights glittered on an array of scalpels, knives, tongs and a wet, blood-sheened mess. The three wore surgical gowns and masks. DeFore's arms were crimson-soaked up to her elbows.

They all looked up curiously as Rouch and Kane appeared. Kane saw Brigid's eyes narrowing, then widening in amusement as Rouch clapped a hand to her mouth, spun on her heel and fled from Kane's side.

Brigid said, "We're performing a little postmortem work on our troll." Barely repressed laughter lurked in the back of her throat.

"You didn't waste any time," he said.

DeFore plunged her hands into the peeled-open chest cavity. "I wanted to get in and out before full rigor set in."

Kane looked at the dissected corpse, at the various wet organs resting in assorted stainless-steel containers. A trick of the light made them look as if they were pulsing, and he felt just a little sick to his stomach. He had seen—and made—a number of corpses, but he had never grown accustomed to the clinical desecration of the dead.

"I'd say you're doing more than a little postmortem," he said quietly. "What discovery have you contributed to the field of pathology?"

"Very little," responded DeFore tersely, "since we know exactly what killed him and approximately when."

"But," put in Brigid, her eyes emerald bright above her white mask, "our ongoing study of genetic nightmares may have been advanced a little."

That captured Kane's attention, made him ignore the pain in his knee as he walked into the room. "How so?"

Brigid waved a rubber-gloved hand over the gaping abdominal area. "See that?"

Kane saw only raw viscera with a few streaks of a leathery brown. "See what?"

"The major organs are enclosed in their own independent shielding of dense tissue," answered DeFore, picking up a probe and inserting it into the fibrous mass. A few semisolid yellow lumps oozed out around the sharp point.

"There's an extra organ a few centimeters behind and below the stomach," she said. "Food-reserve storage, in the form of adiposal deposits."

Seeing Kane's blank look, Brigid supplied helpfully, "Fat."

She pointed to the juncture of the troll's thighs. "See anything?"

Kane craned his head, squinting, seeing only a small, fleshy pouchlike bulge. "Like what?"

"Like genitalia. He has no external apparatus to speak of."

Kane repressed a shudder. "You mean he doesn't have a, uh, a penis?"

"Not a conventional one," DeFore replied. "It's more like a direct valve connection to the bladder rather than a reproductive organ. I might add that his bladder is twice the size it should be, even in an average human male."

Kane flicked curious eyes from DeFore to Brigid. "Meaning?"

"Meaning," spoke up Auerbach, "he could go days, maybe as long as a week, without having to take a leak."

Kane grunted. "Handy."

"Speaking of that—" Brigid lifted the troll's right foot by the ankle "—not only has the form of the bones been modified, but their structural properties, too.

They're not as rigid as our own—they're far more elastic.''

Kane swallowed a sigh. "All right, time for the big revelation. Is he a mutie or hybrid or a what?''

"He's a what,'' Brigid answered confidently.

"What?''

"He appears to be human enough, but the end result of people adapted for life in a low-gravity environment.''

"That's Baptiste's opinion,'' commented DeFore. "I'm not convinced yet.''

Brigid shrugged. "It's a hypothesis, but it's more than provisional.'' She dropped the foot and began ticking off points on bloody fingers. "The vertebrae are modified to the point where the load-bearing function is no longer necessary. They are more like a system of levers.

"The legs and feet don't have to support the full weight of the body, and therefore effectively become a second pair of arms and hands, useful for anchorage in a weightless or near weightless environment.

"The outer epidermis is thick and strengthened, but without a significant loss in its elasticity. The pelvic girdle is very light.''

"And his size?'' Kane asked. "What about that?''

"The smaller and more compact the body structure, the less bulk he has to pack around while coping with low gravity.''

Kane studied the troll's fixed expression of ferocity. "If that's the kind of environment he came from, what the hell was he doing in Redoubt Papa?''

"I would imagine,'' replied Brigid, "he was in a lot of discomfort due to the increased gravity and external atmospheric pressure. He may have even been half-drunk because of the richer oxygen content.''

Kane's brows knitted. ''Just where *did* he come from?''

''Hopefully the imaging scanner's memory will give us an idea.''

As if on cue, Lakesh's voice filtered out of the speaker grid of the wall comm. ''Dearest Brigid, friends Grant and Kane—please join me in the control center as soon as soonest.''

DeFore nodded to Brigid. ''Tell him I'll have a report ready within the hour.''

Stripping off the blood-spattered gown and peeling off the gloves, Brigid crossed the room to a sink and thoroughly washed her hands. ''What were you and Rouch doing here anyway, Kane?''

For a moment, his memory failed him. ''I came to get something for my knee.''

''And Rouch?''

''She was helping me.''

Brigid dried her hands briskly on a towel. ''I guess you aroused her strong female drives toward mothering.'' She smiled when she said it, but her smile didn't reach her eyes.

Kane bit back a retort, and turned toward the door. ''Let's go.''

''Sure you don't need Rouch to get you there?''

''Leather it, Baptiste.''

Grant was already in the control complex, standing behind a seated Lakesh and scowling at the main monitor screen. When they entered, he glanced toward them and growled, ''You two will *love* this.''

On the screen glowed the cutaway outline of a round tube connected to a cylinder by a double array of slender rods. It resembled a narrow wheel or a particularly unappetizing doughnut.

"What is it?" Kane asked.

"Parallax Red," replied Lakesh matter-of-factly.

Kane sighed in irritation. "And what's a *Parallax Red?"*

Brigid intoned, "A space habitat."

"More commonly known as a space station," Lakesh said. "The existence of this one was rumored, hinted at, but never conclusively proven."

All of them knew the stories about predark space settlements, even of bases on the moon. But after the nukecaust, without the transmission of telemetric signals to correct orbits, most of them dropped to Earth over a period of decades. In her former position as an archivist, Brigid had read about a Russian station that had crashed in the vicinity of the Western Islands in the early part of the century. *Shostakovich's Anvil*, its name had been.

Beneath the diagram of the ring-shaped habitat, Brigid swiftly read the specs. *Parallax Red* was based on the Stanford Torus design, built with prestressed concrete, reinforced by vanadium-steel bulkheads and cables. The structure was an astonishing two miles in overall diameter, with a mass of over ten million tons.

"You may be wondering why I direct your attention to this," said Lakesh.

"Not particularly," Kane replied nonchalantly. "It's more than likely where our dead troll came from."

Grant and Lakesh swiveled their heads toward him in astonishment. Kane met their gazes with a bland smile. "Am I close?"

Tersely Brigid explained the findings of the autopsy on the troll and her own theories. Lakesh nodded when she was done. "It makes a reasonable amount of sense."

He touched the keyboard, and the image on the screen shifted to a full-color production painting showing a vast circle of parklike lawns where flowers bloomed and shrubbery grew in neat hedgerows. Fountains splashed here and there between the hedges, and little pools gleamed like polished silver.

Lakesh sighed sadly. "Orbital space stations such as *Skylab* and *Mir* were well-known in the twentieth century, but it stands to reason there may have been others, kept under wraps. *Parallax Red* appears to have been designed as an elite community, with a maximum population of five thousand. Something of a utopia even, as you can see. The best of Earth transported to space."

"Do you think the dwarf beamed down from there?" demanded Grant. "That not only does it have a mat trans, but the place is still functional after all this time?"

"I make no such claims without hard data." He nodded toward the screen. "There is no record that *Parallax Red* was actually built, but inasmuch as the gateway I traced was not indexed and the pathway appears to lead to Lagrange Region 2, I believe the conclusion is as apparent as it is inevitable."

"You're going to explain Lagrange Region 2, right?" Grant inquired darkly.

Lakesh laughed. "My apologies, friend Grant. There are five stable areas in space where the gravity from surrounding masses, the Earth, Moon and Sun, are precisely balanced. An object set to rest at a Lagrange point stays there indefinitely.

"The points known as L1 through L5 are all related to the Moon. The destination lock of the transit path I traced terminated in L2, on the far side, or dark side, of the Moon.''

Kane asked, ''If *Parallax Red* was built, who put it up there?''

''An excellent query, friend Kane, but alas I have no solid answers. The Totality Concept's Overproject Majestic dealt with astrophysics and the mechanics of space travel. There were rumors—'' He broke off, shaking his head wryly.

''What kind of rumors?'' pressed Brigid.

Lakesh forced a rueful smile. ''I was going to say, the 'lunatic kind,' but with two centuries of hindsight at my disposal, I can't afford to dismiss any form of speculation out of hand, no matter how superficially outrageous it appears.''

''Get to it,'' Grant urged impatiently.

Lakesh coughed, eyes shifting behind the lenses of his spectacles as if in embarrassment. ''An exceptionally bizarre conspiratorial premise was put forth in the waning days of the twentieth century, as a means to explain the epidemic of so-called alien abductions.

''The scenario claimed that these people were all lifted off Earth to build secret bases, not only in space but on the Moon and...'' Lakesh's voice trailed off, and he nervously wetted his lips.

''And where else?'' asked Kane.

''And Mars.'' Ignoring the incredulous stares directed at him, Lakesh took a deep breath and spoke rapidly. ''The abductees served as mind-controlled slave-labor construction workers, not for aliens but for a covert, ultrasecret arm of the government. According to this theory, NASA was simply a smoke screen, diverting attention from a U.S. and USSR joint space program.''

Grant rumbled, "That makes no sense."

"It does if the schemers behind the program had advance knowledge of Earth's impending doom," Brigid observed. "Whether caused by an ecological catastrophe or the nukecaust." She paused, then added, "And we know some people did have that forewarning."

No one commented on her statement. All of them were aware that due to the temporal dilations opened by Operation Chronos, a select few predark power-wielders gained advance warning of the atomic megacull.

"Space stations were envisaged as staging points for launching deep-space exploratory craft," continued Lakesh, "but I suspected that once Project Cerberus began mass-producing gateway units in modular form, conventional spacecraft would be rendered obsolete."

"How so?" Kane inquired.

"Think about it. Instead of clumsy, fuel-wasting and slow-moving shuttles taking years to reach one of the outer planets, a mat-trans unit set up on the Moon or a space station could move personnel, matériel and natural resources back and forth with relative ease."

"That might cover mat-trans units on the Moon or in Earth orbit," Brigid argued, "but not any celestial body beyond it."

Lakesh replied, "There was a theory—"

Kane groaned.

"And experiments were conducted," Lakesh continued doggedly, "regarding the teleportation of gateway components through space along carrier-wave guides, placed at equidistant intervals to the projected destination. It's possible that such wave guides were launched from the station."

"But it's only possible and it's only theory," declared Kane stolidly.

"Yes," Lakesh admitted.

Grant gusted out a skeptical breath. "Putting together what you and Brigid have said, do you believe *Parallax Red* is an operable station on the dark side of the Moon, full of monkey-pawed midgets?"

Lakesh inclined his head toward the schematic on the screen. "The diagram for *Parallax Red* was in the database, and it appears to be the only likely destination of the carrier beam from Redoubt Papa. All the evidence points to the existence of the station."

He wheeled his chair around to look at Brigid. "And your postulation regarding the...*troll* living in a low-gravity environment lends more credence to the undeniable reality of *Parallax Red*."

"We don't know for sure where he comes from," Brigid stated. "DeFore is reluctant to agree with me."

"Sounds like her," remarked Grant sourly. "Tell me this, though—is there any tactical reason why we should be concerned about this? If the trolls are visiting redoubts through a space-based gateway, I can't see what difference it makes to us. They can't lock on to our unit and jump in here, right?"

Lakesh's seamed face showed a sudden discomfit.

"Right?" Grant repeated, sharper this time.

Lakesh lifted his hands, palm upward. "I wish I could provide you with a take-it-to-the-bank assurance, but at this juncture, facing a wholly unknown and unexpected random element, I won't pin myself down."

"They've got their hands—all four of 'em—on some pretty nasty tech," Kane declared.

"Like what?" demanded Grant.

Lakesh spoke briefly about the remains of the Magistrates found in the redoubt and his conjecture that a molecular destabilizer was responsible.

Grant's face displayed his difficulty in visualizing such a weapon. He didn't quite believe it, not even comparing it with the commonplace scientific miracles he had witnessed in the past half year.

Kane's lips quirked in a thoughtful smile. "If we could get our own hands on a piece of ordnance like that..."

He didn't complete his sentence, but he didn't need to. Everyone in the room easily pictured what he did. An MD gun could make Cerberus itself not just impregnable to assault, but they could take their war directly to the baronies, even to the Directorate itself.

Lakesh waved the attractive notion away. "It's too soon to make such plans. Let's wait for the good doctor's final report before we embark on a course of action."

Chapter 13

When DeFore announced the autopsy was complete, Lakesh convened a briefing in the dining hall. Although the third level held a formal briefing room, it was depressingly sterile and disturbingly cavernous, with seats for at least a hundred people.

The dining hall was more intimate. Grant, Brigid, Kane, DeFore and Lakesh sat at a table in a corner, sharing a pot of one of the few perks of living in Cerberus. Real coffee was one of the casualties of skydark, almost completely disappearing from the face of the continental United States. A bitter, synthetic gruel known as coffee sub had replaced it. Whether the name derived from *substitute* or *substandard,* no one knew. The Cerberus redoubt had tons of freeze-dried caches of the genuine article, stockpiled for the original residents of Cerberus.

DeFore's report had little to recommend it as the basis for a course of action. The examination of the troll proved that though he possessed more organs than a normal human, and a few that were modified, he was essentially *Homo sapiens.*

"I found signs of decreased blood circulation," she said, "and a reduction of oxygen and nutrients in certain organs, particularly the liver. He also had a small secondary lung connected with the primary two, with very muscular walls to control expansion and collapse.

If the dwarf did not come from a low-gravity environment, he certainly lived in one with a rarefied atmosphere that did not provide the proper electromagnetic fields to ensure healthy cellular growth.''

"Do you have an alternative theory?" Brigid asked.

DeFore folded her arms over her ample chest and eyed both Brigid and Lakesh with an attitude akin to defiance. "I know speculation is almost a religion in this place, but I don't feel comfortable in engaging in it as to the subject's point of origin."

"Understandable," replied Lakesh mildly. "From a medical point of view. However, under the circumstances, I hope you don't object if we do."

DeFore's dark eyes glittered. "It wouldn't matter if I did. There's your report. Speculate, postulate and hypothesize away."

She pushed her chair back from the table and stalked from the hall.

After she was gone, Lakesh remarked conversationally, "Is it my imagination, or do certain members of my staff seem unusually on edge these days?"

Brigid fixed a penetrating gaze on Lakesh. "It's not your imagination, and you don't need me to tell you that."

Kane and Grant glanced curiously from Lakesh to Brigid, but said nothing. Lakesh cleared his throat noisily. "As for the dwarf's most likely point of origin, the database yielded very little on *Parallax Red* itself, beyond what it was supposed to be, not what it became after it was built or what it is at present."

"So you're not absolutely sure it's there." Grant was not asking a question; he was making a statement.

"No, not absolutely. I'll have to qualify my assertion

and say there is a ninety-eight percent certainty that it's there.''

"Why would this space station be kept secret,'' inquired Kane, "if it was supposed to be, as you said, a utopia?''

Lakesh shrugged. "Your question is its own answer. As a citizen of the late twentieth century, imagine how you would feel knowing that a select group of people were allowed to escape all the sociopolitical instabilities, the fear of war or ecological catastrophe, economic hardships, the hunger for food or sex or power.

"If such a floating paradise was built and inhabited, the people in power had very good reasons to conceal it. They feared an uprising among the rank-and-file citizenry, a revolt of the so-called useless eaters that might result in civil war.''

"Judging by the dwarf, *Parallax Red* doesn't seem like much of a paradise to me,'' growled Grant dourly. "Floating around weightless all the time.''

Lakesh chuckled. "The spinning of the station would produce the effect of Earth gravity around its equator, much like a gigantic centrifuge. However, if the rotation cycle was adversely affected, gravity would fall off in proportion to the decrease of the spin, with zero G at the axis. It's likely the revolution cycle was interfered with.''

Kane linked his fingers together on the tabletop. "Presuming we do have a mat-trans jump line to the place, what would we find if we went there?''

Lakesh shrugged. "Worst case, a zero G atmosphere, perhaps only one half of Earth gravity. It may be uncomfortably cold or intolerably hot. The air may be so thin you cannot breathe it.''

"Why don't we teleport a vid probe first?'' asked

Brigid, "just to make certain we can establish a retrieval lock?"

"Like a note in a bottle?" Lakesh smiled at her fondly. "I contemplated that, but if *Parallax Red* is indeed occupied, we would be forewarning its inhabitants of our arrival."

Grant scowled. "If we manage to move around in a weightless environment without puking our guts out, how do you figure we can keep from freezing, burning up or suffocating?"

Lakesh smiled and pushed himself to his feet. "That was the first problem I addressed, friend Grant. All of you follow me, please."

He led them from the dining hall, down the corridor and into the big square room that served as the Cerberus armory. As Lakesh entered, he pressed the flat toggle switch on the door frame, and the overhead fluorescent fixtures flashed with a white light.

Stacked wooden crates and boxes lined the walls. Glass-fronted cases held racks of automatic assault rifles. There were many makes and models of subguns, as well as dozens of semiautomatic blasters, complete with holsters and belts. Heavy-assault weaponry occupied the north wall, bazookas, tripod-mounted M-249 machine guns, mortars and rocket launchers.

All the ordnance had been laid down in hermetically sealed Continuity of Government installations before the nukecaust. Protected from the ravages of the outraged environment, nearly every piece of munitions and hardware was as pristine as the day it was first manufactured.

Lakesh strode purposefully past the two suits of Magistrate body armor mounted on steel frameworks to a row of metal lockers arranged against the far wall.

Kane, Brigid and Grant had noticed them before, but since they had been nearly hidden by boxes of matériel, they assumed they contained nothing of importance.

The crates had been shifted to one side, and Lakesh opened one of the locker doors. He removed a dark one-piece garment from a hook and showed it to them. It was gunmetal gray in color, and the light glinted from the many zippers and metal apertures on the sleeves and legs.

"Suprotect3 and neoprene weave," announced Lakesh. "Damn near indestructible, constructed in a multilayer format, affording atmospheric integrity, thermal and humidity controls. It's lined with a layer of lead foil to prevent radiation contamination. With all the openings sealed and the helmets and breathing apparatus attached, they're airtight."

Kane eyed the suit doubtfully. "How old are they?"

"Over two centuries, but like I said, the material they're composed of has an almost eternal shelf life. Designed as rad-proof environmental suits, the personnel here used them shortly after the nuke whenever they left the installation."

Lakesh unzipped a sleeve, pointing out a network of tiny filaments on the inside lining. "Internal thermostats that will keep you comfortably cool or toasty warm, depending on the external temperature or pressure."

He fingered a cylindrical pouch on a leg. "Secondary oxygen tanks slip inside here. The helmets are equipped with their own self-contained circulation equipment."

"That solves the breathing and temperature problems," Brigid said. "What about the gravity or lack thereof?"

Lakesh returned the garment to the locker. "If these were space suits, they'd have magnetic boots. Unfortunately they aren't, so they don't. However, there should be handholds on the station's bulkheads that you can use in case of zero-G conditions."

He swept his gaze over them. "Any further questions?"

"Just out of curiosity," spoke up Grant, "just how far away is *Parallax Red* from here?"

Lakesh shrugged and smiled wanly. "In astronomical terms, only around the corner. Approximately 250,000 miles."

No one replied. They struggled to conceive of such a vast distance, trying to find personal frames of reference.

Finally Kane ventured, "That seems an awfully long way for a gateway jump."

"Distance is relative when you're dealing with quantum mechanics," said Lakesh. "There is no relativistic range limitation on hyperdimensions."

"That you know of," Brigid argued. "So far, the transit pathways have followed the curvature of the Earth, from jump point A to reception point B. Therefore, measurements can be made from gateway to gateway, so distance is *not* relative."

Lakesh evidently wasn't hearing anything new. Diffidently he responded, "The gateways form interstices and interfaces between linear points, regardless of the distance between them. Utilizing hyperdimensional space, there is little difference between a mat-trans unit in Cuba and one in Australia. The same principle applies to the gateway here and one on the dark side of the Moon."

When no one responded, Lakesh inquired, "Anything else?"

"Just this," Kane replied. "When do we leave? Or is that relative, too?"

AT 0700 THE NEXT MORNING, they convened in the ready room adjoining the jump chamber. Brigid, Kane and Grant had made their preparations the night before, filling flat cases with special equipment, rations and water. All three of them wore the formfitting environmental suits, all the seals zipped up and complete with the secondary oxygen cylinders.

The only modifications Kane and Grant had made to the suits were the additions of their Sin Eaters holstered to their right forearms. Their combat daggers hung in scabbards from web belts.

Brigid carried a stunted Ingram Model 11 subgun, slung over a shoulder by a leather strap. She examined one of the helmets resting on the table, turning it over in her hands. Dark gray in color like the suits, it was made of a lightweight ceramic-alloy compound. The treated Plexiglas faceplates polarized when exposed to light levels above a certain candlepower.

On each suit, squat oxygen tanks were attached to the rearward part of the headpiece. The Suprotect3 lining hung down from inside the helmet, to be attached to the suit's collar by an arrangement of tiny snaps and zippers.

The suits were hot, despite their internal thermostat controls, and none of them felt comfortable. Although the fabric hugged the contours of their bodies, it was stiff and a little unwieldy. The swelling in Kane's knee had gone down overnight, but the suit's tight leggings constricted it to an annoyingly painful degree.

Lakesh and Domi came to see them off. The albino girl's lower lip protruded sullenly, and the up-from-under stare she gave Grant was reproachful. Brigid and Kane wondered if she had tried to persuade him to take her along on the mission. If so, Grant must have adamantly refused. Still healing from the gunshot wound and reconstructive surgery and bound in the body brace, Domi's presence on any op more complicated than drinking a cup of coffee would be a definite liability.

Grant did not make eye contact with her, instead putting into words what his teammates were thinking. "These rigs are hotter than hell, Lakesh. I'm sweating like a pig."

Lakesh smiled patronizingly. "You could stand to lose a few pounds of water weight."

"Maybe it's best we all sweat out a couple of gallons," Kane muttered, "since according to the autopsy, the trolls can go for days without having to pee. There's probably no toilets where we're going."

Brigid started to laugh but stifled it when Lakesh rapped sharply on the table for their attention. Expression grave, he said, "Listen up for a moment. Don't default yourselves into thinking your suits are armor. They're tough, resistant to penetration, but they can be breached by something strong or sharp enough. Be careful.

"Secondarily, since the unit to which you're transporting is not part of the Cerberus network, it may not be equipped with an LD setting."

Kane crooked a quizzical eyebrow. The Last Destination program was a fallback device offering jumpers a way to quickly return to their departure point without entering the exact coordinate codes, providing they activated it within a half hour of materialization.

"Why wouldn't it be?" he challenged. "Even if the unit on the station isn't official, it was still manufactured according to the standard specs, right?"

"More than likely, yes," agreed Lakesh. "But inasmuch as we're dealing with modified humans, we may be dealing with modified tech, too."

Brigid touched her arm. "What about our transponders?"

Lakesh shook his head. "The telemetry won't be able to reach us because it'll be blocked by the Moon, unable to bounce off the Comsat. We won't be able to monitor your vital signs. Therefore, if you find yourselves in difficulty, we won't be able to send a rescue party."

Grant snorted, picking up his helmet. "That'll be the day. Since when have you ever sent out the cavalry?"

Lakesh didn't reply.

Brigid, Kane and Grant slipped on their helmets, helping each other zip the collar attachments securely. Oxygen hissed into the headpieces, and it required a few moments to regulate the flow and adjust their respiration patterns. They heard not only their own, but each other's breathing over the UTEL comms built into the helmets.

Lakesh performed a final check on all the seals, then gave them a thumbs-up sign. Impishly Domi leaned up on her tiptoes to plant a kiss on Grant's faceplate, leaving an impression of her mouth in the aquamarine shade of lipstick she favored.

"Goddammit," he growled, but she couldn't hear him through the helmet. Kane wryly noted that he didn't wipe away the smudge. He would wait to do that when he was out of her range of vision.

They trooped to the jump chamber, all of them a little annoyed by the constant sound of respiration echoing within their helmets.

The translucent armaglass walls of the Cerberus gateway bore a rich brown tint. Right above the keypad encoding panel hung an imprinted notice, dating back to predark days. In faded maroon lettering, it read Entry Absolutely Forbidden To All But B12 Cleared Personnel. Mat-Trans.

Kane used to wonder why Lakesh hadn't removed the sign, but the old man probably applied the same reasons to keeping the illustration of the three-headed hound intact. Nostalgia could take very curious forms.

The destination-lock coordinates had already been entered into the interphase computer program, so simply by closing the chamber door automatic jump-initiator circuits would be engaged.

They took their places, and Kane pulled the door closed. He noted that breathing rates increased, including his own. Traveling the quantum stream always induced apprehension, if not fear.

Kane glanced over toward Grant. "Aren't you going to say it?"

"Say what?" His tone, like his expression, was stony. He used the heel of one gloved hand to wipe away the lipstick on his faceplate and succeeded in only smearing it.

"You know, what you always say before we make a jump."

"It's a bad habit I've been trying to break. Besides, I'm used to it now."

The familiar yet still slightly unnerving hum arose,

muted due to the helmets. The hum climbed in pitch to a whine, then to a cyclonic howl. The hexagonal floor and ceiling plates shimmered silver. A fine, faint mist gathered at their feet and drifted down from the ceiling. Thready static discharges, like tiny lightning bolts, arced through the vapor.

The mist thickened, blotting out everything. Shadows seemed to creep into Kane's vision from all corners. The sound of breathing faded, ebbing away into silence. Right before Kane's hearing shut down altogether, Grant's strained, faraway whisper reached him. "I *hate* these fucking things."

Chapter 14

Stepping into a mat-trans chamber, losing consciousness, then awakening in another always seemed like dying and being born again.

From the hyperdimensional nonspace through which they had been traveling, they seemed to fall through vertiginous abysses. There was a microinstant of nonexistence, then a shock and their senses returned.

Kane stared up at the pattern of silver disks on the ceiling and realized ·sluggishly that something was wrong with them. A moment later, his stumbling thoughts amended that observation. Not wrong, just different. They were smaller, diamond shaped rather than the familiar hexagonal configuration. ·

Trying to focus through the last of the mist wisping over his faceplate, Kane became aware of the rasp of labored respiration in his ears. Nausea churned and rolled in his stomach, and he fought it down, almost panicky at the notion of vomiting inside his helmet.

In a strained, hoarse whisper, Brigid asked, "Is everybody all right?"

Kane turned his head, squeezing his eyes shut against the momentary wave of vertigo that blurred his vision. When he opened them, he saw Grant and Brigid carefully hiking themselves up to sitting positions. The floor-plate pattern duplicated that of the ceiling. The jump chamber was small, about half the standard size.

The dark blue color of the armaglass walls allowed only the dimmest light to penetrate.

Grant got to his feet first. To Kane's eyes, it looked like he kicked himself up from a crouch, as if he were performing a broad jump. He lunged the width of the chamber, slamming a shoulder hard into a wall. Catching himself on the palms of his hands, he pushed himself backward and stumbled, crashing into the back wall.

He snarled in bewilderment. "What the fuck is going on?"

Kane gingerly rose to a knee, realizing his body felt oddly light, as if it weighed half of what it should.

Brigid said, "We're dealing with maybe half a G here. Be careful."

Both she and Kane took care as they stood up. Kane rocked experimentally on the balls of his feet. "I don't feel as hot," he remarked.

"The suits' thermal controls must've adjusted to the external temperature," replied Brigid. "It's probably about twenty or twenty-five degrees colder here than in Cerberus."

"What about the air?" Grant asked.

She opened the kit slung from a shoulder and removed a small air sampler. She waved the sensor stem around, gauging the reading on the glass-covered face. "Thin," she announced. "It's recycled, but breathable. It'd take some getting used to. There's a trifle more carbon dioxide in it, so we'd have headaches for a while."

Grant consulted the motion detector around his left wrist. "No movement. It's safe to leave."

Kane walked the short distance to the door, planting his feet firmly on the floor plates. He heaved up on the staple-shaped handle and used his shoulder to push it open. Even with its counterbalanced hinges, he was surprised by how little effort it required.

A single overhead light, sunk in a ceiling socket, illuminated the familiar anteroom with its prerequisite table. The far door was up, and Kane saw the flickering lights of computer consoles.

Kane, Brigid and Grant moved out in single file, not speaking. Except for the small size of the gateway unit itself, the rest of the layout conformed to the standard dimensions. Most of the computer screens were dark, and the few that glowed displayed only shifting columns of numbers.

Brigid murmured, "This place is clean, in good repair. Somebody's been using it recently."

"That's what I was afraid you were going to say," responded Grant.

Kane passed a large VGA monitor screen, a twin of the one in the Cerberus control complex. The power indicator below it was lit, so on impulse, he stroked a key. Instantly an image flickered across it, filling the four-foot square of ground glass.

The image swiftly acquired sharp focus, but it still took Kane a moment of staring to understand what he was looking at. Brigid said, "An exterior view of the station, probably transmitted from some sort of vid sat in synchronous orbit with it."

Kane realized she was right, but the sight didn't awe or particularly impress him. The screen showed it clearly—a round, slowly rotating mass, like a floating coin seen edge-on. Illuminated by sunlight, it looked ancient, rust pitted, slapped together. Some sections were completely skeletal with no outer sheathings at all, metal frameworks exposed to the void.

"This is really something," said Brigid.

"What is?" Grant wanted to know.

She waved to the image on the screen, then to the room around them. Voice quivering with excitement, Brigid declared, "We may be the first Earth people to step off the planet in two hundred years. It's historic in a way."

Kane glanced at the screen and smiled sourly. *Parallax Red* looked like such an unfinished, godforsaken hunk of junk, he couldn't help but wonder why anyone visualized it as a utopia or even why predark scientists had thought it worth building at all. Visiting it certainly didn't meet his criteria of historic.

A few months back, Lakesh had showed them a satellite shot of Earth, taken from two thousand miles up. The view had depressed Kane, showing a forlorn planet that the rest of the universe had forgotten about a long time ago. *Parallax Red* had that same dismal, bleak look about it.

The upper right corner of the monitor screen showed a sweeping, rocky curve, the white pumice desert of the Moon's far side glaring in the merciless light of Sol. The harsh sunlight reflected from the Moon was so intense it overwhelmed the twinkling specks of stars.

"It doesn't look like much," Grant intoned softly. "Nothing of the historic about it if you ask me."

Brigid sighed wearily and just a bit exasperatedly.

Kane moved on to the closed exit door, his pointman's sixth sense suddenly edgy and restless. A wheel lock jutted out from a circular hatch-port, surrounded by two interlocking collars of dark metal and thick flanges.

"An air lock." Brigid's voice was low. "Probably

to keep the jump chamber isolated if the rest of the station lost atmosphere.''

Grant took a motion reading and clicked his tongue against his teeth. "No readings."

"No movement?" questioned Kane.

"No readings. Whatever that hatch is made of, it's too damn dense for the sensor beam to penetrate it."

"Maybe that's what happened here," Brigid stated. "The station lost its atmosphere and they sealed this part off. If we open the door, we might get sucked out into a vacuum and decompress."

All of them thought that over for a moment, then Kane said with forced cheeriness, "There's only one way to find out. We didn't travel a quarter of a million miles to just look at the front stoop, did we?"

He put both hands on the lock, fancying he could feel the frigid metal even through the insulation of his gloves. "I'll go slow," he said. "At the first sign we've got problems, I'll button her up again."

Slowly he twisted the wheel lock, hand over hand, half turns with a few seconds interval in between. The wheel spun easily, and Kane guessed it had been used frequently and recently.

The lock completed its final cycle, and he heard the metallic snapping of solenoids even through his helmet. Before pushing it open, he threw a questioning glance over his shoulder at his companions.

Pointing the air analyzer at the hatch, she said, "No change in either content or pressure."

Grant shook his wrist. "Still no motion readings."

"All right," declared Kane, leaning his weight against the hatch cover. "Here we go."

The disk of heavy metal swung outward smoothly. As it did, the bottom lip of the encircling collars lowered automatically, making a seamless, flat span of flooring. Kane tensed, hand ready to receive his Sin Eater. The opening of the portal revealed a long, curving stretch of corridor, pitching down at an ever increasing slant.

The passageway resembled the inside of a tube, but with a flat floor. Kane estimated its height and breadth to be twelve by twelve. Halos of ghostly yellow light from ceiling fixtures illuminated it every ten or so feet.

Grant swept the motion detector back and forth. "No movement." Nodding to the corridor, he added, "I guess it's safe to go down there." He didn't sound particularly eager about it.

"We won't really be going down," Brigid assured him. "It feels and looks that way to our senses because of the station's rotation."

Kane took the first tentative step over the threshold, understanding what she meant. It did feel like he was walking down a gentle slope, and he unconsciously leaned his upper body backward.

After a few yards, he grew accustomed to the sensation, and his pace became more confident. The flooring material looked like a kind of shiny plastic, or maybe some sort of porous, varnished concrete. It felt hard and unyielding beneath his boots.

A large, deeply recessed niche on the right-hand wall held a mass of scraggly vegetation, most of it yellow, though bearing a few green patches.

"Looks like moss," Grant observed.

"It is," Brigid replied. "It's an old idea of supplying oxygen to spacecraft and habitats with plants that breathe carbon dioxide and give off oxygen as waste."

She checked her air sampler. "In fact, the oxygen content is a bit richer in this vicinity."

The three of them continued along the curving corridor. Twice they forgot about the low gravity and stumbled forward, nearly sailing headfirst into the ceiling.

They came abreast of a rectangular, round-cornered metal panel spanning a dozen feet of the left wall. Two recessed buttons protruded from a plate beneath it. When Kane paused to examine it, Brigid said, "Probably an observation port."

He thumbed the top button, and the shutter rose swiftly upward into a thin slot. Cold white light exploded from the transparent portal beyond it. The polarized filters of their helmets reacted instantly, but not fast enough to keep their optic nerves from being overwhelmed by the incandescent blaze of the Sun.

Kane's helmet filled with profanity-seasoned outcries from Brigid and Grant, and he frantically groped for the second button. His tear-leaking eyes saw nothing but a steady, flaring radiance. He depressed the button, whirling away from the nova of light, hearing Grant say bitterly, "Real intelligent, Kane. Just because you see a damn button, it isn't an open invitation for you to push it."

The panel slid shut over the port, blocking out the fierce, dazzling blaze.

"Sorry," Kane said. "Won't happen again."

He blinked, trying to clear his vision, wishing he could rub his stinging eyeballs. Even with his lids screwed up tight, all he saw was a molten afterimage of the Sun. By degrees, his sight returned, in a hazy, piecemeal fashion. The first thing his eyes fixed on was the troll.

It—he—crouched on the opposite side of the corridor, his heavy-jawed face sunk between the broad yoke of his shoulders. His beady black eyes glittered from the shadows of deep sockets. Coarse, straight black hair fell over his retreating forehead.

Kane wasn't so much nonplussed by the troll's unexpected presence as he was by the multilinked length of chain he gripped in his gnarled right fist. It terminated in a splayed, three-pronged grapnel. Even to Kane's fogged eyes, the points looked very sharp.

Though the chain looked more like a tool than a weapon, Kane's Sin Eater blurred into his palm, nevertheless. He had no chance to fire it.

Bright floaters still swam in his eyes, so he caught only a glimpse of the troll hunching down, then leaping upward as if shot from a cannon, powerful leg muscles propelling him from the floor.

Something hard yet flexible whipped down across the nerve center in Kane's right arm, just below his elbow. He cried out in anger and pain, seeing only a fragmented image of the grapnel hooks snaking out of his range of vision. His arm seemed to fade out of existence, dropping limply to his side, weighed down by the Sin Eater.

Brigid and Grant were alerted to the danger too late. Their vision still impaired, they heard Kane's outcry, but barely a second before they were struck by the troll and his steel flail.

By Kane's perceptions, the stunted creature moved as if he were on a vid tape sped up to an inhumanly fast, frenzied rhythm. The troll sprang outward, nearly brushing the ceiling with the crown of his head, and whipped the length of chain down at Grant in the same motion. The grapnel claws and links struck sparks from his helmet.

The troll landed on Brigid's shoulders, bouncing off

them, using her body as a springboard to launch another of his fantastic leaps. Grant and Brigid cried out simultaneously, more in alarm than pain. Grant staggered sideways, and Brigid fell to her hands and knees.

The troll landed in a squat, lips writhing over stumpy teeth. His breath puffed out before him in a cloud. He said something, a word Kane couldn't hear through his headpiece, then he bounded at him again, snapping out the hooks in front of him.

Kane kicked himself down the passageway as the prongs missed impacting with his faceplate by a fraction of an inch. He half staggered, half drifted along the corridor, arms windmilling as he tried to regain his balance.

The troll's leap dropped him to within three feet of Kane. He gave the chain an expert, snapping jerk, pulling it back. Kane got his boots planted solidly beneath him, gathered his muscles and dived forward.

The troll tried a backward bound, but Kane's left hand tangled in his dirty jumpsuit, fingers digging into the hard muscles beneath.

Mouth open in a silent snarl, the troll struck at his face with the hooks. As Kane swiftly lowered his head, they clanged loudly against the top of the helmet and the two of them tumbled headlong down the passageway.

The troll fought savagely, with muscles of surprising strength and with reflexes just shy of superhuman swiftness. In a revolving whirl of limbs and bodies, they rolled from one curving wall to the other. Due to the reduced gravity, Kane felt exhilaratingly buoyant.

The troll's free hand clawed for the air-circulation assembly on the back of Kane's helmet, but he forced the little man's hand away. He dropped onto his back, the troll on top of him. Placing both boot soles flat against the troll's pelvis, he bent his knees, then straightened out his legs in a powerful, levering kick.

Like an arrow loosed from a bowstring, the troll shot straight up, the top of his head crashing into a ceiling light. It shattered in a brief flurry of sparks. The troll slammed to the deck, hitting it spread-eagled on his back. A few shards of glass sprinkled down onto him.

The little creature wasn't dead or even unconscious, but his black eyes bore a dazed sheen as he tried to push himself up. He managed to achieve a sitting position, but not before Brigid lunged forward, jamming the short barrel of the Ingram against the side of his head.

"Settle down, Frog-boy," she said, even though he couldn't hear her.

The troll felt the pressure of the blaster bore and remained where he was, chest rising and falling. His respiration rate was ragged, labored.

Getting to his feet, Kane kneaded feeling back into his arm. His knife wounds stung and pulled, and his sore knee throbbed. Grant glared at the little man, pointing his Sin Eater at his face. The troll glared back, fearlessly and defiantly.

"He's one tough little monkey," Kane commented. "Where'd he come from?"

Grant pointed to a double set of open doors a few yards down the corridor. "He must've come from that elevator while we were still blind."

"Think he speaks English—or at all?" Brigid inquired.

"If he does," Grant said dourly, "we'll have to yell so he can hear us through our helmets."

Brigid stood up, gesturing with the Ingram for the

troll to do the same. Regarding them with a sulky stare, he did so. Kane pointed to the open doors, then to the three of them.

Nodding, the troll began a shambling, leg-spraddled walk to the elevator, listing slightly from side to side. If he had slouched a little, his knuckles would have dragged on the floor. Kane attributed his curious gait to the elongated thumb near his heel.

"He looks pretty clumsy," Grant commented.

"He's fast and strong," replied Kane. "Never saw anything like the way he jumped around."

"He knows how to use the lighter gravity to his advantage," Brigid commented.

The elevator car was fairly spacious, and the troll stood impassively against the rear wall, abnormally long arms crossed over his chest. He pretended to take no notice of the three blaster barrels trained on him.

Four glowing buttons studded a stainless-steel panel near the door frame. They were marked, A through D. The B button flashed in a regular rhythm. Raising his eyebrows in a silent question, Kane looked at the dwarf, hand hovering over the buttons.

The troll pointed down and said, "D." At least D was the letter formed by his lips.

Kane pushed the button, the doors slid shut and, with the barest of lurches, the elevator began its descent. He announced, "Next stop, Trollville."

Grant scowled at him. "It better not be."

The elevator eased to a slow stop. Kane fisted his Sin Eater, whispering, "Triple red."

The doors slid open on a very deep dark. They gazed at utter stillness. Kane heard Brigid's and Grant's tense respiration. Nothing moved in the gloom, but out of the corner of his eye, he glimpsed the troll casually squatting down and lowering his head.

Out of nowhere, out of the darkness, a harp began to sing, notes rippling in tuneless melody. Kane's memory jerked back to Ireland, to Newgrange and the deadly harp played by Aifa.

With his head encased in the helmet, he should not have been able to hear much of anything external, let alone a sound as subtle as a harp's.

"I hear music," Brigid blurted in dismay.

Kane whirled toward her, feeling a trip-hammer vibration shivering up and down his body. The harp sang louder, throbbing through his bones. He felt it sweep over him in a wave.

The troll's face was screwed up tight, eyes closed, but he was receiving only a feeble backwash of the harping. Grant cursed thickly, like a man drifting off to unwelcome sleep or fighting the effects of a somatic drug.

Kane swung his Sin Eater toward the troll, crouching in a corner like a gargoyle. His finger crooked around the trigger. Then he fell on his face and lay there, struggling to move but only twitching. He was dimly aware of Brigid sagging to the floor, her knees buckling, collapsing half on top of him.

The harp trilled louder, achieving a jumbled cacophony of notes. Their vibrating echoes trailed off into a silence as deep and impenetrable as death.

Chapter 15

Brigid remembered nothing that had happened since the harp song insinuated itself into her brain, overwhelming her senses. She fought very hard to ward off the clutching fingers of unconsciousness.

She was still fighting when she found herself waking up prone on a flat surface. The air was thin and bitingly cold on her exposed cheeks. She realized with a start that she no longer wore her helmet.

Snapping her eyes open, Brigid saw blank walls of blue surrounding her. She struggled up to her elbows on the raised disk beneath her body. It was of an opaque, plasticlike substance about four feet in diameter. From beneath it, she heard the faintest susurrus of electronic hums.

She slowly pushed herself to a sitting position, squinting around at her surroundings. The blue room had eight walls, enclosing her and the disk in a featureless octagon. She was alone, but she didn't pay attention to the sense of dread the thoughts of Kane and Grant evoked. Without much surprise, she saw her blaster, web belt and equipment case were missing.

Breath rasping in her throat, Brigid climbed to her feet, her lips feeling dry and chapped. She noticed she felt heavier than she had upon arriving at the station. Wherever she was, the gravity was close to that on Earth. She moved to the edge of the disk and looked down. It was elevated a foot above the floor, and she made a motion to step down.

A sudden flash of blue lightning filled her eyes, and for an instant, she glimpsed skeins of electrical current dancing along the metal zippers of her sleeves. She whirled around and slammed back on the disk. She felt no pain, no sensation of shock, only an invisible hand swatting her away from the disk's edge.

She lay for a moment on her side, dragging air into her lungs. She tried to curse, but couldn't find the breath for it.

"Our visitor appears conscious," said a man's voice.

Brigid heard the words in a monotone, with faint fuzzy crackles of static following each *s*. She sat up again, but this time stayed put, hands on her knees. She guessed that some sort of electromagnetic screen surrounded the disk.

"Identify yourself," the voice demanded. Though it had an electronic timbre, the voice was well modulated, with a sonorous tenor quality.

"Where am I?" Brigid asked. "Am I on the station? Where are my friends?"

"You will answer my inquiries first. What is your name?"

Seeing no reason to lie, she said, "Baptiste."

"Baptiste, that's it? No other name?"

"Brigid. Satisfied?"

"By no means. You arrived here via the gateway. From where?"

Repressing a smile, Brigid replied, "Where else? Earth."

The unseen transmitter offered a deep sigh, heavy with annoyance. "Where else indeed. From where on Earth? I was not able to trace the matter-stream carrier wave to its point of origin. Was it a failure on the part of my instruments or a deliberate deception?"

"Your choice."

There was a long pause in the questioning. Presently the voice stated, "I've just been informed that your companions have revived. They are unharmed, but a bit uncomfortable. What is the nature of your visit here?"

"A recce," she answered.

"Recce?" The word was repeated, the pronunciation uncertain. "Explain."

"It's slang, derived from *reconnaissance*."

"Oh." A chuckle floated into the room. "Local vernacular. Lingo. Patois. I'm hip."

"What?"

"Pardon my ignorance, Miss Brigid. I—*we*—have been separated from the mainstream of common humanity for a very long time. We hope to change that."

Getting to her feet again, but maintaining a discreet distance from the edge of the disk, Brigid winced as her lungs burned with the effort of breathing. A slow throb began pounding in her temples.

The voice instantly became solicitous. "I apologize for your discomfort, but we only recently restored marginal power to this section of the station. We're still working out the bugs in the environmental systems. They've been neglected for many years."

It took a moment for the statement to penetrate Brigid's oxygen-deprived reasoning centers. "You only recently restored the power? You mean you don't live here?"

"A small group of us does at present. This is not our home, only a way stop, a staging area."

Brigid gazed around the room, trying to locate the

comm unit from which the voice emanated. "A staging area for what?"

The reply was so long in coming, Brigid almost repeated the question. Then the voice spoke a single word, the tone of it touched with a bitter resolve. "Exodus."

Brigid started to respond, but her throat muscles constricted. She coughed, shoulders shaking, diaphragm contracting. Her chest ached fiercely.

Through amoebalike floaters swimming over her eyes, she saw a dark line form a rectangle in the facing blue wall. The line expanded and became a door. The figure that walked through it was so startling, Brigid feared her air-starved brain was supplying hallucinations.

He was small but so perfectly proportioned her sense of perspective was confused for a moment. He was a three-foot-tall godling of a man. Unlike the trolls, his legs weren't stumpy or his arms too long or his forehead too low.

If he had been three feet taller, a hundred or more pounds heavier, he would have been the most beautiful male Brigid had ever seen. Thick, dark blond hair was swept back from a high forehead and tied in a ponytail at the nape of his neck. Under level brows, big eyes of the clearest, cleanest blue, like the high sky on a cloudless summer's day, regarded her sympathetically. Beneath his finely chiseled nose, a wide, beautifully shaped mouth stretched in an engaging grin, displaying white, even teeth.

He wore a perfectly tailored, fawn-colored bodysuit. A silk foulard of blue swirled at its open collar. A gold stickpin gleamed within its folds. The cuffs of the legs had stirrups that slipped between the arch and heel of polished, black patent leather boots. In his right hand, he carried a miniature black walking stick, with a hammered silver knob and ferrule.

He should have looked ridiculous but he didn't, and Brigid wasn't sure why. Perhaps the confidence, the self-assurance he exuded as he walked across the room had something to do with it. Her eyes fixed on the small metal cylinder in his left hand, with the transparent respiration mask attached to it.

The man stopped at the outside rim of the disk and made a short stamping motion with one foot. Brigid heard a click, then an immediate cessation of the electronic hum beneath her.

The little man handed her up the cylinder and mask. "Put that over your nose and mouth, turn the valve and breathe normally."

She did as he instructed, inhaling the cool stream of oxygen into her straining lungs. Within moments, the fiery pressure in her chest abated and the pounding in her temples ebbed away.

The little man watched her curiously, a friendly smile playing over his lips. Brigid considered using the air tank as a club, but decided that such an action could not only bring about unpleasant repercussions, but it would also be exceptionally bad manners. She noticed his foot hadn't strayed far from the control he had manipulated to turn off the disk's electromagnetic screen. Presumably he could reactivate it quickly if he thought the circumstances warranted it.

Brigid removed the mask long enough to say, "Thank you."

The little man nodded. "My pleasure. I'll keep the sterilizing field down if you promise to govern yourself as a guest, not as an invader."

"I promise. Sterilizing field, you say?"

"Originally this device was designed to sterilize nonterrestrial materials, kill possible alien bacteria and microbes, that sort of thing. I simply altered the voltage capacitors and voilà, I had a small holding cell, with no bars or doors."

She smiled wryly. "Am I your first prisoner?"

He shook his head, returning her smile. "Lamentably no. I've had to place a few of my own people in it when they became..." His eyebrows knit as he searched for an appropriate word. "Overeager is the best way I can describe it."

Brigid took another deep breath, removed the mask and asked, "Who are you? Who are your people?"

The man pressed a narrow, long-fingered hand over his heart and bowed slightly. "My apologies for my breach in manners. I should have introduced myself at once. The name I have taken is Sindri."

"Sindri?"

The little man lifted his cane and rapidly traced letters in the air, as if he were writing them on an invisible chalkboard. "S-I-N-D-R-I. It's spelled the way it's pronounced. Does it mean something to you?"

Brigid flipped through the index file of her eidetic memory. "Only in the classical sense. In Norse mythology, Sindri was the weapon smith of the gods, corresponding roughly to Hephaestus in the Greek pantheon. Sindri fashioned Odin's armring, Frey's golden boar and Thor's hammer, Mjolnir. He was a—"

She bit off the final word, not wanting to utter it.

Sindri smiled mildly. "A troll, Miss Brigid. My namesake was a troll, but an extraordinarily gifted one. As am I."

He extended his left hand toward her. Tentatively

she took it and stepped down off the disk. The crown of his head barely topped her hip.

"As for my people," he said, "I suppose they meet, perhaps even exceed the standard definition of trolls."

Brigid did not respond, pretending to inhale deeply in the respiration mask.

"However," he continued, "it would be far more accurate to call them Martians."

GRANT AND KANE AWOKE more or less simultaneously and both felt like they were falling, plummeting a hundred feet, a thousand feet, ten thousand, a mile—

They kicked and flailed frantically, tumbling through the darkness. Their stomachs lurched; their heads swam. Kane opened his mouth to cry out, but he realized he felt no rush of wind buffeting his speeding body. The air was calm, but very cold. His sinus membranes felt dried out, and the tender tissues of his throat burned. His chest and head ached.

Grant coughed and muttered something. Kane's eyes adjusted to the dim, vinegar-colored light. He stiffened, went rigid with shock.

He and Grant were suspended, floating in the gloom, the lack of gravity providing the illusion of falling when they returned to consciousness. They bobbed gently in an ovular cell with no apparent door or windows. Kane felt as much as heard a steady whine, so high in pitch it was nearly beyond his range of hearing.

Grant's cough turned into a strangulated spasm, and he floated over Kane's head, knees bent double and drawn up to his midriff. Kane reached out, caught an ankle and drew him close. He held him until Grant got his coughing under control.

They still wore their environmental suits, and judg-

ing by how cold the air felt on his face, Kane figured
he and Grant would have succumbed to hypothermia
without them. He didn't see their helmets, blasters, web
belts or Brigid anywhere. He felt a flash of fear, but
he tried to ignore it.

Both of them snapped at air, desperately trying to
drag the thin oxygen into their lungs.

Kane forced himself to speak, though his words issued from his lips in a wheeze. "Where do you figure
we are?"

"Lakesh said the central axis might have no gravity
at all," Grant managed to half gasp. "I figure that's
where we've been stuck."

Kane closed his eyes. He felt thirsty and sleepy.
"Why didn't they chill us?"

Grant shrugged, and the motion sent him drifting
toward the ceiling or the floor. Neither one of them had
any idea which was which, no sense of up or down.
"What did they use on us? I heard something like harp
music."

Kane remembered the op to Ireland and how he had
fled the agony-inducing music strummed by Aifa. Baptiste had theorized that the instrument utilized sound
waves in certain frequencies and harmonies that could
have deleterious or benign effects on matter. Still, it
made no sense that monkey-pawed trolls were mincing
around the enormous space station playing the same
kind of deadly harps.

Grant braced his hands against a curving wall, truc-
ulently knitting his brow. "Don't feel like talking?"

"Not much, I don't."

Grant inhaled harshly. "If there's a way out of this
place, we've got to find it and soon. For all we know,

we're in *Parallax Red*'s trash hatch, left here to die or to be jettisoned into space.''

It wasn't a comforting possibility. Kane stretched out his arms and legs. He floated at the midway point in the chamber, where the curvature of the walls was the deepest. Peering around the darkness, he felt ineffectual, indecisive.

''I don't think that's the plan,'' he said at length. ''I think they put us in storage to give them time to figure out what to do with us.''

Without warning, the ovular room seemed to split open in sections. Bright light dazzled their eyes, and they glimpsed a tumble of shapes, silhouetted black against the white. The cell seemed suddenly filled with a foul smell.

Kane pressed his back against the wall, squinting against the sudden glare. The light actually wasn't all that bright, and his eyes swiftly adjusted to it. Seven trolls floated around them, six men and one woman. Like the males, the female was a squat creature with pushed-in, bulldog features. She wore a threadbare olive smock that left most of her stumpy, thickly thewed legs bare.

Gripped between her unshod feet was an object that resembled a lopsided wedge made of a glassy, iridescent gold. The leading edge was strangely elongated, like the neck of a glass bottle that had been heated and stretched out.

Kane looked at it closely, noting how the device vaguely resembled a small harp, but with a set of double-banked strings. The opposable toes of the woman hovered menacingly over them.

Two of the men grasped a length of heavy rope in their feet, tie bars knotted to it at regular intervals. The rope dangled upward into a star-shaped aperture. The troll Brigid had christened "Frog-boy" paddled close to Kane. He scowled ferociously and pointed at the rope. "Climb."

His voice was a squeak, like that of a small child or an adult who had been sucking on a helium-filled balloon. Despite the situation, Grant and Kane couldn't help but exchange smirks.

The woman's foot-thumb stroked the harp strings. Something rippled out of the bottleneck, a force that shocked both of them. For a sliver of an instant, both had the impression of being stung by a hundred wasps—not the tiny, predark variety, but the big, black mutie brutes with six-inch wingspans. The flaming agony seemed to erupt from the nerve roots outward.

The pain vanished immediately, before either one of them could draw enough breath to gasp.

Frog-boy said again, "Climb."

Neither Kane nor Grant smirked this time. The demonstration of the harp's capabilities proved that a rebellious attitude would earn only agony, if not death. Other than the devices, the two men weren't accustomed to zero gravity and they feared the rarefied air would cause them to faint if they expended much energy in a struggle.

Kane grasped a tie bar and began to climb, though he felt more like a worm wriggling up a string. A troll preceded him, and two placed themselves behind him, between him and Grant. The other three men followed Grant, the female bobbing alongside them, swimming easily through the null gravity.

The rope extended through the opening and into a completely round chamber, featureless except for white-glowing light tubes bracketed to the walls.

Kane's headache worsened once he climbed out of the ovular cell, and he clung to a tie bar, wheezing and panting, his legs drifting upward. Frog-boy floated past him, his foot slapping him lazily across the cheek.

"Let's go," he piped. "Keep it up."

Relaxing his grip, Kane rose upward. In the domed ceiling, Frog-boy clung to a wheel lock by his feet, turning it expertly. His coarse black hair puffed around his head like clot of rancid seaweed stirred by ocean currents.

Grant bobbed up beside Kane, jostling him with a shoulder, sending him into a slow somersault. Kane started to swear, realized he didn't have the breath to waste and tried to straighten himself out. A pair of trolls grabbed him by the shoulders, turned him upright and gently pushed him back toward the hatch.

Frog-boy opened it and kicked himself through the opening. Kane followed a moment later, finding himself staring at the stinking, dirty, callused soles of Frog-boy's feet. They were anchored on a staple-shaped rung bolted to the inside of a long, straight tube, barely wide enough to admit Kane's shoulders. Looking up the shaft past the troll, he was reminded of an unbelievably long blaster barrel.

Frog-boy scampered up the shaft, clutching and kicking off the rungs. Kane came after him, imitating his method of propulsion. It wasn't as easy as it looked. The troll's small stature allowed him more clearance to move around, and Kane scraped his back on the tube wall and banged his chin on the metal rungs more than once.

Grant underwent the same painful experience. The hollow shaft echoed with his breathless curses.

Kane lost all track of time. He had no idea how long

he squirmed his way through the shaft. He focused only on putting one hand after the other on the rungs of cold steel.

After a long, miserable period, he realized the climb was requiring more effort, more muscular tension and strain. He felt a growing pressure against his eardrums. Chains seemed to weigh down his limbs.

Although his thoughts moved sluggishly, he understood his body was reacting to a return of gravity. The longer he climbed, the more it settled on and over him like a heavy cloak. He wasn't certain if he was happy about it, since the increased gravity doubled the difficulty of scaling the ladder. He had to work at it, and the hand-over-hand process became strenuous. His knife cuts stung, and his right knee throbbed.

However, he smelled fresher, richer air, and his respiration slowly became less laborious and painful.

At a scuttling, clanking sound above him, Kane craned his neck, looking up just as Frog-boy's grotesque feet slipped out of sight over the lip of an open hatchway.

Kane sighed in relief, caught himself, fought back a cough and hauled himself up the last yard. He thrust his head out of the metal-socketed hatch and stared directly into the grim, graven face of a god.

Chapter 16

The room was enormous. It had to be in order to contain the gargantuan head. It loomed above Kane, silently judging him and finding him wanting.

Kane blinked, and by degrees he saw the head was a colossal effigy made of stone or rockcrete, supported within a taut webwork of steel cables. He followed them with his eyes, noting how they were anchored to eyebolts driven into metal girders running the length and breadth of the high, domed ceiling.

A hand prodded his rump from below, so he obligingly heaved himself up and out of the shaft. He stood beneath the head, giving it an appraising once-over. It didn't look quite as gigantic as his first impression. Now that he had it in perspective, he realized it was about twenty feet long by fifteen wide.

He detected a raised outline of a headpiece or stylized hair running across the breadth of the massive brow and framing the face on both sides. The eye sockets were deeply, darkly sunk, the nose only an undetailed lump with a straight slash of a lipless mouth beneath it. The mouth was slightly open, as if it were about to utter pronouncements of doom. He noted a suggestion of sculpted teeth between the lips.

Despite its lack of a clearly defined expression, the face exuded an ineffable emotion, either a soul-deep sadness or a profound resignation to ruthless destiny.

A pleasant voice carried to him over the cavernous room. "No need for caution, Mr. Grant. He won't bite."

Kane cast a quick glance backward, expecting to see Grant climbing out of the hatch. Instead, he saw a troll pulling himself up.

The voice spoke again. "My apologies for addressing you incorrectly, Mr. Kane. To Lilliputians, all of you giants tend to look alike, despite insignificant differences in skin pigmentation."

Hearing the rhythmic clacking of boot heels on the hard floor on the other side of the massive head, Kane shifted position so it didn't block his view. A very small man approached him, walking hand in hand with a very tall woman. Brigid gave him a jittery smile, her jade eyes acknowledging her relief at seeing him safe and apparently sound. She looked taller than she actually was because of her hip-to-head proximity with the little man.

His crystal-clear blue eyes stared at Kane boldly, gesturing around him with a black cane. "I trust you're feeling a little more comfortable. I managed to restore optimum oxygen circulation to the warehouse, and since it is located on the far outer ring of the station, the gravity is closer to what you're used to."

Kane didn't answer, but inhaled gratefully. The hatch disgorged another troll, then Grant's head and shoulders. He swept the stone head with a penetrating stare, glanced over at Brigid and the little man, then climbed out.

"Let us get the introductions out of the way," the man said incisively. "According to Miss Brigid, your names are Kane and Grant. She doesn't know your given names, a deficiency to which I can relate, although my lack of one is due to personal choice. I am called Sindri. S-I-N-D-R-I. It's pronounced the way it's spelled. Follow me, please."

He and Brigid started off across the vast room. Grant and Kane exchanged questioning glances. The stunted woman carrying the harp climbed out of the shaft. She gave the two men a sharp, beady-eyed stare. Grant shrugged, falling into step behind Sindri and Brigid.

Now that he had the air for it, Kane vented a deep sigh and followed his companions. He didn't know if the three of them were prisoners, but drawing on their experiences of the past few months, he assumed they were. Like that of Sverdlovsk in Russia and Strongbow in Britain, Sindri's hospitality was probably a facade.

Sunlight flowed down from a round skylight in the high, arched roof, glinting from stacked metal crates and long trestle tables. Elevated boom arms stretched out over the floor, cables and winches dangling from them.

Symbols and lettering were visible on some of crates through the cargo netting draped over them. Kane walked casually on an oblique course that brought him close enough to read them. Some of the cases bore the acronym NASA; others had strings of indecipherable letters that seemed like a deliberate jumbling of the alphabet. Several read Parallax Red—Cydonia Compound.

The symbols differed, too, ranging from stylized eagles gripping olive branches and arrows in their talons, to hammers and sickles. He saw an insignia he immediately recognized, and his belly fluttered in a cold reaction, but not really shock. It was more of a grim I-should-have-known.

The symbol looked like a thick-walled pyramid, enclosing and partially bisected by three elongated but reversed triangles. Small disks topped each one, lending them a resemblance to round-hilted daggers.

It was the unifying insignia of the Archon Directorate, one adopted by Overproject Excalibur, the Totality Concept's division devoted to genetic engineering.

Kane managed to keep the angry revulsion from registering on his face. He knew the symbol was supposed to represent some kind of pseudomystical triad functioning within a greater, all-embracing body.

To him, all it represented was the co-opting and deliberately planned extinction of the human race.

The female troll waddled up beside him, making shooing gestures with the harp. Kane obeyed her, but he took notice of how her gait seemed slightly uncertain and how her black eyes appeared glassy, like damp obsidian. He remembered what Baptiste had said about Earth's oxygen levels having an adverse effect on the trolls, and he wondered if the ugly little bitch might not be a bit tiddly.

Grant was eyeing the contents of the trestle tables when he rejoined him. They both looked at chunks of ores, stones and minerals. Little adhesive labels were stuck to some of them, identifying them as terbium, tantalum, promethium.

Bisymmetrical forms like outlandish sculptures also rested there, made of substances which appeared to be wood overlaid with a metallic lacquer. The labels on these items read ID Pending.

A large number of objects scattered over the tables were completely unrecognizable, bearing no labels or striking any chords of recognition within either man.

They followed Sindri and Brigid down an aisle

formed by plastic-sheet-shrouded banks of equipment.
A few feet beyond lay a small living area, with a low
table, a couple of chairs, a fraying sofa and a small
refrigerator. A few personal items cluttered the table—
a hairbrush, a sheaf of computer spreadsheets, crum-
pled-up self-heat ration packs. A glass-fronted, wire-
shelved case held all of their equipment, from blasters
to their helmets, all within easy reach—if the handles
had not been chained and padlocked.

A scrawny orange cat dozed on the arm of the chair
and regarded their arrival with sleepy yellow eyes. Sindri gestured to the furniture. "Take a load off, but don't
spit on the deck or call the cat a bastard."

Kane, Brigid and Grant exchanged mystified looks.
Sindri uttered a short laugh. "Old Navy talk. Picked it
up from a book, as I have so many things. Forgive the
eclectic mixture of furnishings. They were the best of
a bad lot I was able to salvage."

A quartet of trolls stood by watchfully, including the
woman. Uneasily, the three of them took seats, Kane
easing down on the sofa, at the far end from the cat.
He was moderately fond of animals, but he had not
spent much time in their company, especially cats.

The animal looked his way, made a quizzical noise
that sounded like "Ralph?" rested its chin upon its
paw and fell back asleep.

Sindri said, "Don't mind old Robinson Crusoe there.
He's the latest in a very long line of feline Robinson
Crusoes who took possession of this station after its
bipedal inhabitants fled."

"Cats?" Grant's tone was skeptical. "Cats lived
here?"

Sindri opened the door of the refrigerator and bent
down to peer inside. Distractedly he said, "Evidently

a few of the original colonists of *Parallax Red* brought their pets with them. They and their descendants survived long after their owners perished."

"What did they find to live on?" Kane asked, interested in spite of himself.

"Oh, there was plenty of water still in the reservoir, dripping from pipes in the lower levels. As for actual foodstuffs, the station supported a thriving population of rats."

"Rats?" Grant's tone wasn't skeptical now; it was alarmed.

"Experimental animals that escaped their cages, got into the food stores and were fruitful and multiplied."

Sindri rummaged through the contents of the refrigerator, muttering, "What to offer you, what to offer you..."

With an exclamatory "Ah!" Sindri straightened up, holding a heavy carafe in his hands. Placing it on the table, he said, "Permit me a moment to scare up some glasses."

Kane eyed the carafe distrustfully. "Mind telling us what's in it?"

Sindri plucked three tumblers from a shelf, blew on them and set them down on the table. "No, I don't mind at all, Mr. Kane."

He tipped the carafe, pouring a clear fluid into a tumbler. He smiled disarmingly. "Water. Plain, ordinary distilled water. After your period of weightlessness and exposure to the thin air, you're all touched with dehydration. It would be unwise to offer you anything else, even had I anything else to offer you."

Kane noticed the last remark seemed to be directed at Brigid, but he was too busy gratefully gulping the water to reason out its meaning.

Sindri waited until the three of them had downed two tumblers of water apiece before saying, "I'm certain you have just as many questions for me as I have for you, so allow me—"

"Question one," interrupted Kane. "What do you intend to do with us?"

A puzzled line creased Sindri's high forehead. "I don't understand."

"Are we your prisoners?"

Understanding shone in the little man's eyes. "Not unless you offer violence toward me or my people. I have your weapons locked away so some of my more curious brethren won't be tempted to play with them. No, I fully intend to allow you to return to where you came from—wherever that might be."

No one spoke.

Gently Sindri said, "That was a conversational lead-in. You are to provide me with the name of your place of origin."

"We're not much for polite drawing-room chit-chat," Brigid said dryly. "Just ask us what you want to know outright."

Sindri laughed merrily, his blue eyes alight. "But don't you see, it's more fun this way. I can deduce that wherever on Earth you sprang from, English is the native tongue. You have access to higher technology, else you would not be here. You are also accustomed to treading dark, dangerous ground."

He waved to their blasters on the shelf. "You came prepared. Furthermore, you have a fair amount of education. Or at least—" he inclined his head toward Brigid "—one of you has. It is contraindicated that your arrival here was not simply serendipity. No, it was instigated by our brief occupation of the installation code-named Redoubt Papa.''

Sindri's expression changed suddenly, the smile disappearing from his lips and the humorous light in his eyes turning cold and implacable. ''An occupation from which my cousin Brokk did not return. I was told he was wounded unto death. Is that true?''

Brigid stated frankly, ''True. But we were not responsible for his death. We found his body and removed it from the redoubt.''

Sindri passed long fingers over his brow. ''I am the responsible party. The quantum interphase inducer controls here were computerlocked on to the one in Papa. It was reported to me that the area was not suitable for our needs, but I viewed it only as our first, tentative step on Earth.''

He sighed regretfully. ''I should have devoted more time to searching the database for initiator codes to other gateway units in other places. Instead, I wasted my time with petty administrative details here.''

''How long have you been here?'' asked Kane.

Sindri gave him a detached, preoccupied glance. ''Here?''

''On the station.''

The man's mouth pursed in thought. ''Three months. Or is it four?''

Grant glowered at him. ''Only three or four months?''

Sindri nodded.

''How did you get here?''

''The same way you did. By mat-trans unit.''

''But from where?'' Kane demanded.

Sindri's eyes widened in ingenuous surprise. ''Did I

forget to mention that, Mr. Kane? Forgive me. Mars, Mr. Kane. We came from Mars.''

SINDRI'S REVELATION stopped conversation for the next few moments. Grant was the first to start it up again. ''Do you expect us to believe that you are extraterrestrials? Aliens?''

Sindri chuckled. ''Yes to the former, no the latter.''

''The difference,'' said Kane in a quiet monotone, ''escapes me.''

''You were born on Mars,'' Brigid declared. ''Technically that makes you extraterrestrial, but since you're of obviously human ancestry, you're not aliens.''

Sindri smiled broadly, nodding. ''Precisely, Miss Brigid. I and the twenty people here and the thirty back in the Cydonia Compound comprise all that remains of a human Martian colony, seeded there some 190 years ago.''

''Seeded by who or what?'' Grant demanded.

Sindri fixed him with a direct, unblinking gaze. In a soft voice not much above a whisper, he answered, ''I sometimes wonder about that myself, Mr. Grant. If nothing else, *Parallax Red* supplied me with confirmation of several suspicions I'd harbored all my life.''

''Such as?'' inquired Kane.

Sindri pointed to the cavernous storage facility beyond the living area. ''Come with me, and perhaps together we can work out the knottier problems that plague both our houses.''

He marched purposefully past them, swinging his cane. Robinson Crusoe blinked after him, asking again, ''Ralph?''

As they rose from their seats, Grant said in an aside

to Kane, "He and Lakesh must've attended the same schools."

Overhearing, Brigid shook her head disapprovingly, touching a finger to her lips. Kane felt a flash of annoyance. The oddly dressed little man displayed polished manners, but he was still an enigma and they were still, regardless of what he said, his prisoners.

Brigid's concern that Sindri might take offense at one of Grant's sarcastic asides seemed to be a fairly low priority at the moment.

Flanked by a retinue of trolls, they followed Sindri out into the warehouse. He flung his arms out wide, pirouetting on his toes. "What you see here is all that the Cydonia Plains of Mars yielded in the way of wonders. Hundreds of people labored over the final, pitiful handful of years of the twentieth century digging them out of oxidized soil. They were collected, dusted off and transported here for final identification and conveyance to Earth."

Dropping his arms to his sides, Sindri added dolefully, "Of course, after the month of January 2001, nobody on Earth was too interested in picking over the leavings of a long-vanished race. I imagine the subject struck a bit too close to home."

"Mars was inhabited?" Brigid asked, voice holding a note of excited interest.

"It was indeed, Miss Brigid, although nothing very exact was ever established about who the original inhabitants were or what happened to them."

Sindri strode over to a trestle table and picked up a bizarrely fashioned piece of sculpture. "They were evidently humanoid with a high level of civilization and technology. Philosophically it appears they lived by a certain moral duality, an integrated dichotomy between enlightened self-interest and a readiness, if not a facility for war.''

"What makes you say that?" Grant asked. "You found weapons?"

Sindri turned to face him. "Devices. Instruments that could deal death and bring life, that same moral duality incorporated into one mechanism.''

Kane shook his head. "I don't get you."

"Perhaps you should have a demonstration so you can, as you say, 'get it.'" A thin, bleak smile creased the little man's mobile lips as he turned toward the female troll. "Elle, if you could play a lively air for Mr. Kane?''

The woman grinned and pointed the elongated neck of her harp at Kane's chest. Her fingers strummed the stiff, double-banked strings. Soft notes sounded, weaving and dancing in the air.

Kane received the startled impression that responding notes sounded deep within his body, but disharmonious with the ones struck by Elle.

Like a bolt of lightning, agony ripped through his nervous system. His nerves were aflame with it, and he fell on his face and lay with his mouth opening and closing against the hard deck, too consumed by pain even to scream.

Chapter 17

Over the roaring sleet storm of agony that filled his head, he distantly heard Brigid's and Grant's voices raised in furious, demanding outcries.

The harp song drowned them out, and again he had the impression of his body ringing with answering musical notes. This time, they seemed in harmony, complementing and blending together. He tried to understand how this could be. At the same time the pain left him, his strength and balance were restored.

Elle struck one final note, and Kane levered himself up to a sitting position, astonished by how physically good he felt. Brigid went to one knee beside him, hands on his shoulders, eyes full of questions and anxiety.

"I'm fine." He sounded surprised. He probed the knife wounds in his shoulder and rib cage and felt no twinge, not even a stinging sensation. He stared at Sindri wonderingly. They were nearly face-to-face.

Sindri raised his left hand, palm outward. "Quite remarkable, isn't it? On the one hand, the instrument produces pain so intense you prefer death to tolerating it."

He flipped his hand over, showing the back of it. "And on the other, music so beautiful it heals and restores health. That was the duality I spoke of."

Grimly Brigid said, "You might have told us what you had in mind."

"And spoiled the surprise and diluted the dramatic effect of the demonstration? I fear my showman's spirit would not allow that."

Kane eyed the harp, thinking back to the infrasound wands wielded by the hybrids at Dulce, to the instrument played by Aifa in Ireland. They all seemed related, devices operating on the same principle. He knew it wasn't a coincidence.

Slowly he rose to his feet, towering threateningly over Sindri. "I don't like being used as a fucking guinea pig, little man."

Sindri stared up at him, not in the least intimidated. "Neither do any of us, but it's a situation we had no choice but to accept."

"What did the instrument do?" asked Brigid. "How does it work?"

"Every energy form has its own balanced gap between the upper and lower energy states, each size of the gap giving a particular frequency to the radiation emitted. If the radiation within this particular frequency falls on an energized atom—like living matter—it stimulates it in the same way a gong vibrates when its note is struck on a piano. Harmony and disharmony."

Sindri smiled, displaying his excellent teeth. "I hope you don't think my little demonstration of its principles was a breach of manners."

"Not at all," said Kane. "You have perfect manners."

"And pretty damn imperfect morals," Grant said.

Sindri's face lost its beam. For a second, rage looked out of his eyes as a glare that glittered. It was instantly veiled. He wheeled around and marched across the floor.

Grant whispered to Kane, "You sure you're okay?"

Kane nodded. "Yeah. I actually think I'm better off than I was before."

Brigid's eyes narrowed. "Explain."

Sindri called with quizzical impatience, "Gentlemen and lady, if you will please join me?"

They joined him under the colossal head suspended by the network of cables. Tapping the chin with his cane, Sindri declared, "This morose fellow is who started all the trouble, began the entire sequence of events which led to this moment."

"Who is he?" Brigid asked.

Sindri sighed and shrugged. "His name, if ever he had one, is lost in the mists of prehistory. Perhaps he had many…Ra, Lugh, Odin, Yahweh."

"I have no idea what you mean," said Brigid icily.

Sindri said, "In 1976 the satellite probes of the *Viking* Mars Mission transmitted more than fifty thousand photographic images of the planet's surface back to Earth. The image on frame 35A72 of the Cydonia Plains became the mystery of mysteries of the late twentieth century. A vast stone head, over a mile and a half long by one mile wide."

Waving to the head looming above him, he continued, "This is a model of the mysterious Mars masque built to a fraction of the scale. I can testify the original is much more awe-inspiring. As you may have guessed, the photograph of the face was debunked by the authorities of the day as a result of natural erosion, tricks of light and shadow."

Kane looked the head over again, trying to visualize the size of the original. He found he could not.

"Of course," Sindri continued, "although the possibility of an extraterrestrial civilization in our solar system was publicly sneered at, a furious, concerted and covert campaign began to investigate and lay claim to any artifacts this nonexistent Martian civilization may have left behind.''

Sindri gazed up at the face, and his expression mirrored the majestic sadness etched into it. ''They left behind very little of value. Wherever they went, whatever happened to them, the Danaan took their secrets with them.''

Brigid had worked very hard in her years as an archivist to perfect a poker face, so her reaction was restricted to an almost imperceptibly raised eyebrow. Grant seemed momentarily frozen, and Kane's whole body tightened, as though a jolt of current coursed through him. He echoed, ''The Danaan?''

Sindri cast him a curious glance. ''Yes, that was the name they were known by. Or more accurately, what they were called in Terran mythologies.''

Kane stared at the head with a new intensity, whispering, ''Son of a *bitch*.''

Sindri asked, ''You know of them?''

Grant answered gruffly, ''How could we?''

Ignoring him, Sindri said urgently, ''You must tell me what you know, how you know. I need your cooperation.''

''Cooperation?'' echoed Brigid. ''For what?''

''For the return to Earth of me and my people, to retrieve our long-denied legacy as Terrans.''

''Why should we?'' Grant asked.

Sindri nodded toward the trestle tables. ''There are discoveries here worth taking back to Earth.''

''You're proposing a trade agreement?'' Kane's tone still quivered with barely suppressed surprise at the mention of the Danaan.

''Naturally. You can make it easier for us. You can

tell us the safest places for us to settle, to transplant the colony.''

''Why do you want to come to Earth so badly?'' inquired Brigid. ''It's not exactly an Eden.''

Sindri's features contorted, as if he were struggling to keep himself composed. ''It is not that we want to. We need to.''

''Why?'' Brigid persisted. ''The environmental conditions are not those in which you were raised, the planet is still trying to recover from the war—''

Sindri's words came out in a rush. ''I told you we were all that remains of the Cydonia Compound colony. I meant that literally. We are the last of our kind, the final, dwindling generation. Unless we leave Mars, we will die—there will be no more after us. Utter extinction, Miss Brigid. Thorough and complete.''

He drew in a sharp breath through finely drawn nostrils. ''That is all you need to know, for the moment.''

''The hell it is,'' rumbled Grant. ''The little you've told us so far is through inference, feeding us information in unconnected bits and scraps. If you want anything from any of us, wipe the snake oil off your tongue and speak straight from the shoulder.''

Sindri's face revealed conflicting emotions. Anger, desperation, doubt and something else, raw and primal and not easily identifiable. Finally, in a very hushed tone, he declared, ''I will tell you what you want. But as Mr. Kane mentioned, I seek a trade agreement. I tell you and you tell me. We will barter with information. A fair exchange, I think. Do we have a bargain?''

Brigid, Grant and Kane regarded him silently, with flinty eyes and expressionless faces.

Sindri rapped sharply on the floor with the ferrule of his cane. Elle sidled close, stubby fingers poised over the harp strings. In the same low voice, he said, "Make no mistake. I can put all three of you in so much agony you'd kill each other to be the first to answer my questions. I prefer not to do that. It is coercion, not cooperation, and such actions do not come naturally to me. However, if you leave me with no other option, I will undertake that course. Regretfully, but very, very devotedly."

His eyes flicked back and forth across their faces. "Do we have a bargain?"

When the answer wasn't forthcoming, Sindri clenched his delicate hands, the knuckles standing out against the flesh like ivory knobs. He thrust his head forward and roared furiously, "Answer me! *Do we have a bargain?*"

Lips compressed, Kane glanced into his friends' faces, cast his gaze to the harp, remembered the universe of pain it had put him in and said grimly, "Bargain."

Sindri instantly unknotted his fists. He extended his right hand. Kane reluctantly took it, noting how his almost completely folded over Sindri's. The little man gave his hand two swift, perfunctory pumps and announced, "Done and done."

He laughed, his eyes shining brightly. Kane recognized the quality of the laugh and the light burning in Sindri's eyes. They were those of a madman.

SINDRI SMOOTHLY slipped back into the persona of congenial host. He offered to take them on a tour of the space station, not that there was, he added, anything particularly remarkable to see.

He directed them to a corner of the warehouse where a small, four-wheeled, battery-powered cart was parked. He had rigged an enclosed canopy of sorts with sheets of transparent plastic draped over an aluminum framework. A small tank hissed a steady stream of oxygen into the cramped interior.

Brigid sat beside Sindri in a bucket seat as he manipulated foot pedals and a steering wheel. Grant and Kane sat facing each other in the back, heads low, their knees pressed into each other's.

Sindri drove the cart along the corridors, chatting gaily, as if he were on a Sunday drive in the country with long-lost cousins. He told them about *Parallax Red*, or at least what he knew about it.

Construction on the station began in early 1977, shortly after the photographic discoveries of the *Viking* Mars probe. Originally the project was a covert joint undertaking between America and Russia, but the commanding organizational body had been something called Overproject Majestic.

Some years previously, a small secret base had been established on the Moon in the Manitius Crater region. This site was chosen because of its proximity to artifacts that some scientists speculated were the shattered remains of an incredibly ancient city, once protected by massive geodesic domes.

The early shuttlecraft program ferried construction materials to a point in the Moon's orbit, where they were retrieved by the engineers living there via short-range unmanned vessels. From there, they were conveyed to Lagrange Region 2, on the dark side of the Moon.

Parallax Red had a twofold purpose—to establish a permanent Terran military presence in space and to use the base as a jumping-off point for missions to Mars.

However, the construction project was mind-staggeringly costly and excruciatingly slow.

The loss in life was exceptionally high, as well, due to accidents and the cumulative debilitating effects of zero gravity.

"From what I read in the few journals still extant," Sindri said, "conditions in the first decade of the project were beastly, technical problems nearly insurmountable and the schedule was woefully behind, on the order of three years."

"Something obviously turned it around," Brigid commented.

Sindri nodded, steering the cart around a curve in the passageway wall. "That something was the advent and installation of a gadget colloquially known as a gateway. One was installed in Manitius base in 1990, and another a few months later on the station itself."

Grant and Kane exchanged dour glances. What Sindri said fit with what they knew of the Project Cerberus timeline.

"After that," Sindri declared, "construction on *Parallax Red* resumed, and the major portions of it were completed in a little less than a year. Once that was accomplished, the focus turned to Mars.

"In the intervening years however, the situation had changed. Other unique features had been discovered on the planet. Constructs that were obviously unnatural and that resembled a pyramid city showed up in the photos…the products of design and all that implied.

"The situational change was political. By the mid-1980s, the Soviets had withdrawn their support from the *Parallax Red* project and made their own partisan plans to investigate the so-called Monuments of Mars."

Sindri laughed shortly and went on. "In 1988, Russia launched two probes supposedly to investigate the Martian moon Phobos. Both were lost without revealing anything."

Kane leaned forward. "Lost? How were they lost?"

Sindri turned the wheel and guided the cart up a ramp slanted at a forty-five-degree angle. "More than likely, they were destroyed."

"By who or what?" asked Grant.

The ramp ended in a white, blister-shaped pocket, about the size of the mat-trans control room. Sindri applied the brakes, and the cart squeaked to a halt. "Disembark if you've a mind to, but you will find the quality of air and gravity severely lacking."

All of them saturated their lungs with oxygen before pushing aside the plastic sheets and climbing out of the cart. As Sindri warned them, the gravity was very low, probably a fraction of a G above zero. The air was exceptionally thin and cold.

The chamber was dominated by a ten-foot-high platform surrounding an elongated object shaped in some ways like a cannon, but one that appeared composed of an alchemical fusion of glass, ceramic and metal.

A ladder and a lift led up to the railed platform. Underneath they saw ribbons of circuitry and control consoles. Nestled directly beneath the cannon, enclosed by transparent armaglass partitions, was a humped row of dynamos.

Voice tight so as not to allow more air than necessary to escape his lungs, Grant said, "It's a weapon. A blaster."

Sindri nodded. "I believe it was deployed to destroy the Russian space probes."

"What is it?" Kane asked. "An MD gun?"

Sindri swung his head toward him, regarding him keenly. "No, Mr. Kane, it is not, though I am interested in learning how you know about it."

He pointed to the long barrel of the cannon. "It is a GRASER, a gamma-ray-powered laser projector. Gamma-ray photons are millions of times more powerful than infrared photons produced even by ruby lasers. This is a true death ray, horrifyingly powerful, far worse than a molecular destabilizer. A few billion megawatts of GRASER power might conceivably blow up the Sun, force it to go nova."

Sindri half strode, half drifted to a control panel. He pressed a series of buttons, snapped a toggle switch and the white blister slowly became translucent, then transparent. The outlanders recognized the same microcircuitry system as in the Sandcat's gun turret, where an electric impulse was fed to the treated armaglass bubble. Outside the dome, space spread like a vast, black velvet curtain, dusted with tiny diamonds.

"The GRASER was a major component of the so-called Strategic Defense Initiative," said Sindri, a slight wheeze in his voice. "I refer to it as Thor's Hammer, throwing thunderbolts from the heavens to destroy the cowering sinners below."

"Is it still functional?" Brigid inquired.

"No. The dynamos drew their power from an array of electromagnets. Over the years, they became degaussed."

Sindri put a hand over his mouth, swallowing a cough and waving them back to the cart. He hit the control switches, and the blister turned opaque again.

Back inside the vehicle, they sat for a few moments, breathing deeply, replenishing their lungs. At length,

Brigid asked, "Did the Russians suspect how their spacecraft were destroyed?"

Sindri nodded. "I'm sure they did. They waited until January 20, 2001, to retaliate. Physical evidence here points to explosive decompression of the most strategic points of the station. It's my personal opinion that a swarm of Russian killer satellites attacked *Parallax Red,* severely decreasing its rotation cycle."

"And the people here?" asked Kane. "What happened to them?"

"The ones who didn't die simply fled. Earth certainly didn't offer much in the way of a sanctuary."

"So they went to Mars?" Grant ventured.

"Exactly. I know that much."

"How many survivors?" inquired Brigid.

"Enough," replied Sindri, a cold note of bitterness sounding in his voice.

"Enough for what?"

Sindri didn't respond for a long moment. When he did, it was in the form of a sneering chuckle. "Like the rats left behind here, enough to be fruitful and multiply."

Chapter 18

Sindri turned in his seat to face Kane. "Your casual mention of the molecular destabilizer surprised and intrigued me. How do you know of it?"

"We found its handiwork in Redoubt Papa," he answered. "Three Mags and one of their vehicles unraveled."

"Mags." A line of puzzlement appeared between Sindri's eyes. "What are Mags?"

"Magistrates," Brigid told him.

Sindri shook his head, indicating he didn't understand.

Grant said, "Sec men."

Sindri frowned slightly, then comprehension dawned in his eyes. "You mean security men, like police officers?"

Kane nodded. "Yes."

Sindri turned back around, starting the cart's motor. "Mags and sec men. Have all Terrans been trained to think in shorthand, or are you three special cases?"

As he steered the cart back toward the ramp, he said, "Tell me about Magistrates."

The three of them took turns, choosing their words carefully. Brigid limited herself to a historical background, describing how the Magistrates were the organizational descendants of a proposed global police force of the late twentieth century, one that had judicial, as well as law-enforcement powers.

Grant and Kane supplied a few specifics about the Magistrate Divisions, soft-pedaling the patrilineal traditions and the oaths sworn to wring order out of postnukecaust chaos. They refrained from mentioning their own long associations with the Magistrates.

"Nasty customers," Sindri commented. "But I suppose fascism is always an attractive alternative to the madness of freedom. Had these Mags of yours come to Redoubt Papa because my people accidentally set off an alarm of some sort?"

"No," said Kane slowly. "We aren't really sure why they were there."

"You're not sure." Sindri's voice was gently chiding.

"No."

"I'm sure of one thing, Mr. Kane. You're withholding information in violation of our bargain."

Sindri suddenly wrenched the steering wheel, turning the cart down a side-branching corridor. It dead-ended inside a room that was not much larger than a niche. Within it, resting on a four-wheeled platform, was a totally unfamiliar machine.

"There," said Sindri genially, "is your molecular destabilizer. Not quite as impressive as the GRASER, is it?"

All of them had no choice but to agree. Whereas the GRASER followed the general configurations of a cannon, the MD was a dark metal ovoid with a convex dorsal surface, about three feet long and half that in diameter. On the end facing them, they saw a round, recessed lens. Flexible metal conduits curled, twisted and bent double on all sides of it. Tubes forming concentric circles occupied the rear of the platform.

Pointing to the tubes, Sindri said, "The MD is powered by antiprotons, concentrated and held in those storage rings around which they constantly move. When the discharge setting is activated, a stream of particles are released through that lens, a power of about two thousand joules to a three-second burst. You can squeeze about ten bursts out of it before the batteries need recharging."

"Doesn't seem like a very reliable weapon," Grant observed.

"In truth, it is not. Though developed as such, the MD proved more useful as a tool, to mine buried elements and ores."

"Why did you take it to the redoubt, then?"

Sindri shrugged. "I thought it might be needed to force egress through doors that could not be opened or passages blocked by rubble. My people had no choice but to turn it on your so-called Magistrates. It was their only defense."

"No smaller models were ever built?" asked Kane.

"Not that I am aware of, no." His response was glib, practiced and smooth.

Putting the cart in reverse, Sindri backed it out of the niche and into the main corridor. He drove slowly along it, silently, as if lost in thought. Then he said, "You were lying to me, Mr. Kane. You know why the Magistrates were in the redoubt, don't you?"

Kane didn't reply for a long, tense moment. Carefully he answered, "We aren't sure, Sindri. Believe me."

"But you have suspicions?"

"Yes."

"Do me the honor of presenting them to me, please."

Brigid said, "We suspect they were looking for some signs of us. Your people's paths and theirs crossed at the wrong time. An accident."

Sindri's shoulders stiffened. "Why would Magistrates be looking for you? Are you criminals?"

"In many circles on Earth," answered Brigid, "we most definitely are."

Sindri looked at her wide-eyed. "Miss Brigid, I would have never believed it of a young lady with your refinements. Your companions yes, but not you. I can scarcely credit it."

He smiled conspiratorially, leaning toward her. "What crime did you commit? Did you punish an unfaithful lover, stab him with a jeweled letter opener on the night of the full moon, then dance about naked in his blood?"

Brigid's eyes slitted in confusion, and she drew as far away from him as the bucket seat would allow. "What? No, of course not."

Sindri's face fell in disappointment. "Then what did you do?"

She tried to shrug casually. "I wanted to know a few things that weren't meant to be known."

"Elucidate, kindly. I'm quite fascinated."

"What the hell difference does it make?" broke in Grant harshly.

Kane couldn't help but smile. Out of all the exiles at Cerberus, Grant was still the most sensitive about his criminal status. He didn't like to think about it and he certainly didn't enjoy talking about it.

Sindri turned around to look him reproachfully. "It

makes a very great difference to me, sir. Common ground we all share, you see. I, too, am a criminal.''

Kane angled an eyebrow at him. "What kind?"

"Oh, the very worst, from a philosophical point of view." Sindri's fingers began tapping a nervous ditty on the steering wheel. "An idealist, a savior gone wrong. I kill in order to save.''

Grant's lips twisted in a barely repressed smirk. "Just who did you kill while saving them?''

Sindri laughed. "Ninety-five percent of the population of Mars. I hope you don't want their names, because they've tended to slip my mind.''

THE FOOD at Sindri's table came from self-heat ration packs. The fact that he served it on plastic dinnerware didn't improve its taste, look or smell very much. Kane tried to feed some scraps of a rice-pilaf concoction to Robinson Crusoe. The cat sniffed at it to be polite, but declined to consume any. Kane couldn't blame him.

Grant and Kane were surprised by the fiery wine Elle served them. Brigid drank a little of it, but not much.

The table had been moved out of Sindri's improvised living quarters and into the barnlike warehouse. Trolls stood around it here and there at a respectful distance, but their black eyes never left the three outlanders at the table.

Three females danced in the shaft of sunlight slanting in from the skylight. They moved in hobbling, graceless kick steps to the skirling and twanging of men playing pipes and harps.

Sindri apologized effusively for the food, but felt that it would have been a shame to waste the enormous cache of it on the station.

"The eleventh commandment of the universe," he declaimed. "Thou shalt not waste."

Kane refrained from commenting that by following the eleventh commandment, and eating two-hundred-year-old rations, they were increasing the odds of contracting severe gastrointestinal disorders.

Without preamble, Sindri said, "You were going to tell me how you know, and how much you know about the Danaan."

Brigid lifted a speculative eyebrow. "We were?"

"Our bargain, remember? I showed you around the station, provided you with its history and numerous samples of my good faith."

"And," declared Kane, "there's plenty you haven't told us. The least of which is when we can expect to leave."

"Shortly, Mr. Kane. You will leave shortly. Now, as to my request?"

Brigid took a sip of the wine and repressed a shudder. "There isn't much to tell. A short time ago, in Ireland, we encountered a small group of people who claimed Danaan ancestry."

Sindri leaned forward eagerly. "Did they have any of their technology?"

"Not as such. A few artifacts which were regarded as holy objects, a few places they revered as Danaan power points."

"And a harp," said Kane, casting a sidewise glance at Elle.

Sindri stroked his chin contemplatively. "Harps. Like the ones here?"

"No," Brigid answered. "More conventional in shape, but apparently operating on the same ultra or infrasonic principles."

Sindri's face lit up with a startled smile. "The harmonic and disharmonic resonances? Oh, this is far better than I hoped."

"We were told that the Danaan could manipulate hyperdimensional vortexes," said Grant. "Naturally occurring mat-trans gateways. Is there evidence of such things on Mars?"

Sindri shook his head. "There is only evidence the Danaan wielded a mighty science, the science of energy being moved in precise harmony and in perfect balance."

Kane's nape hairs tingled with suspicion. He knew Sindri was lying by omission. The little man was more than an accomplished dissembler—he was a smooth and practiced actor.

He asked, "How are you going to make it worth our while to help you and your people settle on Earth?"

Sindri smiled coldly. "It is something beyond the limitations of descriptive language. I'll have to show you."

"Then get to it," Grant said with a gruff impatience.

Propping his elbows on the table, steepling his fingers beneath his chin, Sindri gave him a direct, level stare. "I shall, Mr. Grant. But there is more I have to learn from you first. Much, much more."

"Until you start giving us more," said Kane acidly, "your education has come to a stop."

The pipes fluting in the background suddenly fell silent, but the harps continued to sing. The tune subtly changed, the notes octaves lower than they had been.

"I don't think so," Sindri stated calmly. "It has only just begun. I will walk in all your minds, looking at your memories, strolling here and there among the ru-

ins of your broken dreams. Make no mistake about it—
I will find what I need.''

Sleep suddenly came over Kane in waves. He swallowed a yawn, the effort making his ears pop. His eyes began to water. He looked at his companions and saw them blinking their eyes rapidly, straining to keep them open.

Kane realized what was happening. The drugged wine had placed them in a relaxed, receptive state so the vibrations of the harps' notes repressed and controlled areas of the brain. The harp music spoke of sweet, slow winds and deep, comforting night. The music crooned to them, a lullaby urging them to care about nothing but the need to crawl into the embrace of sleep.

It took all of Kane's strength to keep his head upright. He snarled and reached for Sindri with an arm of lead. He forgot he was sitting down.

Although he was distantly aware of sliding from the chair, he was deeply asleep before he hit the floor.

impending danger with every step that took them farther away from the gully. Though hounded by Grant's grim manner and demeanor, he inferred him of his suspicions.

Only hours before Kane had questioned and asked him when surely it was beginning to be possible if they, in the dusty floor, flexing, smile-embroidered

Chapter 19

Kane didn't drift into a dream—he dived into it, shoulder-rolling across loose sand, joining Grant behind a bullet-pocked boulder. The rock wasn't very large, but it was the only decent cover available for yards around. Hazy heat waves shimmered from the Great Sand Dunes hellzone, making visibility uncertain.

Kane looked at the scarlet streaming from between the leg pieces of Grant's armor, like a bubbling spring of blood. The blood wasn't a bright arterial red, but the Roamer land mine had still inflicted serious lacerations, even through the polycarbonate shin guard and Kevlar undersheathing.

Kane reached out to examine the wound, but Grant slapped his hand aside angrily. "Don't waste time on me."

Kane hesitated. He was twenty years old and on his second dark-territory probe. He didn't know Grant very well, and as his squad leader he wasn't supposed to. All he was expected to do was obey the man's orders.

Through helmet comm-links, they heard the shouts and curses of the other four members of the squad pinned down in the gully an eighth of a mile away. The sporadic pop-popping of muzzle loaders interwove with the deeper, steadier stutter of Sin Eaters and Copperheads on full auto.

Grant and Kane had walked point, and Kane sensed

impending danger with every step that took them farther away from the gully. Though intimidated by Grant's grim manner and seniority, he informed him of his suspicions.

Grant ignored him, told him to shut up and march. So when armed Roamers began rising from pits they'd dug in the desert floor, tossing aside sand-covered tarps, it was almost a relief.

The two Mags had heeled around, saw they couldn't backtrack and headed for the boulder. Grant was in the lead. When the black-powder mine detonated under the pressure of his right foot, it ruptured the surrounding earth in a gout of smoke, dirt and flame. The cracking shock wave knocked Kane down, but picked up Grant and cartwheeled him to within a few feet of the boulder.

The primitive mine's low explosive power contained more sound and fury than death. It also provided a pall of smoke and dust, allowing Grant to crawl behind the rock. Kane held his ground, firing his Copperhead in long, left-to-right bursts, then bounded across the smoldering crater and joined Grant behind the boulder. A storm of bullets struck it, chipping off shards and bouncing away.

Grant palmed grit from his helmet's visor and checked the Sin Eater's action. He had lost his Copperhead in the detonation. "How many do you figure?"

"Too many," Kane replied, ducking his head as another rifle ball dug a gouge in the rock. "We're about as outnumbered as we can be."

Grunting and wincing, Grant shifted his leg. More blood flowed out from beneath the polycarbonate shielding. Kane reached for it again.

"Lay off," Grant snapped. "We've got no time for first aid."

"And I've got no time to deal with a stubborn bastard who passes out from loss of blood and expects me to drag his ass back to the Sandcat." Kane's reply was as sharp as Grant's command. "I'm going to take a look at it, try to stop the bleeding. It's that simple. Sir."

Tersely Grant said, "Be quick about it."

Kane loosened the seal and lifted the shin guard away. Crimson spilled over his black-gloved fingers. Pushing aside the torn edges of the Kevlar, he examined the ragged, blood-pulsing gash at the base of the knee.

"Bad?" Grant asked.

"Not really. But not good, either. Bet it hurts like hell."

"You've got a gift for stating the obvious," said Grant between clenched teeth.

Kane opened up pouches on his web belt, removing field dressings and a pressure bandage.

"I should've listened to you," Grant said. "How'd you know?"

"Instinct. Ninety-nine percent of the time I'm wrong, but that one percent makes up for all the time I waste on paranoia."

Grant chuckled, then bit off a groan as Kane began treating his leg.

There was a tap on his shoulder, and Kane felt thrown out of sync with the dream reality. "I'm not really interested in this, you know," Sindri said. "I had already deduced that you and Mr. Grant were Magistrates."

"Fuck off," Kane snapped, unscrewing a vial of

sulfa and blood coagulant. "You wanted me to remember, so I'm remembering."

Sindri clucked disapprovingly. "You've gone too far back. This is what, a dozen years ago?"

Kane nodded, frowning, his thoughts leaping ahead. The Roamers had made a concerted rush to overwhelm their position, hurling their mines as grenades. One had detonated nearly at Kane's feet, deafening him, chunks of the hardened clay case battering him and cracking a couple of ribs. If not for his helmet's visor, he would have been blinded.

Only their superior firepower beat off the attack, routed the Roamers, drove them into the gully and the deadly fusillade laid down by the rest of the hard-contact squad.

A few of the ragbag bastards escaped and disabled the Sandcat. The Mags had been forced to hike a day and a night through the Colorado hellzone, Kane lugging Grant almost the entire distance.

Toward the end of the rugged trek, Kane was so punch-drunk from exhaustion and consumed with pain from his cracked ribs that he had shot a cactus to pulpy pieces, hallucinating that it was an ambushing Roamer. It had taken him nearly a week to remove all the needles from his face.

He looked over his shoulder at Sindri. "What is it you want me to remember, exactly?"

The little man shrugged. "I'll know it when I see it. Now move on."

Kane let his mind go with it. He didn't feel as if he had much of a choice.

THUNDER RUMBLED and the dark clouds flashed with lightning. Grant watched it, listening to the soft pattering of raindrops against the window. He looked at Cobaltville's Administrative Monolith, its white facade shimmering in the downpour, light still shining from the slit-shaped windows on every level.

He glanced down, at the feeble, guttering torchlight in the Tartarus Pits, spread out below the Enclave towers. Tomorrow he would be down there with Kane, searching every cellar and every squat for pregnant outlanders.

Intel section had received information that a group of them were hidden somewhere in those narrow, twisting lanes, hoping against hope to give birth before they were discovered and ejected from the ville.

Ejection was not an option. Salvo had issued termination-on-sight warrants, and so the Magistrates had to serve them. It was their portion of duty and service to the baron.

"Can't you sleep, sweetheart?"

Grant whirled, stomach muscles jumping in adrenaline-fueled spasms. He hadn't heard Olivia come up from behind him. He made himself grin, feeling ashamed that he had almost forgotten she was there. It was her flat, after all, on the top level of the residential Enclaves. Olivia had earned her place there. Grant lived two levels below, and it was something of a bend in rules for him to be in her place at all.

But as a Magistrate who had just been awarded his third meritorious-service citation that very morning, he wasn't too worried about a reprimand. He had other concerns preying on his mind.

Olivia slid her arms around his waist, snuggling her naked body close, the hard nipples of her breasts pressing into his lower chest. Grant enfolded her in an embrace and held her, his cheek muscles aching with the strain of maintaining his grin.

Olivia was a beautiful woman, with her light brown complexion, black hair plaited and beaded and big eyes—wise eyes, yet innocent, deep and brown. The wisdom that had helped her earn a senior engineer's rank of E Level at the age of twenty-four also helped her sense his discomfiture. However, her innocence didn't allow her to understand it.

Tilting her head back, troubled eyes searching his face, she asked, "What is it?"

Gently, hands on her smooth shoulders, he pushed her away, holding her at arm's length. He started to speak, then cleared his throat. She stared at him unblinkingly, waiting.

He inhaled a deep breath, then slowly expelled it. "After the ceremony today, Salvo told me."

"Told you what?" Her question came out as a whisper, full of dread.

"Our contract application was refused. You and me don't meet the profiles, at least not yet. Maybe in a couple of years, once my administrative transfer is scheduled—"

Olivia twisted out of his grasp, turning her back. She stared into the shadows of her apartment. Softly she asked, "Who had the most incompatible scores, me or you?"

Grant squeezed his eyes shut for a moment. "It doesn't matter."

Olivia hugged herself. Flatly she said, "So I guess that's it. We're through."

Grant felt so weak and weary and defeated, he couldn't dredge up a reply. She had spoken the truth. He and Olivia were finished. Submitting a formal mating contract application had been a calculated risk, naming names and listing all pertinent statistics. Now that it had been reviewed and refused, he and Olivia had drawn attention to themselves. Their relationship was now officially unsanctioned and couldn't continue lawfully.

Into the bleak cold of ruined hopes came a jarring intrusion. "Oh, for God's sake," moaned Sindri from his perch on the windowsill. "This is *so* puerile."

Grant whirled on him, feeling the hot prickles of shame rushing to his face. He growled, "You little sawed-off asshole, you wanted me to remember!"

Sindri's face screwed up as if he tasted something exceptionally sour. "Not these old maudlin memories, five or more years old. What can I do with them? I mean, *really*—"

He propped his cane beneath his chin with one hand and made back-and-forth sawing motions across it with the other, miming the playing of a violin. He shook his head ruefully. "All of you are going to have to do much better."

Grant glanced toward Olivia, standing there with her back to him, head bowed, shoulders slumped by the weight of an inconsolable misery. He remembered how he had left her place a few minutes later and, unable to sleep, prowled the promenades of all four levels, seeking a way to escape his own grief. He had considered barging in on Kane, but then he would have been obliged to explain his presence at 3:00 a.m., and he simply didn't have the words.

At dawn, he and the squad made the Pit sweep. They found six pregnant women cowering in a cellar, and at Salvo's terse "Flashblast this slaghole," they opened up with Sin Eaters on full auto. Grant had kept his eyes closed when he fired, praying he didn't hit any of them but knowing he had.

Shuddering, Grant faced Sindri again. In a dead voice, he said, "I don't like it here."

Sindri hopped down from the window. "You and me both. Let's go someplace else."

BRIGID WINCED as the brush caught in a snarl and pulled her scalp. "Ouch, Mom! Are you trying to snatch me bald or what?"

Moira Baptiste chuckled, patting the top of her daughter's head. "If you paid a little more attention to your appearance, brushing your hair wouldn't be like hacking through a jungle."

Brigid sighed in irritation. "I ought to just cut it all off. It's a pain putting it up every day before I go to training."

Moira ran the brush through her daughter's red-gold mane with long, even strokes. "You could, but I think you'd regret it."

"Why? Having it pinned up for twelve hours gives me headaches. And besides—" Brigid's words trailed off.

"Besides what?"

Quietly Brigid said, "It draws attention to me. Some of the men there give me funny looks. Not ha-ha funny, either."

The brush paused in midstroke. Tensely Moira asked, "Is Lakesh one of the men?"

Brigid was startled into laughing. Turning in her chair, she looked up into the slightly weathered beauty of her mother's face. Though her eyes were hazel, her hair was identical to Brigid's own, both in color and texture.

"Him? C'mon, Mom! He looks like he's eighty years old. Besides, he's the senior archivist. He hardly ever comes to the training sessions, except to give a lecture now and then."

The expression of relief on her mother's face was so pronounced that Brigid was mystified. "Why'd you ask about him?"

A smile creased Moira's lips, but it wasn't her characteristic smile, which lit up and transformed a pretty face into something heart-achingly beautiful. It was forced, stitched on.

"No reason." Gently she turned her daughter's head and began brushing again. Very softly she asked, "Is your talent serving you in your studies?"

Brigid knew what she meant. "Talent" was their private euphemism for her ability to produce eidetic images. The talent had first manifested itself when Brigid wasn't much older than an infant, and her mother had carefully coached her not to mention it to anyone.

Imitating her mother's quiet tone, she answered, "Yes."

No more was said. Her mother finished brushing her hair, then began pinning it up for her. "You know," she said casually, "you're really going to have to get into the habit of doing this yourself."

"Why?"

"You can't expect me to be your personal stylist forever." Moira's voice held a teasing lilt. "You'll rise up the ranks in your division and be on your own."

Brigid stood up, automatically smoothing the green bodysuit with the rainbow-colored insignia of the Historical Division on the left breast. "That won't be for a long time, Mom."

Moira smiled again. "Time is a relative thing. Now, off with you."

Brigid saw moisture glisten in the corners of her mother's eyes. She turned quickly, averting her face, swiftly leaving the room. Brigid started after her, heart thudding in her chest in sudden alarm…but something blocked her way.

Sindri was blocking her movement with his walking stick. Pinching the bridge of his nose, he said in weary exasperation, "Again with the banalities. None of you are cooperating. I'm not interested in any of your past melodramatic moments."

Brigid stopped, remembering how when she had returned home that day, over thirteen years ago, her mother was gone. No note, no message, only a framed photograph of her.

Brigid had made no inquiries. People vanished from the villes all the time, as if they had never existed. Asking about it only drew attention.

She looked down at Sindri. "You weren't really specific, you know."

"It's difficult to be so with the unconscious," Sindri retorted defensively. "I had hoped with your orderly mind, I could learn what I wanted without prompting."

"What do you want?"

"Show me, Miss Brigid, those few things you wanted to know that weren't meant to be known."

Brigid felt the surge of memory, felt it stimulate one nerve after another, sliding up and around in her head.…

She sat at her workstation in the Historical Division, inserted a computer disk into her machine and opened it up. The message flashing onto the monitor screen stunned her into momentary immobility. In that numbed moment, she read:

Greetings, fellow scholar. We are the Preservationists. You have distinguished yourself as a seeker and collector of knowledge. Only those deemed most worthy of preserving the hidden history of humanity are selected to join us. We will contact you again very soon.

Then the message faded from the screen, as if it had a preset time-limit program. She remembered how the message had terrified her, yet enthralled her at the same time. Weeks passed before she was contacted a second time, and that message was just as brief, promising to contact her again in the near future. In the weeks that followed, more messages appeared on her screen.

She slowly understood that the Preservationists had intentionally sought her out. Archivists like herself, the Preservationists were scattered throughout the villes, devoted to preserving not just past knowledge, but to piecing together the unrevised history of not only the predark, but also the postholocaust world.

One morning, she found an unfamiliar disk in her work area, and when she opened it, the message said simply "Read only in private."

Shortly thereafter, she had found, retrieved and repaired a cast-off DDC. She slid in the disk and read the data it contained. It contained the journal of a woman named Dr. Mildred Wyeth, a specialist in cryogenics who had entered a hospital in late 2000 for minor surgery. An allergic reaction to the anesthetic left her in a coma, so to save her life, the predark whitecoats had her cryonically frozen.

She was revived over a century later and she joined a band of warrior survivalists led by Ryan Cawdor. Though the journal contained recollections of adventures and wanderings, it dealt in the main with Dr. Wyeth's observations, speculations and theories about the environmental conditions of postnukecaust America.

She also delved deeply into the Totality Concept and her fears and suspicions that the minds behind it were somehow, some way, directly responsible for the nukecaust and the horrors of the Deathlands.

Brigid hadn't known how much of the *Wyeth Codex* to believe or disbelieve, but she was never the same again. Thus began her secret association with the Preservationists.

"The light of understanding begins to pierce my benighted brain," drawled Sindri with a grin, leaning an elbow on her computer console. "Your assignment was to memorize any documents at variance with ville doctrine, put them in cogent form and pass them on. Sedition—I like that. Move ahead now, Miss Brigid. Show me more."

A flow of memories swept her up and along. She sat at her machine, tapping the keys. She had just come from the shower and sat at it naked. She began entering the data she had glimpsed on a Department of Defense document, bearing the date of April 30, 1994. Since she had merely glanced at it, no one would suspect her memory retained almost every word and punctuation mark of the document entitled "Possible Origin of Magistrate Division—Source: DoD Document, Dated 4/30/94."

She input steadily for over half an hour. She raised her arms above her head, arching her back to work out the kinks in her shoulders. She tried to keep her mind empty, visualizing nothing but the rest of the document—

The bedroom door swung open, and her head swiveled toward it so quickly she felt a twinge of tendon pain. Immediately, almost instinctively, she swept her hand across the keyboard, hitting the Escape button, clearing the screen of its data.

She stared at a dark-haired, clean-shaved man in a long black overcoat. Though she couldn't see it, she almost felt the bore of his Sin Eater trained on her naked body.

Sindri waved his hand and walking stick dismissively. "No, no, I don't need to see this. Mr. Kane retains quite vivid memories of your first meeting. Move further up the line."

Gray mist enfolded her bedroom, swallowing up her, Kane and her computer. When it cleared, she sat staring across Lakesh's desk in his small, sparsely furnished office. Grant, Domi and Kane were there, too, listening to the old man's reedy voice.

"They were called many things over many centuries—angels, demons, visitors, E.T.'s, saucer people, grays. Whatever they actually are, what they are called, even where they come from is unimportant at this juncture. The sinister thread linking all of humankind's darkest hours leads back to a nonhuman presence that has conspired to control us through political chaos, staged wars, famines, plagues and 'natural' disasters. It is a conspiracy that continues to this day, aided and abetted by willing human allies...."

"Good," whispered Sindri in exultation. "Good. Take a forward baby step, Miss Brigid. We're almost done."

She took the step and stood staring at a wall constructed of glass panes. Behind it she saw a deeply recessed room, dimly lit by a red light strip.

A shape shifted in the ruddy gloom, and for a fraction of a microsecond, she glimpsed a long, pale head and a high, hairless cranium. Then a fog seemed to whirl inside the recessed chamber, blotting the face from view. Then the mist cleared and two eyes flamed out of the blood-hued murk. The eyes were frighteningly huge, tip-tilted like a cat's, completely black with no pupil or iris.

A thready nonvoice said, *We are old. When your race was wild and bloody and young, we were already ancient. Your tribe has passed, and we are invincible. All of the achievements of man are dust—they are forgotten.*

We stand, we know, we are. We stalked above man ere we raised him from the ape. Long was the earth ours, and now we have reclaimed it. We shall still reign when man is reduced to the ape again. We stand, we know, we are.

Sindri tugged her away from the glass wall and the fathomless eyes. "Thank you, Miss Brigid," he said kindly. "This has been an ordeal for you. Now I can proceed. You may sleep now."

The memories dimmed and faded out of Brigid's mind like smoke wraiths, and she slipped gratefully into a warm sepia sea.

Chapter 20

Blackness not as deep as death acquired colors, muted and dim. Brigid felt her body again as she bobbed out of the sepia sea into the world of three dimensions and physicality.

As consciousness came slowly back, she was aware of mechanical sounds, electric motors whirring and humming. She tried to stir, but she was restrained by several hard and flat bindings pressing against her arms and legs. When she attempted to lift her head, she felt a tight pressure against her forehead.

She managed to open her eyes, forcing the lids apart a micromillimeter at a time. Objects, shapes and shadows swam mistily around her. Figures scuttled to and fro across her limited range of vision. She heard a murmur of voices, metallic clinkings and clackings.

Though she couldn't turn her head, Brigid shifted her gaze to her right. A naked man lay flat on his back on a padded table only a few feet away. He seemed to be deeply asleep, unaware of the arrangement of canvas straps that stretched across his forehead, his chest, his arms and legs.

She squinted, trying to reason out why the long-limbed, hard-muscled man looked so familiar. Then she recognized the dark tousled hair and the profile and realized it was Kane. She had never seen him naked before, and somehow she felt a certain satisfaction in this. Her gaze traveled down his body. It stopped at his pelvis, and her eyes narrowed, then widened.

What appeared to be a bowl of black rubber rested upside down over his groin. A flexible hose extended from a sleeve socket in the center of the bowl and snaked up to a small, glass-walled box hanging from a metal armature. As she watched through blurred eyes, a short stream of milky fluid squirted from the end of the hose, splashing the transparent inner walls of the box.

A piping voice wafted from the shadows. "We've got a strong flow now. More than adequate volume."

A deeper voice responded, "Good. Disconnect him and prepare Grant."

The voice rang a responsive chord in Brigid, but the lethargy in her body and mind prevented her from attaching a name and face to it. Still, the sound of it sent cold chills over her flesh.

Twisting her head, she looked down at herself. She was as naked as Kane, restrained by the same arrangement of straps. The only difference was the position of her legs. They were widely spread, the ankles clamped tightly at the corners of the table. A length of hose lay coiled between them, its nether end attached to a machine mounted on a tripod. The hose had a bulbous, blunt tip.

A wave of fear flooded her and tore a cry from her lips. Sindri's face suddenly appeared at her left shoulder, his smile warm and comforting.

"Dearest Miss Brigid," he said quietly, "I should've taken extra measures with you. You drank the least amount of the wine, and I subjected you to more neocortex stimulation. Of course you would revive first. My apologies."

Brigid jerked against the restraints. In a high, aspirated half sob, she demanded, "What are you doing?"

"Proceeding, Miss Brigid. Elle, if you please..."

Harp strings thrummed and vibrated. Her eyelids fluttered. She struggled to keep them open, fought not to be soothed.

Sindri stroked the side of her face. "Sleep," he crooned. "Sleep."

Brigid's eyes closed, but when she felt a distant, probing pressure, she managed to wrench them open again. They filled with tears of terror and outrage when she saw Sindri very carefully manipulating the tip of the hose between her legs.

Brigid drew in a lungful of air, ready to expel it in a scream. But lulled by the harp song, she allowed herself to sink again into the warm sea of oblivion.

Chapter 21

Kane opened his mouth and tried to yawn, failed and closed it again. His head ached dully, as if he had clogged sinuses. He heard a faint rising-and-falling throb in his ears, and he thought it might be the crash of surf on a distant, rocky beach. But the sound was too steady, too overlaid with a pulsing, mechanical rhythm to be natural.

He felt something soft and yielding beneath his naked shoulders and backside. He shivered and opened his eyes. He lay on his back on a narrow bed, covered with a thin blanket. Staring upward at a blank, domed ceiling, he wondered with a degree of detachment why he felt so groggy. It was as if he had been asleep for a long time, but he didn't feel rested. His slumber had been a chaotic jumble of busy dreams.

Levering himself to a sitting position, he blinked at his surroundings. They didn't go away, so he knew he wasn't dreaming. There wasn't a great deal to see. The room was a small ellipse, like the inside of an eggshell balanced on the broad end. A single overhead light strip provided the illumination. He saw his environmental suit hanging from a hook beside a thin, dark rectangular line spanning half of the facing wall. A small square metal plate studded with two buttons was mounted beneath it.

On the opposite wall, he saw a round hatchway with irislike segments nestled within a thick metal frame.

Slowly Kane swung his legs over the side of the bed, his bare feet recoiling briefly from the cold, hard floor. He remembered sitting at Sindri's table with the dawning realization that the combination of wine and harp song was pushing him into the placid depths of sleep.

He stood up, and the floor heaved beneath him for a moment, then steadied. He took a careful forward step, noting the gravity seemed normal, as did the air. He flexed his leg muscles, lifting and lowering himself on his heels, then he winced at the stinging, slight burning sensation in the vicinity of his groin.

Looking down at himself, Kane gently touched his genitals. His testicles were sore, almost as if they had been roughly squeezed, and his penis felt very sensitive. It was irritated, with reddened marks of chafing on it.

A gauzy scrap of a dream ghosted through his mind, but it was too insubstantial to grasp and it flitted away before he could examine it.

He probed at the knife wound on his ribs, but when his fingers didn't touch the film of liquid bandage, he uttered a wordless exclamation of surprise. The layer of artificial skin was gone, and of the slash, only a pink line remained, looking like an almost healed scratch. The shallow puncture wound on his right shoulder was merely a pink, irregularly shaped dot.

His knee showed the fading yellow blotch of an old bruise. He worked it back and forth, pleased but disturbed there was no corresponding pain or stiffness. As he had already suspected, the demonstration of the harp's powers had healed his injuries.

Running a hand over his jawline, he felt a bristly

growth. He had shaved just yesterday morning, only an hour before climbing into the Cerberus jump chamber. The hair sprouting from his cheeks and chin felt like two days' worth of beard.

Kane didn't devote much thought to it. The longer he stood, the more he experienced hunger pains and a fierce thirst. Taking the environmental suit off the hook, he quickly slipped into it, zipping up the seals and pulling on the boots. He contemplated leaving off the gloves but decided not to risk losing them.

After he dressed, he paced around the small room, seeing no control buttons or knobs on the hatch frame. He yelled, "Hey!"

His voice echoed hollowly. There was no answer.

"Hey! Sindri!"

Again there was no response. For lack of anything else to do, he went to the rectangular shutter, placed his finger on the top button, turned his back, closed his eyes and pressed it. He immediately rested his finger on the second button, ready to push it if undiluted, blinding sunlight cascaded in. He heard the whir of tiny motors as the shutter lifted. What little change he could detect in the light level through his eyelids was minute, so he cautiously slitted them open.

The sunshine shafting through the observation port wasn't intolerably bright. In fact, it looked diffuse and pale, as if filtered through heavy cloud cover. Kane turned around, hand half-lifted to shield his eyes. It was an unnecessary gesture, but he didn't lower his arm. He was too busy being alternately stupefied and terrified.

The light of dawn came through the transparent port, the sun just climbing over the rust red horizon, turning the pumpkin-colored sky a deep rose. In the far distance, Kane saw a range of stone shouldering up from rock-strewed and barren ground. Much closer towered a structure, a mountain in the shape of a pyramid.

It loomed frighteningly high, its gigantic red walls climbing sheer toward the sky. Kane had to tilt his head back to glimpse the apex, even though his wheeling thoughts told him the pyramid was at least half a mile away. It was gargantuan, immensely broad at the base and narrow at the top. He calculated that the bottom covered a square mile and a half and the top rose nearly six thousand feet.

The dawn sun glinted faintly from a metal spire stretching from the pyramid's apex. It looked tiny and threadlike in relation to the structure supporting it, but he figured it had to be a minimum of five hundred feet long.

The side facing him bore a deep V-shaped depression, symmetrical and running the length of the pyramid, from bottom to top. Between the arms of the V, Kane saw great flights of steps leading up from the desert floor.

The pyramid exuded antiquity, a history so incalculably ancient that it couldn't be measured by millennia and perhaps not even aeons. Fragmented memories of the Anasazi's Cliff Palace, the Black City of Kharo-Khoto and the tumulus of Newgrange flitted through his mind. He knew, without knowing how he did, that by the age standards of the immense pyramid, they had been built but an hour ago.

He heard a hissing sound behind him, but he did not, could not turn, not even when Sindri's amused voice said, "Welcome to my hometown, Mr. Kane. Welcome to Cydonia. Welcome to Mars."

KANE WAS SO DAZED, his thought processes so frozen into immobility, he allowed Sindri to nudge him gently away from the window and guide him to the hatch with gentle taps of his walking stick.

"Don't act so startled," Sindri said as they stepped from the room into a narrow, tunnel-like hallway. "I certainly mentioned my birthplace enough times for you to get used to the idea."

Kane didn't reply. Intellectually he had accepted Sindri's claim of extraterrestrial origin, but to wake up on another planet was an emotionally stunning experience.

Hoarsely he said, "You brought us here last night, while we were unconscious?"

"Partly correct and partly incorrect," responded Sindri blithely. "You were definitely unconscious, but I brought you here two days ago—Martian standard time."

Kane's mind reeled. Lakesh had probably given them up for dead by now. "Why?" he rasped.

Sindri, walking a few paces ahead, stopped and turned to face him. "Why did I bring you here or why did I keep you unconscious?"

"Both."

"Remember me saying I had to show you my reasons rather than tell you?"

Kane nodded.

"There is your answer."

A hot flush of anger burned away the last of the paralysis gripping Kane. Teeth bared, he lunged for Sindri, hands outstretched to secure a stranglehold.

Sindri sidestepped with a gliding grace and speed that deceived the eye. The silver knob of his walking stick drove deeply into the pit of Kane's stomach. His breath burst from his lips in an agonized grunt.

Stumbling, Kane tried to keep from bending double. From the corner of his eye, he saw the silver-tipped cane descending. The blow to the back of his head, delivered with a sharp economy, knocked him to his hands and knees, multicolored pinwheels spiraling before his eyes.

The walking stick cracked against his wrists, sweeping his arms out from under him, and he fell face-first to the floor. He struggled to rise, but a bone-deep boring pressure on the clump of ganglia at the base of his skull kept him prone. Sindri leaned his weight on his stick, the ferrule pressing into the back of Kane's neck.

"Very foolish of you," he said in a low voice. "Your reaction is understandable. Naturally you resent the liberties I have taken with you, but cooperation will be in the best interests of all."

Sindri whipped away the stick, taking two swift steps back as Kane pushed himself up by shaky arms. "Besides," he continued, "you are very weak. Other than receiving fluids intravenously, you've had nothing to eat or drink for two full days. I've no wish to take advantage of a man half-dead from want."

Kane climbed to his feet, refusing to give Sindri the satisfaction of seeing him rub the sore spot at the back of his neck. "Where are Baptiste and Grant?"

"Here, where do you think? I'm taking you to them—that is if you can stop being bellicose for just a few moments."

He turned and strode purposefully down the hall. After a moment of glaring after him, Kane followed.

"You brought us here with a gateway?"

"How else could I get you to Mars in less than a year?"

"You kept all of us asleep for two days?"

"It wasn't an arbitrary decision, Mr. Kane. It saved me and my aides a considerable amount of time and trouble."

"You might have asked us," Kane grated, "rather than abduct us."

"And have you refuse me? I couldn't take that chance." Sindri cast him an impish smile. "Besides, the Cydonia Compound has such a long tradition of abduction that it would be remiss of me not to uphold it."

"On the station, you said we could leave shortly."

Sindri stopped in front of another iris hatch. "So I did, and so you did. Didn't you leave *Parallax Red* and in fairly short order, too?"

Kane started to snarl out a curse, but the hatchway irised open and Sindri stepped through. After a second's hesitation, Kane followed suit.

The room was big, dome-shaped and full of furniture, but it smelled of damp and mildew. Old water stains streaked the walls beneath small metal vents. Tall bookshelves stood here and there, and Kane let his eyes rove over the titles visible on bindings as he walked past.

He saw Auerbach's *Mimesis,* seven volumes of *The Cambridge Medieval History,* Tarkington's *Complete Penrod,* Burroughs's *Gods of Mars,* Dickens's *A Tale of Two Cities,* Nietzsche's *Selected Discourses,* Darwin's *Origin of Species,* D'aulaire's *Norse Gods and Giants* and Melville's *Moby Dick.* Two entire shelves appeared to be only technical manuals, most of them spiral bound.

Since Kane wasn't familiar with any of the works, he couldn't glean any insight on Sindri's personality from them. A knowledge of literature, classic or otherwise, hadn't been part of his ville upbringing.

A quartet of male trolls stood stiffly at equidistant points around the room, hands behinds their backs in parade-rest positions. Grant and Brigid sat at a disk-topped table and when they saw Kane, they stood up, their faces reflecting conflicting emotions. In their expressions he read relief, anxiety and anger.

There was another emotion glimmering in Brigid's eyes, a shame she struggled to contain or come to terms with. Grant, like him, sported beard stubble.

Plates of food, plastic dinnerware and bottles of water were on the table, and Sindri pointed Kane toward it. "Dig in, refresh yourself. Your friends refused to eat until you joined them. Mealtime manners are one of the few qualities I admire in Terrans."

Kane pulled out a chair that felt and looked like lightweight plastic and sat down. After exchanging silent glances, they started to eat. If the food was strange, their stomachs, if not their palates, accepted it as adequate.

After a few minutes of silence, broken only by the clicking of eating utensils against plates, Sindri sighed deeply. "Come, come, people! Where is the sprightly conversation? You're on Mars! Aren't you the slightest bit excited by the prospect of exploring a strange new world and seeking out new life and civilizations?"

Grant picked up a plastic, blunt-pointed knife. He pointed it at Sindri like an accusatory finger. "Come over here, and I'll show you how fucking excited I am."

Sindri made a tsk-tsk sound of disapproval and

strode quickly to a wall switch. "Perhaps you need visual aids. A dining room with a view ought to stir the blood."

At a touch of the switch, the walls of the room seemed to vanish in yard-wide, floor-to-ceiling increments. By segments, the room became transparent.

Outside they saw a low collection of buildings, nearly all of them domed and made of a dull, lusterless metal. They were interconnected by tubes composed of the same material.

"Cydonia Compound One," Sindri announced. "A poor place, but mine own—and hopefully for not much longer."

Beyond a fenced-in perimeter spread a seemingly endless desert of orange-red sand. Low ridges rose naked from the desolate landscape and grew into a distant, barren mountain range.

Miles to the west rose a vast bulk of stone, a smoothly contoured formation that resembled a slightly squashed mesa.

"Be calm," said Sindri. "Accept. You are now thirty-five million miles from the planet of your birth. The temperature outside at noon will be a balmy fifty degrees Fahrenheit and around two hundred degrees below zero at midnight.

"The surface gravity is less than half that of Earth, and its atmospheric pressure is about eight millibars. The air is composed mainly of carbon dioxide. If we were not safe inside this pressurized habitat, we would all die within minutes."

Sindri paused, grinning crookedly. "So, as I hope you understand, regardless of the current conditions on Earth, they are far and away superior to that of Mars."

Kane tore his eyes away from the vast panorama of

desolation and focused them on Sindri. "All right, we understand you want to leave. You claimed you *needed* to leave."

Sindri's grin twisted, molding itself into a grimace. "I also said my reasons defied the limitations of descriptive language. Do you three feel strong enough to undertake a little walking tour?"

Before any of them had the opportunity to respond, Sindri flourished his cane in a grand gesture. "Excellent. Let us be off."

Chapter 22

Flanked by the retinue of trolls, they followed Sindri out into the tunnel-like passageway. Walking backward, facing them, he said, "I know what you want to ask." Affecting a childish, ingenuous falsetto, he stated, "'But, Perfessor Sindri, if we is on Mars, how come we can breathe so good an' we ain't floating around, losin' our breakfasts on the ceiling, how come?'"

Reverting to his normal tone, he announced, "This section of the compound is equipped with a network of small, synthetic-gravity generators. The field is created by a controlled stream of gravitons. That hum you hear is produced by the generators.

"Atmospheric processing units are located throughout the compound, maintaining a breathable mixture by removing carbon dioxide and other waste gases. It is recirculated through the system of processors."

He darted into a wide, outward-bulging niche in the tunnel wall, touched a button and a shutter slid up, affording them another view of the compound. It was just as dreary as the first one. Rust-hued sand spread listlessly, piling up in drifts at the bases of the domes. A few of the habitats were larger than others, their exteriors faintly etched with window lines.

Sindri said, "There are the barracks, the manufacturing facilities, the nurseries."

"Nurseries?" echoed Kane. "For what?"

"Children," Sindri replied disdainfully. "Not plants."

Lowering his gaze, Kane saw a small object squatting on the ground between two of the tube tunnels. Flat topped and suspended by an assembly of tread-enclosed rollers, it looked vaguely like a toy version of a Sandcat.

He pointed to it. "What's that? One of the children's playthings?"

Sindri chuckled. "Actually no, but it became one. That is the Mars Pathfinder, landed here by NASA in the late 1990s. It was quite the public-relations coup for them, since it helped to quell rumors they were deliberately concealing facts about Mars from the American citizenry."

He sighed a little sadly. "As a child, I spent many a happy hour romping around with the old Pathfinder. I'd put on an environmental suit and sit on it for hours, imagining it was taking me to all sorts of exciting places. Like Earth."

"That's what you brought us to Mars to see?" Grant growled.

Sindri barked out a laugh, turning around and leaving the niche. "Hardly. Come with me. We'll start out slow, just for you, Mr. Grant."

As they followed Sindri down the tunnel, Kane stepped close to Brigid. "You okay, Baptiste?" he whispered. "You haven't spoken a word."

She shook her head. "Not now, not while he's around."

He didn't argue. Her entire stance telegraphed tension and a barely leashed fear. When she said "he" there was no disguising the loathing in her voice.

They passed many of the irislike hatches. More than one bore plastic signs red-imprinted with the exclamatory notice, Warning! Low Grav And Atmo Conditions Beyond! Transadapts Only!

After seeing several of the sign-adorned hatchways, Kane asked, "What are transadapts?"

"A euphemism," retorted Sindri.

"For what?"

"For my people. Those doors lead to their living areas. You would find them most uncomfortable, not very far removed from the worst conditions aboard *Parallax Red*."

He walked a few more yards down the passage and stopped before a hatch on the right-hand wall. It opened, and he stood by expectantly ushering the three outlanders and the trolls through with waves of his cane. After the last troll had entered, Sindri stepped in and the iris sealed behind him.

They found themselves in a room like a small theater, with two dozen chairs grouped in a double circle around an elevated stage. An array of what appeared to be light fixtures hung above it.

"Take seats anywhere," Sindri instructed.

"Why?" demanded Grant.

"Entertainment and education, a blend that cannot be beat."

Reluctantly they sat down in the chairs, the trolls seating themselves behind them. Sindri climbed to the stage, standing in the center of it. They saw he held a small remote-control box in his left hand, and his thumb pressed one of its buttons. He was instantly cast in a halo of light from one of the overhead fixtures.

Clasping his hands atop the silver knob of his cane, he cleared his throat and stentoriously announced,

"What you are about to see is a presentation made midway in the year 2000, for the oversight funding committee of Overprojects Excalibur and Majestic. Crafted by state-of-the art holographic artists, its sole aim was to impress visiting dignitaries so they would increase the operational budget of the Cydonia Compound. I'm not sure if they ever saw it.

"Certainly, I know it by heart. After you've sat through it, hopefully you will know *my* heart and find it within yours not to judge my actions too harshly."

He bowed his head humbly for a moment. Kane wondered if he was waiting for a round of applause.

As Sindri left the stage, shimmering veils of multicolored light sprang up, expanding to encompass its entire length and breadth. The light shifted in color and shape. One moment the stage was empty, and in the next a man stepped forward. He was completely three-dimensional, and his sudden appearance surprised and confused Kane for a moment. His attention seemed narrowed to a point in the theater slightly to the left and behind Brigid.

The man was fairly young and prosperous, judging by the slight fleshiness around his chin. His dark hair was neatly combed, and his features bore an Asian cast. He wore a tailored one-piece bodysuit of a deep red. The words Cydonia One were worked in yellow thread upon the breast. He looked slightly familiar to Kane.

"I am Dr. Kuo Liang, the overseer of Project Sigma and now serving as a special scientific liaison between Overprojects Majestic and Excalibur."

At the introduction, Kane recognized him. In the disastrous mission to the past, he and Brigid had briefly seen Kuo Liang in Lakesh's company on New Year's

Eve, 2000. But that had been only a version of this man, in an alternate temporal plane.

"I bid all of you the warmest of welcomes to Mars," Kuo Liang continued. "At this time of year, I imagine you don't find it all that different from Washington."

He paused, smiling, waiting for an anticipated wave of appreciative laughter to die down.

"Oh, fucking fireblast," Grant half groaned, scuffling his feet on the floor.

Sindri sat down beside him, whispering fiercely, "Hush! No talking while the feature is in progress. You'll disturb the other patrons."

The hologram of Kuo Liang nodded to the audience politely. "Yes, I am aware that some of you find our undertaking here frightfully costly, especially after the Soviets withdrew their support. I also know how difficult adjusting the budgets to keep this project hidden from congressional bean counters can be. However, the progress we have made here in the last decade makes the expenditure of every dime more than worth it. But enough of words. Pictures speak far louder. Ladies and gentlemen...I give you...*Mars!*"

Kuo Liang vanished instantly, swallowed up in a blaze of light and a brassy musical fanfare, full of horns and heavy kettle drums. Sindri waved his cane in time to the music, as if he were conducting an orchestra.

The three-dimensional image of a rust red planet appeared on the stage, swelling to fill it, seeming to speed toward them. Even though they were sitting down, they had the impression of soaring over a vista of huge craters, mountain ranges, channels cutting through arid ground and dead sea bottoms.

A deep male voice, in rich mahogany tones, declaimed, "Mars, named after the Roman god of war, the fourth planet in orbit from the sun, smaller than Earth, only 4,212 miles in diameter. The oxides trapped in surface mineral deposits give the planet its red tint in the evening sky. Of all the planets in the solar system, Mars is unique—it alone can change its axial direction in space by as much as twenty-four degrees.''

The voice droned on, providing a history of the fascination held by all Earth cultures toward Mars. The three-dimensional image on the stage continued to display a leisurely flyover of monotonous terrain.

"I hope this picks up," said Kane, stifling a yawn.

It didn't. After the novelty of the holovision passed, the presentation became almost intolerably tedious. Sindri sensed their impatience and growing boredom.

"Keep watching," he said. "There's a little secret hidden in this documentary, and it's worth a bit of your time.''

"Don't you have a fast-forward button on your remote?" Grant asked.

"Of course," replied Sindri, sounding a little peeved. "I'd prefer if you watched it through.''

Exterior views of *Parallax Red* appeared with the narrator providing an excruciatingly detailed account of its construction and purpose. The scene shifted to the interior of a manufacturing facility aboard the station, full of forges and presses. People wearing pressure suits swabbed down thick slabs of a translucent substance.

"Utilizing zero gravity," the voice intoned, "the engineers aboard the *Parallax Red* station developed a method of plasticizing metals that could revolutionize every Earth industry that today depends on either material. Indeed, armaglass is already in limited usage.''

The scene suddenly switched to a desolate, wind-swept landscape, with clouds of reddish dust billowing about. Figures in space suits operated heavy machinery, digging and excavating equipment.

"Employing the discoveries made upon *Parallax Red*," said the narrator, "the establishment of Cydonia Compound One began in late 1990. The organic environment of Mars, in all its complexity, presented the most difficult challenges for the brave colonists."

On stage, single-storied, metal-ribbed domes on concrete-slab bases began appearing across the terrain. An interminable number of exterior-construction sequences dissolved into an equally interminable number of interior-construction sequences. Though he felt himself nodding off, it occurred to Kane that no mention of the so-called Monuments of Mars had been made.

The narrator declared, "The colonists had to adapt and they did so with great ingenuity."

The scene changed to a view of a field of rich soil, with leafy vegetation sprouting out of it. The perspective widened, showing that the field was enclosed within a pressure dome.

"Another development made on *Parallax Red* benefited the Cydonia Compound—a method of synthesizing from ordinary soil any kind of vegetable growth. Human ingenuity, adapted to a world not native to humans. However, adapting an alien world to fit human physiologies is only one of the options open to us."

Sindri sat up straight in his chair.

"It might be more convenient to adapt the descendants of our colonists to the alien world. It is certainly more desirable, more cost-effective than terra-forming. If humans are to live on Mars, they must adapt to a low-gravity, oxygen-poor environment. They must stay warm in low temperatures and draw oxygen from the thin atmosphere."

The image jumped to a setting inside of a sterile laboratory. People in white smocks, surgical masks and caps bustled purposefully around pieces of gleaming equipment and racks of test tubes.

"If there are to be humans spending their entire lives in space or on the surface of Mars," the deep voice stated, "we must improve the body's ability to adapt itself and redesign it to suit the new conditions. To this end, Overproject Excalibur's subdivisions have proved exceptionally helpful."

A side view of an upright human skeleton appeared on the stage.

"The fact that human beings stand erect against Earth's gravity poses certain problems that have been solved by skeletal and body-mass modifications."

The image of the skeleton seemed to shrink in size, acquiring a hunched-over posture. At the same time, the length of the arms increased and the foot bones rearranged themselves, the big toe sliding down toward the heel and extending outward, transforming into a double-jointed thumb.

"In a lighter-gravity environment," said the narrator, "strain would no longer be put on the spine by maintaining an erect posture, and our heavy supportive legs would become redundant. Modifying the legs into a second pair of arms would be particularly useful because one of the problems in working in a near weightless environment is anchorage.

"Obviously such an undertaking is difficult, but in the fullness of time, it will be attempted and—"

Sindri pressed a button on the remote-control unit with a stabbing motion. The image on the stage froze, and the monotonous lecture stopped. In an intense tone, he said, "You understand now."

"Understand what?" Brigid demanded. "That you and your people were genetically engineered? We pretty much figured out that much."

"But the banal perfidy of it all!" Sindri's voice hit a high note of fury. He pointed to the stage. "The way that presentation is worded, an uninitiated dolt would think the type of bioengineering discussed was far in the future, just a whim to look into when nothing more urgent was pressing. In truth, when the documentary was made, the first generation of transadapts had been born over five years before."

Grant sighed. "Your point being?"

"My point, Mr. Grant, is that generations of human beings had their birthrights denied, born into government-sanctioned, -funded and -institutionalized slavery. Mr. Kane, remember what I said to you about the Cydonia Compound's long tradition of abduction? The raw genetic material used to create the first generation of transadapts was provided by people taken forcibly, against their will, from Earth. Victims, not volunteers! Can't you grasp the monstrous injustice of it all?"

"Hell, yes," snapped Kane. "Of course we can. Things haven't changed all that much on Earth."

Sindri's eyebrows quirked. "Yes, so I learned."

Kane noticed how Brigid's hands suddenly clenched into fists.

"But what might be *very* different," Sindri went on, "is that the transadapts were the majority in this microcosmic society. They built most of the compound, mined the ores, tilled the fields, maintained the machines. They were the serfs and vassals to a tiny number of royal humans—their royalty bestowed upon them simply by dint of the fact that their antecedents weren't abducted to provide the templates for the transadapt program.

"Eventually, over a period of decades, the transadapts outnumbered them three to one. By the end of 180 years, their population continued to grow, while that of the humans dwindled."

"So far," commented Grant dryly, "this has a familiar ring."

Sindri ignored him. "The transadapts were bred to be the Cydonia Compound's manual labor, its dray animals, its mules, living their lives doing nothing more than slouching through the red dust of Mars. They did not question their place in the scheme of things. They obeyed and did what was expected of them.

"But the humans here feared their growing numbers. They already had instituted a form of apartheid, segregating the transadapts into their own habitats. But due to several factors, only a couple of them environmental, the men had become sterile, the women barren. They couldn't stand the thought of perishing while the sub-human transadapts inherited this planet.

"So, using a medical treatment disguised as necessary vaccinations, they made the transadapts as barren as themselves. It was nothing less than the perpetration of slow-motion genocide. Inasmuch as the transadapts were engineered to have far shorter life spans than human beings—very few live past thirty years of age—it was conceivable that they could all be dead within a single generation."

"They," Brigid argued testily. "You've called the transadapts 'my people,' yet you refer to them as *they.* Which is it?"

The corners of Sindri's mobile mouth turned down.

"I was supposed to be a transadapt. But I was born a mutation, with far more Earth-human characteristics. It happens occasionally."

Brigid inspected Sindri silently, glanced over at the trolls sitting behind them, then back to Sindri. "No mere accident of birth can account for the differences between you and them."

Sindri smiled bleakly. "You're quite correct, Miss Brigid. My father was a human who took a transadapt woman as a lover. Truly a horrific case of miscegenation, at least as far as my father's peers were concerned. You can imagine the reactions when I was born."

"What happened to your mother?" Kane asked.

"She died shortly after giving birth to me. I never knew her."

"And your father?"

"He was shunned, ostracized, exiled from the Cydonia Compound. In a twist of irony that cheap fiction loves so much, only the fact of his exile saved him from death when the revolt occurred."

No one spoke. Sindri looked at them expectantly.

"Do tell us all about it, won't you?" Grant requested with unmistakable sarcasm.

Sindri nodded gravely. "In due time. But first, a bit about myself. I obviously could not live in the transadapts' habitats, so I was tolerated among the humans. I made myself indispensable to them with my mechanical acumen and affinity for electronics. I was very clever with my hands.

"A little over a year ago, I was allowed into the computer database to correct a minor problem. I corrected it, but I stumbled across things of far greater magnitude that had very little do with machines or electronics.''

"And they were?'' asked Kane.

Sindri stared directly into his eyes. "The Tuatha De Danaan and a group with whom you have had prior dealings…the Archon Directorate.''

magnitude that had very little to do with thinness of cigars."

And they nearly died," Kane

Sindri stared at them both in silence. The Trolls, the Danaan and —— Nothing seemed to leave that little theater in the Violet Directorate.

Chapter 23

Kane said grimly, "I don't recall mentioning the Archon Directorate."

"You may not recall it," Sindri replied diffidently, "but you did. All three of you, in fact. Different perspectives on similar experiences."

A fleeting memory of Sindri's words came back to him: "I will walk in all your minds, looking at your memories, strolling here and there among the ruins of your broken dreams. Make no mistake about it—I will find what I need."

Kane lunged to his feet in an angry rush. The trolls rose just as quickly, but Sindri's reaction was to wag his walking stick like a chiding finger.

"An outbreak of violence will accomplish nothing, Mr. Kane. It will not bring our business to a satisfactory conclusion, nor will it get you back home."

Kane scowled around the theater. "Maybe not. But I'm tempted to give it a try just to see what will happen."

Brigid tugged at his sleeve. "He's right, Kane. We've gone this far, let's hear the rest."

Sindri nodded to her gallantly. "Ever the orderly mind."

Kane dropped back heavily in his seat. "What do the Danaan and the Archons have to do with your revolt?"

"In a direct, one-on-one way, almost nothing. But the war they fought here, long ago, still echoes. Evidently the war was more of a skirmish, the continuance of hostilities that began aeons before between the Danaan and the Archons' root race. What did you call them again?"

"The Annunaki," interjected Grant tonelessly.

Sindri nodded. "Just so. They weren't given a name in the data I found within the computer. According to it, a Danaan colony from Earth had settled here, observing the terms of truce wherein both races agreed to leave the planet."

Kane recalled what Brigid had learned in Ireland of the hostilities between the reptilian Annunaki and the humanoid Tuatha De Danaan, which had broken out millennia before. Mankind became embroiled in the conflict, and the conflagration extended even to the outer planets of the solar system, immortalized and much disguised as a war in heaven.

Finally, when it appeared that Earth was threatened with devastation, the war abated under terms. The Danaan and the Annunaki agreed to end it for the sake of all their intertwined futures.

A pact was struck, whereby the two races intermingled to create a new one, to serve as a bridge. Extrapolating from information imparted to her, Brigid had speculated that the Archons might be the spawn of Danaan, Annunaki and even human genes.

The reign of both races came to an end, and they left Earth, yet legends of their long-ago war were retold by various religions, and they themselves were diminished in stature by fanciful myths.

Still, all of it was oral history, legend as reinterpreted through scientific conjecture with only a handful of artifacts as supportive evidence. Kane didn't necessarily believe it.

"The Danaan," continued Sindri, "came here to Mars. When they were attacked, their cities destroyed, they fled again. Where to is anybody's guess. Nor did this war and exodus happen all that long ago."

"If there really was a war between the Annunaki and the Danaan," put in Brigid, "it happened so long ago that even the people who claim descent from them have only the vaguest notion of a date. If the Danaan were driven from Mars, by the Archons and not the Annunaki, you're probably talking in terms of tens of thousands of years."

"No," Sindri responded smoothly. "More like hundreds, as in the midnineteenth century. Beginning in the 1860s and continuing to the 1870s, astronomers on Earth reported monstrous explosions occurring on Mars—visible even with the primitive telescopes of the day. The phenomenon ended rather abruptly in 1872. I believe the astronomers were witnessing aerial bombardments and missile attacks."

"What's this got to do with your revolt?" asked Grant darkly.

"I'm getting to that. I learned that only by following the dictates of the Archon Directive—as it was called in the twentieth century—was man able to establish more than a tenuous toehold here on Mars. They wanted us to plant a colony here."

"Why?" Brigid sounded skeptical. "From what we know of them, the Archons mastered not only hyperdimensional travel, but physical space travel, too. Mars and all the planets in the solar system shouldn't be any more difficult for them to visit than Earth."

Sindri smiled a secret, mocking smile. "True, as far

it goes. But unlike Earth, the Danaan turned Mars into a—what was your quaint term?—hellzone, deadly to the Archons.''

Interest instantly replaced hostile impatience, and three pairs of eyes locked intently on Sindri's face. The little man chuckled appreciatively.

"I thought that might revive your flagging interest. As all of you are aware by now—particularly you, Mr. Kane—the very essence of Danaan science stemmed from music, the controlled manipulation of sound waves, perhaps the 'music of the spheres' as referred to in legend.

"The Danaan, before they left Mars and perhaps even the realm of three dimensions, left a parting gift for the Archons.''

"Which is?"

"A song,'' stated Sindri with a smug simplicity. "A song that plays eternally, borne by the winds, serenading and blanketing this entire planet. The melody is too subtle for our human ears, yet not only can the Archons hear it, but it is deadly to them. It prevents them from ever putting a foot on Martian soil. And that is the real reason for the Cydonia colony...to locate the source of the song and stop it.''

He looked levelly at Kane. "You saw the pyramid?''
"Yes.''

"It is more than a monument. It is a gigantic broadcasting tower, transmitting the song of the Danaan to every nook and cranny of the planet, forming an invisible sonic wall which forever bars Archon entry.

"That is why they supported and abetted a Terran colony here, and aided the bioengineering process. We would, by proxy, conquer Mars for them, reclaim it from the Danaan. A precious ruby in the crown of the cosmos.''

Brigid furrowed her brow. "If the song is deadly to Archons, but not to humans—"

"I didn't say that," Sindri broke in sharply. "True enough, the sonic frequencies were keyed to set up disharmonious resonances in the Archon metabolism. But that was before.''

"Before what?" asked Kane.

"Before arrogant human interference altered the modulations and turned the song into a doomsday dirge for the planet. Remember what I said regarding the factors which caused sterility in the men and women of the colony? The change in the harmonics was one such factor, the primary one."

Sindri sighed, running a hand over his face. "When I learned all of that, a year or so ago, I knew swift and decisive action had to be taken to save the colony, humans and transadapts alike. Extinction for both groups was less than a generation down the road. I double-checked all my data, correlated it, made sure there was no error. Day upon night, pausing for little sleep and less food, I worked on the findings, to make them utterly convincing to the so-called Committee of One Hundred. But I also knew I could not go to them with the tragic news without bringing a solution. In the database, I learned of *Parallax Red,* and of the gateway unit which linked the colony with it. What I didn't know until later, was that I was not meant to know of either one.''

The man's lips twitched, as if he had a nervous tic. "Do you know what the committee did? First they laughed at me. Then they claimed I had lost my mind. In brief, they could not and would not believe me.

When I mentioned the mat-trans unit and the space station, their decision was for me to join my father in exile. Since I saw no way to make them understand, I was determined to make them relinquish their decision-making powers.

"I reached out to the transadapts, persuaded them that we must leave and find a safe new home. They supported me. Since they were the majority of the colony's population, I had hoped the humans would bow to their will."

He shook his head sadly. "They preferred death to ceding to the wishes of creatures they considered inferior. That made a revolution not only necessary, but inevitable. The true tragedy of it all was that no neutrals were permitted in the conflict. Transadapts who wished no part of the revolt were slaughtered by humans as potential foes. The handful of humans who were sympathetic to my cause were killed by enraged transadapts.

"Once the first blood was spilled, there was no turning back. Blood called for blood, vengeance followed vengeance. It lasted a month. At the end of it, all the humans in the Cydonia Compound and three-quarters of the transadapts were dead."

Sindri exhaled a weary breath. "Mars, the god of war indeed."

Grant stated, "Then you went to the gateway and made the jump to *Parallax Red?*"

He shook his head. "If only it were that simple. First I had to find it. When I did, the mat-trans controls defied all of my early attempts to activate them. The process of trial and error lasted for months."

"The jump chamber was hidden?" Kane asked carelessly. "Where?"

"It was in—" Sindri broke off suddenly, favoring Kane with a slit-eyed stare. "Very clever, sir, my congratulations. You almost had me telling you its location. Never fear, if all goes according to plan, I'll take you to it soon enough."

"Let's get to your plan," said Grant impatiently, "unless there's another vid you want us to sit through."

Sindri stood up. "Once again, it's something easier shown than told. Come with me."

Trailed by the trolls, they followed him out of the theater. He commented, "My apologies for running you around so much, but it's for the best. I imagine all of you will be feeling a little limp by the end of the day."

They passed the open observation port that looked out onto the compound. Kane glanced at the Pathfinder and asked, "If the American government knew that Mars had been inhabited only a century before, why did they waste time with dropping things like that here?"

Sindri laughed. "Cover stories, Mr. Kane, nice and neat. In the late '90s, NASA announced the discovery of microbial life in a meteorite that had come from Mars several billion years before, even though they knew more than a few single-celled organisms existed here. So, they broke it to the public gently, watering it down.

"The public could easily accept amoebas might have lived on Mars three billion years ago. The concept that an advanced race, superior to humanity, had inhabited it for thousands of years would end the reign of Earth as the center of universal intelligence. And horrors of horrors, the public might decide that nationalism and partisan politics didn't fit their needs anymore…not if they realized they were citizens of an entire galaxy instead of a subsection on a tiny planet in a backwater solar system.''

The hatch Sindri led them to was not in the wall, but in the floor. When its segments irised open, they saw a metal-runged ladder extending into a barely lit gloom. Without beckoning to them, Sindri swung his body into the opening and climbed down. Grant, Kane and Brigid looked at the hole distrustfully, then to the four trolls standing around them like swart, short sentinels.

"Ah, hell," Grant growled in disgust, and climbed down into the aperture.

The descent was short, less than twelve feet, and they found themselves standing on a low-ceilinged platform. A dim yellow bulb cast its feeble rays upon a dark, bullet-shaped vehicle resting upon a single raised rail. It was about eight feet long, six in overall diameter. The track stretched out of sight down a long round chute.

Sindri touched it, and a man-size section of the hull slid aside, revealing a hollow interior. The door panel lowered to form a short ramp. He walked across it. "I'll take you to the scene and the perpetrator of the human arrogance that brought all this heartbreak about. He's had no visitors for a long time."

Kane peered into the opening of the bullet car. There was nothing inside but four padded seats. Sindri was already strapping himself into one.

"Doesn't appear there's enough room for all of us and your escort," Kane said. "Who stays behind?"

"Oh, get the hell in," Sindri snapped. "The vehicle is automated, so there's nothing you can do once we're under way. We'll arrive at our destination regardless of whether you behave yourselves. However, we will be met there, so it's in your best interests not to attempt anything unpleasant during the journey.''

They climbed in, Kane sitting down beside Sindri. As soon as Brigid cleared the entranceway, the panel slid silently shut behind. Within a moment of buckling their seat belts, they felt a slight shock that pressed them against the padded chair backs.

''Are we moving?'' asked Grant.

As if on cue, a curving section of the forewall became transparent. They saw the walls of the chute racing past and around them at a rate of speed none of them could estimate, but that was obviously quite high. Overhead light fixtures flicked by so fast that they combined with the intervals of darkness between them to acquire a strobing pattern.

''What's our destination?'' Unconsciously Kane had raised his voice a trifle, then realized it was unnecessary. There was no sound of motors or rush of wind to speak over.

Sindri didn't answer for a moment. In that brief beat of time, the bullet car burst out of the tunnel into the full, pink-hued daylight of Mars. The track stretched out far ahead in a straight line, leading to the base of the colossal pyramid.

Sindri nodded toward it. ''There.''

Even though Kane had seen it earlier, he couldn't help but gape a second time, just like Brigid and Grant.

''The so-called D and M Pyramid,'' Sindri said. ''Named after DiPetro and Molenar, a pair of computer photographic analysts in the twentieth century. It is one mile high by 1.6 miles broad. Unlike the classic Egyptian design, this one is a pentahedron. Five sided.''

As the bullet car sped along the rail, Kane saw crumbling ruins around the foot of the immense pyramid. The structures were huge, but dwarfed by the monument. Walls had fallen in, and the stone blocks were scoured smooth by windblown sand.

Kane leaned his head back, studying the long spire affixed to the pyramid's apex. Like an unimaginably huge needle, it seemed to pierce the wispy clouds.

The rail curved lazily to the left, toward a corner of the pyramid. A great cavity occupied a large portion of the base. High heaps of debris were piled on either side of it. The track disappeared into the hole.

Sindri declared, "No, the colonists did not breach the walls. The damage showed up on the Viking photos."

"What caused it?" Brigid asked.

"More than likely, explosive penetration, probably an Archon missile."

The bullet car plunged noiselessly into the cavity. Lights shone intermittently overhead, small splotches of illumination that did little to alleviate the deep shadows.

The track tilted upward at a gradual incline until it reached a ninety-degree angle. The speed of the vehicle did not slacken. Kane felt the same kind of lifting sensation in his belly as when he rode inside a fast-ascending Deathbird.

After a minute, the track's angle decreased in sharpness until the car rode straight and smooth again. Through the foreport, they saw walls constructed of individual stone blocks three times the size of the vehicle that carried them. The bullet car's speed dropped rapidly until it slid to a halt beside a broad platform.

"This part of the pyramid has been adjusted to accommodate humans," said Sindri. "Complete with synthetic-gravity generators and oxygen-circulation pumps. You might find it a bit nippy due to the extreme altitude, but the thermal controls inside your suits should be able to compensate.''

The bullet car darkened inside as the port opaqued. The door panel moved down and extended to the edge of the platform. Sindri disembarked first, standing with three male trolls who'd been waiting for his arrival and watching the others climb out. With a clanking of gears, the section of rail supporting the car rotated on a hidden pivot, turning it around 180 degrees so it faced the way they had come.

After they all stood assembled on the platform, Sindri turned smartly on his heel and marched off. ''We are on the sixth and uppermost level of the pyramid.''

His voice didn't echo. Rather, the grim, gray-red walls seemed to absorb the sound, softening it without muting it. ''All the levels are huge,'' he continued, ''each one with its own distinct architecture. It appears that different strata of Danaan society occupied the levels, perhaps with their own customs and dialects. If so, they couldn't have been any more dogmatic about the rigid observance of social rites and customs than the humans who came after them.''

The three outlanders followed Sindri and the trolls down a wide corridor lit by wall-bracketed light tubes. They passed through a series of triangular archways. Cut into the stone above each one was a plate-sized spiral glyph, the same kind of cup-and-circle design they had seen in Ireland.

The floor slanted slightly upward, and the stone blocks were worn smooth as if by the pressure of many feet. The arches opened occasionally to the left and right, but Sindri kept to the main corridor.

They became aware of a low hum of sound ahead of them, almost like the bass register of a piano that continued to vibrate long after a key had been struck. Presently a brighter light glimmered in the murk just beyond a tall arch. Without hesitation, Sindri passed beneath it.

They entered into a vaulted chamber of huge proportions, so vast that its nether end was lost in the shadows. Six circular tiers descended to the center of the chamber, surrounding a columnlike dais raised six feet from the floor. From it, a metal shaft rose straight up to the shadow-shrouded ceiling.

Rising from the base of the dais, extending at ever increasing angles into the high shadows, was a taut webwork of silver filaments, hundreds, perhaps thousands of them. They were all connected to the series of circular tiers. A dim glow came down from the pointed roof, glittering from the strings.

Kane had the impression of vast energies being drawn down from the metal spire and disseminated through each one of the silvery threads.

Sindri rapped the tip of his cane sharply on the floor. "Hey, Pop! Where are you? You've got visitors."

A robed figure shuffled out of the murk, leaning heavily on a walking stick. The silver knob and ferrule glinted dimly. With a slight start, Kane recognized it as a mate, albeit a longer one, to Sindri's walking stick.

The man who stiffly approached them was stooped and gaunt, his face but a pale blur in the shadow of his cowl. "Who are you?" he demanded, his voice brittle and hollow. "What are you doing here?"

"Focus, Pop, focus," Sindri retorted patronizingly. "It's me. Your boy."

The man halted abruptly. Incisively, in a tone that

brooked no debate, he declared, "Bullshit. I have no son."

Tightly Sindri said, "I told you to focus, old man."

A narrow, trembling hand flung back the cowl. Kane, Grant and Brigid were all slightly startled by the man's appearance. Even by Lakesh's standards, he was old. His face was a network of deep wrinkles, his toothless mouth a straight, slightly quivering line. An untidy mop of white hair that resembled a snarl of thread topped his liver-spotted skull. Only his bright blue eyes showed any sign of vitality.

"This is the esteemed Dr. Micah Harwin," said Sindri with a cryptic smile. "Biologist, psychologist and a self-styled musician. Pop, these are friends of mine, recently arrived from Earth by way of *Parallax Red*."

Harwin's unblinking gaze darted across their faces, his eyes blazing with a cobalt flame. "Earth?" he said scornfully. "Bullshit. A dead world, nuked to a cinder."

In a tone of aggrieved patience, as if he were talking about a not very bright child, Sindri said, "Please forgive Pop's manners. He's fairly inflexible about some matters—he's particularly so about his paternal relationship to me. He denies he sired me, but the DNA tests proved otherwise, didn't they...Pop?"

Harwin ignored the harangue. He shuffled a few feet closer, the weight of his stare almost palpable. "Are you really from Earth?"

"Where else could they be from?" Sindri demanded, no longer sounding patient, but definitely aggrieved. "You fucking knew everybody in the compound. Do these three look familiar?"

Tears brimmed suddenly in Harwin's eyes. Haltingly he said, "I was taught from infancy that my great-

great-grandparents came from Earth. They survived its destruction, but they could never return because there was nothing to return to. It broke their hearts."

In a remarkably gentle tone, Grant said, "Earth's still there. Not exactly the same one your folks came from, but it's still there."

Harwin doddered forward, reaching out with palsied fingers to lightly touch the side of Grant's face, as if he were a work of art. His whispery voice sounded like wind-stirred ashes. "You've come to take me back? Please tell me you've come to take me back."

Sindri placed the end of his walking stick against Harwin's chest and pushed him back half a pace. "You're embarrassing me in front of my friends, Pop. Do what I said—focus. Show them you're a demented old philanderer only part of the time."

Two pairs of blue eyes locked on each other. Tension seemed to crackle around Sindri and Harwin in an almost physical aura of commingled anger, resentment and hatred. But there was a deeper emotional connection between the two of them, a mutually shared grief that neither could acknowledge.

Kane couldn't help but be reminded of Baron Sharpe and Crawler—or himself and Salvo.

Micah Harwin drew himself up in what passed as a posture of indignation. To Sindri, he said, "You keep coming back here. I told you not to, and I meant it. This is my place."

Sindri smiled thinly. "As I keep telling *you*, it's *my* place. You live here at my sufferance."

Harwin returned Sindri's smile, but there was a hint of amused contempt in it. "That, Little Bubba, is nothing more than your insufferable arrogance."

Kane tried to repress a chuckle, but it came out as a laugh. ''Little Bubba? That's your name?''

Harwin smirked. ''His childhood nickname, bestowed upon him when he was still dimpled and cute. His full name is William Paulo, but 'Little Bubba' fitted him best.''

Sindri stood motionless, but flickers of raw, soul-deep fury and shame passed through his eyes. ''Enough, old man. You know why I've come. Stop the song, goddamn you. Stop the song.''

Chapter 24

Harwin's smile didn't alter, but at a slow, dignified pace, he turned around, facing the dais and the network of strings. "You know I've tried to stop it. I've tried every day for a year. What I did, I cannot undo."

Sindri snorted out a scornful laugh. "And you dare to speak to me of arrogance."

To the others, he announced coldly, "As I told you, my father was exiled from the compound. Having few choices of where to go, he came here, hoping to solve the mysteries of the pyramid, which had eluded generations of colonists."

Without turning his head, Harwin declared, "I came far closer to accomplishing that than any before me."

"That I cannot deny," Sindri retorted. "He reasoned out that a science was at work here, the mastery of the vast and subtle forces of nature. He knew that here on Mars, for uncounted centuries, had been those who manipulated them. He had to find out if even a scrap of their knowledge remained.

"In doing so, Pop experimented with the frequencies of the transmitter. And in experimenting, the song of the Danaan became a death ditty for all of us, not just the Archons."

Kane's eyes traveled up and down the mass of stretched-out strings, to the tiny lights sparkling along them. The filaments vibrated gently, continuously, producing the bass note that he sensed rather than heard.

"Pop was here when the revolt broke out in the compound," Sindri went on. "Safe from the blood and death he had caused. I've allowed him to live only on the off chance he can stop the song."

Micah Harwin laughed, a gargling cackle. "I've told you and told you that I cannot. I've told you to go ahead and kill me. But you never do. You keep coming back here to torment me with demands that I do the impossible. I've challenged you, the clever Little Bubba, to stop it. But you haven't even the courage to try."

Sindri pointed the end of his cane at Harwin's back, shouting angrily, "It's *your* responsibility to rectify your error!"

Harwin laughed again, shaking his head in pity. "As I've asked you, ad nauseam, why do you assume I made an error?"

"What do you mean?" Grant demanded loudly. "You *deliberately* caused infertility in the colonists with your tinkering?"

"He's lying," Sindri barked. "It's the cowardly way of avoiding blame, like some kid who screwed up while trying to be smart and saying 'I meant to do that.'"

"How do you know for sure he didn't mean to do it?" Brigid asked.

"Because he's not intelligent enough to control Danaan technology for his own purposes."

Harwin said, "So you keep saying, Little Bubba. Say it often enough, and maybe you'll finally be able to convince yourself. You can't tolerate the notion that someone—*anyone*—may know more than you, may have an agenda that you can't pick apart. You're a textbook example of overcompensating for an inferiority complex that you disguise with overweening pride and ego."

"Spare me the sandbox psychoanalysis, old man," Sindri snapped. "Stop the song."

"You stop it, you little freak bastard."

Sindri glared at the man's robed back, lips writhing over his teeth in a silent snarl. His body trembled. Then, with an inarticulate roar, he lunged forward, cane raised like a bludgeon.

For a helpless second, the outlanders thought he intended to club Micah Harwin to death. Instead, Sindri roughly shouldered the old man aside, bowling him off his feet. He fell to the floor with a bleat of surprise.

Sindri rushed along the stone walkway circling the room and down a narrow passage to the dais. He scrambled up a short flight of steps and began hammering the metal shaft with the knob of his walking stick, holding it in a two-fisted grip like a sledge.

A deep, gonglike chime rang, and the webwork of filaments shivered furiously. Another note, discordant with the first, echoed throughout the huge room. Before it died into silence, another sounded and another, so that the walls filled with vibrating chimes, the dim light glittering from the strings.

Kane was aware that his body resonated to the conglomeration of notes flooding the room. He shook with a jarring dissonance. He felt it as little prickles of pain that would have been torture had they lasted longer. Out of the corner of his eye, he saw Brigid and Grant jerk in reaction to the shock wave of sounds. Kane caught a glimpse of the three trolls twisting in acute pain. One of them opened his mouth to voice a howl no one could hear, clapping his hands over his ears. A trickle of blood crawled from his right nostril.

Sindri shrieked as he beat his cane against the shaft, his face frozen in a mask of fury and frustration. They couldn't hear a word, but they saw spittle flying from his lips. Micah Harwin hiked himself up on his elbows and watched the little man impotently flailing and pounding away. He threw back his white-haired head and laughed uproariously.

At length, Sindri's wild blows became weaker. Finally he stopped altogether and sagged panting against the shaft, his arms at his sides.

The music in the tiered room reached a crescendo and hung there on a long chord. It didn't end, but simply hummed down in pitch, achieving the same bass register note all of them had heard upon entering.

Sindri dragged a sleeve across his sweat-beaded brow. Harwin continued to laugh from his place on the floor, an ugly vocalization with no mirth in it at all.

"Goddamn you, old man," Sindri said between harsh breaths. "Goddamn the Committee of One Hundred. Goddamn the Danaan."

Grant helped Harwin climb stiffly to his feet. The old man muttered a word of thanks then called, "Come away from there, Little Bubba. Tantrums won't change the way things are."

Sindri pushed himself away from the shaft, fingers caressing its gleaming surface. "There's a conductive force inside this metal," he said in a strained voice. "There's got to be a way to tap into the right combination of notes."

"Beating on it like a workman isn't it," said Harwin. "Face facts. It's all over, Little Bubba. Finished. Your future has left the building. Even if you go to

Parallax Red and then to Earth, you and your followers will have what, ten years, perhaps fifteen on the outside, of life?"

The old man drew his robe about him. "Accept your fate with dignity. If you're truly my son, you will do so."

Sindri whirled away from the shaft, stamping noisily down the steps at the side of the dais. "I don't surrender as easily as you, Pop. If you are truly my father, neither would you."

He returned to where they stood, declaring, "Show-and-tell time is over. By now, you should have some understanding of the tragedy I'm trying to avert. Can any of you offer suggestions?"

He spoke in such a way as if he expected no response. To Kane and Grant's surprise, Brigid said mildly, "If the countermeasures you've already undertaken don't bear fruit, you've no choice but to go quietly into the night of extinction."

Sindri peered up at her, head cocked at a quizzical angle. "Indeed, Miss Brigid. What are those countermeasures I've already undertaken?"

Grant and Kane knew Brigid was fast, but even they were taken aback by how swiftly she shot out her left arm. Her fist impacted with a meaty smack on the point of Sindri's chin, sending him reeling backward. His walking stick clattered to the floor, tangling in his feet and causing him to fall unceremoniously on his back.

The three trolls voiced hooting cries of anger and shock, and they pelted forward, their eyes fastened on Brigid.

Two of them just managed to see Kane's right fist and Grant's left boot driving at them. Arms flailing, spurting blood from a nose and a lip, the pair slammed into each other.

The third troll flew over his companions in a steel-springed bound, somersaulting between Grant and Kane and landing feetfirst against the small of Brigid's back. Flinging out her arms, she staggered forward. She would have fallen atop Sindri had he not rolled frantically to one side. As she dropped to her hands and knees, the troll alighted just behind her, small fists raised over the exposed nape of her neck.

Kane went for him, but Sindri bellowed, "Enough!"

The troll immediately dropped his hands to his sides and stepped quickly over to Sindri. Kane kept coming, stopping only when Sindri snatched up his cane and held it before him like a sword. "Enough, I said!"

Turning toward Brigid, he put a hand on her arm and helped her up. Wincing, she fingered her back.

"Why did you strike me, Miss Brigid?" His voice was filled with anger, but full of reproach, too.

She glared at him. "You learned I have an eidetic memory. Did you think I forgot what I saw, or wrote it off as a dream?"

Sindri swallowed hard. Perplexed, Kane asked, "What did you see, Baptiste?"

In a voice quaking with barely controlled fury and disgust, Brigid answered, "That filthy gnome did more than interrogate us while we were unconscious. He experimented on us, violated us. I woke up just long enough to see what he was doing."

"I have the right," Sindri stated firmly. "Any life-form has the right to survive—by any means necessary."

"What are you talking about?" demanded Grant.

Brigid ran unsteady fingers through her hair. "Sterility and infertility. There's absolutely no point to leaving Mars if those conditions can't be reversed."

Without looking at him, Brigid stated, "Kane, I saw you hooked up to a machine. It was milking you of sperm. Grant probably got the same treatment."

Kane instantly became aware of his sore genitals again.

"And with me," Brigid continued in a rush, "Sindri took a personal hand. He inserted something into me. All done against our wills, just like the ancestors of the transadapts he pretends to weep for."

No one moved or spoke for a long moment. The only sound was the deep bass hum. The trolls Kane and Grant had incapacitated stirred, climbing slowly erect. One of them groaned and broke the frozen tableau.

Grant took a threatening step toward Sindri, face an expressionless ebony mask, but his dark eyes held a homicidal glitter.

"Don't be foolish," Sindri said. "Killing me will avail you nothing. You don't know the location of the mat trans, so you can't return to *Parallax Red*."

"We'll find it," grated Grant. "If we have to raze the compound to the ground, we'll find it."

"Not with all my people howling for your blood. You're unarmed, trapped on a hostile world. Like the old man there, you live only at my sufferance."

Kane swung on Harwin. "Do you know where the gateway unit is?"

Harwin's lips parted, but Sindri shouted, "Shut up!"

Shaking his head remorsefully, Harwin said, "He's right. I'm sorry, but he's right. Without him to protect you, if you show up in the compound the transadapts will tear you apart. They hate all humans. He is the only reason you've stayed alive this long."

Grant paused in midstep, uncertainty flickering in his eyes.

Sindri smiled at him with smug self-possession. "Nor will a hostage situation lead to anything but your deaths."

"Maybe dislocating your arms and legs and neck would make you willing to tell us where the gateway is," Grant countered.

Sindri shrugged. "Mr. Grant, believe me when I say that I've lived so long with pain that what you propose would be no more than a minor discomfort to me."

The little man turned to face Brigid, gently touching his chin. Sincerely he said, "Miss Brigid, I apologize for your ordeal from the bottom of my heart. The last thing I wanted was to distress you."

She inhaled sharply, exhaled slowly. She asked bitterly, "Did you find what you were looking for?"

"If it means anything, yes. The sperm samples collected from Mr. Kane and Grant are more than adequate to begin the gene therapy."

"What's the point?" Brigid snapped.

"I don't understand."

"You need healthy ovum for the sperm to fertilize, and your females are barren. Do you have in vitro eggs so the genes can be spliced?"

Sindri shook his head. "No, we do not."

"Then where will you find healthy eggs to implant in the women?"

Squinting up at her, Sindri said, "I presumed you had it all figured out. From you."

Brigid stared at him for a long silent moment, then began to laugh.

Chapter 25

Sindri's frown was deep as he waited for Brigid's outburst to cease. When it did, he said, "Perhaps you will be so courteous as to share the joke with the rest of us."

"No," she replied, eyes jade bright. "It'll keep until you make your first attempt at hybridizing a transadapt with our combined genetic material."

Sindri eyed her curiously. "And that will be funny?"

Brigid presented the image of pondering over the query for a moment. At length, she said, "Only to me."

Tersely Sindri said, "Explain yourself."

She smiled a small, frigid smile. "I thought you enjoyed guessing games."

Sindri stared at her. She stared back. Then he heeled about, striding toward the arched entrance. "Time to leave."

Harwin touched Grant's sleeve. He extended a hand toward him, mumbling, "Pleasure to meet a Terran."

As Grant took his hand and shook it, the old man's lips formed the words *He lies*. His forefinger tickled Grant's palm, the long nail tracing an impression into the fabric of his glove.

Keeping his face composed, Grant said simply, "Same here."

He released the old man's hand and fell into step with the entourage formed by Sindri, Brigid, Kane and the three trolls. They followed the same route as they had when they arrived, passing under the spiral-engraved archways until they reached the bullet-car platform.

Once they were strapped inside with the hatch secured, the vehicle started up, sliding effortlessly along the raised rail. The forewall became transparent again, and they silently watched the interior of the pyramid speed by.

Sindri didn't speak. He stared out of the port, his blue eyes at once fierce and vacant.

Kane wondered at the meaning of Brigid's bitter laughter and mocking words. Such behavior was not normally in her cool, reserved character and made him feel distinctly uneasy.

The bullet car raced out of the cavity in the base of the pyramid, raising a wake of red dust that billowed out on either side of it. Overhead the sky flared with pink and saffron hues.

Kane looked out on the desolation of the Cydonia Plains. It was full of silence and peopled only with the shapes of wind-eroded rock. Far in the distance, he saw the squat, mesa-shaped formation again. He resisted the impulse to ask Sindri if it was the monstrous stone head. He really didn't care if it was. On the horizon, sharp-pointed peaks arose, far too regular in shape to be mountains.

He channeled his thoughts toward finding an avenue of escape. He was mildly surprised by his lack of a desire to punish Sindri, despite what he had done to them. Mad he probably was, obsessed definitely, but Kane had difficulty casting him into the role of an enemy. He was an adversary, but he wasn't like Baron Cobalt, Salvo or even Colonel Thrush.

Sindri radiated a loneliness, a sharp sense of alienation, but also a deep sense of purpose and responsibility.

The bullet car eased into the subterranean chute at the far edge of the compound. Its velocity slowed as it approached the platform. The same quartet of trolls stood there, as if they hadn't stirred an inch in the past hour.

The vehicle slid to a complete stop, and the passengers disembarked. As Sindri made for the ladder, Grant demanded, "Now what?"

Sindri paused, one foot resting on a rung. Not turning his head, he asked dully, "Now what, indeed?"

"Are you going to let us go?"

Sindri sighed. "We'll discuss the subject later, at my convenience. Other matters require my attention."

Grant's nostrils flared, and Kane saw him coiling his muscles. Then he suddenly relaxed. "Whatever you say."

They climbed the ladder and into the tunnel. Frogboy and Elle, still toting her harp, waited there. Sindri said to them, "Escort Mr. Grant and Mr. Kane to the lounge. See that their needs are met. Miss Brigid, I request your company."

Kane made a move to interpose himself between Sindri and Brigid. "For what?"

"That is our affair," retorted the little man broodingly. "None of yours."

Kane almost said *"I'll make it mine,"* but he glimpsed Elle shifting the bottleneck of the harp in his direction.

Quietly Brigid said, "I'll be all right."

"Of course you will," Sindri told her, sounding a bit scandalized. "Why wouldn't you be?"

Stepping aside, Kane watched Sindri, Brigid and the four transadapts walk down the passage, around a bend in the wall and out of sight. Frog-boy piped, "Let's go, big 'uns."

Grant and Kane marched down the hallway, preceded by Elle and trailed by Frog-boy. Kane asked him, "Do you have a name?"

"'Course I do," he replied with a gargoyle sneer. "It's David. What do you think, I'm some kind of bastard foundling? I know all about my family, going back seven generations to Earth."

"And what kind of folks are you descended from?" Grant asked. "People who lived under bridges and took tolls?"

David gazed at him in momentary confusion. "No," he squeaked. "They were gourmet cooks. I inherited all of their recipe books, that's why I'm the cook here."

Considering the quality of their breakfast, Kane didn't think David was much in the way of a chef, but he decided to keep his comments to himself. The little troll was obviously seething with barely tamped down aggression and hostility for all humanity.

"Were you in the recon party to the redoubt on Earth?" inquired Kane.

David nodded enthusiastically, his lips slipping over his stumpy teeth in a proud grin. "I operated the MD. Turned three of them black big 'uns to glop."

"I'm sure you're very proud," Grant commented.

"I am, you bet."

"Of course, those black big 'uns chilled one of you in the process."

David's prideful grin turned to an ugly scowl. "Weren't my fault. Brokk was out of his head, laughin' and dancin' around. Too much oxygen, Sindri said."

"Why aren't you dancing around?" Kane asked. "The oxygen content is about the same here as in the redoubt."

David stopped in front of the hatch. "I got used to it. Sindri—what's the word—he acclimated some of us. Most of us ain't, though, that's why we stay in our quarters. And that's why so many of us got kilt in the revolt. Too damn air-drunk to dodge."

The hatch irised open. Before Grant stepped through, he said, "The humans had weapons, I guess." He spoke as if he were only the slightest bit interested, bringing up the topic just to be polite.

"Old guns," David stated. "Not a lot of ammo. Once that ran out, they were easy to kill…and I'll tell you, did we ever." He smiled at the memory.

"What did you do with the guns—trash 'em?"

"No, Sindri locked 'em up. Said they weren't safe for us to handle, even with no rounds for 'em."

Kane and Grant entered the large dome where they had breakfasted. David stayed outside in the tunnel with Elle. "You two want anything?"

"Not at the moment," Kane answered. "Is there an intercom or something in here so we can let you know if we change our minds?"

David shook his head. "No. Just knock on the door. Elle will be out here."

The hatch hissed shut. Immediately Grant and Kane paced around the chamber, scanning for spy-eye vid lenses or eavesdropping microphones. Since the curving walls were basically featureless, it took only a couple of minutes to decide the room was clean.

"Trusting bunch," Grant muttered, speaking quietly just to be on the safe side.

"Inexperienced," said Kane. "Besides, can you think of a better prison than an alien planet with a toxic environment? Anyway, we know there's some blasters in the compound and only a few of the opposition."

"Define opposition," Grant remarked dourly. "I'm sure we're still outnumbered by a two-to-one margin."

Kane nodded agreeably, looking around the lounge for anything that could be used as a weapon. All the furniture was molded from plastic and a chair leg wouldn't make much of a bludgeon, even if he managed to break one off.

"Right before we left the pyramid," whispered Grant, "the old man, Harwin, told me Sindri was a liar."

Kane snorted. "Big revelation."

"And when he shook my hand, he traced a letter on my palm. I think it was the letter X."

"$X?$" Kane questioned. "What's that supposed to mean?"

Grant's eye went thoughtful. "This is just a guess, but maybe he was trying to tell me where the mat-trans unit was located."

"Hmm," Kane said softly. "Maybe. Construction specs, blueprints use the alphabet when a foundation is being laid out."

"That's what I figured. But we don't know where we are in the compound."

On impulse, Kane strode over to the bookshelves. Swiftly he rifled through the spiral-bound technical manuals, tossing aside volumes devoted to geothermal dynamics, the theory of terra-forming and cybernetic microlinkages. Flaking gold letters on a deep blue cover caught his eye—*Habitat Maintenance/Cydonia Compound One.*

Taking it from the shelf, he carried it over to the table and sat down. Grant leaned over his shoulder as he flipped the volume open and turned the pages. Fortunately they were of slick, coated stock and showed only a little yellowing from mildew.

The majority of the pages contained dense blocks of copy, detailing construction materials and optimum stress points. In the middle of the book, Kane found a trifolded sheet of vellum. When pulled out, it displayed a line-drawing aerial view of the entire compound.

The blueprint showed the Cydonia Compound's layout as a basic wheel, with the tunnel-passages like spokes connecting two dozen domes. All of them radiated out from a central hub, which bore the letter *A.* To Kane's relief, all the domes were alphabetized, but to his disgust, when he located the dome designated X, he had no idea of its location in relation to their position.

"Hell," growled Grant. "We could be in X for all we know. Or B. Or Z."

Kane nodded in irritation. Rising from the table, carrying the book, he went to the wall switch he had seen Sindri manipulate and turned it. The far walls became transparent.

He walked to the window, studying the view, consulting the blueprint, frowning, turning it upside down and sideways, cursing softly.

After a few minutes of watching and listening impatiently, Grant snapped, "Well?"

Gusting out a sigh, Kane replied, "I think we're in U."

"You think?"

Kane jerked a thumb over his shoulder. "Or T. I think X is that way, out the door and to the left."

"You think," Grant muttered. "I wish Brigid was here."

"Even with her photographic memory, she couldn't do any better," Kane retorted acidly. He thrust the book into Grant's hands. "See what you can do."

Grant chuckled mirthlessly. "It doesn't make any difference even if you're right. We're still a long way from X, with God-only-knows how many little goblins between us and it."

Kane ran a hand through his hair. "I know. If there was only some way to get an edge, even a small one, I'd be all for making a break."

Grant forced a grin. "Since David is the cook, I don't think we'd be able to talk him into drugging their food."

"Good idea, though," Kane said gloomily. He stared unfocusedly at the water stain marring the smooth wall beneath the air vent.

Grant followed his gaze, started to look away, then caught the sudden narrowing of Kane's eyes. The idea popped full-blown into both their heads at the same time, and they exchanged swift, derisive smiles.

"It's ridiculous," Grant said.

"Yeah," Kane agreed, stepping quickly over to the wall, examining the slit-baffled vent. The metal frame rattled very faintly.

Grant inspected it with a critical eye. "Too damn small for me."

"Yeah," said Kane again, his gloved fingers exploring the area between the frame and the wall. "Damn tight squeeze for me, too."

"Think you can fit?"

"Let's find out."

Grant visually compared the breadth of Kane's shoulders to the width of the vent. "You'll have to keep your arms together in front of you, like you're diving."

Nodding distractedly, Kane dragged a chair over from the small dinette set, grabbing a plastic knife from the table. He stood on the chair, fitting the blade of the knife between the vent's frame and the wall and carefully pried at it.

"Do you really think this has a chance in hell of working?" Grant asked.

Trying not to exert too much pressure on the flimsy plastic blade, Kane answered, "The air is blowing from some kind of circulation station. Stands to reason that if I follow it, I'll come to the main pumping station, where there's an oxygen supply. If I can increase the mixture—"

The frame popped out, nearly causing Kane to topple backward from the chair. He caught the frame and handed it down to Grant. "If I can increase the mixture," he repeated, "it ought to make the trolls so high they won't be much in the way of opposition."

"Will we be affected?"

Kane stood on his tiptoes, chinning himself up to peer down the square, narrow shaft of dark metal. "I can't say. If we are, not as much as them. Maybe a little light-headedness. Give me a boost."

Grant formed a stirrup with his hands, interlocking the fingers and placing them under the soles of Kane's boots. He heaved at the same time Kane kicked himself upward.

Kane managed to squirm his head and shoulders into the duct before he became lodged. Grant stood up on the chair and lifted his partner's legs, putting a shoulder against his feet and shoving hard. Kane cursed and wriggled, the zippers of his suit scraping loudly against the metal sheathing.

"Think you can make it?" Grant asked anxiously.

"Hell, I don't know." Kane's tense voice held a hollow echo. "This is like being inside a bodybag." He wormed forward a few feet.

"How will I know if you've made it?"

"You're going to have to take your best guess. Monitor the vent. You ought to be able to tell by the airflow and the smell if I've increased the oxygen content."

Grant started to replace the frame over the opening, then asked, "What do you figure the odds?"

"The usual," came the muffled, offhand response. "One percent."

Grant tapped Kane's boot sole with an index finger and slipped the frame back into place. The scratching, thumping sounds of Kane's belly-crawling progress along the duct slowly faded.

Stepping down from the chair, Grant plucked a book at random from the shelves and sat down beneath the vent to wait.

Chapter 26

Brigid wasn't really surprised when Sindri escorted her into a laboratory. He gestured for the transadapts to stay behind in the tunnel and sealed the hatch.

Brigid glanced swiftly around the maze of equipment glittering beneath the sterile light tubes on the high ceiling. She saw a pair of long, black-topped tables holding a glass blood-purification system and petri dishes.

A big electron microscope dominated one table. An oscilloscope, a fluoroscope and a stainless-steel liquid-nitrogen tank were arrayed against the walls. Past a glass partition, she saw a cylindrical hyperbaric chamber.

She recognized one of three cushioned examination tables and the pair of metal rods at one end, which had held her ankles in clamps.

Sindri pulled a pair of stools close to one of the tables. Hopping up on one, he pointed Brigid imperiously toward the other. Face completely expressionless, she complied with his silent command.

Sindri inspected her features with an intense gaze before saying, "Please do me the courtesy of explaining your unseemly display of mirth."

"Why should I?"

"I thought—I *hoped*—you and I had reached common ground based on mutual respect."

Tersely she said, "I experienced the kind of respect you hold me in."

He propped his chin up on his hand. "Necessity drove me to desperate measures. You've done the same for the cause of self-preservation. I didn't want you to remember it."

"You harvested ovum from me." She made a declaration, not an inquiry.

"Yes, in order to create recombinant gametes. Are you familiar with the terminology?"

"Gametes with new gene combinations of chromosomes," Brigid answered curtly, "formed as a result of crossing over. Do you know what polar bodies are?"

Sindri's eyebrows raised a trifle. "Nonfunctional cells resulting from unequal division during the maturation of egg cells. Why do you ask?"

"Because that's what you probably took from me. Your plan to splice Grant's, Kane's and my genes with those of the transadapts and implant them in a female won't work. Like the females here, I'm barren."

Sindri's body and face twitched, as if he had received an electric shock. He groped for something to say, then finally hissed, "You're making that up. You're lying to me."

She shook her head. "I'm telling you the truth. I found out about it right before we left for *Parallax Red*. Not even Kane and Grant know about it. You're the one who is lying—you've been lying to us since the moment we met."

Sindri didn't respond to her last comment. "Is your condition treatable, reversible?"

"I don't know. I was exposed to radiation of an unknown type a couple of months ago."

"There are therapies, treatments, you know. Perhaps—"

Brigid cut him off with a sharp, slashing gesture of her right hand. "What's your real agenda, Sindri? The truth behind all of your martyrdom and devotion to easing the suffering of your people?"

He bristled at her sarcasm, glaring at her. Brigid met his glare, matching it in intensity. Suddenly the little man threw back his head and laughed.

"Yes, I suppose the masquerade was wearing rather thin, wasn't it? I should've have realized that I couldn't gull you indefinitely. The company of transadapts has ruined me for a true test of my intellectual steel."

"What is it you want?"

Sindri shrugged. "What does any man want? Love, security, realized ambitions."

"Which are?"

"To be the master of my own fate, beholden to no one. Certainly you can relate to that, raised in the kind of life you were."

"Of course," Brigid replied. "But we differ on the means of achieving it."

"Perhaps." He reached out to touch her hand, but she pulled it away. She noted the quick flash of anger glinting in his eyes.

"You don't like to have your will, even your whims, thwarted," she observed.

"Who does?" he retorted.

"No one, but it's a simple fact of existence. Only spoiled children and sociopaths can't come to terms with it."

He groaned. "Now you sound like Pop."

"Is he really your father?"

A corner of Sindri's mouth quirked in a sour smile.

"Biologically, yes. In every other aspect of fatherhood, he failed miserably. Although I understand he truly loved my mother, which was in itself not a crime, but the physical expression of it certainly was. After my birth and her death, he accepted his exile gratefully."

"Once in the pyramid, he tampered with the transmitter's frequencies and set up disharmonious resonances in the humans here?"

"He did indeed." Sindri sighed. "He implies now he did it intentionally to punish the compound, so the transadapts could eventually outlive the humans and take over Cydonia."

"You don't believe him?"

He opened his mouth, closed it, shook his head. "For a long time, I did not. Now, especially after today, I'm not so sure. Regardless, the song must be stopped."

"How? I thought he tried many times."

"And failed many times. But a simple solution came to me while exploring *Parallax Red* some months ago. I've yet to test it, because it will have the most deadly of consequences. Now that you've told me my plan to increase the population of the transadapts will fail, I have no other option. Once I embark upon this particular path, there is no turning back."

"Deadly consequences for whom?"

"Everyone."

Brigid lowered her eyebrows in a frown. "Everyone? You mean on Mars?"

Sindri threw his arms wide. "I mean *everyone*. Including the inhabitants of Earth."

She stared at him, confused and puzzled. "You've lost me."

He grinned. "Hardly, Miss Brigid. You've won me many times over."

Grimly she replied, "Stick to the subject."

The grin fled Sindri's face. "You accused me of being a liar, which is no accusation at all, since it is the truth. You told me my plan to revitalize the transadapt population will fail. I presume that is the truth, not a lie to mislead me."

He paused, waiting for her response.

After a moment, she said simply, "It's the truth. Test my egg cells if you doubt me."

"I don't. However, if that plan has failed, then there is no reason to continue the deception. I could give the proverbial rat's ass about the transadapts."

"I suspected as much," Brigid said dryly.

As if he hadn't heard, Sindri plunged on. "Stupid, filthy, childish creatures. The Committee of One Hundred was right. They cannot govern themselves, they should have no decision-making abilities. They are useful only as legs and arms and strong backs. Could you imagine a man like *me* mating with a subhuman troglodyte like Elle?" He shuddered in genuine revulsion.

"Unfortunately," he continued, "they were the only followers I had available. The humans viewed me as a jumped-up transadapt and they refused to acknowledge my superior abilities. I had no choice but to seek the transadapts' aid to accomplish my goals. Despite their other shortcomings, they are easily led."

"What was your goal, to be king of the Fourth Planet?"

Sindri smiled. "Not bad. If I intended to stay here, I might adopt such a title."

"In other words," ventured Brigid, "you weren't

concerned for the welfare of the transadapts due to humane reasons?''

"There is strength in numbers, Miss Brigid. And without sufficient numbers, I do not have sufficient strength to carry out my ambitions."

"Which are?"

He beamed at her, eyes twinkling impishly. "I'll bet you can guess."

She recognized the hungry gleam behind the twinkle and felt nauseous. "You think you can come to Earth and establish your own little empire somewhere?"

"Why not?"

"The barons may have something to say about that, not to mention the Archon Directorate."

Sindri chuckled conspiratorially. "Ah, yes, the barons. I learned from you and Mr. Grant and Kane they are hybrids of human and Archon genetic material."

"They claim to be," she said.

"They have reestablished the ancient god-king system of tyranny. What is needed to unseat them is a leader for disenfranchised Terrans to rally around. After all, from what you three told me, the outlanders aren't too different from my transadapts."

"Rebellions have been tried before," Brigid argued.

"But not in generations, yes? Not since the so-called 'baron blasters'?"

"True," she admitted. "That was nearly ninety years ago. The baronies are far more entrenched now than they were back then, their power bases completely solidified."

"A power base is no more solid than the foundation to which it is attached," Sindri said vehemently.

He jumped off the stool and paced up and down along the length of the table in excitement, tucking his cane under an arm. "What if that foundation shakes and crumbles beneath them? What if the barons had to turn all their resources toward coping with a host of natural disasters—floods, earthquakes, devastating meteor falls? Would they then not be vulnerable to a concerted, well-equipped effort to dethrone them?"

Brigid considered his words for a moment, trying to imagine how the secluded, pampered and fragile baronial hierarchy would react to unremitting disasters.

"I suppose they would," she said. "But how can these catastrophes be arranged?"

Sindri rapped the ferrule of his walking stick sharply against the floor. "Another bit of mendacity I must own up to, Miss Brigid. Thor's Hammer."

"Thor's Hammer? You mean the GRASER cannon on the station?"

"I told Mr. Kane it was inoperable."

"And it isn't?"

"Oh, it most definitely was when I arrived on *Parallax Red.* Over the last few months I've been recharging the dynamos that power it."

Brigid declared incredulously, "Earth is on the other side of the Moon from the station. You can't shoot through it."

"Actually, " he replied confidently, "I probably could. But I have no coordinates for strategic targets on Earth. Besides, the GRASER consumes such an appalling volume of power, I'll have only one chance for a single shot. I can't afford to miss."

Lifting his cane to his shoulder, Sindri sighted down it like a rifle. "I do have coordinates for a target on Mars, however. The pyramid. If my calculations bear out, and there's no reason why they shouldn't, one touch of ten million megawatts of GRASER energy will trigger corresponding and sympathetic vibrations within the transmitter.''

"And then?" Brigid asked flatly.

"And over a period of weeks, perhaps only days, Mars will shake itself to pieces in a cataclysm of Old Testament proportions.''

Sindri lowered the cane, twirled it jauntily and rested it on a shoulder. "Continent-sized pieces of the planet will tear loose and in the form of meteorites and asteroids be drawn in by Earth's gravity well. Their mass will cause slippages in the polar icecaps, creating the rise of oceans and tsunamis. The impact of smaller fragments will trigger earthquakes of immeasurable magnitude. Dormant volcanoes will erupt. It will be world under siege from the heavens.''

Showing his teeth in a wide grin, Sindri added, "Real wrath-of-God-type stuff.''

Brigid listened to his quiet, self-confident litany of catastrophes and the cold fingers of fear crept up, then down the buttons of her spine. If even a fraction of what Sindri said could be believed, then another round of devastation would ravage an Earth still recovering from the nukecaust and skydark.

"You've done no tests," she broke in, "you have no empirical data. You're dreaming.''

Sindri snarled out a superior laugh. "Think of scientific precedent cloaked by myth and legend. The Ark of the Covenant brought down the walls of Jericho when the Israelites gave a great shout. Why wouldn't they fall, if bombarded by amplified sound waves of the right frequency transmitted from the Ark?

"Merlin, who is reputed to be of half-Danaan blood, was said to have 'danced' the megaliths of Stonehenge into place by his music. What I propose is of the same order, but on a far grander scale."

Brigid struggled with visions of Mars breaking up, spewing millions of tons of its crust and bedrock into space. She said faintly, "Your philosophy of destroying in order to save."

"Very perceptive. Think of the long-term benefits, Miss Brigid. Not only will Mars be removed forever from the coveting grasp of the Archon Directorate, they will have no choice but to relinquish their claim on Earth. And I will have stopped the song, as they always wished."

"If what you say comes to pass," she stated, "there won't be much left to relinquish. The loss of life will be incalculable."

Smoothly Sindri replied, "As a point of fact, I have calculated it, at least in percentages. A few human beings will be left alive, of course. Humankind is too tough to be entirely killed off. Consider this—the barons and the hybrids you told me about will suffer the most casualties, living in their villes, the Administrative Monoliths toppling over them. And they are used to acting on orders, but beyond the villes, the outlanders still live by instinct.

"The villes will lie in ruins, overrun by vines and animals. The persecuted outlanders would make up the majority of the survivors. They will be grateful to me, for removing the heel of their oppressors. They would follow me willingly, no matter what kind of empire I wished to build."

"Where will you be during the catastrophes?" asked Brigid.

"On *Parallax Red*. We will sit out the cataclysms that overtake both Mars and Terra."

"Won't you be in just as much danger from asteroids and planetary debris?"

Sindri smiled broadly. "There is an acceptable element of risk. The odds of something as small as *Parallax Red*—speaking in celestial measurements—receiving a direct hit are astronomically high. Pun intended. You and I will be safe, I give you my word."

A second passed before Sindri's last words penetrated Brigid's consciousness. She echoed, "You and I?"

"Well, of course. You don't think I'd leave you behind here or allow you to return to Earth, do you? That would be positively diabolical. You really must give me some credit. I'm not a monster."

He stepped closer to her, placing a hand lightly on her right knee, gazing up earnestly into her face. "All I ask in return is your love."

Brigid's poker face failed her. She felt the muscles of her face contorting and twisting in disbelief and repulsion. She was too shocked to speak.

Voice dropping to an intimate pitch, Sindri continued, "You have a deep wellspring of passion. I desire to plunge into it, to taste the physical love of a human woman. All my life it was denied me. I kept myself pure for a woman like you. I never once, regardless of the temptation, defiled myself with a transadapt female. If you cannot bring new life from my seed, the simple act of implanting it will grant me one of my most heartfelt desires."

Sindri's caressing fingers darted up her leg, toward her thigh. Brigid snapped up a knee, the point of it cracking solidly on the underside of his jaw.

Teeth clacking together, Sindri staggered back a few paces, caught himself on the corner of the table and recovered his balance. He bared his perfect teeth in a ferocious scowl, then by degrees, it turned into a rueful grin.

"Darling Miss Brigid," he said softly, "your assaults upon my person do not have the effect of dampening my ardor. Quite the contrary, I find myself even more aroused by the challenge. I am very accustomed to overcoming adversity when I desire an objective. Nothing has ever come easy to me."

He stepped toward her swiftly. Just as swiftly, Brigid slid off the stool, upending it and holding it by the seat in front of her. Sindri laughed in delight and feinted at her with his walking stick.

Brigid stepped back, feeling frightened and more than a trifle ridiculous. She circled the table, fending off Sindri's cane strokes with the legs of the stool. He chortled, crying out "Ho!" every time he lunged for her.

At the corner of the table, she swept the stool against the miniature glass maze of the purification system. It shattered amid a spray of splinters and foul-smelling chemicals. Sindri scrambled backward to avoid being cut and drenched.

Appraising the damage, he snapped, "You're starting to piss me off. You just ruined the work of two days."

"Then stop this foolishness," she said sternly. "Whatever you want from me is not going to happen."

Sindri's face molded itself into the same mask of demented rage she had seen in the pyramid. He bounded forward, flailing madly with his cane, two-fisting it like a broadsword.

Brigid managed to block and parry his swinging swipes for a few moments. She thrust the stool legs at his face. One of them struck him on the nose, bringing forth a gush of blood from both nostrils.

He didn't react to the pain or the sight of his own blood. Increasing the ferocity of his attack, he drove her steadily backward, around the table again in a flurry of blows.

Glass crunched beneath her boots, and she stepped in a puddle of chemicals. Losing traction for an instant, she stumbled, forced to take one hand off the stool to steady herself against the edge of the table.

That instant was all Sindri needed to leap at her, slapping aside the legs, grabbing the stool by a rung and wrenching it violently from her hand. Holding his cane as if it were a billiard cue, he punched the silver-reinforced tip of it deep into the pit of her stomach.

The impact drove the breath from her lungs in a gasp. Sindri glided to her side, hammering the back of her right knee with the cane's knob, neutralizing the nerve endings in her leg. It buckled beneath her and she fell, catching herself on both hands.

For a second, Sindri was taller than her, and she saw the cruel smirk play over his lips. He delivered a short, savage blow to the base of her neck, right on the carotid artery. Brigid felt a sharp pain, a numbness and her muscles turned to watery mud.

Then the hard floor slapped the side of her face. Sindri grappled with her, wrestling her up and over onto her back. His arms were like compact masses of knotted steel cables. His hands tore at the zippers and seals of her suit. He dug ten vanadium-hard fingers into her arms, her breasts, he shook her, buffeted her, pummeled her to and fro. For a dizzy handful of seconds, she felt as if she were being dismembered in the grip of an earthquake.

The manhandling stopped suddenly, and she lay gasping on the floor, tasting the salty tang of blood at the corner of her mouth. Her body throbbed with a dull, steady ache, and sharper pains let her know of strained ligaments and tendons. She felt the cool touch of air on her torso and shoulders and knew her suit had been opened and peeled down to her waist.

When Brigid's eyes were able to focus again, she saw Sindri standing between her outflung legs. He undid the silk scarf around his throat and unzipped his bodysuit. Gently, smilingly he said "Accept, Miss Brigid. Don't struggle against the inevitable."

Sindri tugged the one-piece garment down over his lean hips, revealing a broad chest with a downlike covering of hair. He stepped out of the suit and kicked it and his boots away. His uncircumcised penis was like a length of heavy rope, uncoiling from a tuft of brown-yellow pubic hair.

Brigid was shocked to see it. It was not erect, but it was enormous, the one disproportion in a small but perfectly proportioned body. It made him a monster.

Still smiling, Sindri bent over her.

Suddenly the atmosphere of the room seemed to give a great upward lurch. Brigid's stomach heaved, and an off-key ringing sounded in her ears. Sindri's eyes flicked back and forth in frantic bewilderment.

Slowly he drifted up from the floor.

Chapter 27

Despite the continuous stream of cool air playing over his face, Kane perspired profusely. Blinking the sweat out of his eyes, he stretched his arms out full-length, shoulders jammed up against his ears, chin dragging on the shaft floor. The crown of his head bumping against the top of the duct, he wormed his way forward with a steady wriggling motion. A burning ache had settled in his hips, the base of his spine and the back of his neck.

Kane had never experienced claustrophobia before, but he battled it now. If not for the slight give in some sections of the ductwork, he would have been trapped, caught fast yards ago. Dim light peeped in from vents where the shaft branched off. He prayed he wouldn't have to turn down one of the side arteries in order to follow the airflow. Trying to negotiate a turn would be almost impossible.

At least the neoprene texture of his gloves helped his fingers to gain some traction on the smooth surface of the duct. Still, after a few minutes of regular flexing, curling and uncurling his fingers, the metacarpal bones and wrist tendons stiffened and shook with the strain.

Although the confines of the shaft were almost intolerably cramped, Kane was grateful he had so far not encountered driving fans, internal grilles or vertical drops. The builders of the compound had gone for straightforward efficiency, with a minimum of accessories requiring maintenance or replacement.

Obviously no one had ever foreseen the ductwork being used as an alternate route of getting around the compound, since the shaft was barely large enough to comfortably accommodate a transadapt.

The deeper he dragged himself into the shaft, the more pronounced became a deep-pitched humming, interwoven with a steady clatter. Somewhere up ahead, machinery was working.

Kane glanced into the side shafts as he passed them. He didn't investigate any of them, continuing to crawl toward the steady airflow. At one point, he heard muffled, distant voices issuing from one of the vents. He thought he heard Baptiste, but he couldn't be sure.

It seemed a long time before a square of light shone in the dimness ahead. He tried but failed to increase his wiggling pace. Then, mercifully, the duct widened and ended. The spinning blades of a big circulating fan, at least four feet in diameter, ruffled his hair.

Peering between the whirring blades, past a protective screen of wire mesh, he saw a large room filled with an array of clattering pumps, their armatures rising and falling in a rapid rhythm. Square ductwork rose vertically from huge, cage-enclosed fan assemblies sunk into the poured-concrete floor.

Kane's perspective on the circulation station was limited. He couldn't move too close to the spinning fan without risking a sliced-off nose.

Examining it closely, he saw a flexible metal conduit snaking down from the exterior of the motor mount. He thought a moment, considering and discarding several methods of interrupting the fan's continuous cycle long enough to disconnect its power source.

Regardless of the virtually indestructible qualities Lakesh had attributed to his environmental suit, Kane knew jamming his arm between the whirling blades wasn't a viable option. Even if the tough fabric wasn't cut, bones were sure to be broken.

Propping up his right leg on his left knee, Kane inspected his boot. Attached to the legging just above the calf by a zipper running all the way around it, the boot appeared to be leather overlaid by layers of neoprene and Kevlar. The heavy, hard rubber treads were nearly an inch thick.

Kane didn't devote much thought to the consequences. He unzipped the attachment and tugged off the boot, nearly poking his elbow into the fan blades in the process. He carefully folded the boot in half, then hitched around on his knees so he faced the fan. Taking a deep breath and holding it, he thrust the boot, sole first, toward the lower edge of the frame.

One of the blades caught it, nearly snatching it from his grasp. Kane strained to hold the boot in place, so it wouldn't be flung into his face. The blade dragged it along the bottom of the frame. The spinning stopped suddenly with a shuddery, mechanical groan.

Leaning forward, Kane thrust his right arm through the narrow gap between two of the blades. The fit was tight, and for a panicky instant, he feared he wouldn't be able to do it. Bending his elbow, he groped for the power conduit, his fingers brushing it twice before closing around it.

The fan groaned again, the blades shifting slightly, pushing the boot forward a fraction of an inch. Exerting all the strength in his arm and shoulder muscles, Kane yanked on the cable. It held fast. Clenching his teeth, upper body trembling from the exertion, he tugged and

snapped at the conduit, up and down, side to side and
then down again.

The tiny screws holding it in place on the mount
sheared away, but Kane continued to jerk and yank,
trying to dislodge the wires connected to the motor.
The mechanical groan stopped for a second, started
again, then settled into a stammering, on-off rhythm.

Finally the wires tore loose, and the fan's noise
ceased altogether. Working his boot free, he noted the
blade-inflicted scars on the surface layer, but the leather
beneath was still intact, as was the zipper. He tugged
it back on and secured the seal.

Worming his way around and leaning back as far as
he could, Kane braced his hands and hips against the
duct and drew up his legs, bending them double. He
straightened them out again with all his strength, landing a powerful double kick against the fan's frame.

The banging sound of impact sounded horrendously
loud, but it couldn't be helped. He continued to launch
kick after kick, even after slivers of pain began piercing
his tendons and ankles. The frame seemed solidly
seated and bolted into place, and he lost count of how
many times his feet slammed against it.

When it shifted, and then the upper left corner
popped out, he could scarcely believe it. He increased
the speed of his kicks, concentrating on that spot.

With a clanging crash, the battered frame and motor
assembly toppled into the room below, landing atop
breakables, judging by the brief jangle of shattering
glass.

Breathing hard, Kane leaned forward and swept the
room with a searching gaze. Aside from the circulation
fans, ductwork and condensers, he saw three huge, hor-
izontally mounted steel tanks in a far corner. The sym-

bol for oxygen was stenciled in black on their dull surfaces. A network of pipes stretched out from the ends of the tanks, feeding into small, box-shaped modules at the bases of the floor fans. Glass meters and valves were attached to the pipes at regular intervals.

Within a chain-link-fenced enclosure rested a metal-walled disk, about eight feet in diameter and three feet thick. The ribbed top consisted of a small, round superstructure of raised flanges surrounding a recessed opening.

On the far side of the disk protruded a sealed yellow cylinder about two feet long and one foot in diameter. The warning painted on it in red letters read Contents Under Pressure—Thorium Chrylon.

It wasn't until he leaned farther out of the shaft that Kane saw the plastic sign bolted to the gate of the enclosure. In blocky blue letters, it read Grav-Stator. Only Authorized Maintenance Personnel Permitted. Must Have C-Class License And Committee-Approved Work Order To Enter.

Looking below the duct, he saw the fan frame had lodged between a pair of pipes, breaking the glass faces of several pressure gauges but apparently causing no other damage. The drop was only ten feet, so he backed out of the shaft, clung to the edge for a moment, then dropped with flexed knees to the floor.

Kane didn't worry about tripping an intruder-detection system or alerting a guard. The racket he had made kicking loose the fan would have resulted in that. Still, he scanned the walls and ceiling for concealed spy-eyes and found none.

He saw the door hatch directly opposite the big oxygen tanks. He made his way across the room to them, studying the different valves, gauges and pressure switches attached to the pipes. He tried to differentiate between the intake and outflow lines. Kane knew he wasn't much of a technician, but he figured the trans-adapts weren't, either. The Cydonia Compound humans had obviously educated them to carry out a diversity of maintenance tasks, and monitoring oxygen content, flow and quality was probably the primary one.

Kane located an L-shaped lever beneath a large, numbered meter. A straight line divided into three color bands, yellow, orange and red, crossed its face. The needle held steady at midyellow.

Grasping the lever, he nudged it toward the right. The needle slowly crept toward the orange band. He waited for a moment, breathing deeply. Finally he caught a faint whiff of an odor reminiscent of ozone. He threw the handle to the far end of the red band and stepped back.

A high hissing emanated from the pipe to which the meter was attached. Within seconds, the metallic odor of pure, undiluted oxygen tickled his nostrils, stimulating the urge to sneeze.

As he turned away, a multipaged chart hanging on the wall near the hatch caught his eyes. He went to it and thumbed through the pages quickly, feeling a rush of elation. Like the blueprints in the manual, the chart displayed schematics of the compound, designating them by letters of the alphabet.

Unlike the manual, the pages bore handwritten descriptions of all the domes, even delineating separate chambers. Within a half minute of serious study, he realized he was in Dome V, only one dome away from X. His guess they were in Dome U wasn't that far off the mark. Judging by the description, the V habitat was primarily a community center, with dining halls, lounges and a medical facility. The facility was located only a few dozen yards down the tunnel from the environmental station.

Dome X had evidently been devoted to administrative duties, since a council chamber, a communications command post and various offices were clearly marked. However, he saw no reference to a mat-trans unit, but he wasn't surprised or dismayed. Sindri had implied the Committee of One Hundred kept its existence a secret.

After memorizing the shortest route to Dome X, Kane walked to the fenced enclosure. The gate didn't have a lock, so he stepped inside. The machine on the floor bore a resemblance to the nuclear generators in Cerberus, but one laid on its side. Circling it, he eyed the control switches studding its surface. Indicators were labeled with the words Rotational Rate Cycle, EPS Channel and Superconductor Stator. A small LED flashed 0.8G.

The disk hummed very purposefully and powerfully. He guessed—and was pretty positive he was correct—that he stood before a synthetic-gravity generator. He felt a gentle field of static electricity surrounding it, one that caused his loose hairs to shift and stir.

Kane had no idea of the effect radius of the generated-graviton field, but the device looked so bulky and heavy he doubted every habitat was equipped with one. More than likely the compound was divided up into sections, with similar environmental and gravity-regulating stations placed at equidistant points that would allow the different fields to bleed into one another for stability.

Bending down, he scrutinized the LED and the small

row of buttons beneath it. He chose one at random and pushed it. Immediately the steady drone of the generator dropped in pitch and the number on the readout screen changed from 0.8 to 0.9. He felt no substantial difference in the gravity.

Kane kept his finger poised over the buttons, face set in lines of concentration, weighing a number of causes and effects. Then he said, "You're doing it again—making up shit as you go along."

He immediately felt a little embarrassed by speaking his thoughts aloud, but he began depressing the buttons in descending order. As the steady hum of the generator altered in pitch, the LED flashed the changing numbers. They went from 0.9 to 0.8 to 0.6 and to 0.5.

When the display glowed with 0.2G, Kane heard an odd ringing in his ears and felt a lifting sensation in his belly that spread throughout his entire body. By the time the LED read 0.0G, his feet were a few inches above the floor. Mars's gravity was a little under half of Earth's, but the generator nullified even that, as he had expected.

He hoped the generator wasn't equipped with an automatic fail-safe reset, which would restore normal gravity, but even if it were, the sudden change to zero-G conditions would give him a small edge.

Most of the time, that was all he ever asked for.

Chapter 28

Grant couldn't be sure if the oxygen content flowing from the air vent was stronger than before. His nose had been broken three times in the past, and always poorly reset. Unless an odor was extraordinarily pleasant or virulently repulsive, he was incapable of detecting subtle smells unless they were right under his nostrils. A running joke during his Mag days had been that Grant could eat a hearty dinner with a dead skunk lying on the table next to his plate.

For twenty minutes or so, he had sat and leafed through volume two of *The Cambridge Medieval History*. He didn't read much of the dense, double columns of copy, but he found the illustrations, particularly the color plates of knights in plate armor, of interest.

Upon taking a deep breath, he caught a very faint odor that hadn't been in the room before. He stood up, turning to face the vent, inhaling the cool air flowing from the duct. Since he couldn't be sure if the new smell meant an increased oxygen content, he decided to wait a few minutes for the mixture to be completely circulated through the habitat. He had no inclination to face Elle or her agony-inducing harp unless she had an additional handicap, even a marginal one.

He returned to his chair and silently counted off three minutes. When he rose, he experienced a brief wave of dizziness, a light-headedness that abated as

quickly as it had come over him. Holding the heavy
hardcover book in his right hand, he went to the hatch
and beat loudly on it with his left fist, shouting, "Hey,
open up! We're hungry!"

He had to repeat his call and hammer even more
forcefully before the hatch finally irised open. Elle
stood blinking up at him, a beatific smile on her
pushed-in face. Though she still held the harp, it wasn't
pointed directly at him.

"Huh?" she asked, words slurred. "Whad you
wan'?"

She swayed a bit from side to side, her long toe-
thumbs crooking and uncrooking on the floor.

Recalling a passage from the book, Grant said
sternly, "We want a haunch of roast mutton with mint
jelly and tankards of ale."

Elle blinked again and tittered girlishly. "You kinda
cute for a big 'un."

Grant managed to control a shiver of horror, muttering, "So I've been told. Can't say the same for
you."

He threw the book straight at Elle's forehead. He
threw it to land spine first, and Elle staggered the width
of the tunnel, uttering a piping squeak of confused pain,
like a mouse with its tail caught in a trap. The wall
kept her from falling, though she struck it hard.

Grant made a dive through the open hatch, both
hands outstretched for the harp. He grabbed the elbow
and wrist of her right arm and the muscles beneath his
fingers felt as solid as steel. Elle squawked, struggling,
wrenching her entire body back and forth. Grant
twisted her arm as though he were wringing out a wet
towel.

Elle's hand opened, and the harp fell to the floor and

bounced, twanging discordantly. Grant flung the little transadapt away from him and lunged for the instrument. Shockingly, his lunge turned into a low-altitude soar. He dived weightlessly along the tunnel, a couple of feet above the floor.

Despite his astonishment, he secured a grip on the harp as he flew over it. He knew, on an instinctive, gut level, that the gravity hadn't vanished due to an accident. Or if it had, the accident's name was Kane.

Squealing in rage, Elle kicked herself off one wall, then the other, powerful leg muscles propelling her toward him in froglike leaps. Despite her drunken state, she still knew how to ambulate in null-G conditions.

Managing to twist over onto his back, Grant pointed the bottleneck of the harp in her direction and plucked frantically at the double-banked strings. The sound exploding out of the instrument bore no resemblance to a melody, but Elle sprang right into its directed, vibrational path.

As if she had slammed headlong into an invisible barrier, the transadapt woman performed a complete somersault, her malformed feet reversing positions with her head. She spun end over end down the passageway, making no outcry or an attempt to check her spinning motion.

Grant stared, nonplussed, wondering if the harp sound had rendered Elle unconscious. When she made another midair turn, he caught a glimpse of her face and winced.

Elle's mouth gaped open, and from between slack lips drifted a scattering of dark ivory crumbs mixed with little scarlet globules. Her teeth and very likely all the bones in her face had been pulverized by his single desperate strumming of the strings.

Grant didn't go after her to find out if she was alive or dead. He extended his arms at a level with his shoulders and paddled the air with his hands, as if he were swimming through the air. He tried to maintain a short, safe distance from the floor in case the gravity returned with the same abruptness with which it had vanished.

BRIGID STARTED TO SPIN and she spread her arms and legs wide to achieve equilibrium. Sindri's expression of befuddlement hadn't changed even as he rose from the floor, his penis bobbing out in front of him.

Loose objects drifted up from the floor. The shattered remains of the glass filtration network and the puddle of chemicals began to float. The liquid formed little mercurylike blobs. Sindri's walking stick arose, twirling end over end.

Angrily Sindri rasped, "The gravity generator has gone out—no, I still hear it. Goddammit, it's been tampered with!"

Brigid kicked her feet, trying to put as much distance between her and Sindri as the size of the room allowed. She struggled to slip her arms back into the sleeves of her suit. The effort sent her bumping into the ceiling.

Sindri regarded her with a hard, humorless grin. "Don't bother, Miss Brigid. I've always wanted to try zero-G copulation. Another item the humans here denied me."

He looked ludicrous floating in midair with his organ drifting out before him, but Brigid didn't feel inclined to laugh. She swam sideways a score of feet, using her arms as rudders. Watching her, Sindri barked out a derisive laugh.

"There's an art to managing weightlessness, Miss

Brigid. One you'll not have the opportunity to master. The generator's reset controls will kick in shortly.''

Smiling scornfully, he worked his legs as if he were running in place. Gracefully he turned to plant his feet against a wall and bounced from it to the ceiling in a zigzag fashion. Brigid swam toward the overhead light fixture hanging from the highest point of the ceiling.

Bracing herself as best she could, she lashed out at it with both feet. Though the motion sent her rocketing backward, the glass shattered explosively. Sharp shards and splinters danced in the air like a cloud between her and Sindri.

Sindri avoided plunging through it by braking himself with hands slapped flat against the ceiling. Brigid hit the wall on her right side with bruising force. Immediately she began pulling herself down toward the floor, using her treaded boot soles to achieve a degree of traction.

Hissing in frustrated fury, Sindri crept along the curved ceiling, circling the outermost edge of broken glass. Brigid knew that once he circumvented it, he would launch himself off the ceiling and swoop down on her like a bird of prey.

KANE HEARD the drunken laughter and cracked, off-key singing before he negotiated a bend in the tunnel wall. The four trolls who had escorted Brigid and Sindri bobbed and pirouetted in the null gravity. One of the little men appeared to be sitting in an invisible boat, making clumsy, jerking, back-and-forth movements with his arms. At the same time, Kane recognized the song they were croaking as a hopelessly mangled rendition of ''Row Your Boat.''

He would have laughed at the scene, except he knew

the hatch they floated before and ostensibly were supposed to guard led to the medical facility. Sindri and Brigid had to be inside.

Reining in his impulse to charge among them and lay them out with his fists and feet, Kane imitated the trolls' slack-jacked, giddy expressions. He floated negligently toward them, singing a song he had heard Lakesh give voice to more than once. He couldn't remember all the lyrics, but as he approached the transadapts, he sang loudly about luck being a lady tonight.

The trolls accepted his participation in their spontaneous sing-along, their hatred of humans subsumed by an overindulgence in oxygen. They greeted him with grins and hoots of appreciative laughter, clapping their hands and feet.

Kane gently bumped a pair of trolls aside as he reached out to trigger the photoelectric sensor beam that would open the hatch.

"Hey, you—fuckin' big 'un," snapped one of the trolls in a surly, challenging tone. "You can't go in there."

Kane turned to face him, maintaining a friendly smile. The little man didn't return it. He scowled ferociously. Kane knew from experience that every group of drunks had at least one member who turned nasty when under the influence, whether the intoxicant was home-brewed whiskey or oxygen-rich air.

This particular transadapt was a mean drunk and, even if a loathsome big 'un hadn't appeared, he probably would have picked a fight with one of his friends.

The troll reached for Kane's shoulder. He struck out at the little man with his left fist. It caught the transadapt in the sternum, and his swart features seemed to squeeze together like a fireplace bellows.

Uttering a strangulated wheeze, the troll catapulted straight back, cannonading against the opposite wall. The double impacts drove consciousness from his gimlet-hard eyes with the suddenness of a light being switched off.

The laughter and singing of the trolls instantly died. They looked at the slumped, floating form of their comrade with dazed eyes and sober faces. They flicked their gaze to Kane, staring at him with mounting horror and realization.

He waved his hand in front of the door sensor, and before the hatch had fully irised open, he lunged through it. The lunge, which began in zero gravity, ended in a limb-heavy, clumsy, face-first collapse to the floor. He realized in midfall that his fear the gravity generator would reset itself had been borne out.

Objects crashed and tinkled all around him. He raised his head just in time to glimpse a small naked man plummet straight down from the highest point of the ceiling. Behind him he heard the surprised grunts and gasps of the transadapts as they dropped heavily to the tunnel floor.

Kane struggled to his feet, turning around to face the enraged troll bounding through the portal. Unsteady on his feet, he leaped straight into Kane's upraised right boot. His jawbone made an eggshell crunching sound as he careened sideways, his body slapping down hard on the floor.

The other two transadapts howled in maddened fury, their teeth champing, as they closed in on Kane from either side. Because of the gravity, they couldn't indulge their habit of high jumping, but they were still strong. One ducked Kane's down-pistoning left hook and head-butted him in the groin. Though the protective suit cushioned the force of the blow somewhat, pain flared through his tender testicles and bile leaped up his throat.

Staggering back, Kane forced himself to remain erect, fighting the impulse to double over. From the corner of his eye, silver flashed in a blurring arc. Metal cracked loudly on bone, and the little man who had butted him wheeled sideways, howling in pain, hands clasped over a bleeding laceration in his scalp. He dropped to his knees, then to his side, curling up in a fetal position.

Brigid stood at Kane's side, half-revealed breasts heaving, eyes blazing with a hot, emerald anger. She gripped Sindri's walking stick in both hands and swung it at the remaining transadapt, bringing it high over her head, then down on his skull.

Despite the rage in her eyes, Kane noted how she checked the swing at the last half instant. The silver knob connected against the crown of the troll's head and knocked him senseless to the floor.

Repressing both a groan and the urge to massage his crotch, Kane wheezed, "Thanks, Baptiste. Are you all right?"

She nodded grimly, fingering away a drop of blood on her lower lip. "You?"

"I won't know for sure until the next time I take a leak. What was going on in here? Where's Sindri?"

In response, she heeled about and strode across the room. Kane followed her to a point where she stopped and stared at a small spattering of wet crimson on the floor.

Brigid pointed the tip of the cane at it, and he saw how it trembled slightly in her grip. "This is where he fell. There must be another way out of here. I guess he's not hurt too badly.''

She sounded disappointed. Half-turning, she indicated the small fawn-colored bodysuit lying on the floor. ''And he didn't have time to get dressed.''

''He's running around naked? What was he doing with his clothes off?''

Brigid zipped up her suit to her throat. Flatly, coldly she replied, ''He was trying to rape me.''

Kane didn't say anything for a moment, considering the comparative sizes of the parties involved and trying to visualize the scene. Finally he said incredulously, ''Little three-foot-tall Sindri?''

''Not all of him is small,'' she retorted, casting away the walking stick as if it had suddenly occurred to her it was contaminated. ''But all of him is twisted. We've got to get out of here, back to *Parallax Red.*''

''No shit,'' rumbled Grant, stepping through the hatch. He rubbed his right shoulder with his left hand. ''Damn near ended up like Domi when the gravity came back on.''

They saw the harp tucked under his right arm and held against his side. Kane demanded, ''Where'd you get that?''

''Where else? Elle. Used it on her, too. I think the payback was terminal.''

He scanned the room quickly, then focused on Kane. ''I sure as hell hope you've done more in the last half hour than to make the trolls drunk and figured out how to dick around with the gravity.''

''Anybody else would think that was enough. But, yeah, I have.''

Kane moved toward the hatch. ''I'll bring you up-to-date as we go.''

As Grant preceded him out into the tunnel, Kane cast a questioning look at Brigid. "You sure you're all right?"

Testily she said, "I said he tried to rape me. He didn't succeed, didn't impregnate me, if that's what's worrying you."

He stepped through the hatch. "It's not."

As Brigid followed him out, she asked, "Would it make much of a difference if he had?"

Kane heard the bitterness in her tone, but rather than inquire about it, he replied matter-of-factly, "To him it would. I would've chilled him long and slow, even it meant I had to spend the rest of my life here."

Chapter 29

They jogged down the tunnel, Grant taking the point, holding the harp in both hands. They encountered no more of the transadapts before the passageway ended in a hatch.

"If the chart was right," Kane said as it hissed open, "this is Dome W. On the other side is X and, if we're lucky, the gateway."

As they piled through the portal, Brigid said tightly, "We'd better be more than lucky. We'd better be blessed."

"Why?" asked Grant as they loped along the hallway.

Quickly, curtly Brigid related what Sindri had revealed to her about how he planned to use the GRASER cannon. Both Grant and Kane were doubtful, if not exactly disbelieving.

"Destroy one planet and wreck another?" Grant's voice held a highly skeptical note. "Damn big order for such a tiny pissant of a man."

"Do you believe him?" Kane asked Brigid.

"I believe he'll try it."

Turning a bend in the tunnel, Kane said musingly, "If it works, it may not be such a bad idea. Sindri would be doing our jobs for us, giving the boot to the barons and the Directorate."

She pierced him with a hard stare. "And most of

humankind, too. Besides, the results he's hoping for
are speculative at best. Even if it all goes according to
plan, do you think Sindri is a better candidate to rule
the planet than the barons or the Directorate?''

"Hell, no," Grant barked. "Then we'd just have to
get rid of him.''

Kane said no more, but he couldn't deny he found
the image of flaming meteors crashing into the villes
and toppling the Administrative Monoliths very ap-
pealing. Still, Sindri was not too far removed, behav-
iorally and emotionally, from Baron Sharpe. Then
again, with his high-handed assumptions that all his
actions were sanctified in the name of the greater good,
he wasn't all that different from Lakesh, either.

The route through Dome W was deserted. Kane suspected Sindri may have gone to the circulation station
to correct the air mixture, and he cautioned his companions that if they met more trolls, they might not be
oxygen drunk.

When they reached the hatch that led to their destination, Kane's sixth sense, his pointman's instinct, suddenly bristled in full, suspicious alert.

"Let me go first," he said, reaching out to take the
harp from Grant.

Distrustfully Grant commented, "You don't know
how to play this thing."

"Neither do you. You just got lucky."

Reluctantly Grant passed over the instrument. Kane
stepped before the sensor, and the iris segments of the
hatch slid open. He stepped into Dome X, sweeping
the bottleneck of the harp in short left-to-right arcs.

Almost immediately he felt his nape hairs prickle.
Although the tunnel stretching before them looked exactly like all the others they had passed through, he felt

a surge of unreasoning fear. Dark stains marred the smooth surface of the floor.

Much blood had been spilled here; many people had died brutally. The dome reeked with the same miasma of terror and despair as Redoubt Papa.

Kane hurried forward and, unconsciously lowering his voice, said over his shoulder, "We'll have to check every room here."

The first hatch they came to opened into a partitioned office suite filled with desks and computer terminals. Tacked on to a bulletin board near the door were dozens of memos, each one bearing the legend By Order Of The Committee Of One Hundred.

Though they knew that it was more than likely a waste of time, they fanned out across the suite, searching for another exit. They found none and returned to the tunnel.

The second hatch opened up into a big room that had apparently served as a council chamber. A raised dais supported a lectern, looking out over ten rows of chairs. They didn't bother to count them, assuming they probably numbered exactly one hundred.

A swift search of the chamber turned up no adjacent room, so they went back into the tunnel. The third hatch they found didn't respond to the blocking of the photoelectric sensor. All three of them made numerous attempts, but the portal stayed shut.

Kane declared, "This has got to be it."

"How are we going to get in there?" Grant demanded.

Aligning the bottleneck of the harp with the center of the iris pattern, he said, "Stand back."

Brigid began to protest, but her words were swallowed up by a discordant wail as Kane stroked the strings, experimentally at first, then harder and faster. The notes rolled, slapping against the hatch metal, building higher and higher until the tunnel seemed to vibrate in unison with them.

Grant and Brigid stood on either side of the frame, hands over their ears, watching pain slowly twisting Kane's face. He stood fast, strumming and plucking the threads of the harp. The disharmonious music flooded the passageway, beating against the portal in invisible waves, splashing back over him.

He felt a crushing weight pressing against his body, and his eardrums seemed to push inward. He labored for breath. It became intolerably hot, heat radiating in hazy shimmers from the hatch.

The metal segments cracked, a pattern of jagged lines bisecting them, widening and lengthening. Flakes of alloy showered down, then small chunks. The panels shivered, a violent tremor shaking them within the frame.

Kane removed his fingers from the strings, but he still felt, if not exactly heard, the echoes of the musical notes. Gritting his teeth, he swung his right foot at the center of the hatch. The sole of his boot struck it hard, and a corresponding vibration jolted up through his leg, like an electrical shock. He almost cried out from the unexpected pain.

The hatch buckled a bit, more pieces crumbling and falling from it. Kane limped back, his leg numb from the tips of his toes to his knee.

Grant pushed him aside, tucked his chin against his shoulder and sprang forward, slamming all of his 220-plus pounds against the portal.

Fatigued metal shrieked and burst inward in a clashing rain of fragments. Grant landed heavily in the room beyond, skidding forward a few feet atop a large curved segment.

Shaking his head, trying to rid his ears of the chiming echoes, Kane stepped over the threshold. The room was small, dimly lit, bare and unfurnished. It looked more like an entrance foyer, not a chamber.

Grant climbed to his feet, grimacing and rubbing his shoulder. "Felt like the door was electrified."

"You intersected with the vibrational field around it," Brigid told him. "Good thing it broke as soon as you hit it or you could've been seriously hurt."

A turnstile security checkpoint occupied most of the opposite wall. Beyond it, they saw a short hallway ending at an open doorway. From it wafted a familiar sound, but Kane wasn't sure if he really heard it or only the ghostly after-chimes of the harp song. It sounded like the distant howl of a gale-force wind.

Brigid rushed forward toward the turnstile, blurting, "It's the gateway! It's activated!"

They pushed through the prongs of the checkpoint and into the narrow corridor. They had taken less than a dozen running steps before a stunted figure appeared in the doorway. All of them recognized David with Brigid's Ingram gripped in his small hands.

He laughed wildly as he triggered a long, stuttering burst, flame wreathing the short muzzle. Grant, Kane and Brigid went to the floor as a raking stream of autofire tore long gouges in the walls and chewed up ceiling tiles. A flurry of plaster dust sifted down on them.

David was a novice with a blaster, hosing the bullets around indiscriminately, the recoil of the full-auto firing rate kicking up the barrel.

Raising the harp, Kane sighted down the bottleneck and stroked the strings. Because of the Ingram's steady hammering, he barely heard the sound his strumming produced, but he saw its effect.

Ragged tongues of flame flared from the blaster in David's grasp as all the rounds in the magazine detonated with a brutal, bone-jarring concussion. The Ingram vanished. Up to the wrists, David's hands vanished with it.

He staggered on wide-braced legs, staring at the blood-spurting stumps at the end of his arms. As if he did not believe what his eyes saw, David lifted his wrists in front of his face. A stream of crimson squirted over his cheek.

By the time he had dragged enough air into his lungs to start screaming, Grant was on his feet and throwing a pile-driver right fist at his head. The scream went back into David's throat as the blow lifted him off his feet and flipped him through the door.

The little man hit the floor spread-eagled and made no movement afterward. Scarlet rivered from his wrists, spreading out around the raised base of the jump chamber, creating a moatlike effect.

The armaglass walls were of the same dark blue shade as that on the station, but Kane had no eyes for it. Resting on the shelves of a glass-fronted case, he saw all of their equipment, including their helmets and Sin Eaters.

On impulse, he aimed the harp at the case and thumbed a single string. The glass shattered with such an explosive, nerve-stinging jangle both Grant and Brigid jumped and cursed.

"You're getting tune-happy with that thing," Grant observed sourly, brushing away shards of glass and removing their possessions from the shelves.

"It would have to be my blaster that got vaporized," said Brigid ruefully.

"David probably couldn't figure out how the Sin Eater holsters worked," Kane replied, strapping his around his right forearm.

They put on their helmets, made sure that each oxygen apparatus was in working order, then sealed them to the collars of their suits.

Grant tapped the keypad affixed to the outer wall of the mat-trans unit. "We're going to *Parallax Red?*"

"If that's where Sindri is," Kane said, "then that's where we'll be."

"How do we know he didn't screw around with the jump controls?" Grant asked. "We may be shunted off into a long trip through the Cerberus network."

"He doesn't have the know-how to do that, or the time," answered Brigid brusquely as she swung open the door. "This unit's destination coordinates are locked on to the station."

They stepped into the chamber, taking up positions on the diamond-shaped floor disks. Kane kept the harp tucked beneath his left arm. Though both he and Grant wanted to, they didn't unleather their blasters. A reflexive jerk of their fingers on the triggers while reviving from the transit could have lethal consequences.

Brigid pulled the door shut, initiating the automatic jump mechanism. Her tense whisper was transmitted into Grant and Kane's helmets: "Mars, *ave atque vale.* 'Hail and farewell.'"

Chapter 30

The outlanders revived quickly and cleanly, more or less simultaneously. Once on her feet, Brigid cast a quick look at the others and made a sensor sweep with the motion detector, and when no movement registered outside the armaglass walls, she opened the door.

Not speaking, they passed through the antechamber and into the control room. It looked exactly the same as when they had first seen it. Even the hatch stood open, just the way Kane had left it. Pausing before it, they exchanged questioning glances.

Finally Grant rumbled, "Now where to? Even retracing our steps won't necessarily take us to Sindri. And this place is what, two miles in diameter?"

"Actually, 2.8 miles." Sindri's voice filtered into their helmets through the UTEL comm-link.

All of them skipped around in shock, half-expecting to see him seated at one of the consoles. Sin Eaters sprang into Kane and Grant's hands.

"I took the liberty of examining your communications system," continued Sindri smoothly, "so I could break into the frequencies if circumstances warranted. I wasn't sure if you had arrived until Mr. Grant spoke."

"Where are you?" Kane demanded.

"That's what I'm about to tell you. By the way, Mr. Kane, were you responsible for interfering with the gravity generator and thus ruining my and Miss Brigid's erotic encounter?''

"That wasn't why I did it," replied Kane, "but now that I know, that seems as good a reason as any."

Sindri's exasperated sigh filled their helmets. "You are truly a most egregious individual, Mr. Kane. I'm putting you at the top of my enemy list."

Dryly Kane retorted, "I'm honored. I'm sure I'm in good company."

"Actually, no. At present your name is the only one on it. I cleared the rest of them off some time ago."

Grant growled, "You little son of a bitch—"

"Tut, tut, Mr. Grant. Have a care, sir, or your name will join Mr. Kane's. Now, as to where you can find me. Go down the promenade for approximately fifty yards. On your left you will see a maintenance accessway. Enter it and climb down. Then I will provide additional instructions."

They did as he directed, leaving the control room and walking along the deceptively down-sloping corridor.

"Can you see us?" Brigid asked at one point.

"Alas, no," answered Sindri. "I never got around to repairing the video security network on your part of the station. However, I presume you retrieved your weapons."

"Neighborly of you to leave them for us," Grant said snidely.

"Such an impulse was furthermost from my mind. I had only a little time to pull myself together, grab what I needed and hie my fair young ass hence to the mattrans chamber."

Sindri paused, then said, "I left David behind to cover my back in case you came calling. If you didn't show, I ordered him to jump to the station with your equipment. Since you're here instead of him, I deduce he failed me.''

"If it's any consolation," said Kane, "he did his best.''

They reached the accessway, entered it and climbed down a metal-runged ladder. The temperature suddenly rose, and Kane guessed that this lower tier of the station was now facing the reflected sunlight from the Moon.

At the bottom of the shaft, they saw a labyrinth of pipes and wheel valves crisscrossing in all directions. Dismantled pieces of machinery lay scattered on the floor.

"We're here, Sindri," Brigid announced.

"Excellent. Look around you. Do you see a pipe painted yellow? Ahead and to your right a bit.''

They searched, spotted the pipe and Brigid said, "Yes.''

"Follow it, no matter where it leads.''

The outlanders moved out, stumbling through the metal maze, bumping their helmets on low-hanging pipes and barking their shins. Grant swore and Sindri laughed.

"Find it a little cramped, do you? Funny, I never have trouble getting around.''

Following the yellow pipe, they navigated around a mass of machinery that had once kept *Parallax Red* alive—heat, light, water, air and cooling systems, as well as huge storage bins.

The longer they walked, the more they noticed how light their bodies began to feel. Jumping over a length of tubing in his path, Kane sailed upward, helmet banging into an overhead elbow joint. He cursed.

Sindri's voice purred with amusement. "Oh, I forgot to mention that the closer you come to the axis, the less the influence of gravity. I suppose you found that out, though."

The pipe suddenly bent downward at a ninety-degree angle, disappearing into a thick iron collar bolted to the deck. They faced a blank and rust-streaked bulkhead.

"Now what?" Grant demanded.

"Turn to your left. Go about ten paces. You'll find another maintenance accessway. It's open." Sindri's tone no longer held a mocking note. "I have faith you'll figure it out from there."

The accessway was a straight chute. They had to stoop over to negotiate it. They exited on the sweeping curve of a corridor. Almost directly opposite them, they saw a narrow ramp slanting upward at a forty-five-degree angle.

They climbed its smooth surface quickly, aided by the light gravity. As they did, a steady deep throb, like the beat of a giant heart, entered their helmets. Near the top of it, Kane set down the harp. Brigid and Grant saw him do it, but they didn't question him. They stepped forward and saw more or less what they expected to see.

Sindri stood in the blister-shaped pocket, leaning indolently against the railing running the length of the raised platform. He twirled his walking stick—or an exact duplicate of it—between the thumb and forefinger of his gloved right hand.

He wore a drab gray environmental suit much like theirs. Only the helmet encasing his head was markedly different. The faceplate was far more rounded and tinted with an amber hue. He watched them walk into the chamber with only mild interest in his eyes. All of them looked around for transadapts, but they saw no one but Sindri.

The domed hollow enclosing the GRASER cannon was transparent, and naked starlight winked from its glossy, elongated barrel. Beneath the platform, lights flashed purposefully on the control consoles. The steady, rhythmic throb emanated from the row of dynamos.

As they approached the base of the platform, Sindri casually reached behind him with his left hand. When he withdrew it, a palm-sized remote-control unit nestled in it. He pressed a button.

Kane caught a flicker of motion at the periphery of his vision and whirled around, leading with his Sin Eater. His belly turned a cold flip-flop.

The dark metal ovoid of the molecular destabilizer rolled out from the far side of the platform. A white halo shimmered above the storage rings at its rear. A deep red light shone from the round, recessed lens facing them.

Sindri said sharply, "At the merest suggestion of hostility, you will learn a new interpretation of the old adage, 'That's you all over.' Drop your weapons."

Kane hesitated only a moment, remembering the black protoplasmic remains of the Magistrates in Redoubt Papa. He unbuckled his Sin Eater from his forearm and dropped it to the deck. Reluctantly Grant followed suit.

"If you fire that thing in here," he said warningly, "you're liable to burn a hole in the hull."

"Since the MD's energy discharges can be fired with pristine precision," Sindri retorted, "the element of risk is acceptable."

Brigid swung her head up, impaling Sindri an emerald glare. "Why did you lure us here—so we can watch you destroy Mars?"

Sindri chuckled. "As much as I adore melodrama, I'm not that far gone. As for the destruction of Mars, the fuse won't be lit for—" he made an exaggerated show of consulting his wrist chron "—another eight hours. It'll take that long for the dynamos to power up."

He stabbed the tip of his walking stick toward them. "Regarding your accusation that I lured you three here, I did no such thing. You came of your own accord, both times. You could have just as easily gone back to that Cerberus place you told me about. I wouldn't have stopped you."

"Go back and wait for you to drop pieces of Mars on us?" exploded Grant angrily. "Not fucking likely, dwarf!"

Sindri's lips compressed in a tight line. "Regardless of the consequences to Earth, I will have, at long last, stopped the song."

"And finally complete the bargain your ancestors struck with the Archons?" Kane snapped.

Sindri brushed aside his question with a sweep of his cane. "I care nothing about the Danaan, the Annunaki or these Archons of yours—if they really exist. I care only about the survival of me and mine."

"That concern has consumed you to the exclusion of all else," Brigid stated in a remarkably calm voice. "It's an obsession that has blinded you to avenues of survival other than what you have planned."

Sindri made a snarling sound deep in his throat. "I *had* other avenues, remember? I counted on you to help me bring them to fruition. You dashed that hope, Miss

Brigid, closed off that avenue, leaving me with no option but to render this final solution.''

Reasonably Brigid said, ''Sindri, I'm not the only human female in the solar system. We can show you methods that will—''

''I don't want another human female!'' Sindri's roar caused all of them to recoil as it filled their helmets. Lowering his voice to a petulant mutter, he said, ''I want only you, polar bodies or not.''

''What's he talking about, Baptiste?'' Kane whispered, forgetting for a moment that Sindri could hear him as clearly as Brigid.

Sindri made a beckoning motion with his cane. ''And I want you up here, beside me.''

''No,'' grated Kane, putting a restraining hand on Brigid's arm.

Sindri touched a key on the remote. The MD rolled forward a few feet, the sparkling lens pointing toward Grant. ''No objections, Mr. Kane, or Mr. Grant will die. Swiftly, painlessly, albeit messily, but he will most certainly be dead.''

After a tense moment, Brigid said flatly, ''Let me go, Kane.''

Slowly he opened his hand. She strode to the platform, scaled the ladder and started to approach Sindri. He waved her back. ''Far enough, Miss Brigid.''

She stopped, staring at him in surprise. ''I thought you wanted me beside you.''

''Oh, very much. But only afterward. I don't want you trying to thwart me. I regret hurting you earlier when you tried to thwart me and I don't want to be forced to do so again.''

Brigid shifted her feet uneasily. ''What do you mean by 'afterward'?''

Sindri smiled at her impishly. "Afterward... following the removal of a pair of exceedingly troublesome factors to our personal equation."

Kane's eyes fixed on the remote-control unit and saw Sindri's index finger curve around to caress a button. Within a microsecond, he kicked himself off the floor, slamming headlong against Grant in a flying tackle, bowling him off his feet.

Grant's breath left his lungs in an explosive whoosh. Both men rolled ten feet across the deck, bouncing lightly. Without the reduced gravity, Kane would not have been able to push Grant away from the red streak that lashed out from the lens of the MD.

Kane heard a sizzling crackle, as if the very molecules of the thin air were seared by its passage. Brigid's shrill shout of fear and anger reverberated within the walls of his helmet.

Pushing himself away from Grant, he spared a half second to look at the section of inner bulkhead that had been sluiced away by the antiproton beam.

On the platform, Brigid struggled with Sindri, attempting to wrench the control unit from his hand while trying to avoid the blows he swung at her with his walking stick.

Crimson radiance sparkled in the lens of the particle-beam emitter. Kane and Grant leaped up and scrambled away from each other, trying to put as much distance between them as the domed chamber would permit.

Kane started an abortive dash for the GRASER cannon platform, but a spear of hell-light spit toward him. He put all his strength into a backward lunge that carried him nearly to the ramp.

The MD shifted back in Grant's direction. He avoided the stream of deadly energy by executing a standing high jump. The beam missed his feet by a fractional margin and turned another section of the bulkhead into bubbling slag.

The low gravity aided them in evading the weapon's beam, but both men knew they couldn't keep ducking and leaping until the molecular destabilizer's batteries were drained. It was only a matter of seconds before one of them made a misstep and was unraveled.

Kane whirled toward the doorway, moving in yards-long bounds.

Sindri's sneering laughter sounded in his ears. "To where do you hope to run, Mr. Kane?"

He reached the top of the ramp, snatched up the harp and spun on his heel. Pointing the bottleneck of the instrument at the rolling molecular destabilizer, he strummed the strings fast and hard. Nothing happened, except that the lens spewed another whiplash of blood-hued light at him. The beam scorched a path across the deck, toward his legs.

Kane jumped but came down on a strip where the alloy turned to slush. His feet slipped out from under him, and he tumbled, cradling the harp in his arms. His roll ended a scant three feet from the front wheels of the MD.

Even as his heart seemed to seize and freeze in his chest, Kane struck the strings of the instrument repeatedly. The lens cracked, sparks spurting out between the splits. The glassy substance fell apart, and a borealis of ghostly light sprayed out from the aperture.

Kane shoulder-rolled away, coming to his feet. He saw Grant at the end of the chamber and Brigid still grappling with Sindri, trying to wrest the remote-control unit from his hand. He desperately pressed the buttons, sending the wheeled weapon careening on a crazy figure-eight course. It shed sparks in its wake.

Brigid stiffened her left wrist, locking the fingers in a half-curled position against the palm. She drove a vicious leopard's-paw strike against the base of Sindri's left hand.

He choked out a pained curse, and the remote dropped from suddenly nerve-dead fingers. He swung his cane like a cudgel at her faceplate, but she checked the blow with a forearm. Her knee flashed up, pounding into Sindri's chest and driving him backward against the railing.

Bracing himself against the rail, he delivered both feet into Brigid's midriff. She staggered, hit the top rail, teetered for a second, then plunged over it. It wasn't really a fall. She twisted her body and managed to alight on her feet in a crouch, catching herself on her hands. She immediately bounced upright.

Keeping one eye on the swerving, circling molecular destabilizer, Kane snatched up his and Grant's blasters. Sindri bellowed, "Go ahead and shoot me, you smug bastard! But the power buildup of Thor's Hammer cannot be stopped by bullets. Whether I'm dead or alive, it will still cast a thunderbolt to the programmed target."

Kane believed him. He pushed the blasters into Brigid's hands and sprang for the madly wheeling MD. Throwing all of his body weight against its bulk, he steered it toward the control consoles beneath the platform. The machine was very heavy, and it wasn't until Grant joined him that it was pushed in the right direction.

The molecular destabilizer trundled forward, snapping sparks and glowing with an eerie aura. Grasping the rail, Sindri leaned over and half screamed, "*Don't,* you idiots! You don't know what you're doing!"

"The hell I don't!" Kane shouted in response. "I'm making up more shit as I go along."

He aimed the harp at the rolling MD and played the strings with fast, violent strokes. The dorsal surface of the machine shuddered, acquiring dents and bulges. A seam popped, spilling out a rainbow-colored nimbus. The concentric storage rings shattered in a cascade of spark-shot vapor.

The harp shivered violently in Kane's hands, the building vibrations stinging his fingers, shooting up his arms into his neck. His vision blurred, but he saw a hairline crack suddenly cross in his helmet's faceplate. Swiftly he hurled the instrument at the console, making sure it landed right beneath it. Gauges on the panels erupted in sprays of glass shards. He turned to run.

Sindri shrieked, "You maniac! You son of a—"

Whatever else he had to say dissolved in a prolonged, screeching rumble that penetrated their helmets. Coruscating light, like a miniature sun going nova, burst up behind them. As Brigid, Grant and Kane sprinted for the ramp, the deck lurched under their feet. They stumbled but didn't fall.

A great, cyclonic wind seemed to gust in front of them, trying to swat them back. They fought against it, bending double, nearly dropping to all fours. When they reached the top of the ramp, Kane glanced back.

Through the flares of light mushrooming up from the dynamos, he saw a ragged, ten-foot-long gash ripped in the blister cupping the GRASER cannon. Enclosed and compressed by the armaglass shielding, the destructive fury unleashed by the overloading dynamos had nowhere to go but up. Like a strip of carpet, a long section of the platform's flooring tore loose from the framework, the alloy fluttering like cloth.

Legs flailing, Sindri clung to a handrail with both hands, his body in a straining vertical posture as he struggled desperately against the relentless drag of depressurization. Splinters of glass and metal scraps swirled around him, trapped by the suction created by the breach in the hull.

Kane would have preferred to wait and watch Sindri be sucked into the vacuum of the void, but he couldn't do so without risking the same fate. He and his companions half rolled and half fell down the ramp. They didn't discuss tactics but simply ran, following the same route that had brought them there.

They were aware of the great groaning shudders that racked the bulkheads around them and jounced the deck beneath their sprinting feet. None of them voiced the dread all of them shared—that the sudden and violent decompression would trigger a chain reaction throughout the rattletrap space station, causing either a total power shutdown or making *Parallax Red* simply fall apart, ejecting them all into space.

By the time they scrambled up the ladder and onto the tier holding the mat-trans unit, the latter hadn't happened, and lights still glowed in the promenade, though they flickered frequently.

They didn't dare slow their pace, dashing flat out and side by side up the corridor. When they entered the control room, Kane paused to catch his breath by the big VGA monitor screen. It still displayed an exterior view of *Parallax Red*.

A white billowing cloud of frozen, escaped atmosphere hung above one of the station's spokes, very near to the axis. Reflected sunlight glittered from pieces of metal wreckage floating around it. To his disappointment, the range was too great to tell if a small body floated among the debris.

"Let's go!" Grant demanded breathlessly.

Kane joined his companions at the jump chamber. Brigid entered the Cerberus unit's destination lock on the keypad, adding the encrypted ID number that informed the redoubt's autosequencing program who was making the transport.

They stepped into the mat-trans chamber, Grant slamming the door behind them. All of them were gratified when the ceiling and floor disks immediately exuded a glow.

As the mist curled up around their feet, Brigid asked quietly, "Do you think he survived?"

Leaning against the wall, Kane released his breath in a sigh of mingled relief and satisfaction. "Not a hope in hell, Baptiste. Not a hope in hell."

Epilogue

Brigid took a breath and raised her arms above her head, arching her back to work out the kinks in her shoulder muscles. She tried to keep her mind empty, visualizing nothing but what she had witnessed over the past few days.

They had arrived safely back in the Cerberus redoubt late in the afternoon of the day before. Lakesh had been almost pathetically happy to see them. Domi had tried to kiss Grant even before he had taken off his helmet. Brigid had been grateful that Rouch wasn't a part of the welcoming committee.

Kane and Grant related a very terse, undetailed overview of the events on *Parallax Red* and Mars. Lakesh seemed shaken by what they told him, even a little awed. "You three may have saved two worlds from destruction. How does that make you feel?"

Kane had frowned, then said dourly, "I haven't really thought about it." Then he left the control complex for his quarters.

As usual, Lakesh put the responsibility for a full report in Brigid's hands, inasmuch as her eidetic memory left little room for misinterpretation. She had been inputting all the events into the main database for the better part of the past two hours.

As she stretched, Lakesh shuffled into the control center, throwing her a smile as he came and stood beside her terminal. The smile fled his lips as he scanned the words glowing on the screen.

Brigid peered up at him over the rims of her eyeglasses. "Something wrong with the report?"

Lakesh shook his head. "Aspects of the contents disturb me. How likely is it that when Sindri probed your unconscious minds, he learned the Cerberus destination code and the ID number?"

She shrugged. "He wasn't interested in information of a technical nature. Besides, he's floating frozen and dead on the dark side of the Moon. And even if he were alive, the ID encoding is encrypted."

Lakesh nodded, as if he agreed with her, but did so reluctantly. "Withal, judging by what you said about him, he was a remarkable man. A genius who never arrived—"

"He was a warped little man with ambitions to challenge God," she broke in, more harshly than she intended. "He won't be missed."

Lakesh patted her shoulder. "Perhaps not. But as friend Kane can attest, hate is often as strong a bond as love."

"I didn't hate him," Brigid protested. "Despite what he did to me, to all of us."

"As you said, he bobs for eternity in the infinite cold of space." Lakesh shivered as if the notion gave him a sudden chill.

Suddenly lights flashed and needles wavered on the consoles. Beyond the anteroom, a humming tone vibrated from the gateway chamber.

She leaped from her chair, and both she and Lakesh gaped at it in astonishment. Bright flashes, like strokes of heat lightning, flared on the other side of the brown-tinted armaglass walls. The low-pitched drone climbed to a hurricane wail, then dropped down to silence.

In a stunned whisper, Lakesh stammered, "Somebody jumped here...to *Cerberus!*"

Eyes wide and wild, he swung around toward the Mercator-relief map, then spun toward a desk, hands fumbling to activate an intercom. Leaning over it, Lakesh shouted stridently, "Armed security detail to the control center! *Stat!*"

Within half a minute, the big, vaulted room milled with people wielding blasters. Kane was among the first to arrive, hefting his Sin Eater. Rouch was right behind him, shouldering an SA80 subgun. Kane pretended not to notice the slit-eyed stare of suspicion Brigid directed toward him.

Auerbach, Farrell and Cotta fanned out around the jump chamber, blasters held at hip level. Kane and Grant cautiously approached the armaglass door from opposite directions. They took up positions on either side of it, exchanged curt nods and Grant heaved up on the handle.

As the door swung open on its counterbalanced hinges, the two men darted inside, Kane going low, Grant going high.

They froze motionless inside the chamber door staring silently at the floor. Anxiously Lakesh snapped, "What is it? Who is it?"

In a flat, unemotional tone, Kane called, "Baptiste, you need to see this."

She warily approached the mat-trans unit, pushing between Grant and Kane. Soberly Grant said to her, "A little gift."

"Or a little message," said Kane grimly.

"Both," Brigid declared.

The last wispy scraps of white vapor dissolved like
early-morning mist. A polished black walking stick lay
at an angle on the hexagonal floor disks. The silver
knob and ferrule gleamed with a mocking light.

After the ashes of the great Reckoning, the warrior survivalists live by one primal instinct

JAMES AXLER
DEATHLANDS®
Way of the Wolf

Unexpectedly dropped into a bleak Arctic landscape by a mat-trans jump, Ryan Cawdor and his companions find themselves the new bounty in a struggle for dominance between a group of Neanderthals and descendants of a military garrison stranded generations ago.

Sinanju software?

#112 Brain Storm
The Fatherland Files Book I

Created by
WARREN MURPHY
and RICHARD SAPIR

Ordinary bank robbery turns into larceny of the highest order as the very secrets of CURE (and the minds of its members) are stolen and laid bare on a computer disk. It's up to Remo and Chiun to find a way to restore CURE's abilities while there's still time.

The first in The Fatherland Files, a miniseries based on a secret fascist organization's attempts to regain the glory of the Third Reich.

Look for it in August 1998 wherever Gold Eagle books are sold.

Or order your copy now by sending your name, address, zip or postal code, along with a check or money order (please do not send cash) for $5.99 for each book ordered ($6.99 in Canada), plus 75¢ postage and handling ($1.00 in Canada), payable to Gold Eagle Books, to:

In the U.S.	In Canada
Gold Eagle Books	Gold Eagle Books
3010 Walden Ave.	P.O. Box 636
P.O. Box 9077	Fort Erie, Ontario
Buffalo, NY 14269-9077	L2A 5X3

GOLD EAGLE ®

Please specify book title with your order.
Canadian residents add applicable federal and provincial taxes.

GDEST112

America faces Armageddon in her own backyard....

STONY MAN™ 35

MESSAGE TO AMERICA

A militia force known as the Sawtooth Patriots have sourced their very own cache of nuclear weapons—and in order to drive their message home, they intend on unleashing them on their neighbors in the United States! It's up to the commandos and cybernetic professionals at Stony Man Farm to prevent this disastrous homegrown Armageddon.

Available in July 1998 at your favorite retail outlet.